THE ROLLING STONES
LIVE 1962-69

You Had To Be There: The Rolling Stones Live 1962–69

Copyright © 2015 Richard Houghton. All rights reserved.
Richard Houghton asserts his moral right to be identified as the author of this book

First hardback edition printed 2015 in the EU

A catalogue record for this book is available from the British Library.

ISBN 978-0-9933781-0-2

No part of this book shall be reproduced or transmitted in any form or by any means, electronic or mechanical, including photocopying, recording, or by any information retrieval system without written permission of the publisher.

Published by Gottahavebooks

To obtain copies of this book, please email: sales@gottahavebooks.co.uk

Designed and set by Bounford.com (www.bounford.com)
Cover image of Rolling Stones © Getty Images/Ullstein Bild

Although every precaution has been taken in the preparation of this book, the publisher and author assume no responsibility for errors or omissions. Neither is any liability assumed for damages resulting from the use of this information contained herein.

The publishers have made every reasonable effort to trace the copyright owners of any and all material in this book. In the event of an omission, the publishers will be pleased to hear from anyone who has not been appropriately acknowledged, and to make a correction in any future reprints and editions.

YOU HAD TO BE THERE!
THE ROLLING STONES
LIVE 1962-69

RICHARD HOUGHTON

GOTTA HAVE BOOKS

Contents

For Bill Houghton. Because he wishes he had been there too.

Introduction

The Rolling Stones first performed in 1962 and, more than 50 years later, are still going strong. Their history as a band is well documented. But much of what has been written about their live shows up to 1967, when they largely withdrew from performing until they re-emerged as a live act in 1969 following the death of Brian Jones, is drawn from newspaper accounts of the time. This book shines a new light on that period of the Stones history. It uses first hand interviews and completely fresh material, garnered from people who saw them as they graduated from performing before a handful of people in small clubs to packed theatres and arenas around the world.

This is not a definitive history of those early concerts and neither does it pretend to be. As an original member of the group, Bill Wyman's account of the band's early days in his autobiography *A Stone Alone*, drawn from his diaries and supplemented by press reports, is as close as we are likely to get to an accurate historical record. Keith Richards' Life is a more impressionistic account of those formative years while neither Mick Jagger, who reportedly returned a £2m publisher's advance when he couldn't remember certain details of the band's career and Bill declined to help him fill in the blanks, nor Charlie Watts, who has generally shunned the spotlight throughout the Stones career, seem likely to write their autobiographies. Brian Jones, of course, is no longer with us.

This is also not a definitive history of the band's early shows because it comprises over 500 individual recollections of encounters with the Stones and it would be unrealistic to expect everyone who saw them or dealt with them in some way to have perfect recall. In some instances the accounts I have reproduced contradict each other. Some tales will have been embellished over the years and other memories will be incomplete. The Rolling Stones have not, of course, been averse to being economical with the truth themselves over the years and the Stones manager Andrew Loog Oldham famously engineered early headlines for the band by encouraging outrageous stories in the popular press. But what I have been most struck by is the number of people who, on seeing my plea for stories, contacted me and began their communication with 'I saw your letter and it brought the memories flooding back' or similar.

The memory can play tricks and support acts or venues will have been misremembered. Where possible I have tried to correct such obvious but understandable errors. In a handful of instances I have had to triangulate the information provided by a contributor (the date, the venue and the supporting artists) to successfully identify a show and have edited the entry accordingly. I was unable to verify one enticing account suggesting that the Stones, Jimi Hendrix, Cliff Richard and

Olivia Newton-John all appeared at the same small club in the west of England and so have omitted it. Everything else is how it has been told to me. I have tried not to rewrite history as it has been recalled.

From their first show outside of the South East of England, at the Outlook Club in Middlesbrough on 13 July 1963 to them topping the US *Billboard* charts with *(I Can't Get No) Satisfaction* on 10 July 1965, took the Rolling Stones just two years. This phenomenal rise was achieved in an age where there was no *YouTube*, Internet or *X Factor*, when – to begin with, at least – there was in Britain no *Radio 1* or *Top Of The Pops*, and when the music industry was still controlled by record company moguls who thought they knew what young people should be listening to better than the young people themselves. The Beatles had opened people's eyes and ears to the possibilities but were, to many teenagers, nice boys and part of the establishment. The Stones were different.

That the Stones achieved their stellar success so rapidly is testament to a number of factors. Not only was Britain ripe for change culturally and socially, emerging as it was from a period of post war austerity, but the band had a wealth of material to draw upon. They played a phenomenal number of concerts, racking up over 800 shows around Britain by the end of 1966, along with countless TV and radio appearances. In this period they were to learn the stagecraft that was later to earn them to accolade the 'Greatest Rock'n'Roll Band In The World'.

It is perhaps hard now to understand the impact the Stones had on teenagers in the early 1960s and the extent to which their arrival challenged the established order. As Tom Wolfe said "The Beatles want to hold your hand but the Stones want to burn your town." This was certainly the view held by my father, who repeatedly stated that there were "only three things wrong with this country – *ITV*, Harold Wilson and Mick Jagger." Dad's sentiments are reflected in the parental opinions of many of the book's contributors.

This book, therefore, is not just about the Rolling Stones. It is a window on the past, a book about what it was like to be a teenager in early 1960s Britain, when you couldn't do things without your parents' permission, when the pubs – if you were old enough to go in them – shut at 10.30pm and when there were only two TV channels. *BBC2* did not begin airing until 20 April 1964 and *Channel 4* was more than 20 years away. Britain in 1962 was still in the clutches of post war austerity, with rationing coupons still a live memory for many. Teenagers hadn't really been invented until the Rolling Stones came along and opened people's eyes to what was possible.

The book also contains accounts of their early appearances and elsewhere in the world, the US and the impact they had on teenagers there. In the US particularly, the impact of the Stones on teenage perspectives on life comes through in people's recollections.

A couple of housekeeping issues:

Keith was born Keith Richards but dropped the 's' from his surname in 1963 at the suggestion of the Stones then manager Andrew Loog Oldham to sound more hip. He only reinstated it in the 1970s but I refer to him, as have most of my contributors, as Keith Richards.

Although ticket prices were often set by the promoter, the Rolling Stones have often attracted criticism for the admission prices they charge. The stories from my contributors demonstrate that this has been a feature of their career since the very early days, whether because ticket prices in the 1960s seemed great value compared with the modern era or because even then the band could command a premium. Where ticket prices are quoted in pounds, shillings and pence I have shown the decimal equivalent. For those readers not familiar with pre decimal currency, one shilling (also shown as 1/-) equals five pence, two shillings ten pence and so on. Half a shilling or 6d equals three pence.

So – this is not a definitive history. It is the recollections and remembrances of the people who were there – in the front row, in the wings, in the side alley waiting for autographs – from fifty or more years ago. Time will have blurred some memories and polished others. But the stories are fascinating, whether you are a Rolling Stones fan or a social historian. They paint a picture of a more innocent time, when five young men from London and the South of England exploded onto the British music scene and shared their enthusiasm for R&B and the blues with an unsuspecting world. This is the story of what it was like to see the Rolling Stones perform in the early 1960s.

Here it is. How it was. Ladies and gentlemen, the Rolling Stones …

Chapter 1

The Rolling Stones first performed as a group on 12 July 1962 when a line up containing Mick Jagger, Keith Richards and Brian Jones appeared at the Marquee Club in London. The band played a further twelve times in the period to the end of October 1962, principally at the Ealing Jazz Club. In November 1962 they began appearing at Studio 51, a club gig hosted by Ken Colyer's Jazz Club in the West End of London.

NOVEMBER 1962

Studio 51, Ken Colyer's Jazz Club, London

Brian Robinson *(age 17)*

When I started getting into music at school I was into blues and – earlier on – rock. I'm talking about Jerry Lee Lewis, Little Richard and people like that. But then I got into trad jazz when I started work. There was a place called the Abracadabra Jazz Club in Coventry which is near where the old Coventry football ground was. I remember going there and seeing people like Acker Bilk and Ken Colyer and Chris Barber and I was very much into that and, of course, with Chris Barber I ended up getting into skiffle with Lonnie Donegan. And, being into that, me and some lads went down to London and we went round to Ken Colyer's Jazz Club which was near Leicester Square. And we were walking past because we wanted to see Chris Barber or Ken Colyer at the time. It was a Sunday and there was a door open and it was in a basement and we went down. There was no one there but we could hear this music downstairs and we went further down, opened this door and it was a bit like I assume the Cavern where The Beatles played – a big basement place, you know, with a

stage. And there was no one there except this band at the end and they were obviously practicing or whatever and my two mates said "eugh, we're not staying here".

Anyway I walked right down to the front – in front of them – and the guy was sitting down playing the slide guitar fantastically. I was the main one interested in that sort of blues music then. When he'd finished I was stood right in front of him and I said "you're really good, you are". I said "what's your name?" And he said "Brian." And I went "oh that's my name. Brian. What's the name of your band?" He said "we are going to be the Rolling Stones".

Brian Robinson

Nikki Bennett

I grew up in north-west Kent in Sidcup and my father was a teacher at Dartford Grammar School, with Mick Jagger being one of his pupils. In later years my father sometimes got called by the press to make a comment on Mick for an article. I remember one account of Mick quickly ditching his school blazer and putting on a shiny jacket just before going on stage to receive a school prize from the headmaster.

I was a great Rolling Stones fan and I and my friends used to see them locally, before they became really well known, plus a girl in my class went out with Mick's brother Chris for a while. Another girl's parents knew Mick's parents quite well and remembered seeing Marianne Faithfull there when having tea once. My father taught French and German and often wondered if Mick's French had come in useful when he married Bianca!

Andrew Crisp

One of the great names in old style jazz in the Fifties and Sixties was Ken Colyer. In fact he was a sort of god amongst the purist enthusiasts. He had a club called Studio 51 in Great Newport Street in the West End of London. As well as the regular evening jazz sessions they had R&B on Sunday afternoons. The Stones were usually featured. Naturally, being a blues lover, I tried to get up to London as often as possible.

At the time I was trying to learn to play the harmonica – the 'harp' – but not making much headway. I just could not make that whining, bending sound that the greats of the instrument such as Little Walter made. So in the interval of a Sunday afternoon Stones session I asked the singer and harp player, whose name wasn't really known then, for some tips. He invited me into the rudimentary dressing room and we sat down and traded harmonica licks. I learned to play the harp thanks to Mick Jagger.

Nikki Bennett

Andrew Crisp

23 NOVEMBER 1962
The Red Lion, Sutton

John Hinton-Styles
I was in a band called the Presidents and we played in Sutton in Surrey every other week with the Stones for about two years. It was the back of a pub called the Red Lion. I went back there fairly recently and I couldn't believe how small it was because it didn't seem that at the time. It was quite the thing in Sutton at the time. They had two damn good groups playing in a pub back room. It was very, very small – a couple of hundred people. They were shoulder to shoulder. You couldn't move. It was a real cook house. It was very, very hot in there. My wife used to do the handbags. She used to turn thruppence. We had a manager who was also very involved with the Stones – Glyn Johns. He was the recording manager up at *Decca* and he later did a lot of their sound work. He was our manager and he was also one of our vocalists. He got us in there but of course we were doing quite a lot of work.

We were probably working four or five times a week. We were playing all over the South East and we were earning quite well but we all had other jobs. I was a hairdresser. We were all zonked out when we were finished because we were working during the day and playing during the night. We played all the latest bloody pop stuff. Being the pianist I did a lot of Jerry Lee Lewis stuff. We were playing sort of pop music. At that time the Stones had a pianist. They were playing sort of more rhythm and blues. The place was packed solid. They would never allow it these days. You couldn't move in there. It was a solid lump of humanity that just enjoyed the music. We used to turn up at theirs and they used to turn up at ours.

Robin Mayhew, The Presidents
I was lead guitar with the Presidents and our link with the Stones goes back to their beginnings. The late pianist Ian Stewart was a good friend of ours and our original bass player Colin Golding often helped out when the Stones did the odd gig. We knew Stu before. Stu. The Chin. He was always noted for his huge chin. Stuey was local to us in Cheam. The Harlequin coffee bar in Cheam was a great centre for all the local music fans and everything else. Stu would come to the Harlequin and we would be talking about gigs and music and things. We saw each other outside of the music side of it – because he was a keen cyclist and we had all our bikes and pushbikes and motorbikes and that sort of thing.

He had this embryo of a band that he was working in with Jagger and Richards and he was always talking to us about it because we were already well established. He'd say "I've got this band starting and it sounds pretty good but come and sing some harmonies for us. That would be good." He'd said to me a couple of times "I wish you'd come and teach our guys how to sing harmony, because they can't. It's hopeless."

> "at that time the Stones had a pianist. They were playing sort of more rhythm and blues"

The Presidents did lots of gigs all around south London. We had a residency which all came about because of a 21st birthday party at the Red Lion in Sutton. The guy who was having the party booked us to play there because we were the local talent. We decided, after the gig which had gone down so well, "we'll see if we can book the hall every Friday". So we did and the landlord was delighted because every Friday it was rammed with people. And Stuey – Ian Stewart – pleaded with us because our bass player used to play with the Stones now and again, because they had no bass player on the odd gigs they did. Stuey said "any chance of us coming down and playing at the Lion?" So we thought about it for a bit and then we thought "ok".

We were so busy we had lots of gigs to do so we weren't going to miss out. So we said "we can do it for a few weeks every other Friday. And you can come in and do it". At that sort of time Bill Wyman had come down and he'd seen the Stones or he might have seen us. He came down probably one night when they were playing bass less because we were playing elsewhere. When The Presidents played the Red Lion, because we were already quite well established and had a good following, it was bursting. It was absolutely rammed. And Mr Edwards the landlord loved it because he was taking loads of money.

I remember one Friday night we weren't busy and we went to the Red Lion. This particular Friday we weren't gigging so a couple of us went down to see the Stones. And there was about six people. Six or eight people! We were getting a full house. It was a bit of a joke. It would be unmiked of course. In those days they used the house PA in there which was really crummy. It was just a couple of twelve inch speakers hanging on the wall, you know? So it was very poor. Stu's piano playing – which you don't really hear on any of the early Stones stuff, it's not sort of there in the foreground at all – was just brilliant. The Red Lion had a crummy old upright piano and he would be great, you know. I went up to the stage because one of the numbers we did was *Sweet Little Sixteen* by Chuck Berry. And I said to Mick Jagger – I'd never met him or spoken to him – but I said "can you play *Sweet Little Sixteen*?" Which they did. And Keith Richards in his autobiography mentioned the Red Lion and said "*Sweet Little Sixteen* went down well" which made me chuckle because, you know, I'd requested it but there were only a handful of people in there.

DECEMBER 1962

Following an audition at the Wetherby Arms pub in Chelsea, London, Bill Wyman joined the Rolling Stones on bass guitar.

12 JANUARY 1963

The Rolling Stones played their first gig with Charlie Watts on the drums at the Ealing Club.

> "in those days they used the house PA in there which was really crummy. It was just a couple of twelve inch speakers hanging on the wall"

9 FEBRUARY 1963
Ealing Club, London

Trevor Baverstock

Dave and I first saw the Stones in early '63. We were living in Ealing near Ealing Common station. We moved into digs, just a room really, near Ealing Common station and we were working at an insurance company in Harrow. We could go one stop to Ealing Broadway. I can remember a fellow there called Bob Jacques saying "there's a good club you should go to in Ealing" and he mentioned the Ealing Club. I remember queuing outside this club.

We were both very familiar with Chuck Berry and Bo Diddley and we had a lot of American records. I heard someone singing *Bye Bye Johnny*. I turned to Dave and said "sounds like a good group and she's got a bloody good voice". I thought it was a woman singer. I don't know if it was the pitch of his voice. So when I got in I went "aah, I thought it was a woman singing!"

It was very crowded. Hot. Smoky. Generally not much air. We'd go in the entrance and the stage was on our left. I think there were just seats around the wall. I don't think there was any seating apart from what was stuck to the wall.

David Colyer *(age 18)*

We went to the Ealing Club, which was absolutely packed. The group was the Rolling Stones and they were fantastic and did a load of Chuck Berry and Bo Diddley numbers. We had a few drinks then found we had no

> "the group was the Rolling Stones and they were fantastic and did a load of Chuck Berry and Bo Diddley numbers"

money left. However, we stayed till 11pm and I was exhausted after some mad dancing.

Trevor Baverstock

Although Dave has written the name in the diary I think he added it afterwards. At the time I'm sure he wrote 'we don't know the name of the group.' There was no way we knew their name at the time.

16 FEBRUARY 1963
Ealing Club, London

David Colyer

We went to the Ealing Club again and paid the four shillings (20p) entrance fee. The Rolling Stones were there again and after getting our drinks we just managed to find a place to stand on the dance floor as it was packed.

Trevor Baverstock

I was queuing for a drink. During the intermission was the only time you could really buy drinks. So I was queuing and I looked behind me and one of the guitarists had come down. It was Keith Richards. So he's standing behind me in the queue for the drinks and I turned around and said "oh, do you want to get in front of me, mate?" I thought it was a nice gesture. And not a thank you. He just walked in front of me. He didn't say thanks or anything. I felt like I wished I hadn't bothered.

MARCH 1963
Studio 51, London

Adele Tinman *(age 16)*

I was quite lucky in my family in that my uncle was a pianist and he had a lot of jazz records and I was into jazz strangely enough, sort of, more than I was into anything else just because I was listening to his stuff and I was sort of into rock'n'roll at that age. There were people like Alexis Korner who were around then and Cyril Davies. Alexis was a blues man and it was him more than anyone else who first introduced people to Muddy Waters and all the American blues legends. I suppose the Stones picked up on that.

Alexis was very well known as a blues man. I certainly remember seeing Cyril Davies. He died very early but I do remember seeing him in Harrow, and Long John Baldry. They were all around and playing that sort of American blues. The other person who brought people over was Chris Barber. They had these early packages where they had people like Sonny Terry and Brownie McGhee. It was so uncommercial then. It was like an underground. You couldn't just get it on *eBay* or whatever.

I would have been at college with my friend Barbara Heasman at that time. Barbara mentioned that there was this band and she was going out with this bloke called Keith and that they played every Sunday afternoon at this club off Leicester Square in Great Newport Street. And I said "oh that sounds good" and that's why I went. All Barbara said to me was "I'm going out with this bloke called Keith who plays the guitar". I just knew her as somebody who I went to college with and she said "come along down to this club". It was Number 51 and it was a basement. It wasn't that big. It was a Sunday afternoon. It wasn't even a Sunday evening. It was an afternoon session at the Studio 51. I probably took my friend Carol.

Why did we go to see them? For me it was always the music. Whenever Mick used to introduce a number he'd always say "this is a Muddy Waters number' or 'this is a Howlin' Wolf number". In other words he'd always mention where he got it from. I always remember them doing that and thinking 'yeah' and then of course it encouraged you to go out and find the originals. That was the thing. I think it was after I'd seen the Stones that then I'd heard of people like Muddy Waters because I wouldn't have heard of him before. It was very different in those days – we didn't have that much American music on radio.

There was a chap who I used to go out with who was a harmonica player called Ray and he used to play in the intervals. He just used to start playing when we were all standing there in the interval and I think Mick didn't like that very much. It was competition! I was quite under age for going in clubs. I think they weren't licensed because I can remember people used to go to the pub next door. Certainly Studio 51 in Great Newport Street wasn't licensed. That was Coca Cola, you know? That's why I probably went – because I didn't have to pass the 'are you 18?' test.

> "whenever Mick used to introduce a number he'd always say 'this is a Muddy Waters number' or 'this is a Howlin' Wolf number' "

In the early months of 1963 the Rolling Stones played a circuit of club and pub gigs. Three to four times a week they would appear at one of Studio 51, the Ealing Jazz Club, the Red Lion in Sutton, the Ricky Tick Club at Windsor's Star and Garter, Harringay Jazz Club at the Manor House pub, the Crawdaddy Club at Richmond's Station Hotel and the Wooden Bridge pub in Guildford.

30 MARCH 1963
The Wooden Bridge, Guildford

Stuart Farrow *(age 24)*
I suppose I was 16 when I started scrambling in 57 with a friend of mine, John Hammond. We used to do our scramble bikes. In the evening it was always traditional jazz. That's all we used to go and listen to, mainly. There was a jazz club near us. We were actually in the garage doing the bikes and suddenly this Bill Haley and the Comets came on with *See You Later Alligator*. And we both looked at each other. It was that good. It was absolutely amazing, the music. And then of course it was all rock'n'roll up until the early Sixties. And then R&B came along.

Somebody said the Rolling Stones were at the Wooden Bridge so we just went down. I went with my brother and his friend. It was all this type of music that we liked. It had a very good rhythm to it. It wasn't very busy. You had your good looking Billy Furys and people like that, but they were a scruffy group and a lot of people didn't bother. There was three or four of us that went. It didn't seem that packed at all. We were dancing. I remember standing around jigging around to the music. It wasn't tremendously busy but the music was very loud.

We were actually talking to Brian in between the numbers. We just had a few words with him. "Where are you playing next?" "Are you playing so and so?" We actually did talk to him about what they were doing and things like that. It was a good atmosphere in the pub. The music was very good. I remember Paul Samwell-Smith telling me he used to go over to Mick Jagger's place at Richmond. He had a flat there. And he said it was the most disgusting flat he'd ever been into. He said it was absolutely filthy. They weren't as big as people think now. I don't think Brian, my son-in-law, believed me when I said they were playing in a pub. He said "I'll go and have a look online so see whether they did". I said "I know they did. Because we were there!"

24 APRIL 1963
Eel Pie Island, Twickenham, London

The Rolling Stones appeared for the first time at Eel Pie Island.

Robin Mayhew
And then, I don't know how it happened, but Stu negotiated – now with Bill Wyman in the band – to get to Eel Pie Island. And the guy there took them on and they got a residency there and from then it took off. For a while we thought we were unlucky that

> "and the guy took them on and they got a residency there and from then it took off"

somebody from Eel Pie Island had come because they'd heard the Red Lion was cooking on a Friday night and they had come on a night when the Stones were on and they got the gig. If they'd come on our Friday we might have got it! I think they got it through Stu's diligence and his negotiating the gigs. And they lived over that way, more towards Richmond. So they probably had a little bit of a following locally and they could do a bit more, you know?

Adele Tinman

I used to go to Eel Pie sometimes. Not very often. It was quite a small elite sort of group that went to the clubs I used to go to, because I liked the music. I went to the Marquee. It used to be in Oxford Street originally. It was the 100 Club on one side and the Marquee on the other.

6 APRIL 1963
Ealing Club, London

David Colyer

The singer with the Stones had a sore throat so they used another singer who 'wasn't good'.

Trevor Baverstock

I wrote to Bill Wyman a few years ago and asked him who sang. He replied 'we probably just winged it.'

27 APRIL 1963
Ealing Club, London

David Colyer

We saw them a lot at the Ealing Club, plus the Station Hotel in Richmond and Studio 51 in Leicester Square and The Marquee in Wardour Street. Their music was great and reproduced the sounds of rhythm and blues classics from America and sometimes sounded better than the original recordings. I didn't always feel their recordings lived up to their live performances and they used to have an excellent piano player in the band – Ian Stewart – but he didn't take part in their success.

Trevor Baverstock

We saw them nine times at the Ealing Club. They also had a pianist who we learned later was Ian Stewart. He was one of the ones who winged it. We also saw them in a pub opposite Richmond station – the Station Hotel – once or twice.

12 MAY 1963
Crawdaddy Club, Station Hotel, Richmond

Tony Donaldson (age 20)

I was living in Twickenham and working in Richmond as a hairstylist in a top hairdressing salon. One lunch time I was in the L'Auberge coffee bar by Richmond Bridge when somebody, possibly the Stones manager, was handing out tickets to see the group play in the back room of The Railway Hotel opposite Richmond Station. I went along with my girl friend to see them that weekend and we were blown away as to how good they were. The music they played was mainly rhythm and blues as they were very influenced by Chuck Berry and to this day my favourite song is Mona. Within

Tony Donaldson and bride

weeks the queue to get in went from the entrance and along the street. It only cost a few shillings to get in. I can't remember exactly how much it was but possibly no more than 25p in today's money. Within a month it became so packed inside they then moved on to the legendary Eel Pie Island in Twickenham, famous as a traditional jazz venue. I had been going there for a couple of years already as I was also very keen on trad jazz and used to go along with my best mate whose uncle, Arthur Chisnall, ran the venue and we used to get in for free.

It was perhaps the most atmospheric venue for live music and dancing you were ever likely to see and I feel privileged to have been there so often. However, within a short time this venue also became so packed that they were again forced to leave and went on to the Athletic Club at Old Deer Park, Richmond. Suffice to say that within a short space of time they left here as their records had started to become hits and they were internationally famous. During all of this period you didn't go along just to listen to the Stones – you went to dance as well. Unfortunately for spectators once they started doing 'proper' concerts this exciting aspect of seeing live bands was lost.

MAY 1963
Eel Pie Island, Twickenham

Jackie Hankins (age 24)
I lived in Epsom then. They lived in Epsom at one time on Upper High Street. They had a bungalow

> " I didn't like the jumping around. It was a bit loud and a bit in your face"

up on the hill and they used to jam out there in the evenings before they were ever known. The youngsters knew where they were. They were just beginning to have a following. I can remember going to see them in Eel Pie Island. It was a hall, quite large, and it had quite a name. There was always a crowd of us. It wasn't a place you'd want to go on your own. There were so many people. They weren't fights, but people had had a drink and were high spirited.

I've got to be honest, although I liked them it wasn't really my type of music. They weren't my favourite band. I liked the Hollies and Searchers and Gerry and the Pacemakers. I didn't like the jumping around. It was a bit loud and a bit in your face. Whereas the Hollies and all those were always dressed in suits, always suited and booted. And then you got to Keith and that lot and they looked like they'd just got out of bed. They didn't look like they'd washed for a month. You see, 17 year olds and 18 year olds, they'd like them because it was all a finger up to society. I was a bit older.

28 JUNE 1963
Ricky Tick Club, Star and Garter Pub, Windsor

Dave Domone (age 19)
I only have a few recollections of seeing them in a building behind a pub in Windsor. My memories were that we paid to get in, had our foreheads – or maybe arms – stamped so we could go back into the pub to get drinks and then

return to the music. They were on a low stage in a corner and people would ask for requests of particular numbers, especially Chuck Berry and Bo Diddley which they dutifully played. As I was, and still am, a fan of rock'n'roll, blues and R&B of the Fifties and Sixties, we were mightily impressed by the fact they knew all these numbers and could play them in what sounded to us then an authentic manner. It's a pity we didn't have cell phones or video cameras then.

Robin Mayhew

Stu used to live in Pittenweem. That's where he was born. He came and stayed with my wife Nadia and I. We had a small hotel in the Scottish borders for a number of years. Stu stayed one or two nights, and we walked along the Tweed because we were right by the river Tweed and we talked not about music but about life in general. It was lovely. And he went on up to Pittenweem and his friends and family. And then he sadly died. Stu was a lovely man and sadly missed. We were living in Scotland at the time and we came down for the funeral in Randall's Park in Leatherhead. And there was a wake held at the Caddington Golf Club and Jagger and Richards were there. No words were exchanged.

The only other opportunity I had to speak to Mick Jagger was when David Bowie executed Ziggy Stardust at the Hammersmith Odeon – 3 July 1973. There was a great big party afterwards at the Café Royal.

Jagger was there with Bianca, and Angie Bowie and Bianca were dancing around and Bowie was with Jagger and I went to say goodbye. It was time to go and I went to see David to say "good luck, mate, whatever you do. It's been great working for you" and Jagger went "neh neh neh neh neh". Taking the piss, you know? I felt like saying to him "remember when I requested *Sweet Little Sixteen*?" It was very crummy – that first gig I saw of the Stones. That early time at the Red Lion – you wouldn't have thought they were going to go anywhere.

> "you wouldn't have thought they were going to go anywhere"

Chapter 2

The Rolling Stones released *Come On*, a cover of a Chuck Berry song, on 7 June 1963. It was a recording that the band was later to disown, complaining that it didn't reflect their sound. But it was their first single and the first opportunity for many people outside of the club circuit in London to hear them on national radio.

John Hinton-Styles

We got to know each other quite well. But when they actually started to get somewhere and get a record out – that was when it all changed.

11 JULY 1963
Scene Club, London

Trevor Baverstock

There was hardly anybody there. The place was empty. There was a stage at the end of a sparse hall-like area. The Stones came down from the stage and were standing around. We were standing very close. They had come down for a break and Jagger, speaking in a sarcastic tone, said "oh Brian Jones – the greatest jazz guitarist in the world!" I heard it clear as a bell. Jones had obviously said something and he was mocking him, you know. We thought Brian Jones was the main man with his guitar work.

Although they continued to gig primarily in clubs around London and the South East, the Rolling Stones began making forays into the Midlands and the North of England. Their first gig outside of the Home Counties was in Middlesbrough.

13 JULY 1963
Outlook Club, Middlesbrough

Peter Wilkinson *(age 21)*

I am virtually the same age as Mick Jagger, give or take a month or two. I have been fortunate enough to see them twice – once in the US – but the first time was at a wonderful club in Middlesbrough called the Outlook which was run by a friend of ours called John McCoy who also had a band called the Crawdaddies. The Stones played on a double bill with the Hollies. Mick Jagger sat at the back of the stage on a stool and played and sang from there.

Dave Connor *(age 17)*

Middlesbrough in them days was so vibrant. It was just unbelievable. The Outlook was on Corporation Road. There used to be a crowd of mates went. That was like our in place at the time. I lived just round the corner from the place. It was only three, four minutes walk. It was downstairs. Only soft drinks. No alcohol whatsoever. The Outlook was only a very, very small place. It was classed as the north vs the south. The Hollies were classed as being the north. And the Rolling Stones did their first gig outside of London. The place was chock-a-block. Because at that point in time the Hollies were the known people. The whole place was just buzzing

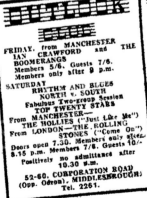

completely. Years later my friend Barry Falconer bought the place. When he went in to it, it was three feet deep in water. There was all these bills, bill heads – everything was just floating about in the water. Because when they moved out of the building they just left it. He even found a receipt there. If they'd paid half a crown more they could have had The Beatles rather than the Stones. It's been knocked down now and there's law courts there.

Barry Jones *(age 16)*
I was an apprentice at Pickerings Lifts. And there was like a gang of us. And there was a lot of clubs around the area that you needed membership for. Obviously all of us couldn't afford them so what we did was split it so we would get different clubs' membership cards. There were about forty or fifty apprentices all of round about the same age. And the majority of us were all into music so, on a Friday, we used to get the *NME* (New Musical Express) and we'd sit outside with fish and chips and then we'd talk about "is there anything on in our area?" because sometimes they advertised in the paper. And then you would say "well I'd like to go and see them – can I borrow your membership card?" so "yes, you could borrow my membership card but I fancy going to the KD Club – can I borrow your membership card?"

That's how a group of us worked, because we couldn't afford to get membership for each club. We just couldn't afford it. So we did as much as we could in terms of helping each other to get

to see these groups and bands. In 1963 *Luxembourg* would be the main radio station but that one used to go off its' station every now and again.

In Stockton we had a shop called Leslie Brown's which was predominantly a toy shop but in the front of the shop they had two booths so if you heard a record or you knew the group's name you could go into Leslie Brown's and say "have you got the latest Shadows record?" and you could go into the booth and listen to it. So when you heard something like *Come On* by the Rolling Stones on the radio and you'd think 'whoa, that's different,' you'd go to Leslie Brown's and say "can I have a listen to it?" And that's how we got into a lot of the groups in the very early days before they were mega.

I was right into the music. I knew both groups – The Hollies and the Rolling Stones – at that time. The atmosphere in our clubs was absolutely electric, to go and see these fellows who had a single out. For that particular night at the Outlook Club there was two of us went. Me and my pal. And we managed to get two membership cards. We went into town first in Stockton, to a pub called the Jockers, and we had a couple of drinks in there and then we got the 55 which was a United bus – it was red, I'll always remember that – and we went direct to the club itself. On the night we had to be there by half past seven. The Hollies came on first. The three songs that I remember them playing were their hit of the time *(Ain't That) Just Like Me, Rockin'*

Barry Jones

Robin and also another song called *Little Lover*. Eric Haydock played a six string bass and he got a helluva sound out of it. When the Rolling Stones came on it was the old style rhythm and blues how I like it. They all had check jackets on. They were quite smart that night. They played *Mona*, and Mick Jagger mentioned that "this was one Bo Diddley did," and Carol and *Come On*. And when you'd go back into work on a Monday, before you started work, everyone would be saying "I went to see so and so at Redcar Ballroom" or Astoria Ballroom or The Globe and things like that and that's how it was back in them days. It was just fantastic.

Mike Gutteridge *(age 17)*
I can remember the date exactly because it was my seventeenth birthday. I was in a band called The DenMen and it was a really popular local band in the North East. It was ten shillings (50p) to get in and that was one of the advantages of being in a really popular band. We got in these places for nothing. I doubt it held more than 150 people. The Stones were paid £35. There was no alcohol. It was orange or coffee or tea. So we got in late – the Hollies were on as well – and this was really just a very small coffee bar. It was quite incredible. It was the Stones first booking outside of London. After it finished Brian Jones gave me a giveaway record of *Come On* signed by all of them which, unfortunately, a lodger I had decided to sell down the pub a few years ago. And after that,

> **"I said 'I like those boots' to Mick Jagger and he said 'yeah, man, these are Chelsea boots' "**

when everybody had gone, me and the other guitarist in my band sat and had an orange juice and coffee with Jagger and Richards on this little stage, literally just sat having a chat and a coffee with them. I can remember asking Keith Richards about the start of *Down The Road Apiece*. It was a little bit of an anathema at the time so he said "yeah, sure I'll show you". So he demonstrated it, not plugged in, with the Epiphone Riviera that he used and then he said 'here' and so I tried it on Keith's guitar. It's just a triad formation on A which is pretty commonplace now but the Stones had it off to a tee at the time. And they were wearing these boots and of course I was in this band from Middlesbrough Art College so I said "I like those boots" to Mick Jagger and he said "yeah, man, these are Chelsea boots."

---

27 JULY 1963
California Ballroom, Dunstable

David Arnold *(age 17)*
I can't recall who amongst my group of friends developed an interest in the Rolling Stones, but one of us read about them in early summer of 1963. Their unkempt appearance and the fact that they played a lot of Chuck Berry and Bo Diddley songs proved to be a lot more appealing than the more conventional image of The Beatles. Five of us went in a car. We were all living in Bedford, 20 miles away. They performed on the second stage – the opposite end of the hall to the main stage – and apart from the girls that

were with them there was just the five of us standing at the stage looking at the first half of their performance. I remember they did *Jaguar and the Thunderbird* which was a Chuck Berry song. They used to do *I'm Moving On* as well, and *Walking The Dog*, *Hi Heeled Sneakers* and *Can I Get A Witness*? At the interval they came and sat in the seats down at the side of the hall and we sat next to them. My friend sat next to Bill Wyman and we were just talking about how things were going and "what time are you on next?" Bill was very co-operative and talkative and happy to exchange pleasantries. The second half of the performance attracted a few more people. People from the other end of the ballroom had thought 'this is quite interesting'. They sang You *Better Move On* and they must have mentioned that it was an Arthur Alexander song. One of the guys remembered that Arthur Alexander had written the song *Anna* on The Beatles' first album and so after that we developed an interest in

Arthur Alexander. It's strange. I probably saw them nine or ten times but I didn't buy one of their records. I've never really gone back and picked up on the Rolling Stones stuff. Looking back on it what jumps out at me is the fact that we saw the transformation because the first time we saw them they were at the secondary stage rather than the main stage when there was literally no one there looking at them. Needless to say the subsequent shows at the Cali became more and more manic. We were lucky in as much that we saw the transformation from virtual unknowns to idols in a period of a couple of months. They never did appear on that minor stage again.

Gerry Parker *(age 19)*
I was a vocalist in a group called the Mavericks in 1963. Top of the bill were Russ Sainty and the Nu-Notes. Second on the smaller side stage were the Stones, with us as back up. I remember Bill Wyman had a home made bass

Gerry Parker, now …

… and then, with The Mavericks

guitar. They played their hit record *Come On* and the crowd went mad. At the time I thought 'what a scruffy lot we have here' but the young girls loved the casual way they dressed. It was the start of a new era.

Margaret Senior *(age 18)*

The California Ballroom was a big dance venue. I sat next to Mick on the corner of the stage while he took a break. I talked to him for a while – I think he was interested in what we thought about them. The place was packed. It was one of the best dance halls around then. He was very friendly and I was flattered, I suppose. Little did anyone know how famous they'd become in time – in less than a year.

16 AUGUST 1963
Winter Gardens, Banbury

Peter Jones *(age 16)*

I was involved in the music industry. There was a band in Warwick called the Talons. They were a couple of school mates, a couple of other people, and their mum used to drive the van. They had a Bedford van in those days and I was their roadie. Their music was very much blues based so they knew of the Stones. I think they'd been down to see them play in Richmond so when we saw they were playing in Banbury we persuaded their mum to drive us. When I told my dad I was going to Banbury he tried to stop me because Banbury was a really, really rough town in those days. Ethel Usher was the lady who owned the Winter Gardens. Ethel

was a great promoter and really far sighted. She told a story that the Stones that night cost her two hundred pounds. That's how much she had to pay the band. And they tried to wiggle out of the booking, because within a week or two of that they were a household name.

Trevor Nevett *(age 22)*

Mrs Usher was the one who owned the Winter Gardens in them days. She used to book loads of names besides the Stones – Freddie and the Dreamers, Helen Shapiro, Chas and Dave when they were with Cliff Bennett and the Rebel Rousers. It was quite the 'in' place. They had boxing, roller skating, everything there. You'd get about 380, 400 in there easily. They were going to have The Beatles there but they were too much money – about four or five hundred quid. So she had the Stones. The Stones weren't a big thing. They were on the way up. They were a bit scruffy. Ethel sent them off to get a haircut. Mick borrowed a leather jacket off a chap who was a friend of mine called Bruce Cox. Banbury would never have got them if they'd been big, you know. They were just about making it, really. It was a sell out.

Doreen Wassell *née Clutton (age 17)*

I lived in Croughton – about nine miles from Banbury. A crowd of us would all pile into one car for the trip there and back. The Winter Gardens was a very popular dance venue drawing teenagers from

Peter Jones

Doreen Wassell

Elizabeth Belcher *(age 17)*

I was at the concert in Banbury Winter Gardens. I went with a school friend who had previously lived in Cheltenham and knew Brian Jones. I have an autograph signed by them all. I remember they did not seem to go down that well. Ann and I chatted to them afterwards by the cloakroom. Ann was talking to Brian about life in Cheltenham.

Elizabeth Belcher

Ken Pratt *(age 15)*

Dressed in smart casual wear myself, I was amazed to see this group on stage not in suit and ties, as all groups tended to dress, but in similar clothes to which we would wear during the week. At the time my hair was fairly blond and to see this guy on stage with blond longish hair – well, Brian Jones straight away became my hero. That night I went into their dressing room after the show and they all managed to cadge one of my *Senior Service* cigarettes

Ken Pratt

far and wide, including American servicemen from the local airbases of Croughton and Heyford. I would have enjoyed wild rabbit stew and dumplings before going out for the evening. The Winter Gardens had a very strict code of dress at that time. If you weren't dressed to the mark you weren't allowed entry. The girls wore pencil slim skirts and the dapper boys wore winkle pickers. After a warm up by the local band on came the Rolling Stones. Shock and horror went across the dance floor. This group of lads were wearing jeans and looking like they hadn't changed their clothes for weeks. They had scruffy hair and were generally very untidy. How could the management allow these youngsters in and on stage when there was such a strict code of dress?

and I had a good chat to them. I never saw them live again until they appeared in Coventry. Dusty Springfield was on the same bill but when the Stones performed you couldn't hear the songs due to all the women screaming. I let my hair grow long and I became a fervent fan of the Stones from then on, buying their first single, EP and LP. I must admit my love for the group faded when Brian left the group.

Joe Freeman (age 16)

The price of the tickets was 7/6 (37p). It was sold out in four days. The Winter Gardens were owned by Mrs Ethel Usher who also owned the Inn Within pub just twenty feet from the dance hall. It was designed in a Spanish style and was a popular watering hole before going to the dance hall. Mrs Usher was a very successful business woman. She would say

Joe Freeman

about an artist "if they're out there I can get them". In 1961 she refused to book The Beatles because they were scruffy. They had not hit the big time then. When the Rolling Stones arrived on the Saturday morning to unload their gear and to meet Mrs Usher she told them to all go and get their hair cut or she would not let them perform. This they all promptly did.

At six o'clock that evening the Stones visited a small night spot just 150 yards from the Winter Gardens. It was called The Gaff. Georgie Fame played piano there before he hit the big time. They only played for one hour but for a treat Mick Jagger got up on stage and sang *Whole Lotta Shakin' Goin' On*. The Gaff was packed to the door as usual and they gave him a great reception. The Astranaughts were Mrs Usher's resident band. They were the best band in town at the time.

The Stones came on stage at about 9.15pm. They were dressed in very smart suits and ties. But Jagger soon removed some of his attire as the sweat started to flow. At the end Mick Jagger shouted to the audience "give me a song to go out on", someone shouted *Shake, Rattle and Roll*, Bill Haley's big hit, so this time accompanied by the Astranaughts Jagger took it on and put it over very well using the full length of the stage. At the end they gave him a chorus of *For He's A Jolly Good Fellow*.

Colin Huckins (age 16)

I was overwhelmed to be seeing them live. They performed very well and the only disappointment for me was that they were only on for a short time in the middle of the evening, whereas I expected them to come back on and close the show

17 AUGUST 1963
Memorial Hall, Northwich

Gay Jinks

My boyfriend Tony (now my husband) read about a new group in the *New Musical Express* or the *Melody Maker*. As a result we went to see the Rolling Stones at Northwich Memorial Hall. When they came on stage we moved to the side of the hall and just watched. Most people were dancing but it wasn't too long before they stopped and moved to the edge of the stage to watch. We were all mesmerised by the group and especially Mick Jagger.

After a while we noticed a young chap standing watching just by us. He was smartly dressed and wore glasses. At the interval he started to speak to my boyfriend and I, asking us if we were enjoying the group and did we think they stood up to The Beatles and other Mersey groups? After a minute or two he said he had to go to the dressing room to see the boys. At this point I asked him who he was. He said his name was Andrew Loog Oldham and that he was their manager.

After a while he came back and asked me if I would like a signed photograph. I said "yes please" and he then asked me my name and returned to the dressing room. When the second part of the show started he returned and gave me a signed photograph. They wore black cord trousers, blue gingham shirts with button down collars, black knitted ties, black leather

Gay Jinks' autographed memento

waistcoats and Cuban heeled boots. For the second half they wore black cords, black and white dog toothed check jackets, shirts and ties and Cuban heeled boots. We have always remembered the show and my husband has been a fan ever since, although we've never managed to see them live since.

20 AUGUST 1963
Ricky Tick Club, Thames Hotel, Windsor

Martin Osborn *(age 18)*
One of my older brothers was working and living in the area at that time and he knew that I liked bands that played Chuck Berry's music so he invited me down to see the Stones. The venue was like a wooden built village hall in the garden of the Thames Hotel pub, next to the Thames, with a lofty raftered ceiling. The Stones had recently signed with *Decca* and, as part of the deal, must have received new Vox AC30 amplifiers and these had been roped up in the rafters.

The stage was a raised wooded area about a foot high which was just about big enough to hold the band and their gear but not large enough for Mick to run around on, so he had to be content with his strange jigging and clapping semi static dance. Bill, who I had the opportunity to chat to in the break, mostly about equipment and set lists, only needed about a square foot to operate in so space was not a problem. There were no tickets for the night. You paid on the door about 2s 6d (13p) and the back of

your hand was stamped with a rubber stamp as proof of payment.

24 AUGUST 1963
Il Rondo Ballroom, Leicester

Susan Alcock *née Measures (age 17)*
It was quite a small venue but one my friends and I visited most weeks. In fact it was the highlight of the week. Six of us went – myself, Joan Brown, Pamela Blakesley, Christine Hunt, Angela Bowey and Lyn Heath. The Stones were all dressed alike in dark trousers and leather jerkins. I can't believe how lucky we were because even at the back of the ballroom we had an excellent view. Who would have thought at that time they would turn into the legends they are now?

Martin Osborn

Susan Allcock

Martin Osborn *(age 18)*

The Il Rondo was a dance venue. I went there with my girlfriend – now my wife and our drummer and his girlfriend. The Stones appearance had been somewhat tidied up from when we saw them at the Station Hotel and they all wore the same outfit, which consisted of a blue open neck shirt, little black leather waistcoat, smart trousers and black Cuban winkle picker boots. They looked like Paso Doble dancers. The music was just as good and they still played Chuck Berry songs better than Chuck himself.

30 AUGUST 1963
Oasis Club, Manchester

Christine Murphy *(age 15)*

My very special memory of them was cycling after school to Manchester, locking my bike up in the city centre near a club called the Oasis then going to Kendals department store where I changed. I wore a red maxi skirt, a navy and white striped shirt which I'd attached a man's starched collar to, and patent shoes. So me and my friend waited outside the Oasis, autograph books in hand, and next minute there they were – our heroes! They wore elephant cord jackets with round necks, college scarves, shirts and ties and jeans and pointed shoes. We went over and they signed our autograph books and we thought how posh they were and how polite too. And, of course, so cool. I got Mick, Keith and Brian's autographs. Next minute they had gone. My autograph book which

Christine Murphy

I still treasure is full of groups' autographs. They were always called groups. We never used the word 'band' in those days.

On 31 August 1963 the Rolling Stones played their first ever show outside of England.

31 AUGUST 1963
Royal Lido, Prestatyn

Trefor Jones *(age 14)*

I had already bought the Stones first single *Come On* but was too young to attend the gig on that Saturday night at the Royal Lido. However my mates – John Ottley and David Owens – and I knew from previous Saturdays that the artistes usually arrived during the afternoon so we made our way to the Lido and stood near a cafe window which overlooked

Trefor Jones

the beach. I think the cafe was closed to the public at that time of day because we never went inside. Inside we could see all the members of the Rolling Stones. The group came to the window grinning and waved to us. My mates and I went home having decided to return to the Lido that night because there was a place to stand outside which was at the back of the stage. We were able to hear the band playing as a window was open, although the sound was a bit muffled. We couldn't really see them. Eventually a jobsworth came along and told us to go or he would get the police. I think he thought we were trying to play on a nearby children's amusement ride.

A family friend called Bill Baines worked as bouncer/doorman at

Richard Austin

the Lido and I had already asked him to try and get autographs. Next day I had all the Rolling Stones autographs. I gave half the autographs away to my girlfriend in 1965 and lost my own half over the years. However when I met my wife to be in 1970 she had an autograph book. She lived in Chester and her grandfather worked at the Chester Royalty Theatre so besides the Stones, the book had many Sixties' artists' autographs in it, including The Beatles. I forgot to smuggle that book away after my divorce so I'm doomed never to have those autographs.

Ian Jones *(age 16)*
My wife to be and I saw the Stones at the Royal Lido. It's now known as the Nova. We saw all the top groups of that golden time including , Gerry and the Pacemakers, Dave Berry, Johnny Kidd and the Pirates and loads more. They were introduced as coming from the Crawdaddy Club in Richmond, Surrey. All of them were untidy but that was becoming the trend with long hair. Jagger wore a grey round neck jumper. My wife commented that he had unkempt teeth.

Richard Austin
I was working at the Prestatyn Holiday Camp during the 1963 season. I recall the concert was advertised around Prestatyn as being 'London's answer to The Beatles'. It was well attended. When the Stones came on everyone clustered to the stage. I recall thinking that this group were rather ugly looking and not

well dressed. I was brought up in Liverpool attending events featuring The Beatles, the Searchers and Billy Fury who were quite well dressed. It was usual for rock bands at the Lido between sessions to have a drink at the bar. I remember trying to speak with the lead singer at the bar. I didn't know who Mick was at the time. He came across as being quite stand offish and aloof. At that time the power in England rested in London and the Home Counties so anyone coming from up North was looked down on.

10 SEPTEMBER 1963

The Rolling Stones were still playing club gigs at Ken Colyer's Studio 51 in Great Newport Street, London. The Beatles dropped in on rehearsals on this date and, on hearing that the Stones were struggling to decide what their next single should be, John Lennon and Paul McCartney retired to Colyer's office and finished writing *I Wanna Be Your Man*, which was to become the Stones next 45.

13 SEPTEMBER 1963
California Ballroom, Dunstable

David Arnold *(age 17)*
Their second performance there was only two months after the first. And obviously they were a bit more well known and they were on the main stage. And the next three gigs there got more and more crowded.

14 SEPTEMBER 1963
Plaza Ballroom, Kings Heath, Birmingham

Tony Lee *(age 18)*
My fiancée Joy and I danced regularly at the Elite in Handsworth and the Ritz in Kings Heath, both converted cinemas, and enjoyed upcoming British groups and occasional American artists. We were so lucky to see Gene Vincent and the Redcaps, Frankie Valli and the Four Seasons and – oh, I wish I could remember them all.

Tony Lee

> "I bought … a black leather waistcoat and a black leather tie. I bought them because the Stones had them"

However, the most mesmerising of them all were The Beatles and the Rolling Stones – both of whom had that special quality and excitement that captured the audience. No one danced when they were on. The Ritz had a bar beneath the dance floor where the turns often went for their drinks. Mick Jagger, who was waiting to be served by my side, cadged a *Disque Bleu* cigarette, which he still owes me!

17 SEPTEMBER 1963
British Legion Hall, Harrow

Barry Marshall *(age 17)*
The British Legion Hall is a local sort of club down here. It had a bar and there was a hall at the back. I saw the Rolling Stones there. I think I'd bought *Come On*. We all wore suits and stuff. I remember that they had a light

and it made the white collars and shirt sleeves always come out blue. I went to Carnaby Street and I bought, and still have, a black leather waistcoat and a black leather tie. I bought them because the Stones had them.

28 SEPTEMBER 1963
Assembly Hall, Walthamstow

Alan Miles
When the Stones played at the Walthamstow Assembly Hall it was packed to capacity. The Stones could not get into their van afterwards due to the masses of fans so they all ran for it up Farnham Avenue along Forest Road and past The Bell pub. They sat on the wall of the car park, obviously waiting for their van, until gone 1am in the morning, signing autographs and cuddling the girls.

In October 1963 the Rolling Stones embarked upon their first UK tour, which was a package tour featuring a number of acts. Each group or artiste would perform twice nightly. Headliners were the Everly Brothers and, depending on the running order, the Stones were advertised as low as fifth on the bill below Bo Diddley, Julie Grant and – when he was added to the tour to help boost flagging ticket sales – Little Richard. The venues were cinemas and theatres in the Gaumont and Odeon chains with a capacity of around 2,000. The tour took in 31 venues in 36 days. The Stones would play a short set of five songs before making way for the next act. Each performer played twice nightly, with an early evening show typically starting at 5.45pm or 6.15pm and concert goers ushered out of the building in time for a second house at 8.30pm or 9.00pm.

1 OCTOBER 1963
Odeon Theatre (aka Astoria), Streatham, London

Susan McLaren *(age 13)*
Before the concert at Streatham Astoria I saw Brian Jones leaning out of an upstairs window – he threw a photo out, which I later got signed by Keith – but also an apple core, which I kept in a tin in the shed until it was full of maggots and my dad made me throw it out! Later I met them all and got their autographs.

I wanted to see. After seeing them I used to go regular to Guildford Odeon to see lots of people. Got lots of autographs doing all sorts of stupid things like nipping round the back, laying under coaches and things. It's horrific when I think of it now. But we loved it! I used to buy tickets for things but if I couldn't I'd go round the back. I met lots of the stars round the back there. I was in love with Mick Jagger, like millions of other girls.

Susan McLaren

4 OCTOBER 1963
Odeon Theatre, Guildford

Veronica Sewell *(age 14)*
I went with my mother. She wouldn't let me go on my own. The Everly Brothers topped the bill and the Stones were first on. It was brilliant and I loved 'em from that day. They all came on and they were all dressed the same in their black ties, black trousers and the black and white jackets. I can't remember who else was on but I wasn't interested. I liked the Everly Brothers but the Stones were who

5 OCTOBER 1963
Gaumont Theatre, Watford

Diana Whitney *(age 22)*
My mother-in-law had a neighbour called Queenie who worked as an usherette at the Gaumont. The Rolling Stones decided to go for a break in the town after rehearsing. When they came back they tried to get in a side entrance. Queenie would not let them in as she thought they were a scruffy bunch of boys that were trying to sneak in. They had to get hold of the manager to get them in.

Gerry Parker *(age 19)*
My wife went to the Gaumont concert. She remembers Wayne Fontana and the Mindbenders. She said the Stones were hard to hear from the screaming.

Diana Whitney

Barry Marshall
At that time I had a Saturday job in a record shop and because of the trade connection managed to get backstage at Watford. I couldn't meet the Everly Brothers but I met the Rolling Stones, Little Richard and Bo Diddley. I remember getting Bo Diddley's *Pretty Thing* single autographed. I really liked Bo Diddley and Chuck Berry. They recorded for *Chess* and their stuff was issued in this country on the *Pye R&B* label. I had a long chat with Bill Wyman. It wasn't until later that I realised that he was that bit older – he actually behaved that bit older. I got the first Stones single autographed by Bill and by Mick Jagger and Brian Jones. I think Keith and Charlie had gone off somewhere.

10 OCTOBER 1963
Gaumont Theatre, Wolverhampton

Ivan Jackson *(age 19)*
I went with a school friend who I lost touch with many years ago. It was possibly the first or second gig that I ever went to. The Stones were bottom of the bill which also included Chuck Berry, Little Richard, Bo Diddley plus others. In those days sets were short – often 20 minutes from the top act. But even at that stage the Stones were so different and a force to be reckoned with, and certainly a band with a big future and an alternative to The Beatles, who were getting a bit too much attention. It was a super line up. That was the only time I have seen the Stones live as I never have been a large venue follower of anyone. Last year I was looking at some Ronnie Wood prints in a local gallery and the gallery assistant asked if I liked the Stones and if I had ever seen them live. I answered, that although I had followed the Stones for many

Ivan Jackson

years, I hadn't seen them live. Prompted by my wife I was able to put the record straight!

11 OCTOBER 1963
Gaumont Theatre, Derby

Moira Allen (age 15)
As a schoolgirl I wasn't allowed to go to the shows, although I didn't have the money anyway, but was able to go down after school to wait at the stage door, see who ventured out after the matinee and collect as many autographs as possible. On this particular day a group of young lads from a group we'd vaguely heard of came out of the stage door, signed a few books, chatted a bit, then casually strolled over to the Wimpy Bar across the road and sat enjoying their coffees. No one had followed them in or approached them inside – perhaps we were too polite in those days. Afterwards they got into the minibus to return to their hotel, which would have been either The York or The Clarendon – both on Midland Road. Of course it was the Stones! We had an advantage over those who'd been at the concert as by the time it was over they were too late to get autographs and have 'real' contact with their idols. I remember thinking that Brian Jones was the best looking, and of course when I decided to sell those autographs a few years ago his signature and the anecdote helped a lot. The fact that when I'd said "thank you" to Mick Jagger for signing he looked straight at me and said "no – thank YOU!" had me telling the tale for ages!

When they became so famous within the next couple of years, it was great to realise that I was there when they were first starting out. I had many other autographs in my book and sold one or two more, but that encounter made the deepest and most lasting impression on me.

Colin Brown (age 17)
When the Rolling Stones appeared at the Gaumont I was living at home. I was into all the latest groups. Other people I remember on the gig were Julie Grant, The Flintstones and Bo Diddley with Jerome and the Duchess. A mystery surprise guest came on and it was the great Little Richard. The Rolling Stones were very good with Mick as usual full of energy and of course the late Brian Jones on guitar. They played their latest release *Not Fade Away*. Good times. Good gigs.

Barbara Castle
Me and a group of friends went to the Gaumont in Derby to see the Rolling Stones. They came on the stage dressed in black trousers and little black and white checked waistcoats. We thought they were fantastic. My friend who was sitting in the row in front turned around and said "shall we scream?" We all fell about laughing.

15 OCTOBER 1963
City Hall, Kingston-upon-Hull

Graeme Middleyard (age 17)
I can recall seeing the Stones in support of Heinz and the main act Johnny Kidd & The Pirates

> "a group of young lads from a group we'd vaguely heard of came out of the stage door"

Graeme Middleyard

at Hull City Hall. The concert took place just a matter of weeks after I had started my second, and last, year in the sixth form. I recall the impact that the Stones had on me and my fellow sixth formers, certainly as far as hair was concerned. On one memorable occasion at the end of morning assembly the school Head left us in no doubt that, if the hair remained as long after the forthcoming weekend, action would be taken. Needless to say, the barbers in Hull were kept very busy on the following Saturday.

16 OCTOBER 1963
Odeon Theatre, Manchester

Jimmy Murphy (age 21)
I went with my girlfriend Pam Felstead, age 23. Top of the bill were the Everly Brothers who were excellent. Bo Diddley was next – OK, but repetitive, although his sister had wonderfully tight trousers. The Stones were on but, apart from *Not Fade Away*, were poor.

Steve Berning (age 11)
My mother took my brother and me – I would have been 11 and Pete was 7. I remember them playing Bo Diddley's *It's Alright* in a set of around 25 minutes. They had a backline of Vox AC30s and not much else. Their sound was almost overwhelmed by the sound of screaming teenage girls. My mother thought it was extremely funny when theatre staff pulled girls, who had been hanging over the edge of the royal boxes, back by hooking a yard brush over each shoulder.

Jimmy Murphy

18 OCTOBER 1963
Odeon Theatre, Newcastle-upon-Tyne

Brian Swales
My memories are of seeing the Stones at Newcastle Odeon. Also on the bill was Bo Diddley and while he was on a couple of the Stones came and watched his act sitting in empty seats in front of us. Sadly I can't remember which two it was! Three of us travelled up to Newcastle mainly to see the Everly Brothers and Bo Diddley and we weren't impressed with this new group supporting the headliners. They appeared lost on the big stage and we thought their sound wasn't good.

Brian Swales

19 OCTOBER 1963
Gaumont Theatre, Bradford

Ken Dorrington (age 19)
By the time the tour got to Bradford, Don Everly had gone home ill and Phil was carrying on alone. The rest of the bill consisted of Bo Diddley, who was very good, Mickie Most, who sang Sea Cruise, and The Flintstones and Julie Grant, of

who I remember nothing at all. I think we paid twelve shillings and sixpence (63p) to see the concert. I remember vividly the Stones performing *Come On* and Keith with his little run across the stage which was a feature at that time. The crowds in those days mostly stayed seated and I don't recall too much in the way of screaming. It was a very different matter when The Beatles appeared at the same venue.

22 OCTOBER 1963
Gaumont Theatre, Sheffield

Gillian Scaife née Bunting (age 16)

I was there that day with Ann and other friends from the Sixth Form at High Storrs Grammar School. I remember we were sat upstairs and I think we went to other shows. Over the years I had begun to doubt that it was the Rolling Stones I saw as they went on to be such global stars, but I definitely remembered Little Richard.

David Roe (age 22)

The thing that sticks in my memory was the fact that they were all dressed in identical black and white dogtooth suits. I don't think I can ever recall seeing them after that time appearing in suits.

David Arnold

I had a houndstooth jacket made. I binned it some time ago. I did actually get one of those made at a local tailor's because I'd seen them wearing them.

Bob Miller (age 16)

Myself and my girlfriend Jenny Holmes went to one of the shows. I was still at Carlton Grammar School. The Stones looked great and their performance was fantastic – what we could hear of it! Jenny was focused on Brian Jones though. We went on to get married in October 1967 and are still together now, 47 years later.

23 OCTOBER 1963
Odeon Theatre, Nottingham

Bill Shelton

I saw the Stones at the Odeon cinema in Nottingham. They only had a ten minute spot and sang *Poison Ivy*, *Fortune Teller*, *Come On* and *Money*.

Martin Osborn

My girlfriend, my band's drummer, his girlfriend and I saw the Stones at the Odeon Theatre, Nottingham. We all had dental appointments or some other excuse and set off from Leicester to Nottingham (no motorways then) in the drummer's dad's Hillman Minx, arriving late. We asked the man on the door if the Stones had been on and he said that they had, but fortunately a band called the Flintstones had opened the night so we had not missed the Rolling Stones, who closed the first half. I don't know what happened to the Flintstones. The Rolling Stones were great as usual, but somewhat overshadowed by Bo Diddley, Little Richard and the Everly Brothers, and particularly the latter. We could not believe that an act could sound so good live with their

Ken Dorrington

Bill Shelton

Gillian Scaife

"when the Stones came on it was absolute mayhem in the audience but we could hear fine"

fantastic close harmonies. I don't have the tickets for this gig, but we paid about 10/- (50p) each. Good value considering that tickets for 'A' listers can now be nearly £100, and you have to pay £35 to see some of the same acts today still doing the rounds and who were on the support bill with the Rolling Stones in the Sixties.

24 OCTOBER 1963
Odeon Theatre, Birmingham

John Tandy *(age 16)*
I bought tickets primarily to see the Everly Brothers. I went with Sandra, my girlfriend of the time. We were both sweet 16. Don Everly wasn't there because he was taken ill at Heathrow when he arrived and had been sent back home. Phil Everly was terrific in performing without his brother and one of the band filled in on vocals. Dionne Warwick was number two on the bill promoting her latest record, Love Letters. The Stones came out wearing those black and white tweed jackets. My lasting impression of Jagger was him shaking his maracas and the band wearing those tweedy jackets. They were promoting their record *Come On*. I still have the single.

26 OCTOBER 1963
Gaumont Theatre, Bournemouth

Norman Squibb
My pal Gary was in a local group and I was sort of roadie to them. They had no gig that night so we went into town just in case we might get a look at the acts

going in or out. There was an alley at the side of the cinema so we were by the side door when the Stones came along. The chap on the door let them in and Keith Richards – who was last in – saw us and, probably thinking we were one of the support acts, held the door open for us. Well, we are going in! Nobody questioned who we were. We did have the hair and fashion of pop stars after all. Anyway, we watched the entire show from the wings, at one time sharing music thoughts with the singer Julie Grant who was on next and watching with us. When the Stones came on it was absolute mayhem in the audience but we could hear fine, which was surprising as we were level with the speakers. Well we never forgot that night as a non performing support act and when we were doing gigs at pubs, etc., in Weymouth, Poole and other places we enjoyed milking that story. I doubt if it could happen now, with security and the safety of stars being what it is. Keith Richards is still my favourite assistant doorman.

Geoff Cooper *(age 16)*
I remember little of the Rolling Stones, the show being completely dominated by Little Richard who closed the first half of the programme with an incredible set. Bo Diddley was also very well received which, alas, was not to be the fate of the Everlys who were booed off stage by a crowd largely made up of motorcyclists. I loved those package tours and got to see and meet some great artists

from that era. For me no-one ever came close to Little Richard in terms of generating atmosphere and energy. Brilliant!

Pat Squibb *née Pearson (age 15)*

That era was a fabulous time to be a teenager. I used to go with my friend Carol Gibbons. On one occasion when seeing the Stones, one of the friends we were with managed to get on the stage and got me Charlie Watts' drum stick – which I still have!

Margaret Gray *(age 17)*

I went to the first concert they played there, and used to have the programme, plus a photo that was sold at that event. Unfortunately I sold it when we moved in 2007 for £40. I also had a great A4 size black and white picture of the group which either came with the programme or I purchased as an extra. I used to see the queues in the Winter Gardens of people waiting for tickets to go to see The Beatles and for some reason I didn't join them. I had seen the Rolling Stones on *Top of the Pops* and was immediately impressed – what a performance! I can remember having a discussion about it in the Poole Wimpy bar with a young man who said, and I quote, "they are scruffy long haired oiks and they will never last." I often wonder if he remembers that conversation.

It was the very first music show that I had ever been to and it was so exciting. I also bought their first LP and EP and used to play them over and over. I don't think I had

to queue for tickets as I was not one to join a queue and I went with my friend Norma. Of course the lovely Brian Jones was there as well. It did seem that most of the audience, and it was packed, were girls of my age. We had seats on the left and in the middle. We watched the show and then the Stones came on the deafening screams. At the time it was Keith who had my attention and I shouted "Keith!" along with all the other screamers. We could not hear much of the music because the noise level was so very loud. We sat down for the Stones. How very civilised.

27 OCTOBER 1963
Gaumont Theatre, Salisbury

Peter Wood *(age 28)*

All the rage then were The Beatles, who were not my 'scene'. I was more into the American Blues, jazz, Bob Dylan, the Stones, and if I wanted something completely different, the Shadows. When the Stones came to the Gaumont Theatre (now the Odeon) in the New Canal, Salisbury they had barely a following out of their London clubs circuit or so it seemed to us.

I went with Anne who I had just married and my best mate Len Watts and his partner Eileen. The only real number I can recall them performing was The Beatles' *I Wanna Be Your Man*. What I'll never forget though is that Len had an A35 van and was giving Anne and I a lift home. We lived at the bottom of Devizes Road. We were holding on in the back.

> "I had seen the Rolling Stones on Top of the Pops and was immediately impressed – what a performance!"

"this was when they were still wearing their matching outfits – the houndstooth checked jackets"

There were no windows except the driver's and the passenger's. The windows were open and I was trying to gauge our whereabouts. I called out "here it is" and he just braked. Behind us there was a squeal of brakes. We held our breaths, wondering if a crunch was coming. Then a heavy reversing, followed by a quick acceleration. We all sat in wonder and then more braking as a large motor pulled up alongside. A person's head literally leaned into the van and shouted "what fucking clown is driving this fucking van?" With that he drew his head back and their car roared off up the road. The silence was broken by Anne saying "that was Mick Jagger!"

29 OCTOBER 1963
Gaumont Theatre, Southampton

John Martin
There was a problem with the sound system during the Stones set for maybe one or two numbers. I'm not sure that they were appreciated by the majority of the crowd as it was a seated venue. My brother collected their autographs plus those of Bo Diddley and the Duchess on a black and white postcard picture of the group in a pub outside the station before they went on and I still have it somewhere to this day.

30 OCTOBER 1963
Odeon Theatre, St Albans

Brenda Parker (age 14)
My friend Annette and I were both huge fans of the Everly Brothers which is why we went,

even though their glory days were behind them by then. My Dad arranged for a friend of his to drive us there and then pick us up afterwards.

We had great seats right in the centre and only a few rows from the front of the stage. I was really only interested in seeing the Everly Brothers but it was clear that things were changing when the show started and the Stones did their 20 minutes or so. This was when they were still wearing their matching outfits – the houndstooth checked jackets – and they weren't polished and slick like all the squeaky clean well scrubbed pop stars on TV. They were rough and raw and, in spite of the matching outfits, edgy and definitely different. They only played a few numbers and such a brief appearance didn't give them time to make much of an impact. The applause was polite but not terribly enthusiastic. Mick didn't have his dance moves down yet so they just did their allotted few numbers and left – but I thought they were great! They were exciting and I'd never heard music like that before. I became a fan on the spot and I credit the Stones with introducing me to what's turned out to be a lifelong love affair with the blues. That was the night it started.

31 OCTOBER 1963
Odeon Theatre, Lewisham, London

Susan McLaren (age 13)
The Stones were having meal at Bettabar near the Odeon. A few of

us waited and chatted to them. It was very exciting for a 13 year old!

As the Stones first British tour was concluding they released *I Wanna Be Your Man*, written for them by John Lennon and Paul McCartney, as a single on 1 November 1963. It would reach Number 12 in the UK charts.

Robin Mayhew
They got that song from The Beatles – *I Wanna Be Your Man* – and just whoosh!

1 NOVEMBER 1963
Odeon Theatre, Rochester

Kay Hunt *(age 15)*
I went with my friend Jackie. I was very young and we tried but failed to climb into their dressing room via the window. The dressing room was on the second floor so it was too high for us to reach even though we tried to bunk each other up to reach. We were too short. We did manage to pass our autograph books up though. I got Bill Wyman's autograph which

I still have. I really wanted Brian Jones' autograph because he was my favourite so I wasn't that impressed with Bill's.

Valerie Groves
I went with my husband, not to see the Stones particularly, but to see the Everly Brothers. The Stones were in small print at the bottom of the bill. I wasn't impressed by the Stones – I wanted them to finish so that we could see the Everly Brothers.

2 NOVEMBER 1963
Gaumont Theatre, Ipswich

Linda Leech *(age 17)*
Bo Diddley opened the first half and Little Richard closed it. The Stones opened the second half and The Everly Brothers closed it. What a line up! The highlight for me was after the show when my boyfriend David – now my husband – and I popped into a pub that was nearly next door to the theatre and all the Stones were in there enjoying a drink and cigarette. How I wished I had got their autographs.

Kay Hunt (left) and friend

Chapter 4

After their first UK tour, the Rolling Stones returned to playing dance halls and ballrooms, attracting more interest as a result of *I Wanna Be Your Man* having been released.

10 NOVEMBER 1963
Town Hall, Crewe

Ray Hulme *(age 16)*

The Rolling Stones in Crewe? I was there. It was called The Sunday Star Club and was 2/6 (13p) to get in. There were four of us – myself, Pete Hilditch, Terry Williams and Steve Buchan. We were all Rolls Royce apprentices. We were there early as there was nothing to do on a Sunday between five and seven. We were outside the town hall when a van pulled up. It was something like an old Bedford van and out got Mick Jagger and Brian Jones. They asked us if this was Crewe Town Hall. We couldn't understand them at first because of their London accents. Then we

helped them unload their gear to take it up the stairs.

I'd never seen long hair like it and Brian Jones was wearing a blue and white hooped tee shirt. They were casually dressed. We at that time were all in suits, shirts and ties. Mine was chocolate brown with bright red lining. We thought we were the bees' knees but seeing the Stones changed my outlook on how to dress. Of us four I was the only Rolling Stones fan and still am. It was a great night for me and one I'll never forget. I was devastated when Brian died.

Mick Hassall *(age 16)*

Me and my mate Chris Buckley went to that gig at the Town Hall. It was five shillings (25p) to get in. It was great. I was already a Stones fan. We had long straight hair, just like Brian Jones. At the halfway break me and my mate went for a pint in the other room. We were at the bar and Jones and Jagger came in and stood right beside me having a drink. A moment I will never forget.

John Edgley

The event was promoted by *Edgley Entertainments* of which I was founder and operated around the North West during the 1960s. We promoted dances at Crewe Town Hall on a weekly basis during this period, initially on Saturdays. We transferred from

Ray Hulme

Saturdays to Sundays under the name The Sunday Star Club in November 1963. We booked the Rolling Stones to top the bill on the grand opening night, supported by the Cresters and Frankenstein and the Monsters. I remember the event for a few reasons. The Rolling Stones fee was very high for the time – £210. *I Wanna Be Your Man* had only just been released and was their first big hit, *Come On* not having been a major success. They did however have a big following in south east England. We had a whole series of major recording stars at this venue, the Rolling Stones being the second highest earners only surpassed by the Searchers in January 1964 who had just released Needles and Pins. The Rolling Stones door attendance on the night was disappointing, being only half of our house records with groups like Freddie and the Dreamers, the Tremeloes, Eden Kane and the Searchers. In fairness, the Stones had competition on the night as The Beatles were on the *Royal Variety Show* on TV that night. But the Stones committed the cardinal sin and blotted their copy book in arriving at the venue late.

John Edgley

11 NOVEMBER 1963
The Pavilion, Bath

Llyn Harrington (age 18)
I grew up in Bath. I wasn't a regular Pav goer but, because Brian Jones used to live near my auntie in Cheltenham and I used to visit her now and again, I liked to think I knew him. I remembered

seeing something about Brian Jones being in the Stones in the paper. My auntie said "that's the little boy who used to live just down the road from us". He would have possibly been one or two years younger than me at that time. They were sometimes billed as Brian Jones and the Rolling Stones. There was a bit of screaming but not a lot. *Come On* had just about charted. I'm pretty

Llyn Harrington
(second from right)
and friends

convinced that they did *Come On*, although I'd read elsewhere that they never did it live on stage.

They had this strange instrument that looked like a kiddie's toy that they used, like a plastic kid's flute, but *Come On* was the only thing they used it on. I remember being slightly bemused. The support act was the Undertakers. They were also very good. Myself and a friend somehow managed to get backstage after the show and I spoke to Brian who said that he could remember my auntie and her nephew – me – but he was probably just being polite! They weren't that famous then so security wasn't very tight.

I've read in some places that Brian Jones wasn't a particularly friendly person but I found him very friendly that night. I got the impression that he was just being polite when he said "I remember you from Cheltenham". I think they were just quite pleased that a couple of people had come to the rear of the stage to see them.

Sheena Hunter-Hedges *(age 13)*

I remember going to the Pav in 1963 to see the Rolling Stones. It was very difficult to get parental permission, particularly from my dad, as these events happened on Monday nights. I was at the girls' grammar school and homework took precedence over everything in those days. I didn't go with my school friends but with a girlfriend who lived just up the road and her school friends. Her older brother was supposed to look after us but I don't recall him doing so!

The support band was the Colin Anthony Combo and Colin Phillips lived two doors away from me, so that might have swung things in my favour with Dad. The support usually came on first, followed by the headline group followed by the support and then a second appearance from the headline group. We were able to get right up to the stage to watch these groups and one of the girls I was with feigned a faint and was lifted up on to the stage to recover just as the Stones were coming on for their second appearance. Mick Jagger was very concerned about her, stopped to ask if she was OK and autographed her arm or her hand.

Brian K Jones, who was a local promoter who always insisted on the 'K' so as not to be confused with the Brian Jones (as if anyone would have!), was very firmly in charge and rushed us off the stage but not before this very enterprising young lady had stolen a kiss from Mick. The Stones were very fledgling in 1963 and

Sheena Hunter-Hedges

they were good entertainment but not, in my opinion, anywhere near subsequent acts I saw there such as Johnny Kidd and the Pirates, Gene Vincent, Jerry Lee Lewis, Alan Price and particularly Joe Brown and the Bruvvers and Screaming Lord Sutch and the Savages. But the greatest of all had to be Little Richard. He was magnificent.

13 NOVEMBER 1963
City Hall, Sheffield,

Julia Taylor *née Barrett (age 16)*

I remember going to the Stones concert at the City Hall with my boyfriend at the time whose name was Philip Battesby. They performed *Come On* and I was impressed – they were different! I thought these lads are going to be big. They had a sound of their own. We were able to listen to them OK. There was no screaming as they were relatively unknown at the time. Joe Cocker was there. At that time he was part of Vance Arnold and the

Julia Taylor

Avengers. I did not know until years later that he was my second cousin. When mum heard of Joe Cocker in the Seventies she said it was her cousin's son, her cousin being Harold Cocker.

16 NOVEMBER 1963
Matrix Ballroom, Coventry

Brian Robinson *(age 18)*

The Rolling Stones were on at a place called the Matrix which was in the Fletchamstead Highway in Coventry. It's not there now. It was a fairly big crowd. I remember Mick Jagger walked rather gay and someone actually shouting up at him "oh what are you doing, you poof?" Charlie Watts stood up on his drums, threw the sticks down and came to the front of the stage and pointed at the bloke and said "I'll have you outside, mate." It was really funny.

Bob Dunthorne *(age 19)*

The Matrix was the local Saturday night dance. I went with my ex wife. In those days you could see all of the main groups for ten bob (50p) or less. No screaming fans. In fact sometimes group members would be at the bar, though I do not recall seeing the Stones off stage.

Mike Russell *(age 18)*

The Matrix Ballroom was really a canteen belonging to the Matrix factory. I was talked into going by a mate who had just bought their first record, Come On. They weren't even famous then so I said ok. What a great night! Brian Jones had his lime green guitar and Mick Jagger was on form. I can understand why the girls liked him. He had an aura about him and great stage presence. There were more boys there than girls so no screaming that I can remember. The local lads were trying to goad them but they took no notice. No roadies then. What a great opportunity lost as it would have been so easy to have met them. They made an impression on me so much that I later went to the same venue to see the original Searchers, the Swinging Blue Jeans, Dave Berry, Cliff Bennett and a young girl called Twinkle. There were only about 75 to 100 people there to see the Stones.

Arthur Warner and girlfriend

Graham Bellamy
I think it was 6 shillings and six pence (33p) to get in. There weren't that many in the audience, maybe 100. This was a week or so before I was due to see The Beatles at Coventry Theatre. That was it for me – a Rolling Stones fan ever since.

Graham Bellamy (second from left) and friends

Arthur Warner *(age 18)*
I remember going to the Matrix Ballroom on the Fletchamstead Highway, Coventry to see Jerry Lee Lewis plus supporting group. The compere introduced the supporting group as a new group from London called the Rolling Stones. They opened up with *I Wanna Be Your Man*. They stood out to me due to their casual stage dress and their enthusiastic singer. Groups I remember in the early Sixties tended to be reasonably dressed on stage – booted and suited. The Stones were different on the night. The second half of the show they backed Jerry Lee all through his act.

21 NOVEMBER 1963
McIlroy's Ballroom, Swindon

Michael Nolan *(age 16)*
I went to all three Rolling Stones gigs at McIlroy's. At the first show the place was nearly empty and

by the last show when they had become better known the place was heaving. I had actually bought the single *Come On* before going to see them so was already a big fan. There was a story that after one of their shows their van had broken down and they were given a lift by a local taxi driver who took them to his house in Penhill to meet his mother and have a cup of tea.

Adrian Heath (age 18)
The Rolling Stones came on stage and with a 'one two three' from the lips of Mick Jagger the beat began with the number *Come On*. When the musicians started to strum their guitars no sound came out and the house electrician had to quickly jump on to the stage to fix the fault. It took about 30 seconds for it to be all systems go. As a young bass guitarist I loved every note.

David Hyde
I knew virtually nothing about them. After they had played a couple of numbers Mick Jagger

announced that they were one member short. As Jagger put it "the blond guy who stands here is on his way". My friend and I didn't even know anybody was missing. The door at the back of the stage opened a bit later and Brian Jones walked on with his guitar. Magic! One number they did was *Poison Ivy*, the old Coasters' number.

Viv Franklin with Christine

Viv Franklin (age 17)
My future wife Christine and I saw two of the three Stones gigs at McIlroy's and can remember them well. Christine was 16 at the time. One thing that we vividly remember was that Mick Jagger told the audience that Brian Jones – the pin up boy of the time – was delayed and might not make it to the gig, only for the crowd to see him peeping through the curtains at the back of the stage, at which everyone went wild.

Jo Poole (age 15)
I went with my sister Helen in 1963. I was dreadfully upset when Brian Jones turned up late and was not on stage at the start of the show. My sister remembers me

David Hyde

Jo Poole

Bernard Linnegar

to Swindon who went on to become household names. I saw a virtually unknown Cilla Black and a better known Johnny Kidd and the Pirates at the Locarno Ballroom, which is now derelict, in another part of town. At McIlroy's we were visited by the likes of Gerry and the Pacemakers, Freddie and the Dreamers and a lesser known group – as they were called then, not bands – also from Liverpool called the Big Three, one of whom I recall received an electric shock from his microphone.

We of course, had to dress like our heroes with fortnightly trips to London to buy the latest fashions in order to slay the local talent on the following Saturday night. I was there on two of the occasions when the Stones played at McIlroy's. The attendance at the first show I saw was about the usual for a Thursday night – just a few hundred. McIlroy's ballroom, which was a restaurant by day, was not huge with a bar at one end and a tiny stage and there crammed on said stage were the Rolling Stones.

My first thoughts, I have to admit, were that they were not the most attractive people I had ever seen, which was perhaps not helped by the fact that there was no smiling, even at each other. They seemed quite morose and made little or no attempt to communicate with the audience. But the music! Wow, it was fabulous – all the old Bo Diddley stuff, which I loved. We called this R&B but I think it means something else now.

disappearing behind the curtain at the back of the stage and leaving her on her own. Afterwards I chatted to Mick and Keith and Mick asked if I was French as my name was Josephine. Brian was leant up against the wall and Bill and Charlie were at the back of the room. I had two promotion *Come On* photos which were signed by Mick and Keith. Luckily Helen still has hers as mine has been lost over time.

Bernard Linnegar *(age 18)*
As a child my contemporaries and I were totally unaware of austerity Britain. It was just there and largely unrecognised apart from some rationing which went on until the Fifties. Indeed I can remember ration books. How things changed once we got to the Sixties. I was 18 in 1963 when a new era in British pop music was emerging with the Stones and the Liverpool Sound. How fascinating it is looking back at all the fresh young acts that came

David Davies

I was the drummer for the Soundcasters. It was the first time they played at McIlroy's. The Stones had only just got into the hit parade. We had some good promoters. McIlroy's had all the top names as did the Locarno. So you could see anybody who was anybody for half a crown. Two and sixpence (13p). And we went to those places every week.

The promoter was a guy from London called Bill Chanel. He was promoting every week there. They were running dances every week. McIlroy's was a big department store – huge. It was a fairly big restaurant during the day and in the evenings for about three days a week they turned it into a bit of a dance hall for people. The stage was on the side. It was a fairly small stage, about three foot off the ground, not very deep and not that wide really.

On the night that we played with the Stones everybody had to set their equipment up but the Stones equipment was pushed to one side while we set up at the front and played our set. There was a door at the back of the stage that went directly into the kitchens so all the drum cases and the other cases were put down there in the kitchens where they prepared everything and we had to change in the chefs' cubicles where they changed out of their chefs' clothes. So we went on and done our spot and the place was beginning to fill up extremely well and we did round about an hour and came off and obviously all the equipment had to be moved around. The Stones amps and drums and Charlie's drums had to be put up on the stage and we moved ours to the side. In the meantime they were playing records as this was going on and the crowd by this time was absolutely heaving. It did break all the fire regulations because people got into trouble afterwards. People at the back were standing on chairs and tables and they had some fairly big windows at McIlroy's with big window ledges so people were stood on those as well so there was no room in the end. If it held 2,000 there would have been 2,000 in there. Whatever the maximum was it was over the maximum. But the crowd itself was huge that night. It was absolutely huge.

So we finished our set and they set the Stones stuff up and started playing records. Unbeknown to the crowd Charlie Watts hadn't turned up. So there was a bit of a panic at the back. The promoter was getting irate about it and a lot of the crowd by this time, because they actually played a lot of records, were getting a bit disgruntled. So Mick Jagger said to me "would you mind sitting in until Charlie Watts arrives?" And I said "no problem at all". So I went on and sat on Charlie's kit. I used my own snare drum because drummers don't like people using their snare drum. I put me own snare drum there. I talked to Bill Wyman for about five minutes. He was going to give me the nod where there were certain breaks going on. He would tell me what the tempos were, where there was a shuffle or a straight eight,

> "so Mick Jagger said to me 'would you mind sitting in until Charlie Watts arrives?' And I said 'no problem at all' "

and that was it. So it was decided I was going to sit in. So I went and sat on the drums. We were going to play after the next record. We were going to start the set, the Rolling Stones set. And Charlie Watts turned up. So I never even got to play a song with them. But that was it. So they had an hour and five minutes and Charlie just went on and played.

After they finished their set we packed all the equipment up. I spent probably half an hour at least with Charlie Watts and Bill Wyman. Two lovely, lovely people – very, very nice. Charlie Watts' drum kit had a big burn mark on the floor tom tom. And when I asked him where he'd got it from, it was when they were on *Top of the Pops*. They were either on the night before or the week before and the lighting crew had put a stage lamp too close to his tom tom and caught it on fire. And the TV appearance is why the crowd was so big. Because they were just starting to get a name even then. My claim to fame is that I nearly played drums with the Rolling Stones.

> **"the lighting crew had put a stage lamp too close to his tom tom and caught it on fire"**

23 NOVEMBER 1963
The Baths, Leyton

Elaine Spinks *(age 13)*
I saw the Rolling Stones at Leyton Baths. I remember going with some school friends and there was a lot of excitement that we could go. There was a fair bit of screaming but nothing on the scale that came later after a few hit records – we were still dancing round our handbags some of the time!

Alan Miles
The Leyton Baths was full to capacity and overflowing with people. Ronnie Kray was putting himself about as he was in charge of the bouncers. I was at the very front row, about three feet away from Brian Jones. He was playing his spearmint green Gretsch guitar and he had a silver band on his finger. I thought he had injured his finger then but later I came to know that it was a silver band used for playing the slide guitar.

As I admired Brian without actually knowing his name, I thought he may have been Mick Jagger and we argued amongst ourselves what the names were of each of the Stones as we didn't really know who was who. I had never seen anyone perform like Mick Jagger. He wriggled and twisted like an eel. They played *Mona* and he played the maracas. Charlie looked bored and half asleep whilst Keith was hopping back and forwards with his Harmony guitar. Bill stood there with his bass guitar held vertically and chewed gum. As I was standing right in front of Bill's bass amp I could hardly hear what songs were being played.

Many, many girls held up pictures of Brian Jones. I remember Brian studying one and his lips seemed to mockingly ask "who's that?" I liked Brian and I still do. I had just begun to grow my hair long. Brian looked straight at me and gave me a couple of nods of approval. I knew the presenter at Leyton Baths. He was called Mick and he wore a nylon Beatles wig. Many girls were being carried up the stairs of the stage past Bill Wyman. Many of them had their blouses and skirts undone and they were being lifted out of the Leyton Baths for safety as they had feinted.

Some rockers to my right were yelling a few insults at the Stones, things like 'queers' and 'bum boys'. The Stones finished with *Route 66*. Afterwards, Mick the presenter said to me "the rest have gone but Bill Wyman's still there" so I went in to see Bill with two of my friends. I sat next to Bill on the table and looked at Keith's Harmony and I said to Bill "that cost a hundred and twenty pound, didn't it?" Bill replied "no, he bought that second hand for thirty quid." Bill then offered me one of his cigarettes which I took and I asked him if he could autograph it for me. He said "no, I gave it to you to smoke, not to autograph." He tore off a piece of his cigarette packet and autographed it. Meanwhile the two idiots who were with me had both got hold of Brian's Gretsch and were pulling it about, both wanting to strum it. I let loose a loud flurry of swear words and told them to "put the effing thing down". I think Bill was a bit miffed by this and said it was time for him to go. So I saved Brian's Gretsch by my temper but we had to say our good nights to Bill. Bill was the nicest person in show business that I have met.

24 NOVEMBER 1963
Majestic Ballroom, Luton

David Arnold (age 17)
It sticks in my mind because I remember being in the queue and a girl behind us said that Lee

Harvey Oswald had just been shot by Jack Ruby. It was two days after JFK.

25 NOVEMBER 1963
Parr Hall, Warrington

Christine Woods
I was there with my friend Janet. We paid 7/6 (37p) in old money for the tickets. We loved the show – it was fab. Myself and Janet were upstairs just chatting about the show before it started – about what it would be like and how good it would be – when a voice from behind said "it will be a good show." When we turned around it was Charlie Watts!

Susan Clive (age 16)
It was a Monday evening and I went with various friends from my school. In those days it was a dance and the Stones played for quite some time as we all jived along. After they had finished one of my friends knew someone back stage and we were ushered into their dressing room. Mick Jagger was so hot he took his shirt off and put on a clean one. His discarded blue shirt lay on the floor near where Brian Jones was standing and I was pressured by my friends to ask Mick if I could have it. He said I could. I picked it up and pushed it underneath my coat and we were ushered out.

We had to push our way out of the door as there were crowds of girls trying to get in. When I eventually arrived home and showed it to my mother she wouldn't let me keep it. I don't know why. So I cut it into small pieces and gave it away to my friends at school.

> "the two idiots who were with me had both got hold of Brian's Gretsch and were pulling it about"

Marion Caswell (age 17)

I went with my friend Patricia, who was 18. According to my mother I was being led astray – after all, they were long haired louts! I think everything was moving too fast for our parents' generation then. It was a great night and we were at the front of the stage. It was quite a crush. We were able to meet them back stage. I don't know how we managed that but security was not an issue then. I managed to get all their autographs – I've still got them – and shared a bottle of Coke with Mick Jagger. I was star struck for months. I treasured the empty Coke bottle and then one day my mother threw it away. I was distraught!

Ken Magill (age 15)

I went with my older brother David. As I recall it was on a Monday night and I paid four shillings (20p) for the ticket. Four shillings represented half of my week's paper money. The hall wasn't jam packed but was quite well attended. The Parr Hall on Monday nights had most of the popular groups/artists on at that time. I can remember seeing Screaming Lord Sutch, Walker Brothers and the Hollies there. We knew a friendly bouncer who would sometimes let us in by the side door when the act had started. Because I really wanted to see the Stones I paid for my ticket to ensure I got in. The Stones had just released the Lennon & McCartney song *I Wanna Be Your Man*. I was transfixed by the length of Brian Jones' hair. He had the longest hair of all the

John Dooley (right) with Brian Jones

Ken Magill

guys by quite some bit. I've seen pictures now of that era and the hair looks quite tame. I was at secondary school then and wrote a piece about the concert and the rhythm and blues music scene for my English homework. To be fair it was well received by our English master Mr. Daniels. Mind you he had long hair, but not in the rock sense. More the mad violinist.

John Dooley (age 23)

It was great. I remember them playing *Roll Over Beethoven* – it was tremendous. A friend of mine had a brother who was a DJ at the time and my pal and myself were invited to the dressing room, which was just a room at the back of stage. My friend was a keen photographer at the time and he took a photo of Brian Jones and me chatting, which I still have. About four or five years ago I copied the photo and e-mailed it to Bill Wyman. He e-mailed me back, thanked me and told me the date. I'd forgotten that and he had forgotten the name of the venue so we were both able to help each other.

26 NOVEMBER 1963
Stamford Hall, Altrincham

Steve Willamson

My dad was an ex-professional boxer known professionally as Frank Johnson. He was a British and Empire Lightweight Champion in the 1950s and he used to work as a doorman at the Stamford Hall. My two brothers and I were young kids at the time and every now and then Dad would take one of us with him to watch some of the bands who played there and we would usually stand in the stage side wings and watch. My brother, also called Frank, got to see the Stones that night. He said it was a fantastic gig despite the fact that you could hardly hear anything over the girls screaming. I was the unlucky one as it was my birthday.

Dad took me to the Stamford Hall the following week and I saw the Merseybeats. No disrespect to them but I am now a big Stones fan. I was talking to an older chap the other day called Shiny Shoes Tom. He said he remembered that day because he was in a pub called the Malt Shovels in Altrincham having a quiet pint when Mick Jagger and Bill Wyman walked in the side door and ordered a pint each at the short bar next to him. He knew their faces as they were at that time just breaking through in popularity after their first single *Come On*. Tom had a chat with them and they said they were in town for a gig later that evening. Apparently the other band members were in the Barrington Hotel further down the road in Altrincham.

Christine Murphy (age 15)

I first saw them at my youth club. This was at the Stamford Hall in Altrincham and was set up by one of the teachers from the boys' school opposite our girls' school in Timperley, Cheshire. The club was called the Young Ones Rock Club and it was run by Mr Bell, the gym teacher and an ex boxer. There they were – all slim, good looking and playing the blues. *Walking The Dog*, *Not Fade Away* and so on. We just danced in front of the stage

as they danced and played away. They were so cool and so good. Mick was so agile and moved about so much. Charlie was nonchalant on the drums. Bill was poker faced and strumming away and Keith was a different Keith then, quite quiet and just playing well. Brian was so cool, his long blond hair moving as he played. I was hooked and have been ever since.

27 NOVEMBER 1963
Empress Ballroom, Wigan

William Blackledge

I was bassist and later band leader with the Wigan Empress Hall band from 1954 until 1969. There were hundreds of great acts that passed through in that time and the Rolling Stones was one of them. I'd like to say that I was overawed but they were just another group passing through.

I still vividly remember arriving at the Empress expecting a standard Wednesday night crowd. I was there as DJ, compere and general dogsbody. There were three groups on that night. Two local groups and the Rolling Stones, who I hadn't heard of. But I had difficulty getting into the place. There must have been 1,500 people in Station Road so I realised the Stones were popular. The evening went well and the Best Boys and the Cheetahs held their own as far as performances go. I'd like to say that I was impressed but my feelings at the time were that groups like the Rolling Stones were threatening the livelihood of pro musicians. It was just another night at Wigan Emp.

> "he was in a pub … having a quiet pint when Mick Jagger and Bill Wyman walked in the side door and ordered a pint each"

Ray Jones

I played lead guitar in a group called the Cheetahs from Widnes. We had an engagement at the Wigan Empress Ballroom, later called the Wigan Casino. I have a diary from that time and all I've got in my diary is Wigan Emp. So it looks like we didn't know when we got the booking we were actually playing on the same bill as the Stones. The Stones were only just coming in then. They'd just released one single and were maybe on their second. It was full. The ballroom hadn't seen anything like that. There were queues outside. It was full to capacity I think.

There were two stages at the Wigan Emp. We didn't play on the main stage. The Stones did. We played on the stage at the other end of the ballroom and we watched the Stones from a balcony looking down onto the stage and it was the first time that any of us had seen some hysterical girls in an audience. And they were being hauled up by the security guys from the Stones or from the theatre. They were pulling them up onto the stage and taking them away back stage. They were getting crushed by the crowds rushing forward so it was quite novel. I'd seen The Beatles and it was a much more orderly organisation. The crowd applauded The Beatles. It went quiet when they spoke. Fellahs in the audience were shouting out "John, can you play – " and they named a tune that they knew. But it was not like that with the Stones. It was squealing and screaming and hysterical really. They'd been on the TV. They were a London group. Therefore they were seen in the north as some of the big guys. There was knowledge of them. I can't remember if it was one or two tracks that had been released. And obviously they were a good band. Mick was a tremendous entertainer in them days so he would get them going. And it was self generation really from the crowd.

30 NOVEMBER 1963
King's Hall, Stoke-on-Trent

June Brown (age 13)

We went to see the Stones in the early Sixties at the King's Hall in Stoke. The fans screamed non stop all through the show so we could not hear them play. They piggy backed on their boyfriends' shoulders so we could not see them either. The room was smoke filled and jam packed. We were glad to get out alive and go home.

June Brown

1 DECEMBER 1963
Oasis Club, Manchester

Bob Lee (age 15)
I couldn't get in. The Oasis was on Lloyd Street, off Albert Square. The queue was from that club right round the block, right round the back, down Brazennose Street which is where the Twisted Wheel was on the corner of, and right past the Twisted Wheel. So there was a queue for the Wheel and a queue for the Rolling Stones at Oasis. All these clubs had very primitive air conditioning just like a fan blowing out so if you ever wanted to hear any group at the Wheel or Oasis you just had to stand outside near the fan and you could hear them as clear as day.

2 DECEMBER 1963
Assembly Rooms, Tamworth

Wendy Burton (age 15)
I attended that concert with my friend Paula – we were 15 years of age at the time and are still good friends now. That night the Assembly Rooms rocked. The screaming nearly drowned out the Stones performance but nevertheless it was a fantastic evening and one I will never forget. I am almost sure their transport was a blue van. I remember it being parked at the side of the Assembly Rooms. I also remember them leaving after the concert and can't remember how many of them I managed to have a snog with. I don't know whether our parents knew where we were that evening but it was certainly

worth any trouble we may have been in when we got home.

Sandra Hale (age 16)
My mates and I were there that night. It was brilliant and I have been a fan ever since. In the interval we went down to the bar and two of my mates were down there. One was with Mick Jagger and the other was with Keith Richards. What really sticks in my mind is Brian Jones and Charlie Watts were sitting down having a drink. Charlie had got his legs stretched out and he hadn't got any socks on. Everybody wore socks then!

Alan Wood (age 16)
My wife Carole and I were both 16 years old at the time and both attended the concert, although we were not a couple then and didn't even know each other. I managed to get Mick Jagger to autograph a ticket. Carole went one better and managed to get a flyer for their latest release autographed by the whole band. The highlight of the night for Carole was snogging Brian Jones in the car park after the concert.

8 DECEMBER 1963
Olympia Ballroom, Reading

Julie Sutton (age 15)
Myself and some friends saw them two or three – firstly I think at the Town Hall and then at the Olympia Ballroom which used to hold a Ricky Tick Club on a Sunday afternoon. The Ricky Tick Club was actually in Windsor but also staged Sunday afternoon shows

Bob Lee

Julie Sutton

Beverley Carruthers

in Reading for a while. We saw lots of Sixties bands including the Animals, the Nashville Teens, the Walker Brothers and the Kinks. In those pre seven day shopping days it was one of the few places open on Sundays. I don't have my membership card any more but I do remember one particular Rolling Stones gig where a few of us managed to climb up on stage – and quickly got thrown off again! We were only about 15 at the time and went into school the next day very proud of this adventure, only to find that a couple of the other girls had actually had a lift back to Woodley with the band. Brian Jones had some family or a girlfriend living in Woodley, East Reading, and spent quite a bit of time there before the Stones really hit the big time.

Beverley Carruthers *(age 15)*
My best friend loved Brian but I was for Mick, so no conflict of interests! The Stones were top of the bill and the supporting band

was the Animals. We had never heard of the Animals. They came on dressed all in denim. Only the bin men wore those clothes. Eric Burdon was chubby and spotty. Their songs were drowned out by all of us chanting "we want the Stones!" until they played *House of the Rising Sun* and suddenly they were more than okay. Then – bliss – the Stones! We didn't really listen. We were too busy shouting "Mick!" and "Brian!" at the top of our voices. Mick looked wonderful – striped top and so skinny and all that hair. Brian – such cute hair and looking sort of shy. The other three – well, they were just there. It cost us 7/6 (38p), which was worth every penny. Afterwards I bought a poster and photo and hung about and Mick signed the photo 'to Bev love Mick x'. I kept it for years and then I grew up, fell in love with David Bowie and threw the poster and photo in the bin.

11 DECEMBER 1963
Kings and Queens Hall, Bradford

Judith Yaxley *née Ackroyd*
I was Student Union Secretary at the Regional College of Art, Bradford. The Art College Union organised a number of social events during each year and participated in planning and delivering the famous Rag Week events with other local student organisations. Our annual college highlight was the student dance held in the Kings and Queens Hall and I was responsible for booking a band for this event in 1963. From a list of options I chose one particular group but

they were unavailable so I chose an alternative at random as I quite liked its' name – the Rolling Stones. Charging approximately £200 we thought we could afford to book this group. It was available so I confirmed the booking.

On the day the union officers worked hard setting up the hall and the band arrived in good time. We supplied them with basic refreshments in the Green Room after they had set up their equipment and the Treasurer and I manned the entrance – praying that our publicity had done its' work and that we would take enough in ticket sales at the door to cover the band's fee. In the event we need not have worried and we were able to hand payment over to Bill Wyman who, even then, seemed to be the chap in charge of the group's finances.

The evening was a great and memorable success and the quality of the band shone through, with Mick Jagger performing as lead singer in the manner for which he was to become so famous very soon after. Only recently I met a man who said no one ever believed him when he told them of his presence at this historic event so he was delighted when I was able to verify that it had actually taken place.

Kevin Holt

I saw them at a student's ball at the Queens Hall in Morley Street before they became so famous. I went with my girlfriend Carol (now my wife of 48 years) and some friends called Anne and Trevor. We got tickets from Anne's brother who was a student at Bradford College. We were walking up the street before we went in and saw them unloading an old Commer van with their instruments in. They gave a great show considering they were an unknown band at the time. I can't remember what they sang at the time but I do remember Mick Jagger gave an announcement over the mike for a young lady to ring her mum.

Judith Yaxley

14 DECEMBER 1963
The Baths Hall, Epsom

John Hinton-Styles, The Presidents

They used to board over the Baths Hall in the winter for this sort of purpose. But unbeknown to them I think there were one or two windows open out the back and people were crawling in. There was a well overload there. We did all the hard work on stage and the Stones followed it up afterwards. But it was a great night. It went off really good. After that of course they moved on and we stayed as we were. It was probably one of the best nights Epsom put on I should think.

Paul Sonnex (age 17)

I was there and remember it well. The Sixties was a great time to be young and the Stones were one of several exciting new groups. I have a vivid recollection of standing in front of the stage watching Mick Jagger strut around and an expressionless Brian Jones strumming his guitar to *You Better Move On*. The volume was tremendous and the atmosphere

Kevin Holt

electric. The room was heaving with young people all having a good time. It was the first gig I had attended and I remember my girl friend and I being transfixed at the edge of the stage totally stunned by the fabulous sound. Truly a night to remember.

Dawn Gozdz *(age 16)*

I was accompanied by my boyfriend, later to become my husband, and my big sister. We had a hard time persuading our dad to let us go but at the time my sister was recovering from a life threatening illness and desperate to have some fun so Dad eventually relented.

The hall was so big and usually used for the big brass band type of dances. Unlike some of the dance halls it lacked in atmosphere. It was brightly lit with normal high watt bulbs. We went into a bare hall with a stage. The hall looked as if it was only about a third full as everyone crowded down by the stage and some of the girls sat on their boyfriend's shoulder to get a better view, leaving loads of space at the back for the keen dancers.

In later years it was nice to be able to say "I saw the Rolling Stones live" but at the time it was just another weekend dance. My sister remembers people climbing in through the toilet windows see the Rolling Stones and to avoid paying an entrance fee. She enjoyed the evening and had a fantastic time and it gave her the boost that life is for living and having fun. And luckily she is still enjoying good health and having fun today.

Karin Stevens *(age 15)*

I was at this performance albeit I should not have been. I was just 15 and a great Rolling Stones fan. My parents did not approve of my choice of band or their music. I was determined to see them but did not have enough money for a ticket. However I knew the baths very well as I had been swimming there every day during the summer opening season for many years.

On the evening of the performance, I and couple of others shimmied up one of the drainpipes and in through a small window. We thoroughly enjoyed the show. The Stones were still in their 'art school look' period and all wore black polo neck jumpers. We did a lot of screaming. I also went to a party they held at the bungalow in Dorking Road that they rented for a while, but that's another story!

Eddie Patterson

I was drummer with the Presidents at the time. I don't remember much of that night over 50 years ago. For sentimental reasons I have hung on to my written record of payments received while playing with the Presidents. My share for that gig in 1963 was the princely sum of £3. I have a vague memory that Ian Stewart played piano on a couple of our numbers but that may have been in rehearsals.

Robin Mayhew

The Presidents were a big local draw all around Sutton, Cheam and Epsom area. Haywood who booked the Stones in to Epsom Baths Hall thought 'well, okay.' He knew that if he booked us as well as the Stones there was a good chance of getting an audience into Epsom Baths Hall, which was quite a big venue. And we were knocked out. And the Stones had just got their first chart success with *I Wanna Be Your Man*. And I think we got two or three quid for the gig. In those days we used to earn between three and five pounds for a gig each which was really a basic wage in those days. And we were doing probably four or five nights a week sometimes, the Presidents. We were really busy all around the north London circuit.

At the Epsom Baths Hall I think we went down better than the Stones actually. I know that sounds very glib. But we had such a following and they were all there. We started our set with Chuck Berry's song *Talking About You* and another friend of our band – none other than Jimmy Page – was in the wings playing harmonica. Jimmy Page was playing harmonica in the wings for us because he knew our bass player Colin Golding and he knew me, and Stu was tinkling away on the piano. It was great. We had a great time. We were rather overwhelmed and I can't really remember much or anything about the Stones performance. It didn't stick in my mind – let's put it that way.

Jane Tomkins
née Shillabeer (age 15)
I was still at school near Epsom. There was a boy in my class called Robert who wanted to be my boyfriend and when he said he wanted to take me to see the Rolling Stones performing at Epsom Baths, I wasn't about to argue! At the time the Stones were not very famous. I seem to remember that they had only produced one EP and one single.

The gig was, of course, fantastic and I decided to leave just before the end in order to find my way backstage to try and meet the boys and get their autographs. I was lucky to be the only fan there and they each walked past me separately, giving me enough time to ask each one to sign their autographs. I handed each of them a card which was available at the gig, with a black and white photograph of them on one side and the name of their early releases on the reverse. As the photo was predominantly black, two of them had to sign on the back. The breathtaking moment was when Brian Jones handed me his famous green Gretsch guitar to hold while he signed his autograph. Little did I realise at the time that his untimely death only a few years later would crystallise that very poignant memory.

I was so excited that I had actually met and spoken to the boys that I can honestly say that I do not remember what happened afterwards. I can't remember how I got home or what happened to the poor boy who had so kindly taken me there – I must have brushed him aside when I next saw him in school!

Jane Tomkins

Brian Howard

Brian Howard

The Stones played the Baths Hall twice – in December 1963 and January 1964. The Fiore Coffee Bar in Bookham was one of a number of coffee bars I used in the Bookham, Leatherhead, Ashtead and Epsom areas to market some of the tickets. Epsom Baths Hall was licensed for music and dancing for 962 persons. Of course, that was for 'old fashioned' dancing and was certainly well below what our sort of event would happily accommodate.

As a consequence I ordered 1,250 unnumbered tickets for the first show and gave 850 to the box office and sold the remaining 112 (read 400!) via the coffee bars and youth clubs. Happily, no one picked up on the discrepancy. When I ordered the posters and tickets the prices shown on them were 5 shillings and 6 pence (28p) in advance and 6 shillings and 6 pence (33p) on the door. By the time they arrived, I knew that I had underpriced the tickets and that I didn't need to offer the 'in advance' incentive. I planned to go through every poster and ticket and cross out the lower price, which would have made me over £60 extra. However my dear mother, bless her, talked me out of it saying "if you were to sell 1,250 tickets at 5/6d each would you be very pleased?" When I said "yes" she told me not to be greedy. So I left them as they were but, 51 years on, it still exercises my mind.

When I arrived at the Baths Hall around 7pm for an 8pm start there were approximately 500 people on the steps, all without tickets. The Hall Manager, a dour Scotsman called John Smith, was very proper and couldn't be encouraged to 'look the other way' so we had to turn these additional punters away – most distressing.

Whilst The Presidents were playing the hall was very nicely full with our uncounted 1,250 punters but when the Stones came on the surge forward left the back third of the hall empty. Plenty of room for that extra 500! Sadly, I don't still have the contract which, I guess, would be worth real money. However, I actually signed the contract in August before the Stones first record *Come On* was released. Whilst their normal Saturday night fee at that time was circa £60 the agent – hedging his bets – asked for 50% of the gate money. I thought about it for a few days, played around with the numbers and went back with an offer of £50 plus 20% of the gate money, which the agent accepted. My recollection is that the gate money (at least the declared level) was £300 so I ended up paying £110 for the Stones rather than the £150 that I would have had to pay on the original offer from the agent. By the time the Presidents and the hall, posters and tickets were paid for I was left with something like £145. So for one night in my life I earned considerably more than the Rolling Stones, who had to pay their agent and roadies and then share the remainder between five of them.

To cap it all in December 2013, 50 years minus one day after the gig itself, I sold at auction a poster advertising the gig and an A4 signed photograph of the Stones from that night. I cleared £7,500 which I then blew on my 70th birthday party last February. What a great party, and we drank a toast to the Rolling Stones!

Mervyn Harper
Being four years older than Mick Jagger, I had already been through the skiffle and trad jazz phases by the time the Stones, The Beatles, etc. started making a name for themselves. My one indulgence in the early Sixties was Wednesday night at the Savoy Ballroom in Catford to hear Brian Poole and the Tremeloes, a band whose records never really came close to their stage act – probably the reason for Ted Lewis's error of judgment in signing them ahead of The Beatles. My contact with the Stones was second hand, when I worked in a south-east London garage. I went to work for Car Mart Sales Limited at 163 Bromley Road, London SE6 opposite the Robertson's jam factory in 1960 after National Service. These days it is a Turkish restaurant. Back then it was a 24 hour petrol service and the regular night pump attendant was a strait-laced northerner, a Mr Mitchell who as far as I know never revealed his first name but who was always immaculate in pressed white overalls and a blue beret. When the Stones had been performing in London they would frequently pull onto the forecourt late at night in their ramshackle Austin J2 van and Mr Mitchell would serve them with 10/- worth of petrol to get them home. To

the surprise of those staff who had never met the Stones, and only heard scurrilous stories, Mr Mitchell would never hear a word against them, got to know them by their first names and, when asked, would declare that they were "a really fine bunch of lads".

17 DECEMBER 1963
Town Hall, High Wycombe

Ruth Bowler née Davy (age 17)
I went with my 20 year old boyfriend – now my husband of 48 years. High Wycombe Town Hall was the place to be seen then. I lived in Marlow and there was nothing else of its type for miles except the Adelphi at Slough, where we saw many famous acts of the time. The hall was so packed with people that we were upstairs trying to get a good look. The sound was amazing as the acoustics were obviously very good. It was deafening and everyone was screaming and rocking to the beat. It was a wonderful evening and they were electrifying. It was a wonderful time to be a teenager.

20 DECEMBER 1963
Lido, Winchester

Elaine Howells née Gilbert (age 17)
I wasn't actually at the Lido – my parents didn't allow me to go. However, I did see the members of the group at very close quarters when they went to the nearby Hyde Tavern during the evening. I was at the youth club in the parish hall next door and word

Ruth Bowler

Elaine Howells

Baz Mort

got around that the Rolling Stones were in the Tavern. I crept in and sat down with a friend. I was so much in awe of them that I didn't know what to say. They were of course very recognisable but there was no big fuss – they were just a group of lads having a much needed drink amongst themselves and I got the feeling they wouldn't welcome attention. I remember thinking that they looked distinctly unwashed! I did register at the time that this was a really big moment in my life, being within touching distance of such famous, notorious celebrities.

Baz Mort *(age 18)*

I remember that they put up the price for this show from the usual 5s (25p) to 7/6 (37p). Also you needed to buy a ticket in advance when normally you could just turn up and get in. Maybe the fifty per cent increase put off a few of my friends as it turned out that I went by myself. In retrospect this was probably the most important gig I'd been to although I was a regular at the Lido and can also boast seeing Cliff Richard and the Shadows in Southampton at the tender age of 14. Anyway, I vividly remember queuing up outside on a dry winter's night having first had a couple of drinks at the Prince of Wales, which has now been converted into flats, and which was down the road from the Lido. Inside the Lido was packed and, not being the tallest of kids, I made my way to the balcony. I managed to find a good spot in the centre with a great view of the stage. The stage wasn't very high

and there were a few long haired lads actually standing on the stage waiting for the Stones to appear. Down below it was packed and girls were being hoisted onto shoulders so they could see. From then on it becomes a bit of blur. I remember the Stones coming onto the stage but the only numbers I can really remember are *Come On* and *I Wanna Be Your Man*, introduced by Mick as "our new single". I guess that they played for maybe 30 to 40 minutes. This has gone down as the legendary Winchester gig and when I tell youngsters that I saw the Stones for about 35 pence in 1963 they are either in awe or disbelieving. My friend John Martin happened to be in another local pub, the Hyde Tavern, that night and in the back bar were Brian Jones, Keith Richard, Bill Wyman and Charlie Watts. He told me that Mick came in and said "right lads, we're on now" and off they went. I only wish that I'd gone to the Hyde that night instead of the Prince!

John Martin

My girlfriend and I walked into the Hyde Tavern public house on Hyde Street and all the Stones bar Mick were lounging around in the back bar. I am sure Keith was lying on a settee. After 15 minutes or so Mick walked in wearing a scarf and a dark Crombie and just said to them all "we're on." We left as well and followed them to the Lido, which was only a couple of minutes away. Tickets were 7/6 (37p). They got a great reception and I remember lots of girls on the shoulders of boyfriends. After a while we went upstairs to the balcony for a much better view. I remember Mick introducing their new record at the time – *I Wanna Be Your Man* – written by The Beatles. They also did a lot of Chuck Berry numbers plus *Hide And Go Seek* by Bunker Hill which I will never forget. I often wonder if any of the Stones even remember that song. Being a smaller venue the atmosphere was brilliant and the sound was very good. It's also difficult to estimate the crowd size but it was a sell out. There was a large following at that time in Winchester of R&B groups rather than the Liverpool/ Manchester groups which often appeared at the Lido such as the Big Three, the Searchers, Billy J Kramer, the Hollies and the Merseybeats. My big regret was missing the chance of seeing the Stones at the Station Hotel in Richmond early that year as I was living and working in Acton and often got invited over by work colleagues but never made it.

22 DECEMBER 1963
St Mary's Hall, Putney, London

Pete Brown *(age 16)*
I saw the Stones at St Mary's Hall, Putney. They lined up along the stage wearing leather waistcoats. Their hair was long and they looked grown up to me. I don't think there was a lot of movement and Mick and Brian shared the vocals and harp playing. The music was Chuck Berry and Bo Diddley plus other R&B of the time. It was very exciting. The whole evening is a bit of a blur

now as most bands at that time became relatively easy to see I but I remember it as one of the best gigs I ever saw.

30 DECEMBER 1963
Studio 51, London

Adele Tinman
The crowds got bigger and bigger. It was a Monday night. I can remember when they did their last gig there. It was the last gig they did at Studio 51 and they were off and so there were more people there by then. They sort of graduated to one evening performance there because I think that that was the time when they were going off to do a tour somewhere. And it was a goodbye farewell thing at the club. It wasn't a huge crowd because you wouldn't have been able to get in the club. It wasn't a big crowd at all.

31 DECEMBER 1963
Drill Hall, Lincoln

Roger Williams *(age 16)*
It was my first year at art college. First term, actually. There were three of us. My friend Max who was studying accountancy. A lady friend of ours – Tolly – who was also at the art college. And me. It was Christmas break. None of us lived in Lincoln at the time. We were commuting students. I was living in a place called Horncastle. I don't know how we got in because I don't think we had any money. But we got in and it was their first tour outside London. I think they'd been somewhere the

> "they lined up along the stage wearing leather waistcoats. Their hair was long and they looked grown up to me"

night before, down in the Fens somewhere. It might have been King's Lynn.

So it's New Year's Eve and we did get in. The band had started playing and it was the blue denim shirts and leather waistcoats because they were in Manchester a couple of days later and they were on *Top of the Pops*. Anyway, we got in and I think it might have been something to do with Tolly snogging one of the bouncers on the door. She snogged us in.

After the show we were in Broadgate heading back to a flat where we were staying the night. Round about midnight we spied the Rolling Stones in a street in front of us – four of them. Not Brian Jones. We had a bottle of cider. So we caught up with them and cigarettes were exchanged. I can remember Keith Richards

offering us cigarettes and we had a bottle of cider and I think we shared that with them. We were sixteen year olds and they were twenty, twenty one year olds, and a bit older in Bill Wyman's case. But they were just making their names then really. They weren't altogether known because they'd only got *I Wanna Be Your Man* as their first release and sixteen was the highest it got, I think.

They were staying in the Grand Hotel – which no longer exists – on St Mary's Street. Somebody said that Brian Jones stayed in the White Hart. That was it – a heady night for young teenagers. Tolly, wherever she is, will be able to tell her grandchildren that she snogged Mick Jagger on New Year's Eve 1963. When we got back to college in January nobody believed us.

4 JANUARY 1964

Town Hall, Oxford

Dave Barden *(age 18)*

Ann and I were courting. She was working at Morris Motors in the trim shop at the time and I was an apprentice toolmaker at the Radiators on Woodstock Road. We travelled in on that Saturday night on my motor bike. I remember parking my motorbike in St Giles, me with my Beatles high buttoned suit and Ann in her trendy Sixties mini skirt and also wearing a leather cap. What a fantastic venue. We paid at the door and walked up the grand staircase in the Town Hall, paying about a shilling to leave my suit coat and Ann's coat in the cloak room. When we got in we were right down at the front of the stage. I remember them coming on stage via what seemed to be stairs coming up the middle of the stage. It was a great night but not a full house. They did numbers by Muddy Waters and also Howling Wolf. A lot of blues numbers with Mick Jagger on mouth organ. Mick said they had just recorded *I Wanna Be Your Man*.

Nigel Molden *(age 15)*

I was a pupil at the City of Oxford High School. My father worked for the company that supplied the bar at the Town Hall for the Saturday night dances. They were organised by a lady called Mrs Osbourne for Bee's Catering. The perk for me was that my father could nearly always obtain two free tickets for me and hence I was able to be at the Rolling Stones appearance with a friend. By this time the popular music explosion had been generally accepted and I do not recall any scenes of hysteria or screaming.

I do have a very clear memory of the band coming on stage and performing with an exotic mixture of equipment. Brian Jones was playing a green, wide body electric guitar and one set of speakers was a very large handmade unit. Interestingly the equipment was a problem almost from the outset. After a few minutes there was a short break as the roadies ran around trying to repair something. Shortly after that a more serious problem developed and there was another break of something like ten minutes whilst more repairs were under way. The band stayed on stage through all of this and Mick Jagger, still playing maracas, mumbled a number of apologies in the almost dismissive style that we have all come to recognise.

I recall that a large audience attended but I doubt that it was a full house. The Saturday night shows were about the best that Oxford had to offer at the time.

Nigel Molden

Everything had to be over before midnight as the Town Hall was a municipal facility. I still have my ticket and another is framed and has been on display on the wall of the Town Hall for some years.

Barbara Bolder *(age 14)*

I was in the Town Hall that night. I wouldn't have missed it. It was quite amazing. Oxford Town Hall was the place to see all the new upcoming groups. My friend Freda and I had arrived early and stood by the stage, all made up in our highest heels and wearing all our latest clothes, as you did at 14. It was the first and only time that everyone was so mesmerised by a group that no one danced – we all just stood and watched. They were so different and so exciting. And a bit scruffy, which was different. At some point Keith Richards' guitar string broke and he had to change it. He walked across the stage to us and handed his plectrum to Freda. She was thrilled – she still has it.

Andrew Crisp *(age 26)*

Traditionally on New Year's Eve in Oxford Town Hall there was a large public dance. In 1964 the Rolling Stones were to be top of the bill and the main attraction. In those days there might be up to six groups performing in one evening, all doing a relatively short slot. The Stones were on last and opening the proceedings was my brother's band the Falling Leaves, who were popular in the Oxford area at the time. The drummer with the Leaves had had rather too much to drink the

day before so, being a drummer, I was asked to step into the breach. No matter that I was a trad jazz musician, I managed to make a fair fist of the blues numbers. With all the bands that were on there was much confusion on the stage with amplifiers, speakers, etc. all over the place. I asked Charlie Watts if I might move his kit so that I had space to set up my meagre equipment. "Don't bother," he said, "use mine." So I played on Charlie Watts' Gretsch kit. Mick Jagger apart, the Stones carried their stuff from the band's van up the Town Hall steps and set it all up themselves. There were very few roadies around then. Mick, however, made an entrance, forcing his way through screaming female admirers. I also spoke to Brian.

I went to art college in Cheltenham in 1961. We students used to frequent a café called the Black Tulip. It had a pinboard and on it was a notice asking for musicians to form an R&B band. I was interested in the American blues stuff (Howling Wolf, Muddy Waters, etc) coming into England at the time, so I wrote to the name on the notice, a certain Brian Jones. He kindly replied, thanking me for my interest but he was wanting to go fully 'pro' which I obviously couldn't do having just started on my art course. When I talked to Brian about his Cheltenham notice he said "I remember. You are the guy with the italic handwriting." What a fine fellow, with none of the big time attitude that rock stars are supposed to have.

"the Stones carried their stuff from the band's van up the Town Hall steps and set it all up themselves"

7 JANUARY 1964
Adelphi Theatre, Slough

Richard Tuck (age 19)
I was chairman of the students union at Slough College of Further Education and we had someone named Dave who knew the Rolling Stones. He acted as an intermediary for booking them. At that time there was inadequate space at the college so we booked the Adelphi. The first time we agreed to pay the Rolling Stones £16 to play and that went so well that we booked them there and then to play another gig for £22. However, they didn't turn up for the second occasion as their first record had come out and they had other things to think about. I like to think we gave them their first big break! It was not part of a tour but before it – a very informal arrangement, demonstrated by the fact that they were able to drop out of the second gig – with notice. Locally they were well known, particularly in Windsor and Eel Pie Island, but not nationally at that time. I remember that it was very loud but they didn't have flashy amplifiers, rather DIY amplifiers and guitars. I think a small wardrobe featured as one of the loud speakers. There were perhaps about five hundred people, and I think they played for the whole evening with two sets of an hour each. The audience all stayed on the dance floor separated from the band, which was on an alcove like low stage with a handrail and gates at the front. The audience was either students or serious fans of the Stones so there was no hysteria but much appreciation.

After starting 1964 with a handful of dance hall shows the Rolling Stones embarked on a second British tour, comprising entirely English towns and cities apart from two shows in Cardiff. This time they appeared second on the bill to all girl group The Ronettes and ahead of the Swinging Blue Jeans, Marty Wilde & The Wildcats and Johnny Kidd & The Pirates. The Ronettes would close the first half of show, with the Stones closing the second half. But even on their nights off from the package tour, the band often played a club or dance hall.

9 JANUARY 1964
Granada Theatre, Kettering

Lesley Smith (age 19)
The night that the Stones were appearing at the Granada my husband was out with his band, so I went to watch the Stones with my friend Janice Chapman. The Ronettes were top of the bill. At the end of the show Rex Smith, who was the manager and knew us, asked if we would like to meet the Stones. This we did, and got all their autographs. I kept them for years but sadly during a house move they were lost. I wonder how much they would have been worth today?

Lesley Smith

Jean Wallace (age 15)
I had just started work when I attended the Rolling Stones concert at Kettering Granada

Dena Hubbard

with my friend Chris. I was not impressed. They were falling about all over the stage. I felt I had wasted my money. It was the worst concert I went to and I saw many in the Sixties at the Granada.

Dena Hubbard *(age 16)*
I went with my friends and we paid about five shillings (25p) in old money. My wage was £4 10s (£4.50) for a 42 hour week. We sat three rows from the stage. They were the best days. The Granada is now a bingo hall.

10 JANUARY 1964
Granada Theatre, Walthamstow

Alan Miles
I saw the Stones play with the Ronettes at the Walthamstow Granada. At the side of the Granada was an alleyway where the Stones' Volkswagen was slowly pulling out. Sitting in the front was Keith Richards. I had a large rolled up photograph of the Stones with me. He beckoned to me through the window so that he could have the photograph. He passed it round inside the van, gave it back to me with every Stones autograph on it and then they drove off to the right towards the West End of London.

Frances Pymont *née Redford* *(age 23)*
It's seared in my memory. I was a bit older than the Stones myself. It was just different – very, very different – from what things had been. These were bands that appealed to teenagers and

previously there hadn't been things like teenagers. There weren't teenager type clothes until the Sixties came in and then they had the short skirts, etc. and things were different. I remember when I was young, when I was 14 or so, we just got something that our mums would have worn and we would have cut a bit off the bottom.

They used to have quite a lot of pop stars at the Granada. I'd seen Bill Haley and the Comets and I'd seen Jerry Lee Lewis but I'd never come across such an atmosphere as the Rolling Stones. Those times you were either Stones or Beatles and quite honestly I never really thought very much of The Beatles. I thought they were the sort that your parents would have approved of if they met them and if you preferred something like that and if your Dad approved of somebody like that coming home with you – well, that was no good. I think with the Stones the fact that they were "a bunch of scruffy gits", as my Dad described them, with long hair – it was a bit of rebellion.

I went to chaperone my sister Monica who was 17. She didn't particularly like the Rolling Stones. Her thing was Marty Wilde and I went to a concert with her and suddenly there was this ear splitting shriek and I looked and there was my sister standing on the seat! We were in the second row from the front for the Stones so we had an extremely good view. Unfortunately when they came on there was this terrible pandemonium that broke out.

There was screaming. Screeching. Stamping, Thumping. I couldn't hear a word of what they were singing about. I couldn't tell you what they sang!

I remember Mick wore a string vest and camouflage trousers. He was obviously singing because he was prancing up and down as ever he did, opening and closing his mouth, but you really couldn't hear a thing.

The people in front of us – it was a family – they were in the front row and they got up and said it was disgusting and they walked out. So the people from behind just climbed over the seats to get a better view in the front. And as it went on it got more and more noisy and then girls started to try and climb up on the stage and there were security men who just sort of chucked them back off the stage and they kept trying to get on there and it was getting a little bit out of hand. At the Granada on either side of the stage there were the Ladies' and Gents' toilets and out of the Ladies' and Gents' came these policemen to assist in keeping some sort or order.

So what they sang I don't know. But it was a very good evening and I thoroughly enjoyed it! When you look at them, the way Mick Jagger sort of prances around now, it's the same as it was then. They seem to have remained – well, obviously his face has gone and the other members of the band look rather dodgy if you look at them – but they've got a certain style about them.

Frances Pymont

11 JANUARY 1964
The Baths Hall, Epsom

John Sutherland
Our next door neighbour's son, Brain Howard from Bookham, was the promoter and hired them. My late father owned the Fiore Coffee Bar in Church Road, Bookham and sold some of the tickets. Needless to say they sold well and sold out very quickly. In their early days the Stones did a lot of Chuck Berry numbers and *Oh Carol* has always been a favourite with me.

Brian Howard
The January 64 date at the Baths Hall in Epsom was part of a week long booking of the Stones by a professional promoter rather than me the gifted amateur. Like the manager of the Baths Hall, he was called John Smith. I believe he came from Reigate and, having booked them for a week, he then put them in different venues each night. John Smith the promoter

John Sutherland

came across John Smith the hall manager and learned that he couldn't be bought. As a consequence he phoned me and asked "how on earth did you cope?" I was flattered that the professional was asking me – I wasn't yet 20 – and when he asked if I could market some tickets through the coffee bar network I was pleased to agree. He got tickets to me and I did the rest.

Then a couple of days before the event he phoned me again and said "can you get the tickets back?" Naturally I said that would be impossible. Whereas I had bought my 1,250 tickets all at the same time he had ordered his in two batches and while the first batch were a browny green in colour the second batch were a greeny brown, ie. similar but different.

One of the Epsom youth clubs was run by a policeman and, when he saw that some of his kids had tickets of different colours, his copper's nose caused him to go and visit the hall and ask questions. That led to the promoter getting a call and the game was up. The outcome was that they had stewards on the door with counters and the first 962 ticket holders were admitted and the remainder received a refund but were then turned away. I've spent the last 51 years feeling ever so slightly smug that I managed to sell 1,250 tickets for the earlier concert.

Trish Cole *(age 14)*

I remember being very excited about it. It was very strange to me as I used to swim at the Baths

Trish Cole

regularly. I lived in the village of Ashtead, about 15 minutes away by car. I went with a friend, whose name I can't remember now. I seem to remember that the friend's father picked us up afterwards. There weren't many people there but the music was very exciting. Cathy McGowan from *Ready Steady Go* was in the seated audience, whereas I was just on the floor. My older sister had lent me a pair of Courrèges' style black boots. I felt like the bees' knees.

14 JANUARY 1964

Granada Theatre, Mansfield

Margaret Audin *(age 15)*

Myself and a couple of friends were avid autograph hunters. We didn't purchase any tickets for the show, but we were hanging about the theatre with lots of others hoping to get a glimpse of the group. Someone got the back doors of the theatre open and we all ran in, up the stairs and onto the balcony. I remember Mick Jagger looking up probably wondering what was going off. We were all soon rounded up and thrown out. The three of us found the van that the Stones were using and the door wasn't locked so we went in. It was full of all sorts of things. We took some clothing. But after about 10 minutes we felt guilty and decided to take the stuff back. When we got back to the van the roadie was inside and he wasn't too happy. We told him that we'd brought the stuff back so he let us in. We persuaded him to get us the Stones autographs so he took our autograph books into the Granada and got them for us. Unfortunately many years later my mum and dad threw out my autograph book when moving house. I had some good autographs including the Ronettes, the Searchers and Billy Fury but the best ones were the Stones.

Estelle Fowden

I went with my friend Angela. We went to the stage door and I asked Brian Jones for his autograph, which I still have. I can see his face now, very pale and drawn with big bags under the eyes. He didn't look at all healthy for a young bloke. I thought that the performance was rubbish (and I also thought this at the concert in Hyde Park a few years later after Brian Jones died) but I remained a fan. I think that to see them do a

gig earlier in their career in a pub would have been great, as would their current high tech concerts, but Mansfield Granada was not the right venue. I would never have said this at the time – I was a big Stones fan. But looking back this is my recollection. Maybe it was the fact that we were screaming and not listening. Why did we do that? How stupid.

David Eames (age 15)

I was a spotty adolescent at the time with an admission ticket to see the Rolling Stones. It cost 11/6 (57p), which swallowed up my paper round money. This type of venue was very small compared to what is expected today. Everybody had a good seat and wasn't that far away from the stage. Everybody felt the raw energy of the Dartford version of US rhythm and blues. The set list from that night included *Come On*, *Mona*, *You Better Move On*, *Roll Over Beethoven* and *I Wanna Be Your Man*. I had to leave as the Stones set ended to make sure that I caught the last bus home.

15 JANUARY 1964
Granada Theatre, Bedford

David Arnold (age 18)

I attended the second performance that evening, a few rows from the front in what I recall as being the eight and sixes (43p seats). The tour was called Group Scene 64 and featured amongst others the Ronettes. They weren't on for long. They played six or seven songs at most. They

> "everybody felt the raw energy of the Dartford version of US rhythm and blues"

did *Come On* as their first record and *I Wanna Be Your Man*. The Ronettes made a lasting impression – we were only 18 after all! One of my friends recalls that the Ronettes apparently had some sort of clothing malfunction – either a strap or a bra.

After the show we made our way to the back of the venue. I remember the sight of the Stones all being in a Mini. These screaming girls had surrounded the Mini as they leapt into it and off they went. The Ronettes were signing autographs at the stage door and the Stones were being ripped apart by several enthusiastic girls. One had a trophy of half of a black knitted tie.

We had a chat with Ian Stewart. He had the Commer van with all the gear and stuff. They'd left him to drive home with it. We said "where have they gone?" thinking they might have gone to a pub in Bedford but he said "no, no, they're on their way back to London."

Dave Howard (age 9)
I was only 9 at the time. Which strikes me now as particularly young, not to be in the St John's ambulance, but to be actually allowed to attend something like this at the age of 9 – I don't think it would happen now. This was two gigs in a day. Seven o'clock and nine fifteen. They only had short sets in those days. And I can't imagine I was allowed out late. I was at the seven o'clock showing. I had to be home

from Bedford to where I lived in Stopfold before it got too late. Dave Berry and the Cruisers performed. Marty Wilde and the Wildcats were also on the gig. And I remember the Swinging Blue Jeans because they were flavour of the month at the month because I think the *Hippy Hippy Shake* was right up in the charts round about then. I remember that one of the Ronettes had a wardrobe malfunction and her bra snapped in the back and one of the other Ronettes danced around the back, sorted her out and danced round again. But that might just be a very young boy's imagination.

Girls were screaming so you could barely hear the Stones and what they were singing. Girls fainting and asking for help and them being carried out on stretchers. Some girls had collapsed. It was a form of hysteria. There was less screaming and fewer people fainting when Dave Berry and the Swinging Blue Jeans were on because I heard more of them than I did the Stones, because with the Stones I was always taking people out. I'd have been lifting people onto stretchers to take them out and giving them water and trying to bring them round if they were still out of it.

Derek Edmunds (age 23)
The Bedford Granada was a premier venue in those days and we saw many new and established acts there. It was located in St Peter's Street and we used to form a queue in a passageway to the left of the

Derek Edmunds

Ricky Porter

in a group from Swindon called The Hummelflugs. His name was John L Watson. I used to lend him my system when they were playing and I wasn't using it. One particular night the group asked me if they could use my gear as they were supporting a band from London called the Rolling Stones. I was working up there that night as well so it was not a problem.

The night arrived, I took my gear and set it up, the Hummelflugs went on and when they finished their set there was an interval. Halfway through the interval the Stones arrived and they had to go on almost immediately. I remember Mick Jagger clearly. He approached me, looking a bit dishevelled and wearing a powder blue pullover with holes in the elbows. I remember him saying "the guys tell me that this is your equipment. We are late. Would you be kind enough to let me use it?" I told him it would be no problem and they quickly changed into their stage gear and did a set. However my gear was nowhere near the quality of the equipment they used and after a set they quickly set up their own gear.

It was a lot of fun, and there were a lot of Yanks there to see John L Watson but they loved the Stones bluesy kind of music too. The girls were really screaming for the Stones, but I'm afraid it was not them that were drowning out the sound of the Stones. It was just that my equipment that Jagger was singing on wasn't powerful enough to cut through the noise the crowd were making. It was no problem once they changed to their own equipment.

building. When I saw the Rolling Stones I thought they were absolutely brilliant. My wife had a different opinion and as we left the Granada she said "who were that scruffy bunch? They were awful" to which I replied "I loved them. They will be big one day."

16 JANUARY 1964
McIlroy's Ballroom, Swindon

Ricky Porter

When I was boxing back in the Sixties, I was out of work as I couldn't get a job at my trade so to make ends meet I had a little club on the corner of Station Road and Bridge Street called the Blues Cellar Club. I also used to make ends meet by working on the door at McIlroy's. Several Yanks from the bases at Fairford, Brize Norton and Burdrop who were friends of mine used the club, and one of them also used to sing

17 JANUARY 1964
City Hall, Salisbury

Geoff Cooper (age 16)
I made an effort to get to a Stones gig in Salisbury Civic Centre. My first attempt was thwarted before I had even left Bournemouth. Having 'borrowed' a friend's Vespa scooter I was apprehended by a Panda car and not being in possession of any of the required paperwork. I was 16 at the time, no licence and carrying a passenger. I was escorted back to the police station. The second time we all went in a pal's car on what turned out to be quite an exciting evening, Brian Jones booting a very persistent girl in the face to prevent her from getting on stage. No security in those days!

18 JANUARY 1964
Pier Ballroom, Hastings

Andre Palfrey-Martin (age 16)
I saw the Stones three times on Hastings pier. They did the three gigs, which were January, April and August 64. In January they were just beginning to cut their teeth in terms of bigger ballrooms. The Pier Ballroom legally can take about 1,400 with all the ante rooms and the bar and everything. Some of them you were getting 2,000 in. But I don't think they ever came in that sort of numbers, not early in the day, because we were talking about *Come On* having been released, possibly the first album. The support would have been a group from a local coffee bar called the Pam Dor and

we'd have been there because it was the only real place to go at that time, because the Witch Doctor and other clubs had not yet opened. So it was the Pier Ballroom or the Happy Ballroom as it was known it featured the longest bar in Hastings and it was at the end of the pier on the promenade end – the nose end right down at the end of the pier. We always used to say it was a sixpenny bus ride to get there in the winter. It would have been bloody cold. It was like an aircraft hangar. It was like a great big aircraft hangar and you expected to see a couple of seaplanes parked in there. That was I think when they wore the leather waistcoats as part of their outfit. They were just another band of the Sixties. It wasn't very full on that first gig. I think it would have been average numbers – five or six hundred, maybe a few more. Very often the promoter wasn't the pier company. It was somebody the pier company was contracted out to and they were putting the packages together. They were supported by the Four Aces. Admission price was 6/6 (33p) in advance, 7/6 (37p) on the door.

19 JANUARY 1964
Coventry Theatre (aka Hippodrome), Coventry

Liz Laurie (age 13)
Like many theatres in the early 1960s, Coventry Theatre hosted pop concerts, usually on Sunday evenings. These consisted of about six current pop acts (groups and single artists) each performing five

> "I think it would have been average numbers – five or six hundred, maybe a few more"

or six numbers. I was very excited to have a ticket for the upper circle for the Rolling Stones: it cost six shillings (30p) and was all I could afford from pocket money. Also on the bill that night were the Ronettes but I cannot remember who else. I went with a school friend, Pam, and can recall the electric atmosphere. The screaming of the girls in the audience meant that almost nothing, musically, could be heard and the upper circle could be felt moving slightly with all of the audience's excitement. They sang *Come On*, *It's All Over Now* and *You Better Move On*, which is still one of my all time favourites. I attended quite a few Sunday pop concerts in those wonderful days but it is the Rolling Stones concert I have always been happiest to have attended. I have always remained very glad to have seen them when Brian Jones was in the group.

Peter Jones (age 16)
We went to see them at the Coventry Hippodrome which is now the Coventry museum of transport. The Stones were third on the bill. The headline act was either the Ronettes or Helen Shapiro. The Stones came on and they all looked incredibly sheepish because it was that period in their history when they wore those black and white hounds tooth jackets. That's what they wore at the gig in Coventry – black trousers and Cuban heels.

Graham Bellamy
I saw the Rolling Stones at Coventry Theatre when they finished the first half and Freddy

and the Dreamers were top of the bill. When the Stones came on I do remember some plonker shouting out "get your hair cut!" To which Mick replied "what, and look like you?"

Dave Jones
We saw Freddie and the Dreamers. It was when he managed to 'accidentally' drop his trousers as part of his act. Not the sort of thing you are likely to forget!

John Crofts (age 16)
I spent the night outside the box office with a bunch of girls from Lyng Hall to be first in the queue for tickets. Highly successful – I got a seat in the middle of the front row. Unfortunately, as I left the box office there was an *Evening Telegraph* cameraman in wait. My ecstatic expression made it onto the front page which was seen that evening by the headmaster of Bablake School. An unpleasant interview followed and a Saturday morning detention was the result. However it was well worth it to see one of the great rock and roll bands early in their career, playing proper rhythm and blues. When the Stones played here again, I was in town with a friend of mine who bore an uncanny resemblance to Mick Jagger and we had to take refuge in what I vaguely remember was the Golden Egg.

Dave Jones
My friend Bernie Spencer and I went to see the Rolling Stones twice at the Coventry Theatre in our teenage years. We were walking

> "it cost six shillings and was all I could afford from pocket money"

Dave Jones

home after one of the shows when we reached a major crossroads about half a mile from the theatre at the junction of Holyhead Road and Queen Victoria Road. As we approached the traffic lights a large black limousine pulled up alongside us. The window was wound down and Mick Jagger appeared and asked "which way to London, mate?" We replied that they should turn left and left again at the next junction – "thanks, mate." And off they drove. We caught a glimpse of Brian Jones on the back seat looking slightly out of it. We were both speechless and stood there for a while. The road layout has completely changed now but I would always tell my daughters Rosie and Angie the story every time we passed the spot, so much so that whenever they are in the vicinity they repeat the tale to their friends.

20 JANUARY 1964
Granada Theatre, Woolwich

Keith Dunwoody *(age 19)*

I was at art school in Gravesend. Prior to the Stones/Beatles era, Chuck Berry and Bo Diddley were the most popular artists in my circle, but that was a time when young peoples' music was everywhere and taking over from the BBC Palm Court Orchestra era, which was awful. Live music was available in all manner of venues – pubs, clubs and even youth clubs – which were usually identified by the day of the week they were open, eg. Wednesday Club, Friday Club, etc. Most of them were run by churches but we did not have

any interest in religion. The most popular local music venue for us was the Black Prince at Bexley, next to the A2, which at this time was merely a cross roads not the three lane dual carriageway it is now. This was also the era when *Radio Luxembourg 208* was being replaced by the pirates just off the coast. They ultimately brought the BBC into the 20th Century and had all their disc jockeys stolen.

I saw the Stones at Woolwich at the Granada cinema by Woolwich Ferry. I remember it cost 5 bob (25p). I went with a couple of friends from art school, Ted Trott and Noela Waghorn, and another girl whose name escapes me. All I remember of the actual show was that they were scruffy. Jagger had a jumper and it looked like a moth had attacked it. I guess that they hadn't managed to get their hands on any money at that stage. However their performance was well up to standard and they managed to produce enough volume to overcome the screaming girls, who were always an annoyance at concerts at that time.

They played *Not Fade Away*, their new record. Marty Wilde was also on the bill. I remember him not because I was a fan of his but because he played *Orange Blossom Special* on the harmonica which was absolutely brilliant. I remain a staunch Stones devotee, having chosen the Stones over The Beatles from the outset. The Beatles appealed to the old people and the Stones to us youngsters in those days. I remember my dad saying "this music will be forgotten in a couple of months."

21 JANUARY 1964
Granada Theatre, Aylesbury

Linda Hailey (age 15)

I went with my mum, her friend and a school friend of mine. I remember standing in the foyer and seeing Mick Jagger talking to one of the staff, then dashing back to my mum to tell her. The show was great – the first time I had been to any show like that. I stayed a fan of theirs for years after.

Bill Hannay (age 13)

As a guitar-mad young adolescent, it was the first time I was allowed out on my own for such an event. I don't think my mother was too keen on them for some reason! The evening was probably notable for the absence of Brian Jones. I remember the official announcement referred to the prevailing foggy conditions and resultant travel problems – what was the real reason, I've always wondered? As far as I was concerned, it didn't seem to detract overly from the tight and punchy sound produced by the quartet of Mick, Keith, Bill and Charlie. Keith was playing his sunburst Harmony

Meteor and Bill his usual Framus Star bass, with the band wearing black leather waistcoats and tab collar shirts, their familiar stage uniform of the period. All exciting stuff, and to think I was part of a live audience witnessing in Aylesbury the early incarnation of a rock and roll phenomenon! I still have the show programme salted away somewhere.

Jilly Williamson (age 15)

It was very foggy and Brian Jones didn't make the show I went to. The *Bucks Herald* newspaper at the time featured a photograph on the front page of two girls kissing the door handle Mick Jagger had touched.

22 JANUARY 1964
Granada Theatre, Shrewsbury

Barbara Roberts

I went with my husband Keith and two friends. Before the show we went into a pub across the road and one of the groups with them was having a drink there. As I walked across the road I found a ticket for the show on the floor. It was a front seat and I handed it in at the box office. As soon as the Stones came on my husband and my friend Bette took hold of my arms – they were afraid I would run to them. My husband was having a good laugh when girls were being half carried, half dragged back into the lobby. And when we came out they were still screaming "Mick! Mick!" It was such a wonderful night and I still think about it. I can't believe that I sat there screaming for them, but I did. It was a night I'll always remember.

Bill Hannay

Barbara Roberts

Sylvia Starkey *(age 18)*
There was no way for me to get home after the concert as I lived in a small town nine miles from Shrewsbury and there was no train or bus after ten o'clock. I was a junior in a fashion shop on Castle Street, Shrewsbury. The day after the concert I was out buying the cakes for the staff tea break, when I bumped into all of the Stones. They had been into a coffee shop called Sidoli's. They stopped and spoke to me and then they all gave me their autographs. Unfortunately, over the years I have lost the autographs, but I can still remember that day.

Sheila Roll

23 JANUARY 1964
The Pavilion, Royal Hotel, Lowestoft

Yvonne Almond *(age 19)*
At the time I was working at the Pye television factory so a crowd of us girls went along. What a night! Being teenagers then, we all went a bit mental as the Rolling Stones left the stage wearing blue shirts, leather waistcoats and dark trousers. We along with many other girls chased them from the stage. As they reached the stairway to their upstairs rooms the girls grabbed them tearing their clothes. My friend came away with a piece of shirt! We often laugh about it now saying if she had kept it then it could have become a collector's item.

Yvonne Almond

Sheila Roll *née Keable (age 13)*
I went with my friend Lynda. It wasn't a concert – we were dancing and I remember being near the stage and noticing how muddy their boots were. They were on a stage about four feet high and we danced to their music. I think they had only had a couple of hits by then – *Come On* and *I Wanna Be Your Man*. They played other hits – Chuck Berry for example.

After the performance my friend and I walked round the building and saw an iron fire escape leading to a window. Bill Wyman was leaning out of the window looking at the sea. He waved to us to come up and happily took our autograph books, passing them around the dressing room. I can't tell who wrote 'love to Sheila from the Rolling Stones' in my autograph book.

25 JANUARY 1964
California Ballroom, Dunstable

David Arnold *(age 18)*
They did four gigs at the Cali. And the fourth one was just pandemonium. That last time

the whole hall was packed to the rafters. When they did *You Better Move On* Jagger said "we've got the heavenly choir in the background" – Brian Jones and Keith Richards. They used to have to make their way from the stage to the dressing room through the crowd. I remember Brian Jones was being held by this girl by his jumper and he just couldn't make any movement at all. He wasn't a big fellah. He was just sort of laughing. Someone had to give him a helping hand to pull him along from the clutches of this girl.

26 JANUARY 1964
de Montfort Hall, Leicester

Wendy Frost (age 17)
The hall was packed solid and all the teenagers were shouting and singing Stones songs. The place was buzzing with excitement. I was there with my boyfriend and we were both wet with sweat at the thought of the Stones music. The curtains opened and the crowd went wild, screaming. The band looked great and Brian Jones, the leader, always looked very smart and well groomed. When the show finished my boyfriend and I left there in a hypnotic haze and walked down London Road where all the other Stones fans were talking and singing and very happy. A Stones fan for life!

Martin Osborn (age 18)
We saw the Stones a number of times after the Station Hotel, mostly at the de Montfort Hall in Leicester where they appeared

with, amongst others, Phil Spector's very sexy girl group the Ronettes, Joe Brown and the Bruvvers and the Spencer Davis Group. We stopped going to see them because we could not hear the band over the screaming girls.

27 JANUARY 1964
Colston Hall, Bristol

John Whelton (age 15)
Tickets for the two concerts went on sale at 9am on a Saturday morning and I was one of five school pals who after leaving school on the Friday afternoon went home and met up later that evening and spent that night on the steps of the Colston Hall queuing for tickets. We obtained front row seats as it was all seated in those days which cost half a crown each (13p). Our parents thought that we were crackers – but it was well worth it.

31 JANUARY 1964
Public Hall, Preston

Susan Grierson (age 15)
My best friend Sandra and I attended the Rolling Stones concert at Preston's Public Hall. The Public Hall was a fabulous building. I went to English Martyrs Girls School and we used to have our school reunion there and I sang on the stage in the choir. When Sandra and I saw the Stones we were very young and our mothers didn't know we were going. We sneaked into the Stones dressing room, spoke with them and got all their autographs. Unfortunately I no longer have the autographs.

> "the band looked great and Brian Jones always looked very smart and well groomed"

Chapter 7

February 1964

The Rolling Stones started their third UK tour on 8 February 1964. As with the first two package tours they had appeared on, they were part of a line up that featured other artists. This time the programme was headed by John Leyton and Mike Sarne and billed as All Stars 64.

11 FEBRUARY 1964
Granada Theatre, Rugby

John Philpott *(age 15)*
You couldn't hear a thing for all the screaming but what struck me was Brian Jones' harmonica – I'd never heard blues harp before and it knocked me out so much that I went out the next day and bought a Hohner Vamper harmonica for ten shillings and sixpence (53p). Half a century later, I have more than 50, in various states of playability.

John Philpott

Janet Skinner *(age 15)*
I went with my 14 year old sister and a friend. The tickets were a Christmas present from my parents. We had never heard of the Stones before they came to

Rugby as they were not top of the bill. Mike Sarne was on the show as well. On the morning of the concert we went up the Granada steps to look at the poster. There were two young men also looking. They turned out to be Mick Jagger and one other of the group. It was a great concert!

Claire Geisberger
née Chadburn
I went to their first concert when they appeared with John Leyton and then again in March 1965. I met them backstage and had two photos taken with them in their dressing room. The photo was published in the Rugby Advertiser together with an article.

Sue McCabe *(age 10)*
Believe it or not I went with my mother and my brother. I *think* the Swinging Blue Jeans wore blue jeans and pink shirts but that may or may not be accurate. Looking back it's funny to think of my mother being at a Stones concert.

Richard Morris *(age 18)*
I joined the English Electric Company in Newbold Road as a graduate apprentice in September 1963. The first six months were at Rugby College of Engineering Technology in Lower Hilmorton Road. Some of the other students

were from London and had seen the Stones at the Crawdaddy Club and Eel Pie Island. At the time they had only released a couple of singles in the UK. I remember the performance at the Granada Cinema although memories of The Swinging Blue Jeans, Billie Davis and Mike Sarne have gone. I do recall Jet Harris, who probably played Diamonds and Scarlet O'Hara.

Most people, especially the girls, only really went to see the Stones who got a rapturous reception and screaming from the girls. I remember they were the next to last act so they must have moved up the list after the start of the two month UK tour with John Leyton. John Leyton was the final act and he was booed harshly after he appeared following the Stones. Based on records to date and about to be released, the play list was probably *Come On*, *Poison Ivy*, *I Wanna Be Your Man*, *Mona*, *Walking the Dog* and *You Better Move On*. Obscure blues numbers would not have gone down well with record buying teenagers. The Sixties was a great time for lots of reasons but especially the live music scene.

Pete Shilton *(age 10)*

I went to this concert as a treat for my tenth birthday. I went to the 6pm early show and my Dad drove me and some mates from my class at Dunchurch School – Richard Harris, Robin Bartlett and Graham Evetts – there in our old Standard Eight car. I think he dropped us off outside the Granada and then picked us up afterwards at about

7.30pm before the second show at 8.30pm or maybe he sat in there with us? I remember us standing up and shouting during the concert which comprised of about ten acts that maybe did three or four songs each.

The acts that I remember particularly were the Stones, the Swinging Blue Jeans and ex-Shadow Jet Harris. I remember a lot of screaming girls, particularly when the Stones came on. I'm sure the Stones did *I Wanna Be Your Man* and *Poison Ivy*. I'd not long bought the Rolling Stones EP so I was looking forward to seeing them. I'm pretty sure that both performances were sold out as I know my mum had to stand in a long queue a couple of weeks prior to it. I still have the programme. Sadly they demolished our great theatre in 2011 and the land currently operates as an ugly interim car park. How short sighted!

David Cumella *(age 14)*

I must have gone to the first show because my parents would have been a bit dodgy about me going to the later one. I remember standing on the top step, slightly offset from the main queue, waiting to go in, when a black Daimler-type black saloon swept onto the forecourt and the group, all in long black coats, piled out of the car and ran straight up the steps at full speed and into the theatre. It's significant to me because, when I say "ran up the steps and into the theatre", the majority did but Keith wasn't really in the moment and crashed right

Pete Shilton

David Cumella

into my left shoulder, knocking me for six. He recovered in a second or two and scrambled to continue his journey on in. I was perfectly alright although very surprised and just a bit bemused that they hadn't gone in through the back door where all the other performers normally went in.

The show was really good. The other thing that I'll never forget was that after it had finished, my mate and I just sat in our seats – ground floor centre – while all the audience made its way out. We then continued to just sit in our seats for another five or ten minutes or so while Charlie Watts carried on tapping his high hat and doing some unmemorable drum practice, totally oblivious to anyone else being in the place. I don't remember being asked to leave but we must've eventually just wandered out in the knowledge that the next lot were just about to come in. I wonder if we'd have been allowed to do that these days? I don't think so with security being what it is now.

They were a very good group even then. I know that because I subsequently played in several groups as a drummer and occasional bad guitarist at working mens' clubs during the Eighties and never managed to do quite as well as they did. Quel domage.

Sue Smylie *(age 15)*

I was still at school when the concert was advertised and, having no money and no chance of getting any from my dad in order to see – in his view – the

Sue Smylie

sons of the Devil 'gyrating' on stage, I had to find some other way to see my favourite group. They weren't known as boy bands in those days. I then discovered that a boy in my acquaintance had two tickets and so I set about charming him into taking me with him to the concert. Admittedly, it was not my finest hour but needs must – I remember his name but not much more about him.

We queued outside the Granada up North Street before being let in. Everybody was highly excited and full of anticipation, including me – this being the first live concert by a famous group that I had ever seen. They were great, especially Mick Jagger, as his dancing was thrilling to a very excited 15 year old girl. They have remained my favourite group ever since.

12 FEBRUARY 1964
Odeon Theatre, Guildford

Veronica Sewell *(age 14)*

I went to the one with Billie Davis and actually met her. I've got all their LPs. All their early stuff I love. *Come On*, their very first record, I remember them singing that. Oh God, that was gorgeous. My favourite is *You Better Move On*. They played that as well. They played that and I shall never, ever forget it.

I was only three rows from the front and – you know what the girls can do – we all try and get on the stage. And I remember security got me and the geezer threw me through the air. I don't know who I landed on. But it didn't deter me. I nearly touched Mick's foot and that was wonderful. It seems stupid now, doesn't it? At the time it was wonderful. I'll always love the Stones.

14 FEBRUARY 1964
Gaumont Theatre, Watford

Susan Ford *(age 11)*

I was there! I can't remember which performance we saw. I went with my cousin Alan who is three years older. I was only allowed to go because his Dad took us and picked us up afterwards.

Oddly, the only thing I really remember, apart from how the Stones looked, was standing on my seat. We were in the stalls, about six or eight rows from the front. In those days it was the height of anti-social behaviour to stand on seats and my cousin kept telling me to get down. I've seen the Stones twice since then but never quite so close.

Anne Waine *(age 13)*

I went with three friends – Janice, Sheila and Vanessa. We all attended Francis Combe

Anne Waine

Secondary Modern in Garston, near Watford. We sat in the front row and one of my friends remembers that the Stones were not top of the bill – that was Gerry and the Pacemakers! All I can remember is them singing *Come On* and possibly *I Wanna Be Your Man*. My friend was quite definite about Gerry and the Pacemakers being top of the bill although I don't remember them being on.

15 FEBRUARY 1964
Odeon Theatre, Rochester

Joan Smith *née Morgan*
(age 19)

I didn't know it was on. I went with a friend. All I remember is the screaming. We couldn't hear the music. I'm no fan of the Rolling Stones.

Joan Smith

18 FEBRUARY, 1964
Regal Theatre, Colchester

Cathy Graham

My family owned a garage and Cafe at Gun Hill in Dedham, Colchester. It was known as Sampsons' Garage Gun Hill at the time. This was on the main London to Ipswich road before the A12 opened. The Stones visited the garage and ate at the cafe twice. My nan, Marjorie, wasn't impressed with them as she took a disliking to Marianne Faithfull who, she explained, was "messing about with them all." She reckoned they were all high! Marjorie didn't have time for "rock stars or nonsense". Her words!

Cynthia Allcock *(age 16)*

I well remember attending all the Rolling Stones concerts at The Regal in February and September 1964. Other pop groups also played there – Eden Kane was one person who performed because I remember him kissing my friend's hand and she didn't wash it for a week!

I think the Rolling Stones played on Friday nights and we screamed all the way through the performance, sang all the words and jumped up and down to the music. It was deafening and obviously better than performances now at the O2 and Wembley, etc. because the audiences were so much smaller and you were much closer to our idols. I recall that after going to these concerts I got my voice fully back in time to go to work on Monday and then we used

to queue up again to re-book for the next concert for the following month. I saved my wages after paying for my keep to my mum to go to these concerts and visiting the coffee bar Boulevard Deux further along Crouch Street.

I think we must have been quite well behaved because I can't recall any trouble with police getting involved or any major incidents that happened. I shared a Dansette record player with my younger sister and there was always a 45rpm record on it – my Rolling Stones or her favourites The Beatles. I used to buy my records from Mann's Music Shop in the High Street because you could take them into the music booths and listen to them before you purchased – or not. Those were the good old days!

Jane Powell *(age 19)*

I don't remember the Rolling Stones being the headline act. I went with a boyfriend of the time and can remember roughly where we sat – it was fairly near the front on the left hand side. I recall that I was not that impressed with them and looked upon them as being just another act. That changed and I became quite a fan although, I must confess, I never went to another concert.

19 FEBRUARY 1964
Odeon Theatre, Stockton-on-Tees

Ann Woodward *(age 13)*

I went to see them on my own. All my friends were Beatles fans (I was also) but I was captivated by the Stones music. My friends thought them too frightening! I will never forget the sound and feeling of that night. The music was raw and undiluted. No backing musicians – just pure magic. My mother was waiting for me to come home. My father, who was a musician, wasn't told where I was going. He certainly wouldn't have approved! I have the original programmes.

George Morland (age 15)
I was in my last six months at school and I and a group of school friends went to see them. The price of a ticket was 9/6 (47p) and John Leyton was top of the bill. I had seen The Beatles three months earlier at the ABC and could hardly hear them for all the screaming. The one thing that sticks in my mind about that Stones gig was the fact that Mick Jagger was sat on a stool on stage backed by the other Stones singing *You Better Move On* and you could have heard a pin drop. Brilliant!

David Degnan (age 18)
During the 1960s I lived in Darlington and every time there was a show at Stockton we went by coach to see many stars including Billy Fury, Eden Kane, the Dave Clark Five and many more. 15 to 20 staff from the TSB bank where I worked went to each show, including the *All Star64* show featuring the Stones. The line up was the Leroys, Billy Boyle, Don Spencer, Billie Davis, the Swinging Blue Jeans, Mike Sarne and, after the interval the Innocents, Jet Harris, the Rolling Stones, Bern Elliott and the

David Degnan

Fenmen, Mike Berry and – topping the bill – John Leyton. According to the programme Mick and Keith and Brian were 19, Charlie was 21 and known as Beau Brummell and Bill was 21! The programme cost 2 shillings (10p) so I must have had a bit of pocket money in those days. I remember Bill Wyman's guitar string snapped and hit him in the eye. He had a little blood on the side of his face.

20 FEBRUARY 1964
Odeon Theatre, Sunderland

Ken Hill (age 15)
I was there at the Odeon Theatre for the *All Stars 64* show. I went with my pal David Hines. The show was great, especially the Stones, who were just like their records.

Joe West (age 19)
I was blown away by the slide guitar of Brian Jones and remember them playing *Not Fade Away* as I had the original record of

Joe West (right) with Sheila (on his right)

Dick Irish *(age 18)*

I went to all their early concerts in Bournemouth except the first one which the Everly Brothers headlined – at that time we didn't know who the Rolling Stones were! John Leyton, as the headliner, appeared on stage after the Stones. The audience wanted the Stones back so you can imagine the atmosphere – screaming and yelling "we want the Stones!"

My mother was a great Stones fan. Of course I discovered that the Stones were playing R&B and moved on to the blues which inspired them in the first place. So I got a guitar and learnt to play. I've been in several local bands and I'm now playing bass.

Dick Irish

that by Buddy Holly. Another they did was a great version of Lennon and McCartney's *I Wanna Be Your Man*. They also played Chuck Berry's *Bye Bye Johnny* and one of my favourites *You Better Move On*. After the concert they stayed at the Scots Corner Hotel and much to the disgust of the older generation they left papers all over the floor with telephone numbers on them and trod biscuits into the carpet. This publicity did them much good as did their later refusal to go on the revolving stage at the London Palladium as they came across as bad boys. The first show had John Leyton and Mike Sarne top of the bill but by the end of the tour the Stones had the biggest following. They still remain one of the best bands I have ever seen.

Thomas Mann

I and two of my friends went. I remember the acts that were also appearing were John Leyton, Mike Sarne, the Swinging Blue Jeans, Jet Harris and Mike Berry. We had a great night, even if it was hard to hear at times because of screaming girls. We sat in the second row and had a good view of all the performance.

22 FEBRUARY 1964

Club Noriek, Tottenham, London

Frances Pymont

There used to be a place called the Club Noriek in Tottenham. It was on the corner of the High Road and Seven Sisters Road and it used to be a converted cinema. It was only a very small sort of gig because the place itself was very small. There were lots of narrow stairs going up and down and they were there one evening and it used to be frequented by the Tottenham Hotspur players, which I was more interested in because I rather liked Dave Mackay at the time.

Dave Colyer (age 22)

One day at work, one of the clients told me he was a security guard at the Club Noreik in Tottenham and that there was a Stones concert on so I invited Linda, a girl from work, along.

We stood outside for about an hour in the queue until they started letting people in and when I approached the security guard he pretended he didn't know me and wouldn't let us in as we didn't have the tickets he'd promised.

We went back in the queue again and as we surged forward I waved some blank pieces of paper at the doormen and we were allowed in, although I still paid for tickets inside.

It was packed inside and we could hardly see the Stones because a group of rockers crowded the stage area.

23 FEBRUARY 1964

Hippodrome, Birmingham

Wendy Cottrell (age 11)

I was there! My mum took my seven year old sister and me. Mum had managed to get tickets in the third row from the front so we had an absolutely brilliant view of the show.

The concert was a sell out and the audience consisted mainly of teenage girls. There was a brilliant atmosphere – the Stones were strutting their stuff but you couldn't hear anything of the music because the majority of girls, myself included, were screaming their heads off! But that was the norm for most pop concerts during that era, so I guess there would have been an air of disappointment if there hadn't been any screaming.

I had a huge crush on Brian Jones and in fact wrote to him several weeks before the show, asking if I could go backstage. Brian himself replied to me – a very nice letter, but no, I couldn't. The Stones must have performed for about an hour or so and that whole period was utterly electrifying. I saw them another couple of times, but I remember the 1964 show as being the most exciting – probably because it was the very first time I saw them and there was so much anticipation there.

Ray Wilkes (age 14)

I paid 7/6 (37p). I was right at the back and could not hear them for the girls screaming. Even through the fog of time I can remember it.

> "I waved some blank pieces of paper at the doormen and we were allowed in, although I still paid for tickets inside"

25 FEBRUARY 1964
Odeon Theatre, Romford

Jill Snowsell (with arm raised)

Jill Snowsell née Goodale (age 15)

I was at Mulleys Commercial College and the Odeon Cinema was opposite. My friends and I at the college wanted to get tickets for the concert but they went on sale at the Odeon on a weekday morning. I was nominated to ask our very strict Head if we could pop out to the Odeon to get our tickets during our mid-morning free study hour. She was extremely cross at such a request but we got permission. There were five of us on the front row of the balcony and my abiding memory is looking to my left and seeing my four friends leaning forward shouting "Briiiaaan!" He wouldn't have heard them above the deafening screaming! And just to add that I didn't know him then but Alan, who became my husband six years later, was also there.

29 FEBRUARY 1964
Hippodrome, Brighton

Paul Cobby

My wife saw them in 1964 at the Hippodrome. There were several others on the bill too. We have the original programme. She and her friend went to see John Leyton – she was not a fan of the Stones.

Frank Hinton (age 20)

I saw the Stones at one of their Hippodrome gigs in 1964. I emphasize "saw" because in those days the girls screamed non-stop while their idols were on stage. I've seen the Stones but I can't really say that I've heard them. I do remember that there were a few others on the bill – John Leyton, Don Spencer and possibly Garry Miller being some of them, I think, and the Stones didn't play for long.

Who did I go with? 18 months or so ago I would not have been able to tell you but, after not seeing her for about 45 years, I saw her in my local library. Her name was Shirley. She wasn't my girlfriend, just one of my near neighbours. She had hardly changed. I approached her and tentatively asked "did I take you to see Gerry and the Pacemakers many years ago?" "No," she said. 'It was the Rolling Stones." So that cleared that up. But now I don't know who I took to the other gig.

Not only did I see the Stones at the Hippodrome but I also saw The Who, possibly in the same year, although they were then called The High Numbers. I have seen two of the best bands in the world for no more than a total of ten shillings (50p). Good value – even if I only actually heard one of them.

Frank Hinton

The Rolling Stones were beginning to attract more of an audience reaction, with scenes of hysteria amongst their predominantly teenage female audience only previously seen at Beatles' concerts.

1 MARCH 1964
Empire Theatre, Liverpool

Trefor Jones
The package tour was billed as *All Stars 64*. My mates and I had bought tickets by post for the first performance and travelled by train from Prestatyn. Inside the theatre we sat near the front and I remember that there were many rows with empty seats so the first house was not a sell out. Not all the artists advertised appeared but I enjoyed Jet Harris and Bern Elliott and the Fenmen. People were shouting for the Stones and when they came on the place came alive. The songs that stick in my mind from that day were *Walking The Dog* and *Not Fade Away*. It was not a very long set compared to later gigs but that's what Sixties package shows were like. When I think back to that day I can still picture each of the guys on stage and feel so glad to have been there.

Gladys Wood
There was a very narrow passageway leading to the stage door. My husband Chas, a police officer, was guarding the stage door while two of his colleagues were trying to clear the passage of a crowd of young ladies as there was a risk of injury to them. Police at the front had cleared the foyer and were trying to disperse them by saying that the group had already left. Suddenly the girls moving out turned back and they were falling over. Chas looked up to where the girls had their eyes on a window, which had Mick Jagger looking out and waving. Chas opened the door, bolting it behind him, rushed upstairs to the room where the band were sitting, pulled Mr Jagger away from the window and slammed it shut. He then took hold of Mick by his lapels and said "if you put your head out of that window again I'll knock it off!" He then left to return to guard the stage door.

PC Chas Wood

Sue Covell

2 MARCH 1964
Albert Hall, Nottingham

Sue Covell *née Burbridge*

My friend Jill and I went to see the Stones at the Albert Hall. We sat on the second or third row. Jet Harris and Billie Davis were on the bill too, along with Mike Berry who sang Sunshine Of My Life. At that time there was seating at the back of the stage and some fans that were sat at the back of the stage pulled Charlie Watts off of his stool. It was a brilliant concert. We had seen The Beatles but this was totally different.

Frank Morgan *(age 17)*

I didn't go to the gig but I remember the bus I was on stopping outside the Albert Hall where a group of girls who had been to see the Stones got on, including one who I quite often used to walk home with from the bus stop as we lived quite close to each other.

What was uncanny that night was that Margaret's character had completely changed. She appeared to be in a trance – she literally couldn't talk! The next time I saw her she had reverted back to her normal self. This showed me the excitement the Stones generated in their live shows – that they could affect a typical 'girl next door' so completely.

Pauline Silvester *(age 15)*

For many years my late mother was best friends with the mum of Sixties pop star Mike Berry and whenever Mike was due to be performing anywhere near our home in Beeston, he came to stay with his 'Auntie Joan', as my mum was affectionately known. Mike was due to appear at the Nottingham Albert Hall as part of a touring show which included Mike Sarne, the Paramounts (later to become Procul Harum), Jet Harris, Billie Davis and, top of the bill, the Stones.

A few days before he was due to arrive Mike contacted my mum and asked if he could bring 'a few friends' with him from the show. My mum was only too happy to agree but secretly doubted it would happen. I subsequently went to the concert with a friend and it was absolutely electrifying. We returned home on the bus and, as we rounded the corner of the cul de sac where I lived, were astounded to see hordes of people everywhere trying to get into the house where I lived.

Well you can probably guess that, indeed, Mike had brought his 'few friends' with him and had been followed from the concert hall. In fact, he brought most of the performers in the show plus three of the Stones - Brian Jones, Bill Wyman and Charlie Watts.

Somewhere I have some newspaper cuttings about the story that appeared in the local press the next day. Whilst they were there, Charlie Watts took a phone call telling him that *Not Fade Away* had just gone to Number One in the hit parade. Needless to say, word got around very quickly and I was certainly the most popular girl at school the next day.

3 MARCH 1964
Opera House, Blackpool

Syd Bloom (age 17)
They were on tour with Eden Kane, Billie Davis, Jet Harris and Tony Meehan. It was that strange tour where they started off almost bottom of the bill and finished up top of the bill. They'd just released the first album, so *Walking the Dog* was a big track at the time.

We actually were sort of old enough to go into the bar and I spent my time ripping beer mats, getting Keith Richards to sign them and flogging them to girls outside. But Jagger was never anywhere to be seen and nor was Brian Jones. But the others were. Richards was the most friendly of them.

Steve Gomersall (age 15)
I had the pleasure of meeting the Rolling Stones in the little Spanish bar in the Winter Gardens during the interval of their first show at the Opera House early in 1964. About four of us from Blackpool had seen The Beatles at the Queens the year before and we were desperate to see how good the Stones were live.

Even though we were only 15 at the time nobody questioned you if you looked 18 so we decided to beat the rush and have a drink before the second half of the concert when to our astonishment in walked the group without any minders or entourage! I couldn't resist such an opportunity so I said "you are going to have fun and games escaping after the show" to which Mick Jagger replied "yea, I think you are right." I didn't wish to

overstay my welcome so I just said "great show, cheers!" to which he modestly replied "well thank you" whilst giving me the thumbs up.

As they were pushing their way through the throng, trying to make their getaway after the gig, he picked me out of the crowd and gestured a knowing sigh with a shrug of the shoulders and waved goodbye. That made my day and, yes, they were very good.

Steve Gomersall

5 MARCH 1964
Odeon Theatre, Blackburn

Jim Taylor
I attended the first of their two shows at Blackburn's Odeon cinema theatre that evening. The place was only half full.Possibly they'd then done only two records – *Come On* and *I Wanna Be Your Man*. Not Fade Away hadn't yet been released. I remember that most people were on their feet grooving to the show. A female friend rushed to the front of the stage calling out "Mick!" Obviously she wouldn't get close to him now. There was no visible security with their show back then.

Denis Neale
My mate said he had managed to get two tickets to see them and I was impressed when he told me that we were on the second row from the stage. The tickets were for the evening concert. They also did a matinee performance in the afternoon that my brother in law, who was a couple of years younger than me, attended. We looked forward to the concert and there was a real air of anticipation. On

the night we took our seats looking forward to seeing, but more so to hearing, the songs that we had listened to on record for the last year or so.

There was an electric atmosphere in the air that night. As the Stones took the stage and launched into their first song, *Come On*, the screams from the many girls in the audience drowned it out completely. They could have been miming for all we knew. It was on a par with Beatlemania. The continuous screaming and hysteria escalated and it wasn't long before there was a surge of girls from the back of the Odeon towards the stage by any means available. Bouncers were throwing girls off the stage as the band was trying its best to play. We were into the music but couldn't hear a note being played!

At some point during the performance someone opened the emergency exit doors and dozens of screaming girls rushed in from outside the cinema and tried to storm the stage. It was total chaos! The band were fending off hysterical girls and gamely trying to play on. The security staff were working overtime hauling people off the stage. The concert ran its course but I was left with an overwhelming feeling of disappointment at not being able to enjoy the music we had gone to hear.

Mick Markham (age 17)
Myself and two mates got into the theatre via the coal chute to the boiler house and ended up in the wings on stage with them during the whole performance. Nobody

Mick Markham (left) and Keith Mercer, who also went to the show

questioned our presence there. We were just amongst them all of the time. I still can't believe it. We didn't get bounced out. We were there for the full gig.

I think the Stones thought we were with the theatre and the management thought we were with the Stones. My wife to be was in the audience and was amazed to see me pop my head round the curtains. She thought she was seeing things. After the concert, with the fans screaming outside the stage door, Mick Jagger pushed me out first. I was quickly rejected by the fans when they realised I was a nobody. My one claim to fame! Happy days.

Peter Forbes (age 12)
Me and a mate had 25 bob (£1.25) front row tickets at the Odeon on Penny Street. Our own nascent pop group The Rotaters had just been joint clapometer winners with a four year old 'Shirley Temple' on the Odeon Saturday morning club talent competition playing Beatles and Stones numbers to 250 kids. On the same day, on the same stage, in the morning! The Yardbirds, with Eric Clapton, were the other support act that day and night. When the Stones came on an avalanche of screaming girls invaded the space between us and the stage in unprecedented Blackburn fashion. The usually gruff and aggressive bouncer, who barked the kids into withering submission at the Saturday morning club, was at a complete loss in the face of that torrent of teenage hormones. We were getting peeved too, having

Peter Forbes (left) and the Rotaters

paid all that money only for our front row privileges being usurped to the point where we could only see and hear jumping girls and their tumultuous cacophony mixed in with a distant rendering of *Not Fade Away*. So we climbed on our expensive seats to restore some consumer justice and get our money's worth of the bad boys. Thwarted by the tide of rampant female youth, the beefy bouncer approached us with refocused wrath and dragged us down from our improvised perches, to our mortified indignation. There was only one thing left to do – we just threw ourselves in amongst all the girls and started jumping and screaming too. And two young lads began to learn some more about the cathartic pleasures of adolescence courtesy of Mick, Brian, Keith et al.

6 MARCH 1964
Gaumont Theatre, Wolverhampton

David Cox *(age 20)*
I went with a pal named Keith Parkes. I don't know what happened to him but the funny

thing about the show was Keith's granny threw our tickets away by mistake so we had to speak to the manager who led us to our seats after everyone was seated and the two spare seats were ours. I always liked the Stones more than The Beatles so that's why I went. It's too long ago for me to remember all the songs but I do remember *Little Red Rooster* and *Walking the Dog* as they were favourites of mine and I think they opened with *It's All Over Now*. Unfortunately it was difficult to hear them properly due to the screams of the girls.

Ben Kirk *(age 18)*
The local Odeon cinema used to open on Sunday evening and put on these shows. I went to quite a few of them and saw artists such as The Beatles, Little Richard, the Everly Brothers and Chris Montez. I would attend with two or three mates at the time and I certainly remember The Beatles supporting Chris Montez. *Please Please Me* had just been released. There was an amazing atmosphere at the Stones show, with plenty of screaming.

17 MARCH 1964
Assembly Hall, Tunbridge Wells

Collie Culmer *(age 15)*
We just couldn't believe that the Rolling Stones were coming to Tunbridge Wells. They were our idols. My friends and I were the local mods and worked in Woolworths and in Boots the Chemists. That night we got to the front of the queue so were able

Collie Culmer and friends

to be in front of the stage. When they came on the screaming was unbelievable. It was so packed with people. I remember leaning onto the stage and grabbing Mick Jagger's leg and then him saying "calm down, girls." After letting go of his leg I noticed that my pink plastic handbag had been melted by the stage lights and a great big hole had appeared in it. When the show had finished we tried to get backstage for their autographs but they had already left.

Lorna Parker *(age 16)*

I must have gone with some girlfriends. Everybody – the whole gang of you – went every Tuesday. Every Tuesday in Tunbridge Wells was on the circuit for the Liverpool groups. It was at the Assembly Hall which is still there. It was a no alcohol affair and it was just the place to go every Tuesday. I'd just started work. For everybody you worked with or knew it was

somewhere where you could go at 16. I left school at 15 because you could do that then.

You couldn't buy tickets online because they didn't have that sort of thing. No one had a mobile. No one had a phone. So we just queued on the night around the block. I can't remember how much it was. It can't have been that much because we went every week. But I suppose if there was no alcohol all you had was a soft drink and it didn't cost you any money once you went in. But I don't think they put the tickets up any more. It was just a set whatever it was. And it was obviously affordable – not like the sort of price now. It wasn't anything like that. We were all living at home. We were all paying our mums. We were all going out to work. You couldn't have afforded a vast amount. It was reasonable. You went over the road to the hotel or down to another pub because people used to go out in the interval to get a drink. But there was no alcohol there. It was just a damn good dance. There were no seats. It was all standing.

It was quite exciting actually. Some weeks there weren't that many people there. I can remember Long John Baldry came one week and there were probably only about fifty people in there. We knew weeks in advance what was coming up. And they were just starting to get really quite well known. I think we probably caught them just before it really took off because it was the busiest ever that I'd seen the place. There was no dancing. It was jammed from the stage – the bit where the orchestra pit is – all the way down the back. Health and safety would probably never have allow it nowadays. It was just jammed with people. There might even have been an intermission.

They were scruffy. And they were somehow naughty. And we all thought "cor, this is the way to go." Because it was so different to what we'd had before with the Liverpool sound. Gerry and the Pacemakers. The Searchers. They were starting to get the bad press as well. They got done for urinating up against some bloke's garage somewhere and all the rest of it.

My favourite Stone was Brian Jones. He had a nice little smile. He looked quite sweet compared to some of the others. You don't realise at the time quite how lucky you are. We did have a really good social life. Even if it was only once a week you had a really good do. The bands were all making their mark and they were all on this never ending circuit of small towns that they would do. Recently I looked up online all the stuff they played. They did a couple of tours of the UK and Tunbridge Wells wasn't mentioned and I thought "I know we bloody well went in March '64." I suppose we didn't realise how lucky we were. It was a lovely atmosphere. And we all thought "well, this is ok."

David Wheeler (age 17)
I and five other lads were there. We lived in a village three miles away and attended most of the gigs that were held there. I'm sure I'm correct in saying none of them were as packed out as that night. In fact I recall we daren't move away as we would never have got back there. We were all around 17 then and it was all so new to us I think I'd be correct in saying we were overwhelmed.

One thing that sticks in my mind was when Brian Jones' guitar string broke and he taunted the fans before he threw it into the middle. I can remember the floor going up and down as the fans jumped up to try and catch it. I'm sure today's health and safety would put paid to that now.

Rick Hodge
My wife Sandy Morgan – as she was then – went to the Tunbridge Wells Concert. She was 19. She remembers the floor bouncing up and down as the audience were dancing. It struck her at the time how skinny and young they looked.

Jenny Gladwish née Bridger (age 15)
I was there! Me and my pal Cecelia Bell had bunked off school early in the afternoon to go to hers to get ready for the evening. We arrived at the Assembly Hall late afternoon with a couple of other friends. We were right at the front of the queue. When the doors opened we rushed to the front, directly next to the stage, to get the best vantage position and stayed put all the way through the performance of the backing group. When they'd finished the compere came on stage to announce "and

> "we were all around 17 then and it was all so new to us I think I'd be correct in saying we were over-whelmed"

here they are – the fabulous Rolling Stones" and all hell then broke loose.

There were so many people, mostly screaming girls, pressed so tightly together – a whole sea of bodies surging forward. The barrier broke and we, who were right at the front, were pushed forward. One of my friends had her blouse ripped and I had that in one hand to protect her modesty whilst I propped up another who I think was on the verge of fainting. There were bouncers and security everywhere and it was complete chaos. So we left school early to get the best position at the concert but ended up watching it all from the rear of the hall.

Linda Walshaw (age 17)

I recall it being a very relaxed evening with less people than I thought would be there, perhaps two hundred. My friend and I danced all the way through the evening. They were very good and we knew they would be big. We felt lucky to have seen them in the early days and the entrance fee, which I can't remember the price of exactly, was not expensive.

My parents were horrified that I went and suggested it might not be the best idea. Mick Jagger did not endear himself to any parents and, after The Beatles who were less of a threat, he showed the face of something quite different. Interestingly, after all those years I went to see them again and it made me smile at the cost. They are the best showmen and in my opinion always have been.

Lynda Pearce (age 17)

Every week there was a dance at the Assembly Hall, I think on a Tuesday or Wednesday, and every week it was a well known Sixties group. I know we saw Freddie and the Dreamers, Gerry and the Pacemakers, the Animals and many more and usually the bands played and we danced. However, when the Stones played everyone just stood and listened and it was a completely different atmosphere. I was lucky enough to see The Beatles in Brighton at much the same time but whilst it was a brilliant concert they really couldn't match the Stones!

I think we only paid the equivalent of about 20p to get in. There never seemed to be any fights or problems that I can remember and it was just a really great time to be young. I cannot remember if there was a bar but my friends and I never drank alcohol and probably just went to the local fish and chip shop for a packet of chips to eat on the way home.

Lynda Pearce

Neil Rowswell (age 15)

I attended with a school friend, Mick Short, who was 14. We both lived nearby in Southborough. I blew an entire week's wages from my paper round which amounted to 6/- (30p) for the admission. It was my first ever live event and the chance to see a rapidly rising group was too good to miss. I think my most vivid memory was of how pale Brian Jones was.

My favourite song of the night was *Poison Ivy*. It was an amazing night and with everything they have achieved since it has now become one of my claims to fame – seeing the Stones twice for 30p as I also saw them at the free concert in Hyde Park in 1969. I have a friend who paid £250 for a pair of tickets to see them perform at one of their London gigs and I take great delight in reminding him of my expenditure and how he never got to see Brian Jones.

Rod Padgham (age 19)

I was there along with two or three friends, a great night mid week and very affordable. It was obviously the early part of their career so we were unaware of what the future held for them. The good thing about the Assembly Hall was that it was a dance rather than a seated concert.

The day after, I went into my local the Foresters Arms in Tonbridge – not Tunbridge Wells – and discovered the Stones had stopped off on the way from the gig but that the landlord, a Mr Les Barret, had refused to serve them, much to the dismay of his young daughter. Last orders

were 10.30pm and, while he was normally flexible with us locals, five long haired teenagers were not welcome.

18 MARCH 1964
City Hall, Salisbury

Wendy Lawrence née Caitlin (age 17)

I was due to attend the concert but my father had died on the 12th and I was unsure whether to go. My mother said that I should and so I agreed to meet friends in the bar at the Cathedral Hotel, including my two closest friends Sally Warner and Gordon Plumb. I was greeted warmly and handed a double vodka on the rocks – I was two months short of my eighteenth birthday!

We then walked to the City Hall where I distinctly remember dancing to *Get Off Of My Cloud*, doing all the actions to illustrate each line, i.e. pointing at someone "Hey you!" and then waving arms about suggesting coming down from a cloud. Sounds mad I know but we were very young! I have only recently discovered that this particular tune was not released until the following year, which almost made me doubt my memory.

Geoff Cooper (age 16)

I made an effort to get to a Stones gig in Salisbury Civic Centre. My first attempt was thwarted before I had even left Bournemouth. Having 'borrowed' a friend's Vespa scooter I was apprehended by a Panda car and not being in possession of any of the required

Rod Padgham

paperwork – I was 16 at the time, no licence and carrying a passenger – I was escorted back to the police station. The second time we all went in a pal's car on what turned out to be quite an exciting evening, with Brian Jones booting a very persistent girl in the face to prevent her from getting on stage. No security in those days.

21 MARCH 1964
Whitehall, East Grinstead

Rick Hodge (age 15)
I went to the Whitehall, East Grinstead. They kicked off with *Walking The Dog* and the place erupted. I remember being pressed against the stage by screaming girls, one of whom gave Bill Wyman a box with scissors in. He promptly cut off a lock of hair, placed it in the box and threw it back to her! No gig I have been to has equalled that evening. I have been a fan ever since. When I got home my parents were appalled that I been to see 'that dreadful group.' Wonderful stuff!

22 MARCH 1964
The Pavilion, Ryde, Isle of Wight

Paul Wavell (age 16)
The concert was organised by my science teacher, Mr Sparks, of Ryde School. It was a private fee paying school which was always thought to be a bit posh. The thought of a master acting as impresario for a rock band did not go down too well with the headmaster and the board of governors. The band started with *Route 66* and played *You Can't*

Paul Wavell

Judge a Book By The Cover, Mona with tambourine and maracas, and *Come On*. There was only one policewoman to control a crowd of hundreds.

Anne Grant (age 15)
I was there at the 4pm performance with my friend Jeanette Butt. I was at school at the time and had to run from the school premises, Ryde County Secondary School in Belvedere Street, to the Pavilion. Fortunately it wasn't a great distance to run but even so we only just made it in time after school finished that day. We didn't have time to change from our compulsory school uniform into civvies but I do recall we removed our school ties and stuffed them into our school bags.

The Cherokees were a well known local group and considered to be the best of all the Isle of Wight bands. They got the show off to a great start and then the Rolling Stones came on. This was amazing for the island, which at the time was very staid to say the least, and we could hardly believe that the Stones were appearing on our little island. It was a great performance and something I've never forgotten.

Loris Valvona (age 14)
The Beatles and the Mersey Sound had swept all before them for a year or so but already there was an emerging new wave of wild rhythm and blues groups with longer hair and a harder image. In the forefront of this new sound, with two hit singles already, were the Rolling Stones, who were

fast becoming the biggest group around and sending audiences wild throughout the land.

The concert was announced and the tickets went on sale. There were going to be two performances – at 4pm and 7pm. I was determined to see them and although the box office queue was big I managed to get a seat for the afternoon show. As the date approached the fame of the Stones seemed to grow daily. It was hard to believe they were actually coming to the Isle of Wight.

On the day I caught the bus to Ryde Esplanade and the sight as I arrived is something I will never forget. It seemed as if every teenager on the island had gathered around the Pavilion Theatre. The Stones were staying at the Ryde Castle Hotel just across the road. A number of fans had got into the hotel and were running around the place amongst the suits of armour, stuffed animal heads and African artefacts, which was the hotel décor at the time.

The Stones transport, a Ford Thames van or similar, was parked nearby and was covered in messages of love from all over England, some in lipstick and others scratched into the paintwork. There were no spray cans in those days. Inside the atmosphere was electric. The Shamrocks and then the Cherokees were the support bands. The highlight of the latter's set was when they announced "one we wrote this afternoon" and launched into a perfect version of The Beatles' *Can't Buy Me Love*,

which had only just been released. The crowd went mad and the excitement went up another notch or two.

The crowd started chanting "we want the Stones!" as we watched equipment being moved around on stage and, as time dragged on, "why are we waiting?" Suddenly there was the biggest collective scream I've ever heard and there they were. A group we had only seen on black and white televisions was now standing on stage in front of us – the Rolling Stones!

What happened next is a bit of a blur. I seemed to be carried forward in the mass hysteria of it all as the crowd rushed the stage. The Stones seemed to be used to this and hardly reacted as order was restored and they could get on with their performance, I can hardly recall any details of the Stones set or anything else, but the excitement and newness of it all is something that has never left me.

The concert was a talking point for weeks. It was great to think the Stones had been to our neck of the woods. One girl at school had a button from Brian Jones' coat, which she had torn off during the chaos in the hotel. Some months later it was rumoured that another young lady had a rather different souvenir of the Stones visit. The Swinging Sixties had definitely arrived on the Isle of Wight!

Angela Hamilton (age 1)
This concert was organised by my Dad. My sister and I have a lot of paperwork from the concert

> "it seemed as if every teenager on the island had gathered around the Pavilion Theatre"

including the original contract agreement signed by Brian Jones, a ticket for the event, a flyer with all five signatures and Charlie Watts' drumstick. My sister, then aged 7, sat on Mick Jagger's lap to watch the supporting band. I was a baby in a pram backstage at the time so I have no memory of the event – only what my parents told me!

25 MARCH 1964
Town Hall, Birmingham

Diane Tubb

As a teenager still at school I couldn't afford to go and see the event. I stood outside the door by the fountain. All of a sudden the door opened and out came Brian Jones. He was amazing. He looked so cool smoking his cigarette – I just took hold of his arm and wouldn't let it go.

A white van arrived and ran over my foot. I couldn't see anything in the van. Brian Jones got into the van and it drove away. It happened so quickly but it was an unforgettable memory.

Neil Reynolds *(age 16)*

I was still in the Sixth Form at Saltley Grammar School at the time and I was also a big fan of Wayne Fontana and the Mindbenders who were on the same bill. When I saw Wayne Fontana perform at other gigs he always referred to them as the Bricks or Rolling Bricks.

My abiding memory of the Stones when I saw them is that they were all dressed the same, in black and white dogtooth

Neil Reynolds

jackets and black trousers. They never dressed alike ever again. I went backstage after the Town Hall show and got their autographs. I've kept it all these years. I thought all five of them had signed it but it looks like there's only four. I'm not sure whether it's Mick or Keith who's missing but Brian Jones' signature is clear so I guess it must be worth a few bob.

Sally Mynott *(age 15)*

I paid five shillings (25p) and sat behind the stage with my school friends Lorna Smith and Jennifer Mellings. We all went to George Dixon Grammar School. There were also other girls from the school in the audience. I must have been 15 as I can't see my parents letting me go at 14, which is why I missed out on The Beatles. I would have had to pay for myself and I had a Saturday job when I was 15.

I can only admit to seeing them as we could not hear them due to us all screaming very, very loudly! When we left the Town Hall it was a bit of a shock as there were loads of rockers waiting to have a go at us in Chamberlain Square so we all scarpered as fast as we could. One girl from school caught her bus home and, when she got off, a rocker had followed her bus, spat at her and drove off on their motorbike.

We managed to get some autographs and I kept the book. However I haven't a clue where it is. I think the Stones played for about 20 minutes. I will never forget the experience.

26 MARCH 1964

Town Hall, Kidderminster

Pat Davies née Such *(age 16)*
I lived on the Comberton estate. I was a mod then and very much in love with Mick Jagger. I remember it was eight shillings and sixpence (43p) entrance fee and they were fantastic. They played *Little Red Rooster* and *It's All Over Now*. I've always been a massive fan. I still think Mick's fantastic.

Pat Davies

28 MARCH 1964

Wilton Hall, Bletchley

Mike Holman *(age 16)*
I was at that concert with a group of friends. Like myself they were all ex Wilton School pupils. The queue for the gig stretched all the way down Church Green Road and around onto Buckingham Road. I also remember being squashed like a sardine in the hall. I'm sure there were many girls sitting on blokes' shoulders to get a better view. The Stones had to stop about half way through their act because it was totally manic in there but they continued after a short while. Anything else about that evening is a bit vague but like most blokes in those days I always wore a suit on Saturday evenings and my hair hung over my collar!

David Arnold *(age 17)*
When they were on at Bletchley Jagger wore a suit. The others were all fairly casual.

Ted Eldred *(age 13)*
The first picture I ever got of them was out of a newspaper. A black and white picture and it was probably only three or four inches by three or four inches. Me and my brother used to have bunk beds and I used to be on the top bunk and then I started collecting pictures of the Rolling Stones there.

My brother wasn't into the Rolling Stones. He was more Beatles. I was a big fan. In those days I always felt that they wrote the music. Obviously they were doing covers then but because you're young you think 'oh, I wonder where they got that from?' They'd had a couple of hit singles but the majority of people I knew then were more into The Beatles and that kind of music. But they were kind of rebels in their way in the beginning. They'd only just brought out their first record.

We used to go to Wilton Hall every Wednesday night. They used to have a dance and I always remember near the end they used to have films. They used to play the music and then they'd have a screen behind and they'd play music and different pieces of film. Old films. I remember I was first in the queue because I didn't want to move. I didn't want to miss anything. I was probably there about half past one in the afternoon. I'm pretty sure a mate of mine – Johnny Carroll – was with me.

All I remember is getting right up in front of the stage and I was on the left hand side of the stage and the piano was there. I'll always remember he got up on top of the piano, Mick Jagger, and Bill Wyman was in his black waistcoat.

I even got to the stage where me and my friend Johnny Carroll were going to start our own group. Because it inspired me a little bit. I bought a set of drums and he had a guitar and I remember cleaning out my dad's coal shed at the side of the house and making it all tidy so that we could try and do some music in there but it didn't come to anything. It petered out after about a year or so.

I always remember I was first in the line and I remember somebody coming up to me and trying to offer me two or three quid for my ticket and I said "no way!" I wasn't giving my ticket away. I was the first person at the front door.

Vivien White *née Wheeler (age 16)*

I was an apprentice hairdresser in Bletchley. I was so excited. I had made a large scrapbook with every picture and newspaper cutting I could lay my hands on. The protocol at the time was to leave autograph books and other stuff at the desk and collect them all, duly signed, at the end of the evening. I handed my scrapbook over and had a great time. The

band was fantastic. At the end I went to the desk to collect my signed masterpiece. What a disappointment! All the autograph books had been signed but my scrapbook had been put on a different shelf because it was bigger and had been missed. Unfortunately the Stones had already left. I was so upset but it hasn't stopped me from going to several Stones concerts since. We had some good times at Wilton Hall in the Sixties and I have very fond memories of my time dancing and watching bands there.

Steve Funnell *(age 17)*

We would visit Wilton Hall once or twice a week. I saw Johnny Kidd there to name just one. When the Rolling Stones came they arrived in a Dormobile covered in lipstick where girls had written all over it.

I think the Stones were wearing blue shirts with black waistcoats. Outside the hall there were lots of mod scooters. I was wearing a Beatle jacket with white jeans and shoes that had fur on them. I can remember having a girl on my

Steve Funnell

shoulders so she could see them. Later on in life I found out that my boss was at school with Andrew Loog Oldham. He said that all he thought about was pop music.

Libby Culshaw (age 14)
I was there! I went with my friend who was also 14. We lived in a village 11 miles from Bletchley and an older boy from the village had a green van in which he was ferrying half the village youngsters to Wilton Hall. My mum came out and quizzed him on his safe driving before we all set off. We all rolled around in the back like a litter of puppies. He could only just have passed his test and in hind sight the grown ups were worried. There weren't so many cars on the road but it was all new world, exciting stuff.

We were in high spirits at the prospect of such an adventure. The Stones were beginning to be heard in our community and across the UK. We surely were the business! We walked into Wilton Hall and looked up in amazement at the balcony. We wandered around and looked down from the balcony. We thought we were the bees' knees being in such a grand place compared to our village hall. We ascertained where the loos were and then went into the main hall to watch everybody else and join in.

Everything was so easy then. You simply walked up the steps at either side of the stage and had a wander and a gander round the back. We spoke to the artists. Basically they were just kids like us but a little older – mainly

curious and innocent. At the break everyone ambled down to the Eight Belles pub, had a few beers and then came back for the second half. I sat in the pub with a half of bitter, terrified every time the door opened in case it was a policeman coming to check my age.

I can't remember how the evening ended except for us all going home elated. After that Wilton Hall hosted great groups. I remember traipsing down to the Eight Belles at half time when the Hollies played there. It was funny sitting in the pub with Alan Clark and co. Just as if we were out with our mates and supporting their music, which we were.

Keith Wheeler (age 17)
I consider myself one of the lucky ones to have been a teenager in the swinging Sixties. You wouldn't believe it but Bletchley was a good place to be if you were into live music. There were two live bands at Wilton Hall every Saturday night and a disco dance midweek. There was also a weekly disco dance at the Labour Hall in Buckingham Road. We also had the option of going to the California Ballroom in Dunstable where you were guaranteed at least two good bands.

The only problem was the lack of transport. There were no buses or trains so you had to have your own transport or hitch a lift. We saw most of the well known artists or bands at these venues and sometimes travelled to surrounding towns if they featured someone we hadn't seen. I remember cycling to Luton to

> "I can't remember how the evening ended except for us all going home elated"

see the Everly Brothers and also managed to get a ticket through Rodex Coats to see The Beatles at Northampton, which turned out to be a complete waste of time as you couldn't hear a thing for girls screaming.

When we heard that the Stones were coming to Wilton Hall we said right it doesn't matter who is on elsewhere we must see the Stones. Just after this I was hit with bad news my parents had booked a holiday in Great Yarmouth which meant I would miss the Stones. I spent the next few weeks pleading to get out of the holiday but there was no way I would be left at home. I must have spent most of the holiday moaning about missing the Stones when my father eventually gave in and said he would drive me back to Bletchley Saturday afternoon and we would return to Yarmouth the next day.

You can imagine how long it took in an old Standard 10 with no main roads as there are now. I got to Wilton Hall just before the Stones came on. The hall was packed to the rafters, the atmosphere was electric and it's a night I will never forget.

Jackie Stevens *née Lane*
(age 16)
I was a Saturday girl at Woolworths and because I lived in New Bradwell I had no time to leave work, get a bath and dressed up. I went to another girl's house in Eaton Avenue where we got ready. I wore a royal blue satin dress which my mother had made for me some weeks earlier when

I had gone to see another band there, which may have been Johnny Kidd and the Pirates.

My father had been killed in a road accident in 1962 and this was my mother's first little holiday since then. She was going to Butlin's somewhere and said that she would have been very worried about me getting home because we used to thumb a lift if we missed the train to Wolverton. She insisted that my grandma came to stay for the weekend to make sure I got home safely. I don't know what she would have done if I hadn't. We had no phone and no transport of our own.

I remember it being 2/6 (13p) to get in. I earned 17/10 (89p) for a Saturday at Woolworths and had 15/4 (77p) left for a drink at Wilton Hall and my 1/6 (7p) train fare home. The remainder was my pocket money for the rest of

Jackie Stevens

the week. I was, after that gig, a massive Mick Jagger fan, and still am. However, I loved their early things best, especially *Not Fade Away*, *It's All Over Now*, *The Last Time* but most of all *Little Red Rooster* and other bluesy numbers. I also saw Big Dee Irwin and The Hollies at Wilton Hall. Happy days.

Bruce Battams *(age 19)*
I was there! As a lifelong Bletchley resident I fondly remember Ron King's gigs at Wilton Hall. Three nights a week with the wrestlers, the bouncers and the Alsatian dogs. Bletchley's golden days. We had two cinemas and work – and prospects!

Brenda Pollard *(age 17)*
I was one of the teenagers who queued to see the Stones at Wilton Hall in 1964. I was at Northampton School of Art at the time and the group had a big following there. We especially loved *Come On*. We were so thrilled that the Stones were coming to Bletchley and told our friends from London, one of whom lived next door to Bill Wyman's brother Paul Perks in Penge.

At the time my sister and I had a Saturday job on Bletchley market on a jeans stall. We were paid the grand sum of £1 a week. The ten shillings (50p) to see the Stones was a vast sum of money then to pay for the dance on a Saturday night. We didn't call it a concert or a gig then. I bought a pair of jeans from the stall and rushed home to undo the hems and fray the bottoms so I could wear them to the dance. This was very 'in' at the time and perfect to wear to college and get covered in paint.

I can't remember much about the queue but I do remember that once inside we could not move. It was one big crush, shoulder to shoulder, but nobody minded. There was no room to move let alone dance. There was also no alcohol sold at all but you didn't need it. It was a fantastic experience and all these years later I cannot believe that we actually saw them in Bletchley and that they still command great audiences today.

We would have caught the bus from Newton Longville to Bletchley – we definitely didn't miss it and would have had a taxi home for the grand sum of 7/6 (38p) which when shared wasn't too bad. The last bus home went at ten past ten. Our dad couldn't stand the Stones and couldn't understand why on earth we would want to spend all that money to see them and wear our 'bloody overalls' to go in. He called them long haired louts.

PC Pat Kenny *(age 36)*
I was in the old Bucks Constabulary – now Thames Valley – at the time based in Bletchley but of course with the crowd expected, I was on duty there, and before proceedings started all the cars were parked on the car park. Towards the back of the hall was a car covered in lipstick – 'love you Brian'. Obviously it was Brian Jones' car.

Now the doors were insecure and the windows were wound down and of course there was a lot of expensive gear on the

> "I cannot believe that we actually saw them in Bletchley and that they still command great audiences today"

"all round the stage were these bodyguards – I could see why they were there"

back seat. There was two special constables there and I said to them "has anybody gone in to tell Brian Jones about it?" They said "no". On the stage door were two bodyguards and they reckoned they wouldn't let anybody in. I said "unauthorised persons they're there to keep out but we're authorised. Anyway, leave it to me. I'll go." I go to the back door and explain what I'm coming to see Brian Jones about. "Certainly" they said and opened the door for me and in I go. And they said "they're in the dressing room under the stage – all of them." I thought "blimey, I'll be lucky here."

So I go into the dressing room and there they are – the four of them – with the girl fans all around them of course and I told Brian Jones what I'd come for and he thanked me and off he goes to make the car secure. And Mick Jagger calls out to one of the roadies "give the officer one of our photos and we'll sign it for him." I thought "ooh, I'm in here." Anyway, back comes one of these postcard-sized photos and he says "no, not one of them – those we got yesterday" and of course when he came back with it, it was a large

photo about 22 inches wide and about 10 inches in depth. It was like a panoramic photo and of course there were big pictures of them on there and he said we'll sign it for you. Well by this time Brian Jones had come back and each one of them signed it.

I couldn't believe my luck. I was in there about ten minutes chatting with them. Although they looked scruffy I found them very polite. When they were prepared to start their performance I was in the ballroom at the back of the hall. The hall was packed. You couldn't move. And of course all round the stage were these bodyguards. I could see why they were there. As soon as they started playing there was a surge forward of those trying to get onto the stage. And they were throwing them back and anyway they got it under control.

As far as I know there weren't any casualties. There certainly weren't any reported to us. Afterwards I got several offers of five pounds for the photo. We put it up for auction some years afterwards. When it went up for sale it raised £420. One of my daughters said "oh, you've got rid of our inheritance!"

April 1964 saw the Rolling Stones fulfilling a number of ballroom and dance hall commitments that had been entered into before the success of *Not Fade Away*, which was released in Britain on 21 February 1964 by their record label Decca and which peaked at Number 3 in the UK charts. 17 April 1964 saw the release of the Stones debut album.

chapter 9

1 APRIL 1964
Locarno Ballroom, Stevenage

Lynne Walters *(age 16)*
The Locarno Ballroom, or the Mecca as we all called it, was an old fashioned ballroom with a mirrored glitter ball even though it was quite a new building. There was a proper wooden dance floor with a low semi-circular stage at one side for the band. The dance floor was surrounded by a carpeted area with tables and chairs and the bar. There was also a balcony upstairs with tables and chairs. On Saturday nights they had proper dances but for teenagers the important night was Wednesday as that was when there were live bands.

Looking back it was quite incredible that we saw all the important bands of the Sixties there – I can remember seeing the Searchers, the Swinging Blue Jeans, the Dave Clark Five, the Who (or the High Numbers as they were then), Geno Washington and the Ram Jam Band, the Small Faces, Spencer Davis, Georgie Fame, Them and many others.

Stevenage was very much a mod town and mostly the kids who went on Wednesday nights were mods who liked to dance and show off their latest outfits. I guess the Stones had been booked before they had become as big as they were by the time they played. I was a mod and with my boyfriend. All the usual crowd of mods were there but there were also a lot of girls who were desperate to get as close to the stage as possible. As the stage was only just about a couple of feet high the Stones themselves were quite vulnerable to being grabbed so the management got all the bouncers who were usually on the door and patrolling the dance floor to surround the stage and link their arms to form a barrier between the screaming girls and the band.

I had seen The Beatles a few months before at Hammersmith so had heard that sort of screaming before but it was quite unusual at the Mecca because, as I have already said, we were mostly mods and therefore super cool! I don't really remember much about the music as I probably couldn't hear very much of it.

My most vivid memory is afterwards when I saw one of the bouncers – all them had to wear a sort of uniform of white shirt, black jacket and bow tie – looking totally shocked as all the buttons had been ripped off his shirt. That night stands out in my memory as it was quite wild. I hasten to add that I was not one of the screaming girls!

Lynne Walters

Penny Scoot with friend Jacky More

Penny Scoot *née Racher (age 17)*
My late dad Stanley was publicity and advertising manager at Geo. W. King, Argyle Way, Stevenage until 1966. My dad told me that my favourite group the Rolling Stones was going to perform at the All Fools Charity Beat Ball on 1st April 1964, which was going to be organised by the Geo. W. King Apprentice Association. He asked if I would I like to sell raffle tickets at the Locarno Ballroom that night and as a reward would probably be able to meet the Stones back stage.

My oldest friend and next door neighbour Jacky More (nee Jenkins) who was also 17 was invited to come with me. We were both very excited to be present at this event and remember selling a lot of raffle tickets as well as being able to watch the Rolling Stones and accompanying bands. We remember seeing Big Dee Irwin and the Diamonds and also the League of Gentlemen, Terry Judge and the Barristers and the Deltics. Both Jacky and I were then privileged enough to go back

stage and meet the group. They all signed my autograph book, which I still have. Afterwards my Dad picked us up and took us back to Hitchin. Both Jacky and I remember them as being very polite and courteous.

Roger Glazebrook *(age 18)*
I went with my mate Mick. It was a Geo. King Apprentice Association dance. The tickets cost 21 shillings (£1.05). It was perhaps the Mecca's greatest moment. Obviously it was packed but as 18 year olds we thought 'what a great night – it would be all girls.' Big mistake. Yes there were girls but no one was dancing. They were all screaming around the stage and so we ended up just going to the bar. The day the Stones turned up in Stevenage was a great talking point in town. About two years later my old firm booked Cream at the Hermitage in Hitchin – Eric Clapton, etc. We also had The Who. Geno Washington. Manfred Mann. But nobody topped the Stones.

Pat Kingsland *(age 17)*
We weren't supposed to be there because Wednesday nights were for over 18s because they had a bar. But Monday nights was a disco night – it was called a DJ night in those days – and it was for the younger ones really. I don't think my mother would have let me go if I was 16. The girl I worked with had been a school friend and actually lived opposite us. She and I went together. And we worked in the local hairdressers and neither of us at the beginning

of the day had got a penny to our names but we obviously did well with our customers that day because as apprentices you didn't get much pay but we'd had good tips so we had enough money to actually have a drink that evening.

The King's Apprentices put on an event each year to raise money for charity. It was called the All Fools Charity Beat Ball of the Year and it was on April Fools' Day 1964. The ticket price was six shillings (30p). And there were loads of other groups there. I don't remember any of the other groups. I think it was just that the Stones were so good. The Rolling Stones were absolutely just like their records. It was a great night. My brother was a King's apprentice and he said the Rolling Stones were only paid £50 that night because when they booked them they hadn't had a hit record. They got them really cheap.

My boyfriend Ceri – who is my husband now and has been for 47 years – decided that night that he didn't want to go. I had a ticket for him and I kept the ticket. When I came home my brother said to me "you're stupid – you should have sold it on the door for 10/6". (53p) I think the ticket price at the time was only six or seven shillings (30p – 35p). And a few years ago we sold it because it had the Rolling Stones autographs on the back and we got nearly £800 for it.

Anna Askew (age 15)
I was in the Red Cross in Stevenage. As a cadet I used to come to the Mecca for emergency aid and saw all these stars who visited

the town. I used to stand on the side of the stage and I was there when the Stones played. There's a photograph of me on the night with a girl who collapsed after screaming too much and trying to get at Mick Jagger. I went with my mother and had a drink with all the group.

Peewee Cochlan (age 17)
I went with my mate Mitch – John Mitchell. We were both number one fans of the Stones. I can't remember if we pulled that night or not. I do remember that we paid 7/6 (37p) and that they were dressed in smart casual clothes.

Roger Comley (age 19)
I was one of the 115 apprentices that year at Geo. W King. Another apprentice named Tom Clitheroe managed a local band in Stevenage and we were members of the G W King Apprentice Association who organised visits to many shows like the Stones, Freddie and the Dreamers, The Beatles' Christmas Show and others at the Empire, Finsbury Park.

Tom Clitheroe booked the Stones for £500 and we sold tickets for the Locarno show at 15 shillings (75p) each for the apprentices to buy. I had about 20 apprentices to contact at work to advertise events and sell tickets. I was given a job to help marshall the balcony and clear up the chairs after. It was mostly a boys' night out with some girls as guests of the boys.

Mike Peg (age 14)
I was there with my first girlfriend – Susan Gunning from the Chells. She went to Heathcote School.

Peewee Cochlan (right) with John Mitchell

I lived in Shephalbury. Stevenage was great in those days. The Stones were my favourites and that day lives in my memory. We were young mods and the Mecca was our regular. That night was special and the place was packed. We stood in the middle of the dance floor, not far from the stage and just jumped up and down and joined in the noise – as you do. It was crazy. We saw the Who at the Mecca around the same time in an equipment smashing mode, but the Stones were the best.

Derek Turner

I was an apprentice at that time at the (now closed) Geo. W King factory and on the committee that organised the dance at the then Mecca ballroom. I remember the night, turning up in my best suit as you did in those days, to help administer the event. We formed a cordon completely around the stage in order to keep the frenzied mass of teenage girls from overrunning the stage. As it was there were many girls fainting and being passed over the top of the crowd to safety. A bonus to us as they were in their short skirts!

I remember wondering whether we could hold the crowd back from the stage as the pressure of the masses was huge. We had to brace ourselves against the stage to keep the cordon together. The Stones were a scruffy bunch compared to us teenagers at the time. I thought, with all the tugging and pulling, 'will my best – and only – suit survive the night?' and 'what the hell are we doing protecting such an outfit?'

Mary Abra *(age 15)*

None of my friends wanted to go but I was determined so went alone. I remember there was a line of bouncers with their arms linked at the front of the dance floor before the stage. I was right at the front and quite small and the crowds were pushing forward. The bouncers were worried that I would get squashed so they let me and a few other girls who were also in danger of getting squashed go through and onto the stage and to the back of the stage to safety. However when I got onto the stage I took the opportunity of sitting next to Charlie Watts and his drum kit. I was soon hauled off and taken to the back of the revolving stage. My idol at the time was Brian Jones. I loved his floppy hair style. I can't remember how much I had to save up for the ticket – probably something like 17/6 (87p).

Mary Abra

My next encounter with the Stones was in the summer of 1976 when they appeared at Knebworth. I was working as a waitress at the Blakemore Hotel, Little Wymondley which was where the Stones stayed. I was on duty on the Sunday morning when they turned up. Mick Jagger came bounding into the foyer, where there was only myself and the receptionist. I stood at the reception and signed in the casual waitress book whilst Mick Jagger booked in. The receptionist said to him "name please." He replied "Jagger." Then she said "initial'" as if she didn't know, and he said "M" and disappeared up to his room. I thought "gosh, he's quite short!" I seemed to remember him as being tall all those years ago when I'd seen him at the Locarno.

The other Stones all came into the dining room where I served them breakfast. They were friendly, polite and no trouble at all. I didn't ask any of them for their autographs, I don't know why – I wish I had! 1976 was a very hot summer. I was living in Bude Crescent in Symonds Green, not far from Knebworth as the crow flies. That evening, standing in my garden, I could hear the Stones music from Knebworth. It was pure magic.

Margaret Senior (age 19)
They were well on their way when they appeared there. At the Locarno, on the Saturday nights when different bands use to play, us girls were usually eyeing up the talent as were the boys. I recall several bands that went on to

Margaret Senior

become really famous who use to play at the Locarno – The Beatles and the Rolling Stones being the most popular.

The Locarno had a half-circle shaped stage and not much room but a huge dance floor that had a balcony all around it where some just stayed up there watching the dancers. The memory I have of the Rolling Stones was skinny, hippy looking boys who looked scruffy compared to other bands. Their music was different and wasn't everyone's cup of tea.

Francis Croucher (age 14)
It was every other Wednesday night that they would have a top Sixties group. We would go to the Black and White café in the High Street before it started. That's where the groups would go before the show. One night whilst walking to the town to see Manfred Mann there was a van parked about 200 yards from

my house in South Road and as I walked passed one of the group got out and asked the way to the Kayser Bondor – what a shock! We saw the Swinging Blue Jeans, Johnny Kidd and the Pirates and others. But the top group was the Rolling Stones. The place was packed – you couldn't move in there. I remember their van because the girls there had written all over it. It was an old Bedford.

Don Maxwell
I had a band called the League of Gentlemen named after one of my favourite films at that time. I had a good relationship with the then manager of the Locarno – Mr Dijon. He liked the League of Gentlemen very much and always gave us the opportunity to support up and coming acts at that time so when he phoned me and asked if we would be interested in supporting the Stones I accepted straight away.

I rolled up early evening to set up and walked into the dressing back stage whereupon I met Charlie Watts. He had arrived on his own and was sitting by himself drinking from a large bottle of alcohol. He looked up and I said "hello" and he acknowledged me. He didn't seem to have much to say so I didn't indulge in conversation. The rest of the Stones turned up later that evening and by the time they went on the whole place was buzzing.

The Locarno had a revolving stage and as it began to turn they were introduced. At this point the whole crowd surged forward.

> "I had climbed onto a photo booth and had a perfect view of their show"

Safety barriers were unheard of in those days – there was just a row of bouncers trying to keep the girls off the stage. During the show many girls were fainting and being transferred to the back of the stage by the bouncers. The crush was really heavy and my soon to be wife and her friend had to force their way to the side of the room. I had climbed onto a photo booth on the left of the stage and had a perfect view of their show. It was a very electric atmosphere and their performance was excellent.

I went backstage afterwards and got them to sign my future wife's autograph book. They didn't hang around for very long and were not the most talkative but it was obvious that their career was beginning to take off rapidly and they were living life at a very fast pace. All in all it was a great night and at that time no one really knew just how big rock'n'roll would become.

Colin Standring *(age 17)*
The Stones were the first band to sell out the Locarno – over 2,000 tickets. They were also the first band I saw that ignored the 'revolving stage' procedure. The stage was built on a large revolving disk format with a backdrop in the middle. When the support band finished the stage would revolve with the band playing out and the new band would come around already playing their first number. Not the Stones. The stage revolved around to reveal just the equipment. Jagger and Co then walked on nonchalantly, picked

up their instruments, tuned up at leisure and started to play. In those conservative days that was a sensation.

Brenda Parker

I saw them when they played at the Locarno Ballroom in Stevenage. By this time they'd had a hit with *I Wanna Be Your Man* and released *Not Fade Away* too. The show was organised by a company called George W King which is where my dad worked and when he heard that they were looking for someone to sell raffle tickets at the show and that the reward for doing so would be actually getting to meet the Stones, he volunteered me immediately! Mums and dads may have hated the Stones at that time, but my dad was cool and he knew I was a huge fan and how excited I'd be. Annette and I dutifully sold our fair share of raffle tickets but no one told us when and where we were supposed to go to meet the Stones and by the time we found out how to get backstage there was no one there to introduce us so it was all a bit of an anti climax. I was very shy back then so I just stammered something about how much I liked their records and they just smiled politely.

Apparently there was a photographer from the local paper there and although I didn't see him take it, a picture appeared in the next edition showing Annette, another girl who I didn't know and me with Keith. Keith was reading the *NME* when I approached him and in the picture he's reaching out to sign a photo of the Stones that I'm holding out to him. One thing I remember very clearly and which I thought was very odd at the time was that Brian wasn't with the others. He was all by himself in a very small space not much bigger than a closet. Now that all the animosity they felt towards him because of him originally negotiating more money for himself has come out it makes sense that he wasn't with them, but I had no idea they'd started to isolate him and freeze him out as early as that. He was very sweet, but I remember feeling sorry for him because he was just being ignored. It's really quite shocking how Brian's been

Brenda Parker

relegated to the dustbin of history when he was so talented and played such an integral part in the Stones' story. He was my favourite Stone, I think, because I never forgot how lonely and isolated he looked stuck there all by himself in that little space and being ignored by all the others and how genuinely grateful he seemed to be that someone had found him there and actually wanted to talk to him.

Unfortunately we had to leave a few minutes later so they could do the show. And the show was great! By now they'd given up on the matching outfits and I remember Brian was wearing a striped waistcoat. I've no idea why that stuck in my mind! The stage was pretty small and there was a huge crush of people all pushing and shoving and trying to get as close as possible.

Mick had learned how to strut his stuff by now and he was vigorously shaking a pair of maracas and Brian had a tambourine and kept coming dangerously close to the edge of the stage to shake it in people's faces. He may have been persona non grata backstage, but he really came alive during the show and seemed to be having a great time taunting people with that tambourine. People kept reaching up to grab him and Mick but at the last seconds they'd both somehow skip back just in time. At this time Brian was very much in the forefront of the group and people were screaming and reaching out to him just as much, if not more so, than to Mick. Bill never moved

but just stood there like a statue holding his bass almost vertical to the ground and pretty much ignoring all the chaos going on all around him.

It was really an exciting show – the best one of all the times I saw them. That's why the 'All Fools' gig at the Locarno was so memorable, apart from the obvious reason for me. It wasn't a theatre so it was possible to get really close to the stage and was much more of an intimate experience than sitting in a big theatre with such a big gulf between the audience and the stage. In April '64 the Stones weren't the huge superstars they went on to become so although there was a massive crush of bodies pressing forward to try to get to them and some girls calling out the names of their favourite Stone, you could still hear the music and feel the raw energy they were generating from it.

A lot of that got lost as they became genuine pop stars and started appearing regularly on TV and headlining their own tours. Don't get me wrong – they were still wonderful! But when Mick stopped singing "I just wanna make love to you" with a salacious sneer on his face and switched to lamenting about 19th nervous breakdowns, a lot of the danger and the edginess that had set them apart was gone.

3 APRIL 1964
Palais, Wimbledon

Jane Tomkins
By the time I went to see the Stones again, at Wimbledon Palais,

they had become much more famous and I found the whole experience quite an eye-opener. Girls were going crazy and it was extremely crowded and hot. With a great degree of determination I managed to force myself quite near to the stage and was so excited to see the group up close. Some girls were fainting and being hauled across our heads and onto the stage by security. Nearer the end of the show we were all soaking wet because it was so hot. I remember laughing as one girl said that her brand new outfit had shrunk as she had been sweating so much. I smile when I remember having to explain to my bemused mother the following morning why my brand new white shoes had become completely black and wrecked by the stampeding fans. I saw quite a lot of other famous groups back then, as they even appeared local village halls. I remember seeing the Animals, the Yardbirds and the Who in Wallington Public – it all seems so improbable now!

Malcolm Clare

right up against the left hand side of the stage and could touch Brian Jones. I was that close. He was playing his lime green f hole Gretsch guitar. Charlie Watts was a joy to watch as he was an excellent jazz drummer, which was my instrument of choice. The supporting group on the night was a local band called the Whispers who had Justin Hayward in their line up pre-Moody Blues as he was a Swindon lad in those days.

9 APRIL 1964
McIlroy's Ballroom, Swindon

Malcolm Clare

I was in a group called Rob and the Rockettes. I was there for the night with all our other group members. It was a full house. I remember queuing up Regent Street to get in and was overjoyed to see the bad boys of rock as this was my first time at any rock concert and I would not have missed it for the world. I was extremely lucky to have a spot

Bernard Linnegar

The second Stones gig I went to at McIlroy's was a completely different kettle of fish from the first. Some hit records had been produced in the interim and obviously the situation had changed somewhat. The place was heaving. There were a record number of people in that room. There was talk at the time of there being 2,000 which would never be allowed now. I can remember just about getting through the door but no further and because of the lack of floor space people were standing on the window sills. I followed suit. There was a large single sheet of glass – there was no double glazing then – between me and the street below. Imagine what the health and safety police would have to say about that these days. At some point I had a pass out to get a drink at a nearby pub, it being impossible to get to McIlroy's bar. It was then that I witnessed what was to become my most enduring memory of the whole evening. In the street outside was fleet of vehicles from Leighfields, a now defunct local building company, who had a team of workmen inside the department store busily propping up the ballroom floor above them with Acrow props. Can you imagine?

Vivien Edwards *née Croxon (age 17)*

We used to go to the Locarno in Old Town in Swindon Old Town and they had all sorts – Lulu and Cilla Black. At McIlroy's I went to see Kenny Ball and his Jazzmen. When the Rolling Stones came to town that was a big event. They played three shows at McIlroy's. I went to the last one. I can remember queuing for a long, long time outside and when we actually got in McIlroy's you had to go up this lovely staircase to the ballroom and then there was more queuing upstairs for the cloakroom to put your coats. I remember we thought 'no, blow that we're not gonna wait that long!' So we put our coats on the floor in the corner. But everyone else had the same idea. So when we came back to get our coats everyone else had done the same and there was a great big pile

Vivien Edwards

of coats on top and ours were at the bottom and it took us ages to find them and then we had to get the last bus home. So I suspect we missed it and probably had to walk home that day. I think it was about five shillings to get in. I went with friends.

I can even remember what I was wearing. I was wearing a brown suede dress with lace up the front with criss cross and then it was fashionable to put your cardigan on back to front so the buttons were at the back. I can remember sitting on someone's lap. I was right at the front. Because it was so packed you couldn't really dance. I can remember being so close I could touch them and obviously screaming maybe at one stage. My picture was in the Adver, the local newspaper. Looking at the picture now I can see that I'm mesmerised by them and some of the audience are really screaming.

11 APRIL 1964
Pier Ballroom, Hastings

Christine Toms *(age 16)*

They arrived late and my boyfriend at the time helped to run the speedboat, so they were brought in on that from the beach as all the fans were packing the pier. I helped them up the steps and took them into the dressing rooms at the back of stage. I managed to get their autographs of course. Then a lot of girls broke in and it was chaos for a while. They were very tired already having already done a few gigs down the coast, possibly Brighton, and I seem to remember they only stayed for about 20 minutes as they were headlining that evening.

16 APRIL 1964
Cubi Klub, Rochdale

The Stones were scheduled to appear at the Cubi Klub but, with the venue full and the band back stage, the decision was taken to cancel the concert for health and safety reasons due to the huge numbers of people in the audience.

Peter Oldham (age 18)

I was at the Cubi Klub in Rochdale that night. I remember going into this basement of this factory or warehouse and thinking that it was a disaster waiting to happen. I cannot remember the size of the room although I feel it was not that high and had pillars but it was hot with body heat so I can only presume there was limited ventilation. I was at the front right up to the stage and the barrier was made out of church pews where the backs can be moved over to sit either way. There was no security staff or bouncers.

The stage entrance was to my right little more than ten feet away. I could not see what was happening behind the curtain but I recall at one point a cheer and messages passed down the line that the group was there and had been seen by those who could see behind the curtain. I cannot remember how long I was there until a guy came on stage and said the Rolling Stones would not appear. I seem to think we exited peacefully. In retrospect any sort of stampede, crowd rush or maybe a fire and the loss of life would have been substantial.

Bob Lee

There was the famous club appearance that wasn't, at Rochdale. I went to that. My take on it is that there was almost a riot. Thousands of us turned up there. You could book in advance and I'd done so – I'd booked in advance. But when we got there they said they couldn't go on because it was our fault – they'd sold too many tickets. The police had stopped them because of the fire regulations. They couldn't have that many people in. That's what they said. I just thought, like everybody did at the time, that it was just a con to get people there.

It had been done before in Manchester with other groups. Some years after, a club in Oldham advertised the Cream at the Stax Club and I've got the ticket for that. That was another club where everyone turned up and the group didn't. It was only afterwards that I found out that they did turn up – the Rolling Stones did turn up – but they were advised it wasn't safe for them to perform. Another group was going to be the support and the club still opened that night and the other group played. I believe it was a fantastic Manchester group called the Stylos. I only found out that they'd played and the club had opened later after I'd made my way back from Rochdale to Manchester. But the Stones apparently were there.

> "the Rolling Stones did turn up – but they were advised it wasn't safe for them to perform"

17 APRIL 1964
Locarno Ballroom, Coventry

Susan Brown *(age 17)*
I bought myself a blue mini dress with see-through nylon sleeves and eight buttons at the cuffs. It was so in fashion at the time and it cost me three weeks' wages to buy from C&A. Plus I put on my silver charm bracelet. I'd collected loads of charms. I was really proud of it. With my long red hair which was back combed into a beehive I was, I must say, looking great. Well we got to the concert. I've never seen so many girls in one place.

The music started, on the stage came the Stones. It was so magical. They were so, so good. Everyone was screaming including myself. All I wanted to do was to get nearer the front. We pushed and shoved until we were right on the front row. As I looked up

Mick Jagger was just picking up his tambourine from the floor. I lent in to touch his leg, pulling myself onto the stage, when my charm bracelet got stuck on his trouser leg. He had started his song running across the stage with me at the bottom of his trouser leg and they started to slip down at one side! The next moment a gang of men were there with fire extinguishers trying to control us.

There were a lot of other girls trying to get on too, but we all got off in the end. When outside I was like a drowned rat. We tried to get on the last bus but missed it, so with stiletto shoes in hand we walked home. Luckily Mum and Dad were in bed. I had a job the next day explaining about my dress, which was never the same again. It was one of the greatest times ever.

Tony Campbell
I ran a band called the Mighty Avengers. We started up in about '61. We were working for Reg Talbot a lot. Reg Talbot ran a load venues all around the Midlands. He ran what was the old Co-op Hall in Rugby and then changed it to the Town Hall. He ran Nuneaton Co-op Hall for many years.

We played with the Stones at the Locarno in Coventry. We got taken on by a Manchester agency which was Kennedy Street Artists who got us a recording contract with *Decca* and eventually we recorded three Mick Jagger and Keith Richards' songs, one of which did very well for us called *So Much In Love*. Our recording

The Mighty Avengers

"WHEN BLUES TURN TO GREY"

THE MIGHTY AVENGERS

118

manager was Andrew Oldham who was the Stones manager. And that's when we got to know Mick and Keith quite well and actually recorded with them. In fact on *So Much In Love* the two session men were John Paul Jones and Jimmy Page. Jimmy played guitar and John Paul Jones played piano on two of our sessions. Most of the work we did was at Regent Sound in Denmark Street. We were working all over the country but we did the Locarno with the Stones and I did another job with them but I can't remember where it was.

We met them personally more than worked with them because we used to go down to Andrew Oldham's flat in north London when we were rehearsing songs. Mick Jagger and Keith Richards were there and they went through the songs with us and Marianne Faithfull was there one weekend.

24 APRIL 1964
Gaumont Theatre, Norwich

Margaret Lee-Caston *(age 15)*
I was there! At the time I lived 20 miles out of Norwich so we went to the gig on an organised coach trip with lots of other Stones fans. I can't believe my parents allowed me to go – my father was a Church of England vicar and rural Dean and I was a day pupil at the Convent of the Sacred Heart in Swaffham, Norfolk. In our class we had two camps. You were either in the Rolling Stones camp or The Beatles' camp. We were not allowed to like or support both bands.

Margaret Lee-Caston

I went with my then best friend Linda and the main thing I remember about the concert was you couldn't hear the Stones performance very well because of all the screaming girls in the audience. It was all extremely exciting. I mainly wanted to see Brian Jones who I thought was amazing, talented and very attractive.

After the gig everyone hung around outside the building hoping for a glimpse of the band as they left. Unfortunately we were disappointed. The next day I had a sore throat but all my class mates were very envious. From the day I first saw the Rolling Stones on Top of the Pops I was hooked and despite now being aged 65 that is still the case. The Gaumont Theatre is currently being demolished due to safety and structural problems.

Rosemary Bruce *(age 10)*

It was against my mother's wishes and I saved up all my pocket money to go. I was in the very back row. I don't really have many other memories apart from going with my best friend and a lot of screaming going on! Of course, no big screens then so they looked very small figures on the stage.

Mervyn Blakeway

Mervyn Blakeway *(age 18)*

At the time I lived in Beccles and my girlfriend was a lovely 17 year old girl named Jeanne Salluyts who lived in Shipmeadow. We had travelled to the city on my trusty BSA Gold Flash. The Stones were amazing. We were about two rows from the front. Obviously Brian Jones was still alive then.

Performing with the Stones were several other artists – Mike Berry, the Leroys, Jet Harris the ex-Shadow, Millie Davis and Heinz, who usually did Eddie Cochran material. I recall the audience were well behaved although a few girls who ventured too close to the stage were stopped by the security guards. It was a great evening. My diary reads I finally reached indoors at 2.30am.

28 APRIL 1964
Public Hall, Wallington

John Fletcher *(age 17)*

I saw them at Wallington Public Hall. They had released their first LP and were amazing. I was right up front and have an abiding memory of Bill chewing gum and holding his bass vertically. When they did *Mona* we had never heard anything like it – brilliant!

John Fletcher

30 APRIL 1964
The Majestic Theatre, Birkenhead

Jenny Wilson (age 17)
We used to go every Thursday and Sunday and danced most of the night to all the local groups, including The Beatles. It was a fantastic night until the stage was besieged by fans and the Stones went off. They were singing *Time Is On My Side* – one of my favourites. I have never forgotten this event and was so upset when they went off.

Sue Hammond (age 17)
It turned out to be a non-event. They came on stage, sang a couple of numbers, the crowd moved forward and they went off and that was it! Not sure whether it was their decision to go off or the management. We had seen The Beatles there on several occasions with no problems. I don't know the reason why they went off. The stage was very near the audience and not very high. We were not very concerned about the reason, just disappointed.

Marj Kurthausen née Cross (age 14)
My friends and I had gone to see what we thought would be The Beatles with the Stones as the supporting act. I had it in my mind to marry one of The Beatles. In fact we dyed our hair in the hope that they would see us and fall madly in love. We also changed our names so that they would sound more exciting. I was to be called Sherie. Imagine

my surprise when another group of boys arrived on stage like a thunderbolt. I was horrified – it was so sexy! The lead singer Mick Jagger had make up on. It was called pan stick in those days. He was so scary but mesmerizing and the music was fantastic. Raunchy was only a word I would know later but I still think dangerous was the word that came to my mind then. I knew then that they were the bad boys of rock. I would always be in love with The Beatles because they were my first crush but the music of the Stones makes me want to move and I love it. I still dance around the kitchen to *Brown Sugar* with my air guitar.

Barbara Palmer
They were fantastic, as they still are to this day. I remember it as if it were yesterday. Mick with his fabulous dancing. Brian Jones as cool as a cucumber. And the lovely Keith, my favourite Stone. Bill and Charlie were fab as well of course. What a view I had. My friend and I saw them from a side door. We were actually on the street and in our school uniforms.

You can imagine how full of ourselves we were when we told all our friends about it next day at school. Yes we were on a real high until one of the teachers gave us a real good telling off. Would you believe we had been seen by one of the other teachers coming away from the Majestic after the show had finished. We were told we should have been at home doing our homework instead of watching pop groups!

> "dangerous was the word that came to my mind ... I knew then that they were the bad boys of rock"

Chapter 10

2 MAY 1964

Spa, Bridlington

Helen Smalley *(age 12)*

I remember it well or rather – not! I was besotted by Brian Jones with pictures from *Jackie* magazine on my bedroom wall. I had nagged my dad for weeks to let me go to the concert only to be told I was too young, which I suppose I was. However he did relent and take me down to the Spa on the night and in those days you could walk to the back entrance and watch the acts go in.

Of course I was not the only one to have that idea but being there early was one of the ones near the front of the barrier. In due course the Stones arrived and alighted from their transport inside the barrier. Well, all hell broke loose and I remember being crushed against the barrier. The next thing I remember was being lifted up and plonked down by one of the bouncers – right next to Brian Jones! He said, and I remember it well, "you alright love?" My one moment of fame, only I was tongue tied and just nodded. I've regretted it ever since. But the highlight was he touched my hand – imagine how many weeks that tale was retold at school.

Bruce Gee *(age 14)*

I went to see the Stones with a friend. I remember buying a couple of tickets for the concert as soon as it was announced. It was 7s/6d (37p) instead of the five shillings (25p) we paid for the lesser known groups. I would have been wearing jeans, tee shirt and Cuban heel boots. We met up in the Spa with some school mates, the big lads all of 16. We had arrived at the Spa about two hours before the doors were opened to savour the atmosphere. Nearly opposite the Spa we saw a couple of lads climbing up the drain pipe of a four storey B&B to get to one or two of the Stones who were waving from the top floor window. The police stopped any further progress up the drain pipe when the girls tried to join in.

We walked round to the back of the Spa near the stage door and spotted a dark blue Mk 1 transit van covered with graffiti – Mick, Keith and Brian in lipstick or scratched on the van. Unbeknown to us at the time it was Ian Stewart unloading amps, guitars, etc. "Dinnae go near the van, lads," he said. We didn't. When the Stones appeared on stage it seemed strange to me when Mick raised his arm to wave to the crowd. His jumper had a bloody great hole under the arm which was not usual with the trendy clothes they were seen with in magazines, unless he got ragged by the fans before he got on stage. I don't think the Stones were on stage for more than 45 minutes and we only heard the opening bars of the songs they played, such was the noise of the girls packed at the stage front.

Michael Gaunt

It was a night I have never forgotten as I was back stage with the supporting group the Avengers. I did not play in the group. I was what they now call a roadie.

Elaine Wilson (age 17)

When I was in the sixth form at Scarborough Girls' High School, for one winter season only the Bridlington Spa ran monthly all night dances. We saw the Rolling Stones, the Hollies and the Animals twice. It cost 12/6 (63p). I hired a coach from Scarborough and collected the money beforehand to pay for the coach. We did not need to book beforehand – we just turned up and paid at the door.

When I saw The Beatles in concert at the Futurist in Scarborough they all wore pale grey mohair suits with Chanel style high necks without collars, white shirts and narrow black bootlace ties. In contrast, the Stones wore casual clothing. Charlie Watts alone wore a suit. Mick Jagger wore a pale grey marl crew necked sweater and danced around on stage wearing bell bottom jeans. We all wore them but girls then did not wear jeans in the evening.

Large posters of them in black and white were sold for five shillings (25p) and I had one. I could not hear anything of The Beatles singing as girls in front of me just stood up and screamed. The Rolling Stones were playing at an all night dance, not a concert. Everyone walked around and sat and chatted whilst they played. When they played the Spa, we saw the Animals in the bar drinking like everyone else. I could not afford a drink!

3 MAY 1964
Palace Theatre, Manchester

Christine McDermott (age 12)

I was a massive fan of the Stones back then and lived in Ardwick, Manchester. Memories I have of all of the concerts I went to are of queuing up for nights on end to get tickets. Hence I got seats near the front, in this case seat F28 in the stalls. This was always a fabulous social thing to do.

I actually managed to climb and jump on to the stage and grab hold of Mick's ankles. Eventually two big blokes came on stage and extrapolated me from Mick's legs and took me off stage and out through the stage door I went. It was worth it to be able to touch Mick. I waited out side the front and at the end of the concert the staff let me back in to get my bag from under my seat. Amazingly, it was still there. When I jumped I landed in the foot lights on my knees. As I was wearing fishnet tights I had diamond shaped scabs on my knees for weeks afterwards.

9 MAY 1964
Savoy Ballroom, Catford, London

Lynne Phillips (age 18)

I went with a boyfriend (I forget his name!) who played guitar in a local group in the Bromley area and who had a scooter, much to my parents' dismay. I often went to the Savoy to dance with various friends. This time we went to see what the fuss was about, not expecting very much. There were lots of groups around – some good, some awful – but we were smitten and came out dedicated fans!

Lynne Phillips

Clive Chase

The group that I was with was called Bobby King and the Sabres. We played covers of just about everything that was in the hit parade. As such many Saturday and Friday evening gigs saw us playing second fiddle to a chart group. Although we seemed to play alongside groups like the Hollies, the Merseybeats and Tony Rivers and the Castaways quite a number of times, we only played with the Stones once and that was a first floor dance club or ballroom in Catford, South London – one of our regular Saturday night places. It generally held about 700 to 800 on a good night. The night the Stones played there we were told by the bouncers "they've let 1,200 kids in" which was probably true because it was shoulder to shoulder pushing. Anyone who wanted to go to the loo would have had a half hour shove through the throng to get there. Dancing? No chance! In fact a number fainted with the heat. The bouncers said there were twelve ambulances in attendance outside taking the unconscious and minor wounded away.

It was a fairly usual evening's schedule in that the DJ would kick off at around 7.15pm or so and then we would come on at around 8pm to 9pm. The Stones were then due to appear at 9pm for an hour, and then the DJ and then us, finishing with the DJ again. But it didn't happen like that. Equipment had been set up by around 5.30 to 6pm. Nothing seemed too out of the ordinary as there were occasions when top groups would

make their entrance just a few minutes before they were due to start, their roadies having set everything up. That said in that era many top groups would be there and want to sound check things themselves and certainly not act the celebrity. But no Stones! We played our first set from 8pm till 9pm. It was hot! Still no Stones. The management got a message to us – play on, play on! So we did. 9.30pm. Nothing. 10pm. Nothing.

Having played for two hours and with the steam rising almost literally we were told the DJ would do a stint. The management must have been having kittens. Remember there were no mobile phones back then. We retired to the only dressing room – that's a polite word for it. It was a sizeable area backstage. I can't be sure of the time but at some juncture in burst the five of them. They had arrived. They seemed a mix of out of breath and giggly. They were late – very late. They had clearly been hurrying on foot across an area behind the venue and then up into the rear as they would have been totally unable to enter through the throng of 1,200 or so kids. Remember this hall was on the first floor, so I'm not sure how they got up from the ground floor. There was a long concrete staircase at the rear from the road behind where groups brought their stuff in but that staircase led to the main auditorium.

So, as I say, a bit out of breath but clearly either loving the fun of it or maybe enhanced by other things! One of the management

"the management must have been having kittens"

was asking – telling – them they had to get on as the kids were starting to turn a tantrum. I recall both Jagger and Jones saying in a very nonchalant way that he should – well the equivalent of – 'keep your hair on.' But they did then get into gear a bit. They had a small attaché case each which seemed to hold odd clothes that would be worn on stage. Not all of them changed. Some decorative bits were pulled out – a scarf, for example – and thrust around the neck. For Jagger I seem to recall there was a pair of very, very sparkly tight trousers. But the thing that made me smile the most was that in these small bags, as well as the clothes, there were also the remains of old food. In one, I can't recall whose it was, was the best part of a cold fish and chip meal still trying to closet itself partially inside the newspaper wrapping it had been bought in at some earlier date. What a way to live, we thought to ourselves, glancing over at each other.

There we were, five kids of around 18 years of age, each driving our own almost new car and each fairly impeccably dressed in our matching mohair suits and ties. Maybe that's where we were going wrong! The Stones finished what they were doing and they were gone – onto the stage. I remember the sheer vibe of their music as it hit. It was good – very good. Bill Wyman had two Vox Foundation speakers with 18 inch units in each and had one either side of the stage. As a bass player I was amazed how good the sound was. That said you could

not actually hear the individual notes that he was playing but the sheer depth made such a tremendous impact.

We never did see them again. When they finished they were escorted off by bouncers to the concrete steps which exited from the hall itself and not that far from the stage and they were gone – job done. I later learned that the reason that were late was because, rather than come to the gig they were booked for, they made the decision to go and see Chuck Berry at the Finsbury Park Astoria.

John Richardson (age 18)

I lived in Greenwich at the time. I didn't live in Catford. It was like the Savoy was the best place around at the time. Saturday night they used to have Johnny Gray and his Band of the Day. That was fun because he was a boozer and we used to enjoy boozing with him. I got involved only because I used to go up there regularly. I went up there with a friend of mine, Dave Harris, who now lives in Australia. We only used to go up there for the birds, you know, like you did.

How they used to run it was, upstairs on a Wednesday night – which I think that's the night the Stones came – and downstairs on a Saturday the bar was open and you had to be a member to get in there and that's what it was all about really. Downstairs was the in place if you know what I mean. You used to get in and upstairs was really just groups.

Brian Poole and the Tremeloes were the resident band. We had

"you could not actually hear the individual notes that he was playing but the sheer depth made such a tremendous impact"

all sorts. Freddie and the Dreamers were there. The Undertakers. They used to have some good groups there during the week. We used to go down in the bar afterwards and chat to 'em. Freddie and the Dreamers. I was talking to him. Course he's dead now. He was good fun – Freddie Garritty.

We was members of the Savoy and we were sort of talking to the bouncers and things like that and when the Stones eventually come on they did about half hour or three quarters of an hour. They weren't on all night. People weren't there regularly. They were there just to see the Stones and it got very crowded and we happened to be at the front. The bouncers started pushing 'em back and we just helped 'em out because we knew 'em. What the girls were doing in the end was fainting to get out because the only way out was over the stage.

The Stones were the Stones, you know, very professional even then. They performed all the way through it but the looks these girls got when they were being dragged across the stage said it all really. Joe, a Turkish or Greek lad, took it upon himself to stand on the stage and take 'em over the stage. That sort of encouraged 'em to do it all the more. These girls seemed to be faking passing out just to get close, you know?

They played all the usual things. I remember I was singing *I Just Want To Make Love To You*. Me an' Dave were singing that all week cause it was stuck in our head. The Stones – they went straight home. They didn't stay.

They did their gig. It wasn't an hour, I don't think. They usually had two groups on when there was a star band there and I can't remember who the other band was. And then they came on and the place got more and more crowded and we just happened to be at the front and we started helping out. Good job we did, I think. They'd have got mobbed otherwise.

I remember Mick looking down at these people, you know. Just glaring at 'em. The Stones were great but the gig was chaos. It turned into Mr Smiths after that, when they had that very famous gun fight between the Richardsons and the Krays. I stopped going after that. I wasn't there that night and I didn't wanna be. I think it's the Co-op funeral parlour now.

10 MAY 1964
Colston Hall, Bristol

Keith Gwinnell (age 15)
I attended the show with a number of friends from school. The original plan was to see The Beatles but the tickets had sold out. The friend who had been given the task of buying the tickets used his initiative and purchased tickets for the Stones instead. It turned out to be a good move. The show by the Stones was the first live show that I had attended and what a first! It was a most exciting experience – the noise, the music and the energy was mind blowing. The Colston Hall is not the largest of venues so even though I was in the balcony I felt very close to the action on stage. I still have the ticket stub

> "it was a most exciting experience – the noise, the music and the energy was mind blowing"

for the concert – 7.45pm for the second house. I paid ten shillings and sixpence (53p) for the ticket which was a fair amount as my only income was as a Saturday boy at Woolworths which paid the grand sum of £1 for 8 hours work. An hourly rate of 2/6 (13p). Fifty years on I am still able to recall the energetic performances especially of Mick Jagger and Keith Richards and the accompanying hysteria of the audience.

Mary King *(age 15)*

I went with my friend, Gaynor. We were both 15. The support acts included Gene Vincent. He was clad in black leather. He had had a car accident and he played extensively on his bad leg, striking convulsive poses during his act. He was brilliant, but a lot of the very young audience such as I didn't really know who he was. I wasn't really interested in seeing him but actually his performance was something else!

Next came Millie of *My Boy Lollipop* fame. We all expected her to be good but she sang sharp and to our unsophisticated ears it really jarred! Knowing what I do today about West Indian music it is the trend to sing slightly sharp. If you listen to Susan Cadogan singing *Hurt So Good*, and in many other renditions of West Indian music, you will hear it again. It has become acceptable to my ears now as I am a bit of a music geek. But everybody chatted throughout her performance, which was quite rude I thought.

Anyhow, then came the Stones. The stage went dark and

somebody came on. Everybody started screaming but it was only a roadie or one of the stage crew. They certainly kept us waiting. Some one else came on and we thought it was Bill Wyman, but he went off again. Some time later the lights went up and Bill Wyman was on stage. I went ballistic as he was my favourite. Everybody was screaming and me and my friend looked at each other and burst out laughing as we were both screaming. We ended up laughing throughout most of the performance but were delighted to be there. Then the other three came on – I don't remember in which order – then last of all Mick.

They played a set lasting about 40 minutes. I was a bit fed up because there was so much screaming I couldn't hear them properly. I really enjoy music of all sorts and I was studying music and theory at the time and I wanted to hear how they performed live. I was hoping for them to play *Little Red Rooster*, which was my favourite. I don't remember what they played as it was impossible to hear but I did enjoy seeing them and it was great to be able to say that I was there. I am sure that they just went through the motions as there was so much noise. I don't blame The Beatles for giving up touring under such circumstances but I admire the Stones for sticking it out and reaping the benefits, as nowadays audiences are far better behaved.

I have little recollection of events after the concert. It took so long to get out of the hall that there was no chance of getting autographs. I expect they were whisked away.

Keith Gwinnell

Mary King

11 MAY 1964
Winter Gardens, Bournemouth

Andrew Philpott *(age 19)*
It seems incredible now but the lead act on the poster was Heinz Burt, formerly of the Tornados, and the name Heinz occupied most of the left side of the poster. Jerry Lee Lewis was on the same bill and was the most exciting performer I ever saw. Gene Vincent and the Outlaws were also on the bill – what an incredible line up! The Rolling Stones name was in small print half way down the right side of the poster and when my mates and I saw Mick Jagger prancing around in his tight trousers I have to say we had a job not to laugh. It seemed so over the top even to us but we enjoyed them and one of my mates from those days who I saw recently reminded me that I was told to get back in my seat by the manager when dancing in the isle. I never told my parents when I went to pop concerts as they strongly disapproved of pop music and if they had seen the Rolling Stones performing they would have been horrified.

Roger Gibbins *(age 16)*
I worked in the camera shop in Brights, a big store in Bournemouth at the time. I remember it being a beautiful summer's day. I went with my friends Margaret Stockley, Maureen Felsed and John Elliott, who was really mad on the Stones. I admit I was more into The Beatles but the first Stones LP still remains one of my all time favourite

Andrew Philpott

albums as do their first half a dozen singles. As usual with most parents, mine thought they were dirty and unwashed. We didn't hear a thing – just screaming.

13 MAY 1964
City Hall, Newcastle

Roz Slater *née Gibbons (age 23)*
At the time I was a youth worker at the Borough Road hall youth club, initiated by St Paul's Church, Jarrow and which met every Friday night. Ninety-eight members expressed an interest in this concert for which they paid 5/6 (27p), 6/6 (33p) and 8/- (40p) each. I remember going to pay and collect their tickets with a bag full of cash. I organised three coaches to take us from York Avenue to Newcastle. The air of expectation was great – as was the crowd. The presenter did all in his power to build up the atmosphere for the Stones. When they finally appeared on stage the whole audience stood up and being small I had to move around to see the event. It was for me one of noise, noise and more noise! It was impossible for hear the words at all. When they left the stage – they didn't come back for an encore – the silence was punctuated by the click of the seats as people sat down again. Many of the girls were sobbing from sheer exhaustion and exuberance. Then the task began for me of collecting my 98 members who were all over the venue due to the different ticket prices. Finally we located our three coaches. It was the first concert I had ever been

to. The members were aged 16 to 20 and, even a week later, were still reeling as a result of the event they had been a part of. The gig changed the running of the club. It used to be 7pm to 10pm, 6d (3p) to get in and free tea, coffee, juice and biscuits with games like table tennis, darts, etc. and closing with a barn dance until everyone had paired off and left for home. As a result of seeing the Stones we started to arrange a monthly dance with people paying 2/- (10p) admission and local groups playing.

14 MAY 1964
St George's Hall, Bradford

Ann Holmes (age 14)

I went to the concert with a group of school friends from Belle Vue Girls' Grammar – heaven knows how we persuaded our parents to let us go. We sat up on the first tier of the balcony and it all just seemed so unbelievable that we were actually seeing the Stones. As usual in those days we just screamed through the performance! My real memory though is after the concert, when we went round to the stage door to see if we could catch a glimpse of them. I don't know how, but Brian Jones got separated from the rest and to get away started running up Bridge Street past the Victoria Hotel. It must have been awful to have a load of hysterical, screaming teenagers chasing you. Unfortunately for him, he fell on the pavement in front of us! At this point those screaming teenagers turned into an embarrassed group

of schoolgirls, all looking at each other, as if to say 'oh dear, what do we do now?' Luckily his security men soon caught up with him and got him back to the rest of the group. As you can imagine, this was the talking point for a long time to come at school – how we had touched Brian Jones! It just seems so unreal now to think and tell people that the Rolling Stones came to Bradford of all places. And I was there!

Bob Miller (age 16)

Myself and my girlfriend Jenny Holmes went to one of the shows. We were both 16 and I was still at Carlton Grammar School. The Stones looked great and their performance was fantastic, what we could hear of it! Jenny was focused on Brian Jones though we went on to get married in October 1967 and are still together now, nearly 47 years later.

Bob Miller with Jenny, then … and now.

Leslie Smith

I was a serving police officer in the Traffic Division and I was on night duty. Whilst most officers were out on patrol, it was procedure for two or three to be kept in reserve in the police garage only to be turned out in emergencies. On the night of one of their concerts I was on reserve and after the show the Stones were escorted back to the police garage. After alighting from their car, I went to speak to them and asked for their autographs, which they duly gave me. Mick Jagger was not amongst them and I was told he was still recovering in the back of the car. I went and sat in the car with him and he asked for two or three minutes to come round. After a short while he signed for me. I must say he was exhausted and sweat was all over him.

17 MAY 1964
Odeon Theatre, Folkestone

Michael Prater

Jean Gatehouse *née Saunders (age 15)*
My mum bought me and my friend Sandra Perry tickets for my 16th birthday on 24 May. It was amazing. We were mods in those days but we got very friendly with a group of rockers and we all enjoyed the night and met up again on the Sunday down the harbour. The Pretty Things were a support band for them.

Danuta Pierce

Danuta Pierce *née Krawczyk*
My best friend Julia Tappenden and her older sisters Marion and Gloria and I attended. We were both still at the Girls' Grammar School and talked Julia's mother into queuing for tickets. We found a way in through a fire door round the back of the Odeon and met some of the other acts and – still my beating heart – some of the

Stones. Not, unfortunately, Bill – my favourite. Mick was carrying some wrapped parcels of fish and chips in a bucket. He said "you wanna chip, mate?" My claim to fame!

18 MAY 1964
Changtinghall Hotel, Hamilton

Michael Prater *(age 10)*
I stood outside, unable to get in. There was a riot at the show due to forged tickets and the place was packed solid. There was chicken wire around the stage and the Stones played stripped to the waist due to the heat. Cars were damaged and there was a lot of unruly behaviour. I have seen the Stones seventeen times now and remain a huge fan.

Patrick McCue *(age 15)*
What a night it was! Though an ardent Beatles fan at that time two of my friends who were into the Stones music managed to get three tickets and persuaded me to accompany them to the gig. There we were, three mods, all decked out in our black plastic coats and trilby hats to match. We thought we were the bees' knees. On arriving at the hotel it was obvious the crowd was way in excess of what the hotel could cope with so we made it our aim to get in as quick as possible. As we entered the hotel it was obvious to the three of us that this night was going to be somewhat hot and so we duly checked our coats into the cloakroom. Though it was May it was still a bit chilly and many people who had coats on did

likewise. My endearing memory of that evening after what can only be described as the best gig I've ever been to is the chaos following it. Yes, before it there was a lot of disruption due to the word going around that there had been a lot of forged tickets being shown at the entry points, and this caused a degree of mayhem, but there was more to come.

At the end, when the crowd including myself and my two friends were heading for the cloakroom, it was announced that the cloakroom staff had lost the ticket stubs and it was to be 50 people at one time to go into the cloakroom and pick up their coats. I was lucky enough to be in the first 50 and I duly picked out my wee fav black plastic coat and headed on outside to the cold night.

After about 20 minutes or so my two friends hadn't appeared and I began to worry if they were okay. Needless to say, about 30 minutes after I had got myself out they arrived, both sporting what could only be described as expensive Crombie coats. When they noted I had chosen my cheap plastic coat they both fell about laughing, saying "Pat, what an opportunity you missed. You must be freezing." So much for honesty, eh?

23 MAY 1964
University Students' Union Bar, Leicester

David Sneath (age 19)
The Stones' university booking had been agreed before the Stones made big, which their management honoured. Girls

I knew in the audience found themselves onstage in the wings and when Mick Jagger stubbed out a cigarette and put his heel on it the girls raced to pick up what was left of it. For some reason there was unimportant barracking from the audience to which Mick Jagger replied that the barracker should "get on down to your Palais de Dance where you'll find things ain't no different".

Dawn Young
They all seemed fatigued, worn out from their tour. But once the curtain went up it was as if everything else in the world was erased. The boys became their alter ego, 'The Rolling Stones'. Mick owned the stage, strutting clapping and gazing into the audience with his bedroom eyes. Bill, Keith and Brian backed him up on guitars, while Charlie kept the beat moving on the drums.

25 APRIL 1964
Granada Theatre, East Ham, London

Michael Bailey (age 19)
I have lived in East Ham for most of my life and have fond memories of the Granada and events held there. I remember seeing the Rolling Stones and all those screaming girls.

Mike Byron (age 16)
The ticket cost ten shillings and I had to choose whether to see The Beatles or the Stones. I couldn't afford both. There were girls jumping up and down and screaming. Oh the screaming!

"when Mick Jagger stubbed out a cigarette and put his heel on it the girls raced to pick up what was left of it"

I saw and heard hardly anything of the Stones. When they were announced, after the support acts, someone in front of me stood up and left. Obviously not a fan.

26 MAY 1964
Town Hall, Birmingham

Diane Carey *(age 26)*
It was a fantastic show and full of energy but every number they played was completely drowned by girls screaming. I was with my Mom, who was always a fan of popular music, and my two younger brothers, who at that time were in their early teens. We were surprised to find that Mick Jagger – always a snazzy dresser, we believed – was wearing what we described at the time as a tweed sports jacket.

When we got back home our dad said "were they good?" to which we replied "yes". "What did they sing?" Well, we hadn't got a clue because we couldn't

hear a word. Even so, we had a wonderful night out and yes we enjoyed the show!

Elizabeth Knapp *(age 15)*
All I can remember is screaming my head off with all the others.

28 MAY 1964
Essoldo Theatre, Stockport

David Massey *(age 15)*
I saw the Stones at the Essoldo with my mate Wilf. One thing that sticks in my mind was the electric atmosphere. The girls were screaming and gave it all they had but, because of the size of the speakers on stage and our position about four rows from the front, we could hear ok.

Shirley Broom *(age 17)*
I went to that concert with my boyfriend who later became my husband. I have a souvenir programme of the show. Peter and Gordon were also on the bill along with the Barron Knights, Julie Grant, The Overlanders and David John and the Mood. But I don't remember the other groups as I only went to see the Stones. We were dressed in our mod gear. I also remember the rockers being outside as the concert finished and the fire brigade coming and turning the hose pipes on us all.

Jean Walker
My boyfriend and I were the first in the queue for those tickets at the Essoldo for the Stones concert and we got into trouble for being late for work. However did we care? Not back then! What great

Diane Carey

days they were - absolute magic. We were advised to get on the third row from the front so that we could see better, and we did. And even thought the screaming was deafening – who cared? I caught the attention of Bill Wyman who waved at me and then Mick Jagger did too.

Sandra Stronge (age 14)

My dad was the commissioner at the Essoldo. I had been to see lots of stars there like the Shadows and Gene Vincent, to name but two. Well when my dad said the Rolling Stones were coming and he had two tickets for me and a friend I could hardly believe it. I took my best mate at the time, Sylvia. We were at school together. Our seats were fantastic – just a couple of rows from the stage.

I remember the excitement when the Stones came out. Mick was about 19, I think, and on seeing him screaming just seemed to happen. I remember it being a fabulous show and I have been a fan ever since. We bought posters of the group – they did not sell merchandise like these days. My dad had taken my autograph book back stage and got all the group's autographs, including Brian Jones. I must have impressed my mates at school when I took it to show them. I have kept the book all these years.

Jenny Bentley (age 13)

A few months before they came I was walking down Wellington Road South towards Mersey Square when I saw a poster outside the Essoldo advertising the concert. I stopped in my tracks, unable to believe that they were actually going to come to Stockport. Very bravely, I crossed over the cinema and went into the foyer and asked if they had any leaflets on it and they gave me one. I couldn't wait to get home so that I could write a letter and send it along with the leaflet to their fan club, requesting their autographs. A few weeks later my self-addressed envelope was returned and I almost screamed the house down with excitement when I saw the leaflet returned to me with all their signatures on! Next day I took it to school to show my friends and was very put out when one of them asked me to cut up the leaflet so that I could share the autographs with them. I didn't, of course – I told them to send off for their own.

I went to see them at the Essoldo with two other girls from school. We were all 13 at the time. I wouldn't be 14 until September. When we arrived on St Petersgate the queue to get in was going right round the block about three or four deep – and mainly girls. We saw several girls passing out with excitement and being tended to by St. John's ambulance staff. We had tickets for the stalls and were on the right hand side facing the stage.

It was the first concert any of us had ever been to and we were all keyed up and wished the other acts would hurry up so that it would be time for who we had gone to see to be on the stage. I can't remember who else was on except Peter and Gordon who

> "when my dad said the Rolling Stones were coming and he had two tickets for me and a friend I could hardly believe it"

> "it was Mick Jagger with his weird hand clapping strutting routine … but he was timid then compared to the showman we know nowadays"

sang *World Without Love*. The roar that went up when Mick came onto the stage was deafening. Everyone was standing on their seats screaming and calling out the names of their favourites. I loved Brian Jones too but it was Mick whose name I was screaming like almost all the other girls. Although we could see the boys on stage, it was impossible to hear them because of all the noise we were making. Mick's moves got all of us in a frenzy!

When we came out I had to walk all the way home by myself and I was in such turmoil that I cried all the way home. My mum couldn't get any sense out of me and said "that's the last time you ever go to see them". But it wasn't. I saw them at least another three times in Manchester. I was so upset after that first concert that I had to have the next day off school and spent the day alternately sobbing and reliving the night before.

Colin Joy *(age 8)*
We had heard about the Stones but seen very little of them as we only had two TV channels – ITV and BBC. There was no *Top of the Pops* then or *Radio 1*, but the BBC did have *Juke Box Jury* which played some of the latest tunes, plus some artists would manage to get a slot on children's TV shows like *Blue Peter* and *Crackerjack*. Granada TV catered for the Mersey Beat and Manchester scenes, with The Beatles and Gerry and the Pacemakers getting maximum exposure on local news programmes. But the London

Scene received very little coverage unless you lived in those areas.

Our next door neighbour Geoff was the chief projectionist for the cinema and wangled his son David, my brother Brian, and me, through the back door of the Essoldo and we were allowed to watch the show from the comfort of the projector slots on the rear walls.

I say "watch" as, once the Rolling Stones came on, we couldn't hear a bloody thing as all the girls started screaming non-stop throughout. All the Stones were smartly dressed in casual pants and shirts – no jeans in those days – and very clean cut. The audience were the same. Dress code was observed at all times.

The Stones were on stage for just over 30 minutes. Keith Richards, Brian Jones, and Bill Wyman mainly stood posing and strutting without moving, with Charlie Watts looking bored drumming – as he still does today! It was Mick Jagger with his weird hand clapping strutting routine dancing around the stage who was the main attraction but he was timid then compared to the showman we know nowadays.

As the night came to a close and the curtain came down after the Stones had finished, I remember there was an incident which caused the audience to suddenly surge towards the stage trapping those at the front. It was a fully seated venue. The safety curtain went up again and the Stones reappeared on stage and started pulling those trapped at the front on to the stage and filtering them away to safety towards the back. We were asked to vacate the theatre as quickly as possible.

We later found out that a load of mods had turned up on scooters and were fighting rockers, or greasers as we used to call them, outside the Essoldo and police had been called to join in the battle. The riot had started outside the cinema as the mods tried to force their way into the venue, hence the surge, but police truncheoned both parties back toward Mersey Square as the bikers continued knocking hell out of each other.

29 MAY 1964
City Hall, Sheffield

Andy Thompson (age 15)
Mates of mine from school were postering for Pete Stringfellow's brother who was a promoter and I remember being in the school yard one day and he fetched this out of his blazer and it was a flyer – a picture of the Rolling Stones – and they'd got the black leather waistcoats on and he said "Pete's on about booking them" and that was the first time I'd heard of them. And then they had a couple of showings on *Ready Steady Go*. I don't think I heard them on the radio.

There used to be the Light Programme and the Third Programme and you'd get up to go to school in the morning and you'd have like orchestras playing light songs and music. There were no pop channels at all. They did have something on a Saturday morning called *Uncle Mack*. It used to be on between 9 and 10 on a Saturday morning and he used to play requests for pop music like Anthony Newley and stuff that was popular at that time. And then you got your commercial radio stations like *Caroline*. *Luxembourg* you could tune into on your little transistor radio under the bedclothes. They were no bigger than an old mobile phone. Everyone used to do it. They used to have the top 20 on a Sunday night so you could listen to it on that. I saw them in '64 at the second house. The only artists I can remember being on with them were Peter and Gordon. They'd just released *World Without Love*.

As we were going in some of me mates were going out and they said that Gordon Waller got hit in the eye with a jelly baby – because they used to throw jelly babies at The Beatles when they were on stage. We were up in the balcony and you couldn't really hear the Stones because of the screaming. To be honest Sheffield City Hall doesn't lend itself particularly to bands. Or it certainly didn't in the Sixties. Sheffield City Hall is more for orchestras so you go from that to putting pop bands on with a couple of 150 watt amps or whatever – well, the sound quality wasn't always that great. They were doing a lot of stuff off the first album. A lot of rhythm and blues. *It's All Over Now*. *Not Fade Away*. I remember them doing *I Wanna Be Your Man*. There's a lot of good stuff on that first album. The Stones were on for an hour or perhaps 45 minutes.

> "we later found out that a load of mods had turned up on scooters and were fighting rockers"

30 MAY 1964

Adelphi Theatre, Slough

Pam Morgan-Brown (age 12)

I haven't a lot of memories of the actual performance, but I do remember that the supporting act was the Barron Knights. In the audience were quite a number of uniformed armed forces. They listened to the Barron Knights and when the Stones came on they made a lot of noise getting out of their seats and leaving the theatre. The Stones waited until they'd left and then Mick thanked the armed forces for 'their support'.

My sister was also at the concert but she recalls even less than me – and she was 15. I can only presume that she was screaming so much she didn't notice much else. I lived in Burnham in Buckinghamshire, where Chrissie Shrimpton – Mick's girlfriend at the time – lived.

We were driving down the High Street one Saturday on the way to the hairdresser's and I suddenly spotted Mick and shrieked! My Dad wouldn't stop and took me to hairdresser's for my appointment. However, while I was there he searched the High Street and found Mick delving into a freezer in a shop. He said to Mick "Mr Jagger, I have two young daughters at home who would love your autograph". You can imagine my delight when he presented me with the piece of paper with the autograph on.

June 1964 saw the Rolling Stones undertaking their inaugural tour of the United States and the release of their fourth UK single *It's All Over Now*.

12 JUNE 1964

Big Reggie's Danceland, Excelsior Amusement Park, Minneapolis, MI

Bob Roepke (age 17)

We were just out of high school. There were three or four of us. I don't remember if it was a Friday or a Saturday night but it was a weekend night and we were just going out. And part of that amusement park had what was called Big Reggie's Danceland. Local bands and other bands would perform there and so you'd run into other young folks – young girls – and so it was a popular place to go.

We were out on the fringe of Minneapolis and pretty rural – still cornfields and small towns. The population of Excelsior was only a handful of thousands of people – less than ten thousand, five thousand. Maybe not even that big. The Excelsior amusement park was just that – an amusement park with all kinds of rides and a big wooden roller coaster ride and circus rides. Back in the Fifties and Sixties dance halls were pretty popular. You'd find dance halls in a lot of small towns, and they were the popular gathering place. And so the Excelsior dance hall, which was close to a big lake – Lake Minnetonka, which is always an attraction with a big boating area – was a gathering place, a magnet for younger people. And Big Reggie – I don't even know the guy's last name – he'd bring the young bands in there and that was

good for folks like us. There were local bands that we'd follow and they'd play in those places and in those little towns and that's where we'd go.

So that night about nine o'clock we went over there because one of the guys heard that there was a band playing. We didn't know much about it. So we went over there and there was quite a large crowd outside, milling around. We hung around there and talked with others and asked the question "who's this band?" "It's a band from England." "What's their name?" "Oh, it's the Rolling Stones." And then we asked "what is it to get in there? How much was it to get in?" And one of the guys asked and it was either $6 or $8. I think it was $6. And we said "are you crazy? We're not paying $6 to get in there for a band we've never heard of." We hadn't heard of the band before then. We had some curiosity about them because they were a band from England coming over here – now that was something we hadn't seen or experienced, so there was curiosity – but not for $6! Because nobody really knew the Stones back then they just didn't have that early draw. And we asked "how many are in there?" And he said "there's not too many people in there." Others have reported that at one point there were maybe a couple hundred people in there but it was a big dance hall so maybe there was more than that. But it was a small number

> **"so we went in there and – I'm not kidding – there were I think thirty five, forty, forty five people"**

regardless. So we said "oh, let's go, let's take off" and so we went some other places and other hangouts and did whatever we did back then on Friday, Saturday weekend nights.

We came back at maybe a quarter to twelve – 11.45pm – that night. It was not as big a crowd outside but there were still people milling around outside. And we said "are they still goin'?" "Yes, they're still goin'." "Many people in there?" "Not too many." "How much to get in?" And they said "50 cents." So we went in. I said "I'm gonna go in there for 50 cents." And so we went in there and – I'm not kidding – there were I think thirty five, forty, forty five people. I mean, it wasn't many people and they were just kinda off to the side. There was nobody dancing, nobody out in front of them. And I actually walked over there in front of them to take a look because there was nobody on the dance floor.

Now they were not very happy. They weren't the happiest of campers, that was pretty obvious, but they continued to play. We were standing off to the side, talking to some other folks. We probably stayed fifteen minutes and then said "let's go" and we left. And the only thing we ever experienced was watching their success after that.

I would have loved to have taken a selfie. Can you imagine what it would have been like to take a picture with them in that empty hall back then? I'm sure if they'd come back a year or two later the place would have been

booked full. But not that night. Mick Jagger signed autographs at the University of Minnesota recently. How cool would it have been to just wait in line and go up to him and say "do you remember the Excelsior amusement park in 1964?" He had to remember Excelsior. It would have been just a fun conversation to have because I could have said "I was there. I was one of those handful of people that was there!"

17 JUNE 1964
Danceland, West View Park, Pittsburgh, Pennsylvania

Philip Lando (age 21)
I attended with a friend from school – Duquesne University in Pittsburgh – whose name was Tony Gentilcore. We went because we were already fans of British Invasion bands, even though this was before the actual popularity of the Liverpool and other bands in the United States. The two of us were deejaying dances following basketball games at the school, and had been supplied demo records by a local radio station called *KDKA*. These were usually records that were not then on the station's playlist, and included records by Freddie and the Dreamers (*I'm Telling You Now*), Gerry and the Pacemakers and other British bands. We liked what we heard and read all we could about The Beatles and other British bands.

When the Rolling Stones came out with their first album, England's Newest Hitmakers, I bought it and liked it. So we knew who the Stones were well before anybody else we knew has heard of them and we were fans. Their initial concert tour was not accompanied with the kind of publicity that greeted The Beatles. I don't recall how we got the tickets exactly but there was no great competition to buy them.

I remember that we enjoyed the show. The Stones had already assumed their bad boy image, and Mick Jagger had already mastered some of his moves. A highlight was the performance of *Not Fade Away*. The venue was actually a dance hall, and there were no seats that I recall. We stood within twenty feet of the stage. There were no more than two hundred in attendance, generally our age or thereabouts. The crowd was attentive and appeared to enjoy the performance.

After a few days off in early July to recover from their American trip the Stones were gigging again in Britain as *It's All Over Now* became their first UK Number 1.

12 JULY 1964
Queens Hall, Leeds

Cliff Watson *(age 16)*
I saw the Stones at Queens Hall, an old ex-tram shed in Leeds. It had a stage which was in the centre of the large room with no tiers and it turned at 90 degrees after each song. We were lucky to be sat on the second row from the stage. I went with my then girlfriend for her 16th birthday. I remember my parents being a bit

miffed about me going to see a 'long haired group of layabouts' and taking a girl with me. Their attitude was also similar for The Beatles. It was the end of music as my parents had known it and they never took to any of the 'new' groups at all. A couple of the support acts were Lulu and the Luvvers, who had just recorded *Shout*, and a Liverpool group whose name was the Rustics.

The seats were all loose and girls were still seated as they shook their coats or cardigans as they screamed at the Stones. They had just recorded *It's All Over Now* and finished the show with it. I went and bought their first LP the following week. At that time most young people were either Beatles or Stones although anyone with sense appreciated them both.

Pauline Haydock *(age 21)*
I became an avid fan when the group emerged, soon knowing all the lyrics of their early hits. I still do! So when they appeared at a large venue in Leeds I eagerly arranged for a group of us, all aged 21 to 23, to go from York –

Pauline Haydock

a big deal for us in those days. We were sitting about halfway back but still had a good view. However immediately they came on stage all the surrounding fans – mainly young teenaged girls – jumped onto their seats and started screaming and shouting. We all remained seated for a while, looking stupefied, and then realised it was a case of 'if you can't beat them, join them'. So we got up there for the whole performance. We barely caught a glimpse of the band or heard much either but I wouldn't have missed this early, exciting experience of those heady times.

18 JULY 1964
Beat City, 79 Oxford Street, London

Shirley Rawstorne

My older brother, who was at this time political journalist for The Guardian, had bought his first house in Nazeing, Essex on the outskirts of North London. Alice and I went for a weeks' holiday and were taken to see the sights of London by my sister-in-law. Initially we spent our free time at a local swimming pool listening to the small radio we had brought along with us. The Rolling Stones were a particular favourite. We loved the rebellious blues sound of the Stones. Somehow we noticed the Rolling Stones were playing at a club in London and after some deliberation my brother agreed to get us tickets if he could. Philip is much older than me and a very responsible person – not at all rock n roll – but during a break from

work he queued up to get us the tickets. It is still one of his many stories over dinner. Alice and I went on the train to the concert.

We managed to get right at the front. The stage was very close and low and we were in easy reach of the group. We were just amazed with the music and the atmosphere. I remember hearing I'm a King Bee for the first time and being totally bowled over by it. The club was crowded, hot and sweaty, and a young bloke came along the front with a bucket of water and sponge. He wiped all the faces of the group and wiped ours also. What we looked like was insignificant – we had been wiped with the same sponge as the Stones. When we left the club and caught the train back to Nazeing we vowed never to wash our faces again.

Shirley Rawstorne (right) with friend Alice

19 JULY 1964

Hippodrome, Brighton

Keith Tapscott (age 14)

Things were easy and uncomplicated then. No call centres. I simply wrote to the Brighton Hippodrome enclosing a postal order, asking for the best seats possible for me and my girlfriend. It was about 10/6 (53p) for centre seats in about the seventh row.

We arrived at the venue and it was swarming with teenagers outside, a fairly even mix of boys and girls. I endeavoured to copy the appearance of Mick Jagger – crew neck lambswool sweater, light grey slacks and long hairstyle. I was very pleased when several people said I looked like Mick and my girlfriend was chuffed too. Vendors were selling large black and white photos of the band. I bought a large one of Brian, a slightly smaller one of Mick and one of the entire band. Once inside I also bought a programme, which I still have to this day.

We entered the theatre and everyone sat down and remained so throughout. There were lots of attendants to keep control and St John's ambulance volunteers to carry out the girls who fainted during the Stones performance. Each act was politely applauded and there was a few screams for Marty Wilde, but at the age of 24 he was a bit old by then in comparison.

As the show progressed the tension, anticipation, and excitement built up and up. There were no fancy light shows or dramatic music played through the PA, but there were curtains which were lowered between each act. The roadie at the time was called Spike Thompson and he had long hair like the band and occasionally lowered his head, poked it through the gap in the curtains and shook it to tumultuous screams! When the time came you could feel it in the pit of your stomach – the compere's introduction was lost in a cacophony of screaming and shouting and the place erupted.

The first thing that struck me was just how ghostly white they all were, presumably a result of their lifestyle of playing and partying at night and sleeping by day. For most of the time the screaming was louder than the music but that only added to an electrifying performance. They opened with *Walking The Dog* and ended with *It's All Over Now*. Mick shook the maracas on *Not Fade Away* while Brian played harmonica on that and on *I Just Want To Make Love To You*. Between songs Mick would check the set list written on a scrap of paper. Mick very much played to the audience while Brian teased it, Bill appeared aloof and Keith grinned and moved with the music.

Mick and Brian were wearing sports jackets, Bill a waistcoat, Keith a casual jacket and Charlie a sweater. Sadly, too soon it was all over. In those days they played for around 25 minutes and there was no encore. As we left some were animated, others dazed. My ears were ringing and then hissing from the screaming. It somehow felt a little unreal as it was all over so quickly. There were crowds of people outside, queuing for the second performance, eagerly enquiring what it had been like and, in a lot of cases, what were the Stones wearing.

24 JULY 1964
Empress Ballroom, Blackpool

The Stones concert at the Empress Ballroom in Blackpool was held during Glasgow Fair, when the seaside resort saw a seasonal influx of factory workers and their families travelling down from Scotland to take their two week summer holiday as many Glasgow businesses closed. The events that unfolded at the concert led to Blackpool Council imposing a ban on the Stones performing in their town, a ban that was not lifted until 2008.

Eileen Cornes (age 16)

I was on holiday in Blackpool with my parents from Shropshire. It was a stand up concert. I attended with my cousin Jean and an older Scottish girl who we had befriended at the hotel. The waiters at the hotel obtained the tickets for us as well as tickets for a Beatles concert which was held in a different theatre during the same week and for which we had seats.

Approximately three quarters of the way through the Stones concert the venue seemed to get rowdy. Our Scottish friend advised us to take off our shoes and run to the back of the venue as she feared that there was going to be trouble ahead. I hesitated at first, not really sensing danger, and she screamed at me to move. Without

more ado I did what I was told and we all went back to the hotel. The following day we found out the Stones' piano had been thrown off the stage into the crowd. I don't know who did it and I don't know if there were any serious injuries.

Peter Fielding

The band I was with when the Stones came to the Empress Ballroom at Blackpool was called the Executives and we were the support band for the Stones concert. It was the night when the crowd wrecked the ballroom and they got on the stage and pulled all their stuff off and kicked it to pieces and the band ran off for their lives. They didn't get much playing done to be quite honest. One of the audience tried to spit at Keith Richards and I think he tried to push him off with his foot or something on the front of the stage. There was a bit of a fracas that went on and it erupted into them throwing bottles and all sorts and then we ran on to get our gear off and it just went bananas. And the only number I saw them do if I remember rightly was an early rhythm and blues thing called Mona, a Bo Diddley type thing. We sort of heard one and a half numbers off in the wings, you know, after we'd been on.

I can't remember what we got paid for it. It wasn't a right lot. They would be on a pretty good fee, you know. I don't know what we received that night, to be quite honest. In those days you would sort of work locally for roughly about £5 each in 1964. We probably got something like that

> "it erupted into them throwing bottles and all sorts and then we ran on to get our gear off and it just went bananas"

or possibly slightly more. Not a lot more. Our manager was in touch with an agency that was putting them on and he must have said we'll be the support band or they wanted a support band and we were very popular in Blackpool at the time because we had a record out. We were on and the crowd were throwing pennies at us – coins – and shouting "we want the Stones! We want the Stones!" They weren't interested in what we were doing at all. And so we did our first set and came off and – well, we didn't quite do a full set because they were throwing coins and we thought we'd cut it short, you know. And we came off and then they were shouting for the Stones and they came on and they did that number and they started another one and this trouble started flaring up and that was it. We never saw anything else. They'd gone and we got most of our gear off the stage. I don't know whether Charlie got his drum kit. He possibly did because it was right at the back of the Empress Ballroom. The roadies got the drum kit off. Well it was the amps really that got jumped on and stamped on.

There was a grand piano on the corner of the stage, a big one and a very valuable one. They ended up pulling that onto the floor and smashing that. It just went mental. It just went daft, you know? They were wrecking anything they could find. There were so many of them. The attendants and bouncers were overwhelmed. We buggered off as well – as quick as we could. We actually got most of

our gear off. The bass player got his amp smashed. We went back the next day. The debris was all over the place. They ripped the ballroom apart, you know. It was unbelievable. It was the only scary experience of my career. It was menacing. It was really bad. You could have been killed, trampled to death or something. They're usually overwhelmed by engaging with not so much wanting to kill the band. It was triggered off by this thing with Keith Richards at the front. The audience member had all his mates with him. That's what started it. A lot of other people didn't want a fight and told them to bugger off but they insisted on fighting them and in the end the whole ballroom would be fighting.

Syd Bloom

I've been to thousands of gigs in my life and I've never been to one like that. It was Glasgow weekend. It was ten bob in and no tickets or anything. Just anybody who came got in. I've never ever, ever been in a worse situation in my life. The place was beyond belief. It was just absolutely ridiculous. I knew Pete Fielding who was in the Executives. And the Executives were doing the support for the Stones. What happened was that Roy Carr was fronting the band. I knew the guitarist Pete Fielding who was a big mate of Tony Ashton. Tony Ashton lived down St Leonards Avenue in Blackpool and played in the Picador Club with the strippers. He played keyboards. Because they were local the Executives opened and

> "I've been to thousands of gigs in my life and I've never been to one like that"

did a spot. And then the Stones came on. And unusually they went off after their first spot.

The Executives came back on and then the Stones were coming on for a second spot. Now Roy Carr wound everybody up by doing *I've Got My Mojo Working* and every time we thought he'd finished and I'd think "thank Christ, get the Stones back on" he'd start up again. So there was a bit of a tension because people were telling him to "fuck off and get the Stones back on."

Allegedly what happened was there was two or three Scots guys got their way to the front right by the stage and one of them threw a fork at Keith Richards who promptly went forward and kicked his teeth out with his Cuban heel and it just kicked off from there. So the Stones ran for it. Then the police came and it was suddenly mayhem. Guys were lobbing bloody bottles at the chandeliers which were about thirty five foot up.

Girls had lost their shoes. They were running around cutting their feet to shreds on broken glass. It was just absolutely ridiculous. The police came first of all and sort of occupied the stage. But under a hail off missiles they all buggered off. The Winter Gardens is connected to the Tower. And they brought all the bouncers from the Winter Gardens and the Tower onto the stage because the police had buggered off, you know, "pouf! You're on your own here." And because there were a lot of locals there and a lot of the locals had had a load of grief with these guys, a history of being given a

good hiding, one guy jumped on the stage and grabbed hold of a ginger haired bouncer and pulled him off the stage and the guy just got kicked to shreds. A lot of guys up there who were bouncers for the Tower company were just absolute nutters. And they got what they deserved. And they got a good kicking because the locals couldn't be doing with it. Then the grand piano got thrown off the stage. Anything that was there got trashed. Absolutely, completely trashed. The cymbals were being thrown around – if you can imagine a more deadly weapon than a cymbal.

It was a dance hall, like an open ballroom. Around the edge of the room is the equivalent of cinema seating. Rows of seating. And they ripped those up and used them as a battering ram. The stage was empty and it just got trashed, absolutely trashed. They just over filled it. I shudder to think how many people were in that ballroom. The people were like sardines. All the way back and all the way up the sides. And it's quite a wide, large ballroom. I would suggest there was two and a half thousand easily in there if not, probably, nearer four. It was just crazy. People were lobbing glasses and bottles all over the place. They were actually aiming to see if they could get the chandeliers and they did.

It was bloody terrifying. I just wanted to get the hell out of the place. It was reported in a way that it became front page of the papers. And the Stones almost immediately did a gig in Paris and there was another riot there. And one wondered whether this was because it had been reported that way. I was pretty bloody scared at the time.

I got a bus home later and I'd got a jacket that was a purple colour that I'd worn quite a few times. My shirt was still wringing wet and my white shirt was purple from the dye off the jacket because I'd sweated that much. It was just absolutely beyond belief. The Tower Company was clearly to blame. They just let anybody and everybody in for the equivalent now of fifty pence apiece. There was no such thing as booking because there were no seats. Hence it was their second and last appearance in Blackpool.

David Clark (age 21)

It's one concert I will never forget. I took my sister Joyce, who was 16, and her friend Sheena Gow. We managed to get to the very front of the stage to the right of Mick Jagger and it was a seething mass of a crowd with not much elbow room at all. Jagger was wearing a green striped blazer of the type you imagine Oxbridge students would be wearing at that time. The others were not smartly dressed. We had seen The Beatles at Kings George's Hall in Blackburn and they were much more uniform and smart but I guess that was part of the Stones attraction.

Whilst we were at the front I became aware of hostility towards the band from many of the crowd around us, who seemed to have Scottish accents. When the

David Clark

interval came I told my sister and her friend that it wasn't safe to remain there for the second half as I could feel trouble brewing so they reluctantly followed me to the upstairs balcony looking down on the stage. Not long into the second half the people at the front appeared to start spitting at Keith Richards and Mick Jagger. I next saw Keith Richards take a swing at one of the offenders with his guitar. I could not tell if he connected with his target from where we were, but from that moment on all hell broke loose.

One minute the band were on stage and next second they were gone. The people at the front then stormed the stage. Some security men who were far too old to be in the job were dragged from the stage. The amplifiers and mikes became the first targets and these were smashed into the smallest pieces that they could break them into in their rage. They then dragged the curtains off the walls and even the Empress Ballroom clock above the stage became a target.

PC David Benson (back row, second from right)

There was pandemonium on the dance floor as there was no seating except on the balcony and at the sides and normal fans began to flee. Then a long row of policemen appeared and baton charged the offenders. They can't have been far away as it seemed such a short time from trouble starting to them appearing on the scene. I suspect they were expecting trouble and had received a tip off about what was going to happen. We watched the dance floor clearance and baton bashing for a while then said we had better go home as there would obviously be no further performance that night. Everybody leaving the building was stopped and searched by the police including us.

The following day I was driving my travelling shop around Penwortham outside Preston when I saw a crowd gathered round a bungalow off Marshall's Brow and I discovered that it was the house of the Stones northern agent, John Dell. He had an indoor swimming pool tagged onto his house and the band were swimming in it, thus attracting local fans.

David Benson

I joined Preston Borough Police in 1963 and started real policing in 1964. There was an infamous concert in Blackpool that year, on a Friday night. I was on earlies in Preston on the Saturday. The Stones were whisked away from Blackpool and taken to the Bull and Royal Hotel, Preston. I remember seeing Mick leave in a minibus on the Saturday around lunch time. I was detailed to patrol outside the Bull and Royal but there weren't many people there and there were no incidents.

Margaret Johnson *(age 12)*

I have never been to a Stones concert but I do recall them coming to Park Lane in Penwortham just outside Preston. At the time it was said that their manager lived there and he had an indoor swimming pool. I was living just up the road in the council houses in Studholme Crescent. Park Lane was considered very posh and there was a great crowd of us outside screaming our heads off!

25 JULY 1964
Imperial Ballroom, Nelson

Fiona Coombes *(age 16)*

I was there, unbelievably with my father. I had bought *Come On* as soon as the record had come out and was totally committed to the Stones and was determined to see them live. But none of my friends wanted to go with me to see them. They all thought they were dreadful compared with the shiny, mop haired Beatles.

I was determined to go and threatened my parents that I would just go and make my way somehow from Whalley to Nelson. My father, a local GP, sighed and said that, OK, he would take me there and bring me back home. So my father, then in his mid fifties, sat at the bar in the Imperial drinking brandy while I screamed at the front of the stage. This was well before the breathalyser and there were far, far fewer cars on the road in this area.

My father found the whole evening ear splitting and never wanted to experience such a night again. I remember them singing *Come On*. Mick was fantastic but I was mesmerised by Charlie too. I always think it is so amusing that a middle aged country GP was in there at a Rolling Stones concert way back at the beginning of their world domination.

31 JULY 1964
Ulster Hall, Belfast

Lyn Morrison *(age 16)*

My friend Christine and I queued all day to be sure of getting in.

It was great fun. We grouped together with strangers and elected someone to go to a shop to get sandwiches. We were eventually admitted into the hall. There was no seating in the hall and Christine and I were thrust forward in a tidal surge to a position right at the front, close to the stage which spanned the full width of the hall about shoulder height.

The moment the Stones ran on there was another surge forward and we got squashed. Christine passed out and the next thing I saw was St John's ambulance men heaving her onto the stage before carting her off into the wings, where my brother Peter found her. It is as well he was there, but I was sickened that he had been able to walk in at the last minute without having to queue. I'm told the concert was abandoned after three songs. I don't remember that. I just recall that the crowd noise was deafening and drowned out the band. Christine heard nothing of course. I see her every week. We play bridge together.

Mik Davidson

I queued up all nights for tickets with my friends. We went to a place called the Spanish Rooms and bought really harsh scrumpy. We sat out all night and eventually got our seats. Great show – not a dry seat in the house! Girls fainting everywhere.

Jim Shaw *(age 16)*

I left school a just over a year before. On that particular day I was working in Bangor, Co Down. I was serving an apprenticeship

Lyn Morrison

as a sheet metal worker and was helping to erect ventilation in Bangor Dairies. I had no transport of my own but at around eleven in the morning I asked could I go home early as I was going to the doctor's – not! My request was granted and I got on the bus to Belfast and joined the queue outside the Ulster Hall along with a few of my friends – Ed Lindop from Holywood, Brian Irvine from Denmark Street, Billy Barnes from West Circular Road, Ann Denver from Crumlin Road, Veronica Jackson from Creagh and a few others.

Long hair was the order of the day. Well we thought it was long then – oh I wish I had it now! We wore coloured shirts and some of us had roll neck sweaters. Bell bottom jeans had made their way in the fashion scene and boots with heels, and that was just for us males! It was a standing concert and I was fortunate we were near top of queue so as soon as the doors opened we made a mad dash to just in front of stage. The next few hours were bedlam, mainly due to the crowd pushing and shoving and trying to get in front of others.

I cannot remember if there was a supporting group because the anticipation of seeing Mick and company close up meant I was oblivious to what was happening prior to their appearance. When they appeared it was just a mad push from the rear of hall and you just about could hear them going through their set. People were attempting to get on stage and a few girls did manage to get close

to Mick but the next thing they knew, they were being led away by the bouncers. I remember well one of the girls who was with us fainted, as did lots of others because of the heat. I lifted her over my shoulders and carried her through the crowd to the back of the hall where a St John's ambulance man helped to bring her round but believe it or not as soon as she was up she headed straight back into the crowd. When the concert was over there were lots of people lying around the hall exhausted by the heat. I made my way home that night by walking the whole way from Bedford Street to Dunmurry where I lived. I was one of the fortunate ones as both my father and mother were quite liberal in their way with me and all they asked "did I enjoy the concert?" Enjoy was perhaps not how I would not have described the experience. To this day I can remember the total joy I got from going.

Grainger Allen *(age 16)*

We had to camp outside the ticket office all night to be able to buy our tickets. The ticket cost 12/6 (38p). Even though the show was short it was worth the wait. They opened with Not Fade Away. One clear memory is of the police having to clear the stage after only four or five numbers as the girl fans were going frantic and were in danger of getting crushed.

After performing in Belfast, the Stones made the 28 mile journey to Ballymena to play a ballroom show the same evening.

31 JULY 1964

Flamingo Ballroom, Ballymena

Martin Stewart with
the Vampires

Martin Stewart (age 18)

In the Sixties many famous or up and coming singers or groups came over here. A phenomenon of Northern Ireland in the period before the Troubles was the ballroom. Ireland north and south was covered in them. Most weekends saw dancing taking place to showbands but once a month or so the promoters would bring in a big act from the UK or the US.

My local haunt was the Flamingo Ballroom in Ballymena, owned and run by the late Sammy Barr. In 1964, the Rolling Stones came to Northern Ireland. They appeared at the Ulster Hall in Belfast but they also appeared at the Flamingo, playing for about an hour. They arrived late from the Belfast venue. As usual, a showband was playing for the bulk of the evening.

The ballroom was packed to capacity that night. We had paid the princely sum of less than £1 to see them. They came in through the back door behind the stage. They used the amps and mikes belonging to the showband, bringing only their own guitars. I think Charlie Watts brought his own snare drum.

They were playing on the stage at the front of the ballroom, about three feet above floor level, with no barriers, etc, to keep the crowds back. I was less than ten feet from Mick Jagger as he Brian, Keith, Bill and Charlie belted out their programme. It was all very restrained on the floor. A few girls fainted, more from the heat than the music. At the end the Stones went out through the back door and that was that. The supporting showband resumed the stage for the remainder of the night. I had seen the Rolling Stones at first hand. I was to play on that same stage many times as a member of a local supporting group for both show bands and headline acts from the UK and the US. Great times.

Pamela Parker (age 14)

I was there with my friends. My mum was in hospital and I cried to her to get going because my friends were going.

James Brown (age 19)

Sammy Barr owned the Flamingo Ballroom. He used to run a little coffee shop and then he built the Flamingo. He used to put on shows at the Town Hall. Marty Wilde and the Wildcats. Adam Faith. Them kind of people.

Then he built the Flamingo and brought over the top stars. Tom Jones. The Stones. Roy Orbison. The Merseybeats. Gerry and the

Pacemakers. And all the famous show bands of Ireland. Every weekend, Friday or Saturday, there was always a top show band. These people were stars. There was a big gateway and they would drive down the back and close the gate, unload all their equipment and go onto the stage.

Sammy used to let me get in early. The bands used to drive down the back of the ballroom. Sammy would let me go in and I would help set up the amplifiers. I remember that night very, very well. Ballymoney Street was all cordoned off. Sammy let me stand at the front door. At the front door you'd go up the stairs to the ballroom. *It's All Over Now* was the top record at the time. Instead of the tour manager bringing the big van with all their gear, two large Mark X Jags drew up and stopped in the street. Mick Jagger got out. Keith Richards. Brian Jones. Bill Wyman. They all jumped out of the Jags and ran in through the front door past me. And they were all carrying their guitars. I could never understand it because the roadies brought their AC30 amps up that way. They ran past me carrying their guitars. Bill Wyman was carrying his bass and Brian Jones was carrying his tear drop guitar. I could never figure that out. Maybe because the street was closed and everything was barricaded off and they knew no one was going to get near them to tear them apart. I think Sammy squeezed in two or three thousand that night because no way you could get moving. Not in a million years. They were just terrific.

The Flamingo Club, Ballymena

1 AUGUST 1964
Pier Ballroom, Hastings

Andre Palfrey-Martin (age 16)
It's All Over Now had just been number 1. It was branded the second Battle of Hastings – the mods and rockers were just about to kick off. The Stones were escorted on and off the pier in an old ambulance by the police as a security measure. We originally thought that someone had tried to get them off the pier on a fishing boat or a speed boat.

The police report from that time gives details of when they appeared on stage, time-wise, and when they were taken off and subsequently dispersed. They went on and did something like a 35 to 40 minute set and that was it and they were brought off. The police report from the time says 'the Rolling Stones beat group was scheduled to give a performance at Hastings Pier Ballroom from 9pm to 9.30pm. This was extensively advertised. The manager arranged for the rendezvous at the Central Police Station in Hastings at 8pm that evening. Several thousand people were congregating on or in the vicinity of the pier.'

So there were a lot of people outside as well as on the pier itself. 'By 10pm the Rolling Stones were transported off the pier in the disused ambulance, conveyed to the central police station and subsequently escorted out of the borough in their private cars.' Prices had gone up in August to ten shillings.

Maurice Viney (age 35)
The boys on the stage were very young but their music was excellent. The main point I remember was that a very nice young lady removed her pants and threw them at Mick in the centre of the stage.

2 AUGUST 1964
Longleat House, Warminster

John Leighton (age 14)
Three or friends and I cycled from Bath to go and see them in Longleat. That was a cycle of 20 or 25 miles on these tatty old bikes. It was chaos, absolute pandemonium. You couldn't see and you couldn't hear them. I can remember the Marquis of Bath looking totally bemused on the steps with it all going on because he'd obviously never seen anything like it before. It was a good day out but for 14 and 15 year olds cycling there and getting pushed around it was a little bit scary.

David Hyde (age 16)
I remember the concert being in front of the house. With everybody waiting with great anticipation for the start a figure ran out of the house with long hair and people at the front went mad until they realised it was not a Stone but somebody with a wig on who we were led to believe was Lord Bath! When I got back to Swindon that night my parents were concerned that I was ok because the news on TV had reported disturbances and people being thrown into ponds outside

> "a very nice young lady removed her pants and threw them at Mick"

the house. I can honestly say I saw none of this but it was always good to report anything bad to do with the Stones. My parents didn't like The Beatles until the Stones came on the scene and then they thought The Beatles were ok!

Jean Goodland

The Rolling Stones first television appearance was on *Thank Your Lucky Stars*, promoting their first single *Come On*. As soon as I saw them on the screen my life changed. In a flash, I knew that there was 'another way' and that I didn't have to stay in a small town thinking or living or following the traditional route of engagement at 18, marriage at 21 and motherhood thereafter. This image told me I could be free and live how I wanted to live. And I did, so it's their fault!

Jean Goodland

They were wild. The newspapers around the country in the following days reflected the horror of parents and all things establishment at this piece of terrible and threatening audacity. Suddenly The Beatles were bordering on acceptability. We saw them live when they played as part of various package concerts touring the UK after that. But my most vivid memory is when they played at Longleat House in 1964. Longleat House was 20 or 30 miles away, deep in the Wiltshire countryside. We always hitch hiked everywhere in those days, so myself and two intrepid friends set off in total excitement. Thinking back on this hitch-hiking malarkey, we took lots of risks but we were fearless. I was wearing denim jeans, striped T shirt and a denim waistcoat. We had duffle coats and what were called duffle bags with us too.

Tension was rife, as with all Stones concerts in those days. Excitement was growing and the crowds were gathering. It was an outside event – one of the first ever rock concerts – so there were no seats. The band was going to play on a sort of patio at the grand entrance to the stately home. There was a chicken wire fence about six feet high all round the house. Within the wire were St John's ambulance and officials and outside were the fans. The crowd pressed up closer and closer to the wire.

The band came from nowhere onto the porch and started playing and everyone went mental. Girls were fainting and being lifted over the wire to the safety of the first aiders' arms. Hmm – I noted that these girls were getting to be on the inside of the wire, near the band. So I got a little plan going. We were right at the front and one by one the three of us all pretended to faint. People moved back and allowed us to be carried over the fence. As soon as we were on the other side we got up and ran up the steps. Suddenly we were on the stage, to the bemusement of the uniformed ambulance staff.

There were a lot of people up there – sound people, security and Longleat staff but only one or two other fans. Not many had managed to slip past the officials as slickly as we did. It was breathtaking, looking out at the thousands in the crowd screaming, waving, shouting, pushing and shaking their hair in a Jaggeresque mime. But we also noticed that more and more people were being carried over the fence in waves and taken to the emergency unit at the back of the house. We were silently standing at the side of the stage, totally stunned at our closeness to them. Brian's tambourine was sitting on an amp right next to me. Wow – what treasure! It seemed sacrilege to even touch it.

We didn't have long to wallow in our good fortune. The organisers came out in front of the stage and suddenly announced that the concert would have to end prematurely. The pressure of the crowd was increasing, fans were in danger of being crushed and no one had anticipated this level of excitement and frenzy. For some reason, we were ordered to go inside the hallway of the house. There seemed to be an air of chaos. Bodyguards were surrounding the boys. There was pushing and shoving and they looked genuinely puzzled.

Then I saw Mick Jagger coming towards me and he walked past me. I remember having a fleeting thought that I should at least touch him as he was so close – not an opportunity to be missed. So I stroked his back as he was marched past. To my surprise he grabbed my hand from behind and pulled me along but I pulled away as Brian Jones was coming next. He had his eyes closed. Another fan mobbed him and without opening his eyes he said

"please don't." He looked in a bad way. He passed by. Next came a lolloping, grinning Keith. He grabbed both myself and one of my friends, pulled us down the corridor and then proceeded to kiss – like, properly kiss – both of us, one at a time. I don't think we responded very well, to be honest. I think we were both in a state of shock. And then, in a millisecond, he had disappeared behind closed doors and a guard of security. My friend and me just looked at each other – what just happened?

We rushed back out to the front of the stage. The crowd were quiet, completely emptied, trying to recover from a short but brilliant live Rolling Stones concert and its' abrupt end. It was a blend of despondency and disturbance and confusion and total disbelief. It was there at all their early concerts after they went off stage – a sort of vacuum of some minutes where people were really trying to process what they had seen. Could anybody sound that good, that sexy, that connected with something so deeply primordial within us all? It was an unwitting release from what would turn out to be outmoded conventions, traditions, sensible clothes and hair cuts.

These were defining moments. We waved to the crowd – "we kissed Keith" we shouted. We screamed. The faces pressed up against the chicken wire were disappointed and envious and spent. We were eventually escorted down the steps to the now dispersing crowd. Exhaustion set in. It had probably been not

> "suddenly The Beatles were bordering on acceptability"

much more than an hour but what emotion for us young teenagers. The world was definitely changing both within us and without. We felt on the edge of a precipice. And, of course, we were.

The sunshine started fading and dusk was not far away – we had to get home. I grabbed a teddy bear that someone had tried to throw at Mick, discarded on the grass. We started down the road and thumbed a lift. Someone stopped, picked us up and we got in but there was something sinister about him. Suffice to say, there was a scuffle and I asked him to stop so we could get out. I literally tore my friend away from him and we ran and ran. He seemed to give up eventually and drove off, leaving us in pitch black darkness. We had no idea where we were. Cars were in short supply in those country lanes.

Eventually we did get another lift, from some parents who were looking for their daughter who had also gone to the concert but had not returned. They dropped us off somewhere in a village near Bristol. A young man was our next driving host. He took us to his flat, parked outside and said we could sleep in the car over night, which we did. We talked all night about the Rolling Stones, their music, their hair, their clothes, their attitude. We finally realised that we really loved them.

In the morning we found other lifts to our small town in Somerset and got home on a Sunday afternoon and boasted to our friends. I left the teddy bear on the dashboard of our overnight

> "... the Rolling Stones, their music, their hair, their clothes, their attitude"

accommodation with a thank you note for the young man. Our parents believed we had had a sleep-over at each others' houses.

10 AUGUST 1964
Tower Ballroom, New Brighton

Gordon Valentine
In the Sixties I played bass and sang with the Teesside group The Johnny Taylor Five. Along with a lot of other stuff we played the Liverpool Cavern a couple of times and beat the Liverpool groups in a competition. We ended up having to appear in the finals at the Tower Ballroom, New Brighton. The compere was the late Jimmy Savile and top of the bill were the Rolling Stones. What a night!

Jenny Wilson *(age 16)*
My boyfriend Terry Wilson and I remember being crushed on the balcony. It was very dangerous by today's standards but another fantastic night. There were huge crowds queuing to get in but we managed to jump the queue with our tickets.

Nadia Davies *(age 16)*
I went to Egremont with my mum for a few days as the landlady was emigrating. I saw a poster advertising the show. I didn't have much money but it was the Sixties and I loved pop. I had no one to go with so I went and queued up outside the hall. I only had enough cash to get in and didn't want to lose my place in the queue so I stood all day – no food or drink. I was at the front of the stage. There were lots of groups playing. It was

Nadia Davis

the hall and the show finished. I then had to run home along the seafront. It was dark and late and I didn't hang about. My mum was a bit of a dragon for telling me off. I have never forgotten this show.

Dave Price *(age 15)*
I was a Beatles fan first. To me everything in the world started with *Love Me Do*. I loved The Beatles and The Beatles got more and more successful. Then the Stones came along. I bought *Come On* when it first came out and I bought everything subsequently. The Beatles versus the Stones was only really a thing used by the teenage magazines like *Rave* and that sort of thing. It just made press. The more middle of the road fans didn't like the Stones. It was just too much for them, whereas you could take The Beatles home with you. It was a little bit outrageous when it first started but gradually everybody came to love The Beatles. With the *Royal Variety* performance with John Lennon and the rattling the jewellery joke, everyone's mum and grandma could say "oh well, they're quite nice lads really. It's not my sort of thing but I can see why you like them." But they were never going to say that about the Stones. It was a much more generational thing.

The Stones had appeared at the Cavern in Liverpool in the November prior to that. The queue went all the way around the block and people were camping out overnight for that. You had no chance of getting into that at all. It was

some sort of competition. The groups were great but I cannot remember their names. I am sure Jimmy Savile was the emcee. We knew his name – this was before he was the big name.

The Stones were brilliant. Their music was like their records which was good in those days. So many other groups didn't do live very well. Mick was like always jumping about all over the stage. He wasn't bad looking in the early days. I was hot and my arms were crossed to stop me from being crushed. I fainted and remember being picked up and carried over the heads of others to the side of the hall where the first-aiders were. My arms were stuck, crossed over my chest. They gave me a drink and I relaxed. They were surprised to hear I'd had no food or drink. I went back into

"when you were in it, it was more or less a riot"

a big deal. The Stones were raved about. Everyone was, y'know – The Yardbirds, Long John Baldry. Everybody that came up from London to play at the Cavern was raved about and the Stones were the number one band. The Beatles had been and gone. Cavern DJ Bob Wooler was always playing the Stones records.

New Brighton Tower Ballroom was a huge Victorian ballroom and it had a balcony which went round but for this Stones show it was purely ground floor, purely standing. So there were no seats or anything like that. It wasn't like one of the cinema shows that they were doing. I went with a friend of mine and our two then girlfriends. And the preliminary to it was a thing that had been going on for some weeks in conjunction with the Cavern which was a competition of twelve local bands playing ten minutes each. The prize at the end of it was supposedly a recording contract and it was done by a company called Rael Brook who were famous for making drip dry shirts which was quite a thing at the time. Part of the reward if you won this competition is that your group would be renamed The Toplins, because that was the name of the material that was used. And that was on a low stage. It was not very high.

We were about two or three rows back standing when this thing started but by the time the Stones were starting we were about twenty rows back. It was

just a maelstrom of people. It was absolute havoc. I've got the Liverpool Echo press cuttings for it which praised the fans for their behaviour and said 'there were only a few arrests' and all that sort of thing. But when you were in it, it was more or less a riot. There were girls being passed over heads who'd fainted. There were people on the stage fainting in the spotlights. And there were police dogs behind. Obviously you couldn't see what was going on but it was generally pretty much a riot.

The Stones didn't appear on this low stage. They were on a much higher raised stage at the back and you couldn't actually get anywhere near them. The compere for it was Jimmy Savile. Back then he was the zany DJ emcee. You couldn't hear anything. You would hear little wafts of songs but basically you couldn't hear anything. It was just like a non stop riot really.

There was girls screaming. There was fighting. The whole thing was liquid. The whole crowd was moving. We started off near the front but we ended up twenty rows back and you had to fight to keep your feet because if you'd gone down under that you'd probably have been trampled to death. There was 4,000 people there apparently. It was a huge venue.

They were probably relieved that they were so far from the crowd. There was no chance of anybody getting at them. There were bouncers everywhere, and uniformed stewards. There were police. Policewomen. There was dogs. You couldn't get near them.

13 AUGUST 1964
Palace Ballroom, Douglas, Isle of Man

Susan Smith *(age 10)*
I would have been nearly 11 but because of their bad boy reputation my mother wouldn't let me go. She said it would be too violent. I was heartbroken.

Sandra Lord *(age 18)*
I went with my friends Pam and Jane. My late father was Bob Wilkinson, Managing Director of the Palace Derby & Castle Company, and he did all the bookings for the summer shows and cinemas on the Island. I well remember that night and people saying to me "is that your father at the corner of the stage?" as the girls were being thrown out. Of course I denied it. I have a great photo of Dad at the Fairy Bridge with the very bored looking Stones and also a postcard they autographed. Dad kept notes from those times and the following is an extract:

After the 'Big Band' era in the Palace Ballroom came the Groups. One of the biggest attractions was The Rolling Stones. That night we had 6,500 paid admissions and what a night it was! I had to have a 'cage-like' barrier built in front of the stage to keep the fans from climbing onto it. The police dog with its handler was there along with many extra security staff for the night. However the girls still managed to fight their way onto the stage, but as fast as they got on they were thrown out through the stage door.

That night when I arrived in the Palace Ballroom there was nearly a riot starting. The crowd was chanting 'we want the Stones. I asked my manager what had happened as the Stones should have been on by then. It transpired that Mick Jagger had decided that they wouldn't go on until they had been paid. I soon got them on by giving Mick my personal cheque for the group's guaranteed share of the gate money!

19 AUGUST 1964
New Theatre Ballroom, St Peter Port, Guernsey

Keith Tapscott *(age 15)*
My uncle was a flower grower and one of his staff was married to a man who worked for British European Airways. After several days of badgering her for information she told me that the Stones were flying in from Heathrow on the afternoon flight. I spent the whole afternoon at the airport waiting. At that time you could sit at ground level and look out from huge windows on to the runway close to where the planes parked. There were not too many fans around and so I had a great view when they arrived, rather like looking at a vast television screen in 3D. They were greeted by a relatively large number of people, some of whom were lucky enough to have been allowed to join the welcoming party.

The band sauntered down the steps, signed a few autograph books and were soon whisked away via one of the airport

Susan Smith

157

perimeter gates. I got the bus back looking forward to seeing them the following two evenings. I didn't go to the first evening as I had originally planned to go to the second of their three concerts owing to a lack of money. Tickets were in the region of 12/- (63p). I'm not sure what this equates to in today's money, but it represented about 6% of a weekly wage in 1964. My uncle, however, came to the rescue and bought extra tickets for my cousin and me so we saw them twice.

"my real memories of that night are of the tomato throwing incident"

The Westcoasters warmed up the audience and very good they were too but the excitement started to build the nearer we got to the Stones taking the stage. There were more males than females and there was no seating. As a result it all seemed more intense, rhythmic and louder and the band seemed closer. There was no pushing and shoving – everyone was there to have a good time.

Keith was playing a Gibson Les Paul guitar which he had acquired during their June tour of the US. Brian was playing a blonde Fender Telecaster and there was no sign of the Vox Teardrop. As soon as I saw that guitar I knew it was the guitar for me. Many years later I now have three of them. The set list was more or less the same as when I'd seen them in Brighton – from *Walking The Dog* to *It's All Over Now*. Shortly before this performance the band had released *Five by Five* and I think they played *Around and Around* from that EP. It was over far too soon. When they left Guernsey

for Jersey there was trouble. They got into an argument with an air hostess on the 15 minute flight which resulted in their being banned from flying British United. Great publicity but rather tame compared with subsequent years.

22 AUGUST 1964
Springfield Hall, St Helier, Jersey

Geraldine Lawrie (age 16)
I was spending a month in Jersey and staying with relatives, having just taken my 'O' levels in Bude in Cornwall. I got a summer job in a shop called Macey's in La Colomberie in St Helier. It was a tourist gift shop selling drinks, cigarettes and souvenirs. Just before 1pm one day the manager rushed and closed the shop and in came the Rolling Stones. I served Charlie Watts and got all their autographs. I was so excited, as you can imagine. That evening I went to their concert at the Springfield Stadium. I will never forget that day!

Bob Lamb
I was in the Army and on leave waiting to be posted to Malaya. The concert was at Springfield which in those days was the main venue on the island. The main auditorium was very packed so we sneaked up onto the balcony to get away from the screaming girls. There were only a couple of others up there, but no security guards. About ten feet away from me to my right was a guy in a brown leather jacket. Suddenly he took a brown paper bag from his jacket and started throwing tomatoes

at the Stones at the same time shouting something about Buddy Holly. Everyone was taken by surprise but he very quickly disappeared. The few security guards there were there ran up to us and ask what happened. We told them and they went away. The Jersey Evening Post later carried an article about the tomato throwing – apparently the guy didn't like their versions of Buddy Holly numbers.

Bill du Heaume (age 20)
My real memories of that night are of the tomato throwing incident. The person responsible was a Peter Smith, known to everyone as Biffo and somewhat of a character in those days. For Biffo and myself the music had died after the death of Buddy Holly and Eddie Cochran. In Peter's case he remained locked into the Fifties era. Unfortunately with the rise of the groups in the Sixties Peter could not come to

terms with the cover versions of the legends' songs. After the Stones recording of *Come On* we heard that their next record release was to be Buddy Holly's *Not Fade Away*.

I knew Peter would get up to something when they came to Jersey, such as stand at the front and heckle the group. So although we were very close friends I avoided him. As soon as the intro to *Not Fade Away* started the tomatoes followed. Peter should have stayed at home that night. He couldn't of course – he had to make a statement. That was probably his 15 minutes of fame as he was interviewed on our local *ITV* channel.

23 AUGUST 1964
Gaumont Theatre, Bournemouth

Tricia Fowler (age 16)
I went with my friend June Cole. I touched Mick Jagger's shoe and was taken back to my front row seat by security. We were both sixteen years old – I don't think my parents were very keen on me going but I went anyway!

26 AUGUST 1964
Odeon Theatre, Exeter

Maureen Metherell
née Gormley (age 14)
I went with my friend Geraldine Balac and it was great. We screamed so much an usherette came over and put her hands on our foreheads and asked if we were ok. What a laugh!

Tricia Fowler

Bill du Heaume

Chris Gale

Chris Gale (age 17)

Despite all the media tosh at the time about rivalry between mods and rockers and the Stones and The Beatles, I was a great fan of both. I attended the Stones concert on my own. As soon as the music hit us everyone shot out of their seats and surged forward. It was our music and, because my dad did not like it, I did.

27 AUGUST 1964

ABC Theatre, Plymouth

Jacki Downing (age 17)

I went with my friend Carol Staverdes, her boyfriend Jim, Pat Jones, Francesca Dadela, Pat Hooper and Jeanette. Jim and Carole called for me in the morning and we had lunch in Littlewoods. We wandered over to the theatre where we found the Overlanders unpacking their gear. We also met Millie's back group, the Five Embers, and the Barron Knights.

When the Stones came on stage the place erupted. It was electric and the atmosphere was fab. The Stones belted out *Not Fade Away*, *I'm A King Bee*, *It's All Over Now* and *I Just Want To Make Love To You*. Some girls tried to climb onto the stage and policemen prevented them. St John's ambulance were also in attendance. Mick was all over the stage while singing and Brian was good looking. Charlie, on the drums, did not smile and Bill stood stock still with his guitar looking upwards. Keith looked like a little boy – so young. It was a really wonderful show.

8 SEPTEMBER 1964
Odeon Theatre, Colchester

Derek Broadbent (age 13)

I went with a friend at the time whose name was Paul Blomefield. I can't remember who else was on the bill but I do remember some of them being out the front on the pavement having a smoke while we were waiting to get in. I was upstairs in the circle and when the Rolling Stones came on we were pushed to the front of the balcony. It was very scary with lots of screaming and you could hardly hear the group. It must have been an afternoon performance if that is possible as it was still day light when we went in. One song sticks in my mind and that was *Little Red Rooster*.

Penny Stone née Phillips
(age 16)

I had started work at Alexis, a hairdressing salon in Colchester High Street, in August and all the girls went to see the Rolling Stones. It was a magical evening. The Stones were fantastic and have stayed in my mind ever since. I was going out with my boyfriend Colin Stone who was 18. I thought his name and the Rolling Stones name being the same were great. We are still together after 51 years of courting and marriage.

Susan Tunstall née Bonner
(age 17)

I was with my best friend at the time Diane Reeve. We were thrilled to be there on the day the Rolling Stones were voted the number one group in the UK. The

atmosphere was electric and the young female audience was manic with screaming and weeping girls. It was our first pop concert and we were rather overwhelmed by the experience. We tried to get out to the front of the Odeon to see them leave but we were too late as they had been whisked away in their car.

Heather Wickenden (age 13)

It was the evening I met my future husband and the evening which set the path our lives would take. Me and my best friend Brenda, both aged 13, decided to go along to the show. We were very excited to see the Rolling Stones but when we got there we were also just as excited to see three boys sitting behind us! They were Michael, Des and Ian – all aged 15 and school friends. They started to chat to us and shared not only their thoughts about the show but also their sweets too. We carried on chatting after the show and arranged to meet them later that week. Michael and I got engaged four years later and married in 1971. They don't know it but the Rolling Stones have a lot to answer for – we thank them very much!

Susan Larner (age 16)

I had met my boyfriend John – now my husband – while at St Helena School in May 1964. John was 15 and a school year below me when we met. I left school in July and started work the following week, having had a choice of three jobs. The Rolling Stones gig was the first

Penny Stone

one we went to as a couple and it seemed to cost a lot out of our wages. An elderly work colleague said I would catch fleas from them as they were not clean. I didn't catch anything, but I couldn't hear the show very well because of the fans screaming.

Penny Gill *(age 13)*

I went with my best friend Pat. We were both 13. Lulu was a support act and we had to queue for hours in the cold and pouring rain to get in!

Teresa Wilkins *(age 20)*

The Stones were my favourite group of the Sixties – much to my father's disgust. I wasn't a fan of The Beatles. For me the Sixties was much more about Bob Dylan, Joan Baez and Peter, Paul and Mary. I saw the Stones play at Colchester Odeon.

We had front row seats which I was very excited about but – alas – we couldn't hear a single word they sang as the mainly female audience screamed loudly and non stop throughout the whole concert. It takes a lot to drown out Mick Jagger but I assure you they did. Jagger oozed sex appeal. I can still see him as clear as anything in my mind as he looked that night. He wore a sloppy sweater and cord jeans.

Due to the screaming of the girls I just have a quaint memory and can boast that I once had front row seats for the Rolling Stones and didn't hear a word. I went with my boyfriend. He became my husband the following year. And still is!

Teresa Wilkins

9 SEPTEMBER 1964

Odeon Cinema, Luton

Mark Tolman *(age 13)*

It was exactly a week before my 14th birthday. I went on my own. It remains a puzzle to me how my parents allowed me to go unaccompanied. The most expensive tickets were 12/6 (63p) which were, naturally, for the front row seats. I managed to buy a ticket for 10/6 (53p), which secured a seat two or three rows from the front, so I had a good view of the acts.

There were cheaper prices to be paid, which allowed a fellow grammar school mate of mine and his elder brother positions some way behind mine. I remember feeling smug that this friend and his sibling didn't have as good a view as yours truly, and I would occasionally look over my shoulder and give him a wave.

I recall a couple of the supporting acts, namely the Mojos from Liverpool and Charlie and Inez Foxx from the States, the latter of whom provided some trans-Atlantic excitement! Needless to say, when the stars of the show appeared the noise level from the audience rose appreciably. I felt quite grown up for having attended such an occasion without any adult supervision.

David Arnold *(age 18)*

We saw them at the Odeon in Luton. My mate shouted out for I'm Moving On and Jagger's response was "no, it's *You Better Move On*".

Brenda Parker

You couldn't hear the music anymore because everyone was screaming so much. These were the years when people rushed the stage at every opportunity and big, burly bouncers struggled mightily to hold them back and people often got hurt in the process. I was never a screamer or a stage rusher. You couldn't hear a thing except for everyone screaming their heads off. Just knowing that you were in the same room as the Stones was enough to join everyone together in one big communal bout of near hysteria.

When they toured with Charlie and Inez Foxx I saw them with my friend Pat who had a huge crush on Keith. By this time they'd become big stars and we were lucky to get tickets and were really excited and talked about nothing else for weeks beforehand. A man who worked with my dad took us. He was probably in his mid twenties but seemed ancient to us and how or why he volunteered to take two teenage girls to what turned out to be a scream fest is a mystery to this day, but I was always grateful that he did because Pat and I had a great time. Not so sure if he did though!

There already seemed a big difference from the April 64 show at Stevenage Locarno as the dynamic had changed and Mick was definitely becoming the main focus of attention. I remember he was wearing a long fluffy white cardigan and at some point someone threw bright green confetti and it went all over him and stuck to his sweater so he did the rest of the show covered with green splotches. Apart from the noise and the atmosphere, that's all I really remember about the show. I suppose, as he was the singer, it was easy to see why people would pay more attention to Mick. He was always prancing about and it was hard to take your eyes off him. He perfected a truly great stage persona and was totally unlike anyone else I ever saw. Sadly, there was never any sign again of the ecstatic tambourine-waving Brian dancing around at the edge of the stage with such a big smile on his face or wailing away on his blues harmonica.

10 SEPTEMBER 1964
Odeon Theatre, Cheltenham

Orville Matthews

I was at all four gigs they did in Cheltenham on package tours that toured the country at the Odeon cinema. I always did the second show. The Stones were top of the bill with Inez Foxx who wore a green suit and was a mix of Little Richard and Prince in looks back in 1964. Brian Jones was certainly the foundation of what the Stones became and was a couple of years older than me and a Cheltenham boy. It was a long time ago but to me they were electric and exciting and are still in my mind.

Orville Matthews

11 SEPTEMBER 1964
Capitol Theatre, Cardiff

John Richards *(age 14)*

I saw the Stones in a sort of package tour. I was with a friend. We were about 15 rows back, just

> "the four of us just rushed up the stairs overtaking everyone and got seats in the front row of the circle"

to the right of the stage. We'd not seen anything like it before. It was pure excitement. I have followed the Stones since *Come On* and The Beatles since *Please Please Me*. It was the decade of change in so many ways. Looking back we had the music and bands that the whole world was following, the weather, plentiful work. What a shame we didn't have digital cameras back then. Can you imagine what we could have captured?

14 SEPTEMBER 1964
The Twisted Wheel, Manchester

Bob Lee

It was my birthday and I went to the Twisted Wheel. That was the night that the Stones, because they were in Manchester staying at the Queen's Hotel, came to the Twisted Wheel. They walked in and Roger Eagle the DJ saw them and proceeded to play all the tracks off their first album, the originals, in the order they were on the LP. He was having a dig in some ways because he really was a purist, Roger Eagle, but they took it in good faith.

15 SEPTEMBER 1964
Odeon Theatre, Manchester

Christine McDermott (age 12)

I was on the front row in the stalls – seat A22. I had such a good seat because I queued with friends from school, one being Chris Lee who was a great friend of mine from the High School of Art in Cheetham Hill and who was also a great Bob Dylan fan. When we

were queuing a Bob Dylan LP had just been released and Chris and I saved each other's place in the queue to each go and buy it.

Penny Whitney (age 15)

My father was very anti the Stones, which was a good reason to be a fan. "Get them in the army and get their hair cut" was his response whenever they were on *Top Of The Pops*. I went with a friend, Mel, and two boys who were friends of our younger brothers. Mel would have been in her 'O' level year and I was a year younger. Dick and Lewis were in the third year and were mad keen Stones fans.

We went by train from Knutsford to Manchester. My biggest memory was that, when the doors of the theatre opened, the four of us just rushed up the stairs overtaking everyone and got seats in the front row of the circle – the tickets weren't numbered and we'd paid six shillings for them. I still have my ticket and my programme from the show.

Bob Lee

I'd booked to go and see them and decided that I'd go to both shows. So I'd already bought one ticket and I went and bought another ticket. And when I got the second ticket to the Odeon I actually asked to speak to the manager and I told him what I was doing because it was quite unusual to do that at the time and I said "would it be possible for me, instead of going out and queuing up again, to just move upstairs?" Because I was in the stalls for the first show and in the balcony for the second show and I said "could I just stay in and do that?" And he said "certainly you can."

So the great day came and I saw them from the stalls and it was absolutely fantastic. I was buzzing. It was incredible. So I started making my way up the stairs. I was about halfway up the stairs and in front of me was a policeman and an inspector. They used to carry a stick in them days. They were walking in front of me with arms behind their backs. And one of them said to the other "funny that, I could have sworn I saw a customer still in the auditorium" and the other one said "yes, I think I did" and I was walking behind them and before I could get a chance to explain they just turned around and said "out!" So I said "no, it's okay" and tried to explain.

It wasn't happening. They said "you're not staying in here while we're on duty" or words to that effect. So I tried to argue with them and they got physical and started pushing me. And then one of them got me by the scruff of the neck, marched me down the flight of carpeted stairs, pushed the fire door and proceeded to throw me down the stone steps down to the ground floor. So I was down these steps and he followed me down. I was a bit battered and bruised and he just kicked me against the push bar, pushed the thing open and pushed me out into the street.

It had been raining and the pavement was wet. The queue was past the point at which I came hurtling out. People saw me and said "what's happened?"

and I explained it to them and word passed down the queue and I ended up at the front of the queue so I got in again. And as soon as I got in I complained to the manager. The manager apologised and said there wasn't much he could do about it. The police in them days were a law unto themselves.

So I saw the second show in the balcony and, as on their previous two visits, I went to the Queen's Hotel. The Stones always stayed at the Queen's Hotel on Piccadilly Gardens in Manchester and I knew this so I went up just to see if I could get a glimpse or whatever. And another reason was there were always lots of young ladies hanging around the hotel as well, which is always good. If they ever were in Liverpool or Sheffield invariably they used to make their way and stay in the Queen's Hotel in Manchester. One of the reasons the Stones used to like going there was because the security was crap and the girls could get into the rooms.

So anyway I went up and I was just talking to people and everything and I saw Ian Stewart and I recognised him and said "hello" to him. And that was it and I thought nothing of it. About half an hour later he came out looking for me and he said "did you have trouble at the concert?" And I said "yes" and the Stones had heard about it. And I was invited in and got to talk to Mick and Keith and Brian in one of their rooms. I can't remember whose room it was. I got talking to them, told them I was in the fan club

"the Stones used to like going there because the security was crap and the girls could get into the rooms"

> "a girl stood up and with the athleticism of an Olympian and with no thought to her own safety, took off over the seats shouting 'Keithhhhh!' "

and all this sort of thing. And they were really good, really nice and pleasant about it and I told them I worked at the AA. And the following year, in 65, they were playing Manchester again and they'd just been given some sort of sponsorship and they'd been given cars. Two of them could drive and they were going to pick these cars up in Manchester and they were going to drive to Sheffield. So they did no more than call in to the AA offices on York Street in Manchester and ask for me because they wanted a road map. Well I tell you my street credibility leapt! I could do no wrong with the girls in there for months afterwards.

17 SEPTEMBER 1964
ABC Lonsdale Theatre, Carlisle

David Hanabury *(age 15)*
I was still at school and starting GCEs and the engineering exam G1. Those were the days. My elder brother worked at the BATA shoe factory in Maryport and some of the girls there had got together and organised a bus to see the Stones. My brother Michael was no fan of the Stones but to me they were the best thing to have happened since Tommy Steel and his little white bull, but I had been six at the time!

The 25 miles or so between Maryport and Carlisle seemed like they would never end. Being the son of a face working miner we always travelled to Carlisle by train – buses were for the working class! However we did finally arrive and by then the journey had

become very tolerable. There was an aroma and an atmosphere on the bus I had never experienced at this intensity – excited women and rock and roll. We were booked to see the first of two shows. It was one of those rock and roll tours of the day with a compere. I can remember Mick Berry with his Buddy Holly tribute. There may have been some other support acts but to be honest I can't remember – my mind was just about to be blown away by Charlie and Inez Foxx. I was a fledgling mod and the Stones were my band but this brother and sister act were the best thing I had ever heard or seen – and their dancing! Their soul opened up another world of music and my side of the theatre just could not get enough and would not let them go. The other side of the ABC were shouting 'we want the Stones but we drowned them out. We wanted Inez and Charlie!

Guitars and drums were being tuned. The female throng around me were on their feet with excitement, anticipation, screams and – yes – some wet seats. The curtain opened – my heroes – 'going round and round'. A girl who travelled with us from Maryport stood up and with the athleticism of an Olympian, and with no thought to her own safety, took off over the seats. She covered the distance to the stage in the blink of an eye shouting "Keithhhhhhhhhhh!" and vaulted impressively onto the stage. Her flight was halted by security and she was escorted straight out of the theatre. The Stones were fab.

The following day my feeling of euphoria was somewhat dented when a games teacher found out I was at the concert and sought me out. I thought I was in trouble when he finally found me. What did I think of the bloody Rolling Stones? "Fab sir," was my reply. He informed me he was there. "What?" He then informed me he had taken his daughter and lectured me on these degenerates and particularly the moron on the drums who, he said, "could not drum his way out of a paper bag."

Marj Birbeck (age 17)
I worked at Sekers Silk Mill at Hensingham near Whitehaven and someone said about getting a coach to go and see the Stones. We filled it easily and away we went. It was wonderful. The place was packed and there was that much screaming and shouting that some of the plaster fell from the ceiling but everything just carried on. The plaster fell in the aisle so no one was hurt. I do not think any one would have bothered anyway. A couple of days later one of my friends came to see me and gave me a photo she had taken of Mick and Keith sitting in the back of a car after they had finished and were leaving. A truly amazing night and one I will always remember. That time in Carlisle when we were all so young was something else.

Linda Nicholson (age 13)
I was a school girl and a massive Stones fan. My friend, Janice Raphael, was a Beatles fan but we went to both Stones concerts at the ABC. I seem to remember they turned up late for the second gig and the emcee had to fill in as the other acts had done their stints, getting us to shout "we want the Stones!" There was a coffee bar opposite the Stage Door in Cecil Street called the Fresco. We got wind that some of the other stars of that first Stones concert would be in there before the show, so we arranged to get down early, autograph books at the ready. Alas we weren't lucky but at some point I acquired Charlie Watts' signature and remember the torn piece of paper stuck in my little blue book – where did that go I wonder? He was always my favourite. It was big news in a small city to have big stars appearing and we went to many more concerts where many stars were on the bill with one headline act. The Stones were the biggest in my book.

Ellen Knight (age 14)
I went with my friend Carol who was three years older than me. One of the local guys had organised a bus from Penrith along with two tickets for the show. I was so excited when my mam said I could go with Carol and her friends. When we went into the ABC the place was buzzing with other people as excited as me. We took our seats to the right of the stage.

Appearing with the Stones were the Mojos and Inez & Charlie Foxx who sang *Mocking Bird*. There was an interval before the Stones came on stage. One of Carol's friends was so excited. The Stones were ready for the second half of

Linda Nicholson and her sister

the concert. The curtains opened. The stage was quite dark. Mick had his back to the audience. Everyone was screaming. He clapped his hands and wiggled his bum and with that Carol's friend fainted! She was carried out by the St John's ambulance men and taken to the foyer with lots of other girls who were overcome by it all. She never got to see the Stones. We just took a quick glance at her before she was taken out – we weren't going to miss the Stones! We screamed and shouted as the Stones sang songs like *Around and Around*, *Not Fade Away* and *Time Is On My Side*. It was one of the best times of my life. All very affordable – not like concerts today – and very special memories.

Dennis Hodgson (age 14)
My mother used to organise a mini bus and twelve of us used to go to Carlisle from Maryport. What I remember of the gig was quite a lot of screaming ladies.

18 SEPTEMBER 1964
Odeon Theatre, Newcastle

Thomas Mann
My aunt and uncle used to manage the Percy Arms in the Haymarket in Newcastle. The Rolling Stones were appearing at the Odeon. That night in the Percy Arms there was a bit of a commotion. A group of young men the worse for wear were insulting and arguing with the pub regulars. My uncle, an ex Royal Navy member, asked them to leave. One in particular took offence at this saying "do you not know who I am?" As my uncle

grabbed him and was ejecting him from the pub he was shouting and screaming "I AM MICK JAGGER! YOU CAN'T DO THIS!" My uncle then went back into the pub and asked the rest of the band members if they wanted the same or were going to leave quietly. They left by themselves without any help.

21 SEPTEMBER 1964
ABC Theatre, Kingston-upon-Hull

Christine Pinder (age 14)
I went with my school friend Jean Baldwin. Her mum had queued overnight to get us some tickets as we weren't allowed to. The Stones did two performances and we went to the second house, as it was called then. The cinema had an orchestra pit in front of the stage with a velvet covered wooden balustrade around it. Whilst we were queuing outside to get into the cinema, word went round that during the first performance Mick Jagger decided to strut along the top of

Christine Pinder

this balustrade. This caused the audience in the stalls to surge forward and Mick was knocked off the balustrade and into the orchestra pit! Because this caused such a riot he wasn't allowed to do it in the second performance, much to our disappointment.

We sat in the circle, about three rows from the front. I remember the Stones coming onstage. I screamed, burst into tears and came to with my head between my knees, having missed quite a lot of their performance! I was still crying on the top of the double decker bus on the way home, but had to come to in order to properly face Mum and Dad at home.

John Brant (age 15)

My mother wouldn't let me queue all night for tickets. However, my girlfriend Carol did and followed them around the area. The performance in Hull was the first of their concerts to be filmed. Mick Jagger caused a near riot by strutting his stuff around the orchestra pit instead of staying on stage. I fell out with Carol after I found out she had gone backstage into the dressing room. I had suspicions that Jagger had had his wicked way with her. I still can't fathom out why she preferred a millionaire rock star to a five pound a week shipping clerk.

26 SEPTEMBER 1964
Gaumont Theatre, Bradford

Mike Roberts (age 17)

I went with my girlfriend, Maureen – now my wife of almost 50 years. The package included

Mike Berry and Inez & Charlie Foxx. The particular memory I have is of watching Bill Wyman who, throughout the entire Stones performance, kept turning to chat to a stagehand standing in the wings. He progressively sidled towards him to such an extent that he became obscured from the audience's view leaving only the fingerboard of his bass guitar in sight!

Mike Roberts

Margaret Marshall *née White* (age 14)

My friend Glynis Mallows (nee Jones) and I were both 14 and we have vivid memories of seeing the Stones. We remember our excitement at purchasing the tickets and waiting for the date. We still talk about it these days when we meet up. After the show the police turned up as there were so many fans in the roads around the theatre.

John Heffron (age 20)

My wife Pat and I remember it well as our daughter was born two weeks after. The night of the concert we were returning home by bus. We lived in Manningham, two or three miles from the centre of Bradford. We noticed crowds of teenagers screaming and running about outside the Gaumont and the bus slowed down and eventually stopped as the kids were running across the road. Whether they had spotted one of their idols we did not know. As we stopped I noticed a big poster advertising the Rolling Stones and supporting artists in concert that night.

Margaret Marshall

Pat and I were both staunch Stones fans and I said to her "we have to have our tea and come back down and see if we can get tickets and go to the concert". Pat, despite being eight and a half months pregnant and ginormous, agreed straightaway. We got back about 7pm and went to the ticket office and I said "have you got two tickets for tonight as near the front as possible?" The lady said "oh I'm sorry but all those tickets have gone". She gave Pat a look over and said "these are the best I can do. There will be nobody sat next to you. Your wife will have a bit of extra room". How nice! We had a brilliant seat about half way back and bang in the middle with a superb view.

There were four supporting artists. I remember Charlie and

William Martin

Inez Foxx and The Mojos. And, obviously, the fabulous Rolling Stones. Their first Number One *It's All Over Now* was still rocking the charts. One of the music papers must have done an article about the Stones likes and dislikes and one of them liking jelly babies. Well when they started playing they got bombarded with jelly babies. The fans had brought bags of these in with them. Charlie Watts' drum kit was covered with them and the Stones were laughing their heads off. What a fabulous night. The Stones were at their raw, hungry best. Simply the tops!

Janet Auty *(age 17)*

I remember going to see the Stones at the Gaumont as it was known as, now the old Odeon building, next to the Alhambra Theatre in the centre of Bradford. I started my working life at Busby's department store in Bradford and I went with some of the girls from there.

29 SEPTEMBER 1964
Odeon Theatre, Guildford

William Martin

I saw the second show at the Odeon Theatre. It was a brilliant concert – complete mayhem and non stop screaming with people rushing the stage. I remember we tried to gate crash the doors for the first performance but soon got thrown out!

1 OCTOBER 1964
Colston Hall, Bristol

Diane Kenyon (age 15)

I went with my two best friends at the time – Valerie Evans and Valerie Coombes. It was the first time I had ever queued for hours to get tickets. The other acts were the Innocents, Mike Berry, the Mojos, the Le Roys, Simon Scott and Charlie and Inez Foxx. Don Spencer was the compere. I would probably have enjoyed most of these another time but I just wanted to see the Stones.

I can remember the review in the paper the next day saying that the audience were all cheering Inez and Charlie Foxx when everyone was really trying to hurry them off as we knew the Stones were on next! They didn't disappoint and I can remember screaming along with everyone else. It was the best concert I'd ever been to.

4 OCTOBER 1964
Gaumont Theatre, Southampton

Graham Kesby (age 14)

I went with friends of mine. A whole gang of us went along. I've no idea what they did. They only did twenty minutes. Half an hour max. It was just one mass of noise. Not just for the Stones but for everybody else that was on the bill also. It did reach a crescendo when the Stones came on obviously. It was, from a 14 year old's perspective, something I'd never experienced before. It was quite something else.

Gill Horn

My husband Bruce saw the Rolling Stones in Southampton with some mates. He recalls they couldn't hear them for the girls screaming. His mate Alan tapped a girl on the head with his shoe to quieten her. She and her friend moved to other seats.

6 OCTOBER 1964
Gaumont Theatre, Watford

David Buckland

I went to both shows with my girlfriend Wendy whom I later married and we have been together ever since. At that time it was fashionable to say that you preferred the Rolling Stones to The Beatles as it made you feel a bit of a rebel, although in all honesty both groups were terrific.

Mary Galvin (age 14)

I wasn't allowed to go to the gig in Watford but my friend Madeleine went and brought me back an autograph from Mick Jagger which said 'to Mary quite contrary' – now a treasured possession. She also had an autograph from Mick on her stomach. She didn't wash it for weeks and we were all so envious!

Chris Day

I can still remember that fantastic night in Watford. Four of us went – myself, Jim Halpin, my girlfriend Carol Jordan and Sue Theobald. Carol and Sue camped out all night in the freezing cold to be first in the queue for tickets. We were in the front row. What an atmosphere. There were hordes of girls screaming and running down the aisles trying to get on the stage. I can still remember a very young Mick Jagger gyrating right in front of us.

Chapter 14

Carole Saunders *(age 17)*
My husband, who was 19 at the time, and I were at the second performance. It was a Sunday and the Nashville Teens were on the same bill. My husband says it was great. I cannot remember it but hubby still lives in the Sixties.

Jan Holding
Dad was in the RAF and we were stationed at RAF Northolt. The scenes featuring Pussy Galore's Flying Circus in *Goldfinger* were filmed there and we saw the filming! I was a Lancastrian, living in London, loving the Rolling Stones when all the other girls in my class loved The Beatles. I still remember those concerts – the raw energy and the screaming girls. I couldn't speak for days after. I still have my tickets and a flyer for the Watford concert framed and hanging on the wall. Wonderful times!

11 OCTOBER 1964
Hippodrome, Brighton

Hazel Smith *(age 14)*
Growing up in Brighton in the Sixties was an amazing time and I and my friends saw many groups in the town. My memories of the concert were that we couldn't hear a thing. The screaming was so loud but I remember being excited to see Mick Jagger clapping and dancing his way around the stage! My other memory was a man behind me starting rubbing my back. I was a little alarmed but it turned out he had dropped ash all down my back from his cigarette. We thoroughly enjoyed our experience of seeing the Stones – it's just a shame we couldn't hear much!

Barbara Awcock *(age 15)*
Like Hazel, I remember the screaming and really enjoying seeing the Stones. My brother Jeff was in the Brighton Police. Hazel and I went around the back after the show to try and get to the stage door for autographs and my big brother was there on crowd control duty. When he saw us amongst the scrum he told us to go home! Being a bit afraid we scuttled out of there.

Don McBeth
I went with Lynda, my wife to be. We sat in the stalls, close to the stage. My lasting memory of the show was not of the Stones, who were good, but one of the supporting groups called the Mojos. They sang their hit record *Everything's Alright*, a number 9 hit record that they had written. During the performance the lead singer accompanied himself with a pair of maracas and at the end of the session he tossed the maracas into the audience. My wife caught one of them and politely passed it to the front, where a girl now had the pair. We assumed that the maracas were given away at every performance but we were wrong. During the interval the lead singer of the Mojos came into the audience and apologised for throwing the maracas away and politely asked for them back. It seems that he had only borrowed them. They belonged to Mick Jagger, who had told him to go and retrieve them.

Hazel Smith

In mid October 1964 the Stones made a quick foray into Europe, playing one show in Paris and making appearances on French and Belgian TV shows.

20 OCTOBER 1964
L'Olympia, Paris, France

Dominic Lamblin (age 19)

I love the Rolling Stones. I spent a lot of time with them. Not as a fan. I was not chasing them. I was with them and being chased! The way I interacted with them was through work working at *Decca*. I was a kid. I think they were 20 or 21. I was hanging around *Decca Records* in France. *Decca Records* was a pretty old company with Sir Edward, etc. so in France they were not too eager to go and deal with all the new bands because they didn't really know what to do with them. In England they had acts like Mantovani, Bert Kaempfert, all the classical stuff.

The first time the Stones came to France I was there and I was the record company representative. I think France was the only country where they sent a guy who was the same generation as them to look after them. In England all the guys who worked with the Rolling Stones were much older than them. Les Perrin was not a young kid, Tito Burns. The only guy who was the same generation as them was Andrew. Most of the places they went it was usually people much older than them. Even the guy in America – Bob Bonis – who took those incredible photographs of The Beatles and the Stones. He was much older than them.

They played the Olympia in '64. In actual fact in the Sixties they only played the Olympia. They came back for three dates at the Olympia in '65 and played it again in '66 and '67. And they played there in 1995 and 2003. I was at all of those concerts. We used to ride in paddy wagons. I ran from the fans all the time. So we'd be riding in paddy wagons to get to the Olympia although they would stay in a hotel which doesn't exist any more, the Hotel de Paris, which was about two hundred metres, three hundred metres from the Olympia. So some stupid guy thought 'oh it's near. We're gonna put them in the hotel so they'd be able to walk from the hotel to the theatre' which was totally crazy because there's no way that we could walk or anything so many times. Even in 1964 they were already big stars. So that was pretty exciting when you think about it.

For me it was a very exciting time, it was really amazing. They would be in Paris for two days. And then they'd be gone and it would get back to normal. And to them it was like that every day. It was constant excitement. I remember I took some photos of the Stones on about four or five occasions and I gave one photo that I took to Charlie and I said "do you remember where that took place?" and he said "no" because it was just another

"Brian was leader, no doubt about it, in my mind in 1964 and also in 1965 as well. And then by 1966 he had started slipping a bit"

gig or another rehearsal. It was just one instance amongst many, many other similar events. So he told me he loved the photo. The same thing with Keith. I gave one to Keith but he didn't remember when the actual concert was. In fact, it was not a concert. It was when they were filming a TV show in Montreux, Switzerland. That's when I took a lot of photos. From a record company angle it was very exciting, and very fast. Very much of a rush. They were very professional. We didn't have any problems with them.

Brian was leader, no doubt about it, in my mind in 1964 and also in 1965 as well. And then by 1966 he had started slipping a bit and he was no longer in charge. The band had been taken over by Mick and Keith. But in '64 he was definitely leader of the band and taking all the decisions. I remember, for instance, the first time that they arrived in Paris and they went to the Locomotive which was a club and they were not supposed to play. They were just supposed to show up on stage, wave and say "hi" to the fans and then leave. And the fans were really almost rioting so when they arrived the owner of the club came up to them and said "oh you've got to play, you've got to play." So we translated this to them and said "well, he wants you to play" and Brian said "no fucking way. We're not playing." And that was it, you know? And we went back to a club, to Castels, that same evening. And we rode around Paris.

We showed them the billboard that we had paid for and then

we went to the Golf Drouot for another appearance. They did a TV show where they did Carol and *It's All Over Now* without their gear because their gear had not arrived because it got held up with all the equipment. If you look at the TV show which you can find on YouTube they don't even have straps on their guitars. Keith's got this funny leather cap on his head. It's a French TV show and it's totally mimed. But then we're at the Olympia which in those days was like twenty minutes and then we were off and the next day they were gone.

After their European visit the Stones headed off on their second US tour.

24 OCTOBER 1964
Academy of Music, New York, NY

Gerrianne Bizan *(age 14)*
My friends and I had watched them on the *Ed Sullivan Show* and we were head over heels in love. We found out that they were appearing in Manhattan at the Academy of Music. We went down and waited on a long line. When she went in to get orchestra seats he gave us row W. My friend came out with the tickets and swapped clothes with a friend and went back in thinking that they were doing something funny with the tickets. She told the man he gave her the wrong row. The man gave her tickets in row U.

At the concert the Stones were great. This was before sound systems. My friends and I climbed over the backs of the seats and balanced on our seats to get a better view. After the concert my friend insisted to go backstage stating that in her excitement she threw her wallet on stage. Of course this was a lie.

Barbara Neumann Beals
(age 14)

My sister Lynne and I were in the record store and we saw this album England's Newest Hitmakers, The Rolling Stones. We knew nothing about them but the album cover was enough. We bought it, we took it home, we listened to it ten times and she said "I've got to meet the group. I've got to see them." We were absolutely intrigued and we loved them and started to like them more than The Beatles.

Back in those days before the mega concerts and the stadiums it was so much more innocent and funny. There was nothing groupie-ish. The name hadn't come up yet. There wasn't sex and drugs and rock'n'roll. It was just 'we want to meet them', that's all. At that time she was doing a little modelling and a little PR work for a small magazine and she was just a word of mouth kind of person. So she found out they were coming to the city – the Academy of Music in Brooklyn – a very small venue. So before they came she found out what hotel they were staying at. It was the Astor Hotel, which is no longer there. We dressed up as models and we pretended we were from Sweden and knew nothing about what was going on because we

walked in the Astor Hotel and they said "excuse me, girls, are you here to see the Stones?" "No, no, we're from Sweden. We're doing modelling here." And the guy believed us for some reason. And we got a room, we actually got a room, and later that day my father found out and he made me go home. But the next day Lynne and her friends, one of whom was called Sandy, dressed up as maids. They went into the closet in the hallway and they found maids' uniforms and they pushed the whole trolley thing down the hall and found out what room the Stones were in. Once they found out what room they were in they took off the maids' clothes, put their regular clothes on and just knocked on the door. And that was it. Lynne said "I just want to introduce myself. You know, I work at blah–blah–blah magazine and you know we're models and we just want to say hello."

It was all very simple and very sweet, not 'oh, you want to go to bed?' It wasn't like that. Lynne was 23. She was quite stunning. She was welcomed in. They talked blah-blah. And the next thing you know they're like old buddies. They're like "Do you think people like us in New York?" "Oh my gosh, yes. My sister's dying to see you." This was before they were hugely famous. And so out of that my sister got me front row center tickets in that little Academy of Music Theater. And my sister and I used to look back and say "can you believe we ever did that? That we could do that?" She said "I can't believe I dressed

> "they found maids' uniforms and they pushed the whole trolley thing down the hall and found out what room the Stones were in"

up as a maid and found their room with my friend Sandy and knocked on the door and walked in.'" It was that simple. She had a lot of nerve. They could have just said "oh, leave us alone and stop bothering us" but they didn't. She just made up some story – you know, she was good at double speak. She made it sound like she had a reason to be here. She was quite a character.

Everything was like that back then. You didn't have to show the contents of your bags. There was no security issues. It was all very innocent. Very simple. It was a different world. It was wonderful while it lasted.

1 NOVEMBER 1964
Civic Auditorium, Long Beach, California

Andrea Tarr *(age 14)*
I went with my friend. Because Long Beach was known to be an unsafe area at that time and because we were rather young her mother – who loved The Beatles and Rolling Stones as much as we did – decided to accompany us. This was a wild concert. A girl from the audience climbed up near the stage and was climbing the drapes in order to get closer to the Stones. Billy Preston and the Soul Brothers opened the show. We couldn't see because a lot of the audience were standing on their seats so we did the same. There was lots of screaming but we all enjoyed this concert and actually thought the songs seemed like what we'd heard on the album and the radio.

"a few of my surf and car turf friends were willing to see the Stones and what 'that scene' was all about"

Kent E Fisher *(age 16)*
The Stones performed at Santa Monica Civic Center three days before, closing the Teenage Awards Music International (TAMI) concert after a show stopping performance of James Brown. The show was filmed and then aired nationally on 14 November 1964. Locally, it played at the Strand Theatre in Long Beach, a stone's throw from the Civic Auditorium. I chose to go and see the Long Beach Auditorium concert rather than sit in a movie theatre to view a film of the much larger TAMI concert or buy a ticket for the much smaller Bob Dylan concert at the local Wilson High School in December. I couldn't afford to go to all three, let alone arrange for transportation. No one but me wanted to go to the TAMI show, but a few of my surf and car turf friends were willing to see the Stones and what 'that scene' was all about.

The tour was in support of The Rolling Stones, *Now!* album but the play list leaned heavily on the first LP, England's Newest Hitmakers. I was in the nose bleed section and the girls in the crowd just got louder and louder the longer the band played. I remember them playing *Not Fade Away*, *Walking The Dog*, *Time Is On My Side* and some Chuck Berry strutting before the band began to close it down with *I'm A King Bee* and wind up with *I'm Alright*. I also recall Otis Redding opening the show and giving an outstanding performance. He got a good response but the Stones gave a performance that no one could hear. They were drowned out by the crowd from the opening lines of *Not Fade Away*.

Tina McKiney *(age 13)*

I took my little sister, who was 10 at the time. We had to take the bus. I remember them trying to escape in their car. My sister was smashed up against one of the car windows. She got the best view. We laugh about it now, but at the time it was scary. It was just sheer pandemonium and chaos. We were lucky we didn't get injured. It was absolutely crazy. I wish I had a picture. I can still see her little face squished against the glass of the car window.

Kathleen Robb *(age 15)*

I sat in the front row at the 1964 concert. I was a sophomore in high school – tenth grade. One of my close friends Cecilia and I snuck out of her house in the middle of the night and walked to downtown Long Beach to camp out to buy tickets for their concert at the Long Beach Auditorium. She lived two to three miles away.

We had front row tickets. The auditorium was not large. We were left front. I think they may have started off with *Not Fade Away* because we were screaming our heads off. Mick used maracas. I remember him dancing from one side of the stage to the other. Brian Jones and Bill Wyman were right before our eyes and Charlie Watts was in the back on the drums. I had on white go-go boots. I took off one white boot and threw it on the stage and Brian held it up. We went crazy. Next thing I knew my friend Cecilia was on the stage hiding behind

Kathleen Robb

the curtain and peeking out. She was only ten feet from me. We got separated and after the concert she followed the Stones to the Long Beach airport and they signed my boot.

Later, my mom threw the boot out. It would probably be of value if I had it now. My brother, Kevin Gannon, was also at the concert and sat in the balcony level six rows back. He saw my boot go on the stage and he saw Cecilia on the stage. He said the opening act was Dick and Dee Dee. His ticket to the concert was $4.

3 NOVEMBER 1964
Public Hall, Cleveland, Ohio

George Shuba *(age 21)*

I was a freelance journalist in Cleveland. I worked for the newspapers and the radio stations. I'd just gotten out of the air force and my first gig was The Beatles. And they said "are you good?" and I said "I'm the greatest thing that ever happened to Cleveland, Ohio" and they said "ok, prove it to us" and "we want you to shoot The Beatles." My partner and I were in the air force together in the United States. I said to my partner Don "why the hell are we shooting bugs?" I didn't know who the hell The Beatles were. I was listening to Perry Como, the Four Lads, the Four Aces. People like that. I did not know who The Beatles were and I had to watch American television in order to find out.

When the Stones came in for their concert we were supposed to meet with them up in their room but we went up there with the disc jockey from the radio station which was WHK and they were too busy entertaining some young ladies so we never got the interview. But I did some shots with Mick and some with the group. I got maybe 30, 40 shots. I had the chance to be as close as a couple of feet. I didn't have any problems with them. And no negativity. They were very co-operative.

Sometimes I didn't understand what they were saying. Mick would say something and I would have him repeat something because I couldn't understand. I wasn't used to the language. The dialect, I should say, not the language. They were at the Public Hall which was the same venue as The Beatles played. The Beatles said "do not throw jelly beans at us because they could hurt us." So what the kids did was they got very inventive and took marshmallows. Now you cannot throw a marshmallow more than four feet, maybe five at the most. But if you put four or five jelly beans inside – now you've got a projectile! Anyhow, there was a balcony so that's what they did at the Stones show. What a good waste of marshmallows.

Shelley Hussey *(age 13)*

I was at the show along with my mom, who would have been 35, and my 12 year old friend Flora. We had missed The Beatles' first appearance in Cleveland that year, which in our minds was a horrendous and unforgiveable tragedy, but thought 'hey, the Stones are the next best thing.' So I convinced my mother to take us. Tickets were $4. We were there the second night of the Stones concerts at Public Hall.

During the first concert a teenage girl had fallen from the balcony with minor injuries. I was stunned to be part of what looked like just a handful of mostly pubescent girls in that 13,000 – 14,000 seat auditorium. There were roughly 800 of us there that night. I remember the DJ, Bob Friend of WHK Radio, inviting all of us to move up close to the stage. We were in Row 59 or 61. My girlfriend Flora and I cried, moaned, shrieked, and screamed at the top of our lungs throughout the entire

Shelley Hussey

"you put four or five jelly beans inside a marshmallow – now you've got a projectile!"

concert, but especially when Mick Jagger began singing his hits *Time Is On My Side* and *(I Can't Get No) Satisfaction*. I believe he was about 20 years old at the time and I tell you there was nothing better than seeing Mick Jagger at age 20!

Author's note: Records suggest that the Stones only played one show in Cleveland in 1964 and that the accident Shelley refers to happened at the concert she attended.

Returning to Britain the Rolling Stones fifth UK single, *Little Red Rooster*, was released on 19 November 1964. It would spend three weeks at Number One.

4 DECEMBER 1964
Fairfield Halls, Croydon

Keith Tapscott
Just before Christmas I saw them at Fairfield Halls, Croydon. By then my hair was even longer and I felt very proud when once again I was told I looked like Mick Jagger! I got there early in the afternoon and had to go the box office to collect my ticket. As I walked in I could hear them doing a sound check – but without Mick singing. It sounded strange to hear them live, crystal clear but without being dominated by screaming.

I was never a particularly over confident person and I didn't have the courage to try sneaking up the stairs to the theatre to watch them. I was frightened that I'd be caught and thrown out and not allowed to see them in the evening. I was seated quite close to the front and became a little unnerved as Mick stared at me several times in a disparaging way. Presumably he thought imitation was not the best form of flattery. Whilst they gave yet another excellent performance they were clearly tired and worn out.

> "he was about 20 years old at the time and I tell you there was nothing better than seeing Mick Jagger at age 20!"

Chapter 16

After gigging extensively around Britain in 1963 and 1964, performing over 300 times each year, 1965 was to be a slightly quieter year for the Rolling Stones but no less hectic for all that. The year was to see them perform more than 240 shows, of which barely 100 were in Britain. Australia, the USA and continental Europe were the focus of much of their live activity. Part of the reason for this was the success of *(I Can't Get No) Satisfaction*, which was released in the USA in June 1965 and reached Number 1 there in July, enjoying a 14 week run in the charts. It was to top the charts around the world. The Stones were undergoing their transformation into global stars.

8 JANUARY 1965
Savoy Theatre, Cork

Sean Gleeson *(age 15)*
I was working as a helper on a lorry at the time so I wasn't in Cork when the tickets went on sale at the Savoy during the week. When I did get a chance to buy a ticket, the 8pm show was sold out so I got one for the 5pm show. At the time I was disappointed as I really wanted to see the 8pm show. However things turned out better than I could have hoped. When I took my seat for the 5pm show only half the tickets had been sold – the Savoy was only about half full.

When I was shown to my seat it was an aisle seat in the front row right hand side so I was directly centre stage. There were about three people in the front row on the left hand side. The rest of the audience were seated throughout the theatre. I can remember the supporting acts – the Checkmates, Twinkle, who had a big hit at the time called Terry, and the Chessmen, who were one of the best Irish showbands. When the Stones

Sean Gleeson

came on the curtains opened to just a smattering of applause and went straight into their act. I can remember Mick Jagger using a pair of maracas and Brian Jones playing his Vox teardrop guitar and his Vox amp. He also used two harmonicas during the show and played slide guitar. Charlie Watts just sat behind them as if it was so easy playing drums and Bill Wyman stood there playing bass. It was then that I realised the audience could hear the music and instruments very clearly. There wasn't the usual screaming mayhem which accompanied a Stones concert at the time or indeed any concert by any of the top groups at the time. Any time I had seen the Stones on news clips all you could hear was screaming.

They played for thirty minutes. I can remember some of the songs – *Little Red Rooster*, *It's All Over Now*, *Around and Around*, *Off The Hook*. They were very, very good – Keith Richards and Brian Jones swapping guitar parts on songs, Brian Jones playing slide and letting his guitar hang from his shoulders when he played harmonica, Mick Jagger swapping the maracas for a tambourine, Bill Wyman holding his bass in an upright position and behind it all Charlie Watts keeping that incredible beat on the drums. They gave a great show. You could hear every instrument and song very clearly. It was amazing.

Olive O'Sullivan

I attended both performances. I even sat in the same seat in the front row for both shows. During the interval between the shows I went backstage and obtained all their autographs. A boy from the grammar school did an interview with them for his school magazine.

I remember my mother was in hospital waiting to have her gall stones removed – I found it funny that we were both concerned with 'our Stones'. The Stones were very nice to speak to – Mick offered me a Coke, when coke came in a bottle. It was Elvis' birthday and they played a tribute to him. The crowd were respectful and appreciated the music. I was on my own but enjoyed the evening as everyone was there for the same reason – to see their idols.

Joe O'Callaghan (age 16)

I was at the later concert. The Stones really knocked me out. I was in a band so I was very impressed by the harp playing of Brian and also his pear shaped guitar. In those days Mick was just throwing shapes – the running around came later. Keith crouching over his guitar licks was great. This was all new to us. The girls were screaming and one guy got up on the house organ in front of the stage. We left our seats and went up to get a better view. Twinkle had a song called Terry. She was a one hit wonder. She got mobbed after the show outside the Savoy. We had to run for the last bus home. We had school the next day.

Jean Kearney née McClement (age 12)

I was there with my friend Daphne. We were in for the 6pm show – given that we were only 12 at the time I suppose that explains why. Certainly they were more trusting times if our respective mothers had no issue allowing us go. The support acts included a young girl called Twinkle. My memory is that there weren't many at the 6pm gig, not more than 300. Daphne and I hid under the seats during the break and then stayed to enjoy the second show too – which had a big crowd, maybe even a capacity one.

Oonagh O'Hare (age 15)

Cork was a great venue because the Savoy was a two thousand or so seater. It was one of the big old art deco cinemas. And it could take big crowds. A lot of great bands came to Cork. The Kinks came. Pink Floyd came. Tom Jones came. The Bee Gees came. Big, big bands of the time came to Cork. We weren't the little backwater that people thought we were.

The changes that came at the time were very big. Ireland previous to that was show band music and boys on one side of the room and girls on the other. So this was quite a thing for these long haired guys to come to Cork.

Olive O'Sullivan

My parents were quite liberal and were okay about me going to see the Rolling Stones but I had to be home for nine o'clock. I saw the matinee, the afternoon show. There was no screaming and no shouting. There was screaming but not like The Beatles' thing where they couldn't be heard. It got treated like a movie because the ushers and usherettes in the cinema couldn't even stand up.

We were very near the front downstairs. My friend Jill Aitken bought a box of Milk Tray to throw at Mick Jagger and when she did we were almost thrown out. Jill said if we got this box of chocolates on stage they would see us and they would want to marry us because we were the coolest girls in the place. We were absolutely, totally convinced that if they saw us and if we got the box of chocolates onto the stage they'd think 'oh my God look at those girls' and want to marry us. But the chocolates went into the orchestra pit and we were almost thrown out. Not because we were being aggressive or anything but because we did actually stand up.

I'll always remember Charlie Watts came up to the front of the stage and announced a number. He got out from behind his kit and announced a number. And he was a big hit with the ladies. The drummers always are. My husband was there and I didn't even know him.

I remember I asked my mother if she would lend me some money for the ticket. I can't remember

Mícheál Ó Geallabháin

what I paid for the ticket. I think it was possibly five shillings (25p). My husband said it was twelve and six (63p) but that seems a lot of money for the time when the average wage was only about five pounds a week. When we made our confirmations as young girls in Ireland our long hair was cut to make us more frown up and our plaits were kept and I sold mine for the money. I sold my plaits to see the Stones.

Paul Gibbons *(age 24)*
I still have vivid memories of a fantastic concert. Cork's Savoy Theatre was really rocking on the night. The Stones gave a thrilling performance with their driving raucous sounds. The concert was a sit down one and I was seated in the top area of the theatre, an area known as The Gods because of the amount of steps to climb up to that area. I remember as well having to leave the concert before the end as I had arranged to meet my girlfriend Eileen (now my wife of 47 years) as she finished her evening shift at 10.45pm in Dunlops factory so I missed the finale of the show.

Mícheál Ó Geallabháin *(age 19)*
My ticket cost 12/6 (63p), the dearest in the house. The cheapest was five shillings (25p). The second house was full but it seems the first house had a lot of empty seats. One of the support acts was a group called the Gonks. At the end of the second house I saw the Stones manager Andrew Loog Oldham carrying the young singer in his arms and saying he

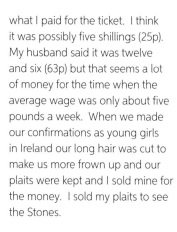

would never come back to Cork again. And he never did. Did he lose money on the concert? What screaming there was wasn't spontaneous – it seemed it was what you were supposed to do at a Stones concert.

They sang all their hits but at the beginning of the eighth song some people rushed down towards the stage, at which point the Stones disappeared and the concert ended. I felt a bit cheated at only hearing eight songs. I felt that those who rushed the stage were not acting spontaneously but had read in the papers that that was what was happening in England. The one who impressed me the most was Brian Jones. I thought his guitar playing was exquisite, while the bass player was very strong.

Greg Ahern (age 15)
The Rolling Stones played in Cork on a school night. In the Cork of 1965 at 15 years of age you were obliged to obey your parents – 'no going out on a school night' – so it was permission denied. I really wanted to go, and was trying to figure a way out, when the sound of a Volkswagen engine starting brought a glimmer of hope. A quick check out the window revealed that both parents were on board as it reversed out the drive!

Whether it was good fortune or fate, within 15 minutes I was outside the Savoy where a friend was waiting with a ticket, bless her. We joined the expectant throng and made our way inside. Rolling Stones here we come – I

would deal with the domestic consequences later. Sitting in the front row with all thoughts of homework forgotten, the anticipation was building. Then the emcee introduced a singer from England: Twinkle. The big red curtain went up and we beheld a vision – blonde hair, big eyelashes, dressed all in white. She sang of motorbikes and young love and as she called his name into the darkness "Terry...Terry..." the excitement of the night was taking hold and my sense of amazement at having transitioned from homework to biker angel in such a short time continued to grow. Are such things possible?

The evening was building. The emcee was doing his thing. The big red curtain went up and came down. We waited for the main event. Then there was noise and commotion from the stage behind the curtain where there was usually quietness. We felt the excitement. The music started. Rock and roll! "I'm gonna tell you how it's gonna be, you're gonna give your love to me." No emcee, no introduction, no curtain, no rules. The curtain was hastily raised and there they were – the Rolling Stones, Mick Jagger at the microphone, maracas in hand. This was amazing. The songs, the electric sound, the energy and the newness entranced us. The 'we don't give a shit how you judge us' attitude was palpable.

They played *Little Red Rooster*. *Satisfaction*. The concert rolled on. The songs merged one into the other. The electric guitars, the electricity of the band, the long

"and the newness entranced us. The 'we don't give a shit how you judge us' attitude was palpable"

hair, the wildness of the drums, the energy, movement and the face of Jagger as he ponced, gyrated and strutted the stage, alert, sensuous and edgy. It captivated us.

As the music filled the auditorium I looked up and around at the huge dark space and at the crowd, pumping and carried by the beat of this thumping rock band. I became uneasy with a vague sense of fear and guilt which I could not explain. I sensed, or imagined, something moving in the dark cavernous space, generated or invited in by the band – something dangerous, uncontrollable and unknown but known about. Then I became calmer when logic told me that 'they' could not see what was going on inside the building.

When it was over and we spilled out onto Patrick's Street we were buzzing and filled with the event. We were elated. We had never been at anything like it before. I bade goodbye to friends and headed home to face the (other) music. My run of good luck continued. The Beetle was not back home yet. What a night.

After this short Irish tour the Stones headed off on their first Australian tour.

25 JANUARY 1965
City Hall, Brisbane, Australia

Barbara Baker *(age 16)*
I remember Mick singing Heart of Stone and him lifting the microphone up when he sang

"never break, never break, never break – this heart of stone." It drove all of us girls into an absolute frenzy. I stood on my seat screaming my head off. I don't remember there being a hand held mic so Mick just took the microphone stand along with him.

10 FEBRUARY 1965
Palais Theatre, St Kilda, Melbourne, Australia

Trevor Searle *(age 15)*
I saw the Stones in 65 and 66 at the Palais in Melbourne. Great shows and, with the exception of Roy Orbison, they blew everyone off stage. Shows were short by later standards but for a 15 year old they were great. In 65 I had never heard She Said Yeah as it hadn't yet been released in Oz. Why can't they do this number again? I have seen every tour since then and thought the sound quality for the 14 On Fire tour was fantastic. Pity they played the same old warhorses though.

11 FEBRUARY 1965
Centennial Hall, Adelaide

Gus Howard *(age 17)*
I saw the Stones in a barn like place called Centennial Hall, where most visiting rock acts played. Brian played a white Vox Phantom lute-shaped guitar, a lovely looking thing. The Stones arrangements depended as much on hearing Brian's guitar voice as Keith's. They played Not Fade Away, Walking the Dog, Under the Boardwalk, Around and Around, Heart of Stone, Time Is On My Side and

It's All Over Now. I think the lead break on *Heart of Stone* was played by Brian. All these songs had strong air play in Australian cities. Everybody had the singles, and the same Chicago and delta blues material was being mined by many Australian bands.

The sound of the Stones was at that time not a lot different to many good generic bands of the time but the charisma and attitude was very powerfully delivered and that was it. Brian wore the 'look Ma' expression he often seem to display, but concentrated when he stepped up. In the whistle stop circumstances, they played really well.

The large crowd included the usual proportion of screaming young girls but there were also a lot of decidedly cool people there as well as many eagle eyed fretboard watchers. It was summer in Australia and the Stones wore clothes that were more California than London. The crowd was dressed pretty much the same.

13 FEBRUARY 1965
Capitol Theatre, Perth, Western Australia

Robert McGowan *(age 34)*
It was a Saturday. I was the head machinist at the theatre so I worked the three shows they played there that day. The first show started about 2.30pm, then 6pm and 9pm but I had to start work at 8am and did not finish until after midnight. The theatre held 2,300 people and was sold out for the three shows. This was the biggest theatre in Perth at this time.

Gus Howard

Chris Antill *(age 14)*
I went with my sister and brother. I was already very much into R&B and rock'n'roll. The Stones shared the bill with Roy Orbison and the Honeycombs. Roy just sat on his stool wearing his dark glasses and sang and was very cool, and received a huge ovation. The female drummer for the Honeycombs had been to the beach that day and had a very sunburnt bum. She had trouble sitting. The Stones were, as they say, not at their best that night and received a lukewarm reception. The word was that they were stoned. A lot of people booed.

Chris Lalor *(age 21)*
There were six of us. We all married the girls we took to the show and we are all still close friends, although one is now deceased. I still have the ticket butt. Sadly the Capitol theatre is long gone. There were seats but

Robert McGowan

most of the girls just went down to the front area and danced away. No drugs, no booze – just the music. The Stones were in full flight and Ray Columbus and the Invaders from New Zealand were the support act.

But I have to tell you that my gang went to the theatre primarily to see the Big O, who stole the show. Fancy that, the Stones and Orbison on the same bill in little old Perth in '65. It was a fantastic time for my generation's music – Elvis, Buddy Holly, Beatles et al. I tell my own boys, now 42 and 40, that they have pinched our music because they both still listen to all of the above.

Dave Perrie *(age 18)*

They played second to Roy Orbison. Also on the show were the Everly Brothers. A few days after Christmas 1999 we and 38 other families lost our homes in a fierce bushfire. I lost a huge collection of vinyl LPs and a lot of memorabilia including tickets, programmes, etc collected over many years including that from the 65 Stones concert.

Derek Bruins

I went to the first show, a Saturday afternoon matinee, with my first real girlfriend Lyn. I was playing in a band at the time called the Wanderers, so to go and see these superstars was the ultimate for a budding muso. We sat in the nosebleed seats up the top but that didn't matter much. If my memory serves me

well, the show was opened by the original Troubadours (Rick Selby, Peter Bull et al), followed by Ray Columbus and the Invaders. The Big O then came out. His stage presentation was uninspiring but when he sang that was forgotten. He did all the favourites and then just left the stage. Due to the fact they had just got off the plane and pretty much came straight to the theatre the Stones seemed to go through the motions, but at the time we didn't really care. As an aspiring guitarist, I wanted to see Keith Richards close up and he didn't disappoint. It was a great time in our lives in Perth, as not too may international acts came here because of the tyranny of distance.

Charles Brader *(age 19)*

I went with the company's social club. My memories of the gig are that the Rolling Stones were the warm up act for the main artist, who was Roy Orbison. I vividly remember Mick Jagger prancing about the stage doing *Little Red Rooster*. It was such a contrast

Charles Brader

to Roy Orbison, who just stood centre stage with his black suit and sun glasses, guitar in hand, singing *Pretty Woman*. Looking back, it seems amazing that I saw Roy the Boy and the Stones on the same bill.

Marlene Mayfield (age 18)
My girlfriend and I went along to see the Stones as the lead up act to the star of the show Roy Orbison. I recall they got a great ovation with fans wanting more. My friend and I sussed out the girls around us. The two in front who looked the wildest were in fact reasonably quiet during the show while the two behind us who looked so quiet just about blew out our eardrums with their constant screaming, proving one can't judge a book by its cover. It's quite incredible to think now that that we could see two fantastic entertainers on the one billing and that the Stones would actually be just the warm up to Roy Orbison.

Peter Roper (age 16)
I was there as a young mod with my high neck button down collar purple shirt, about 20 rows from the front. Everyone was 16 through to 20 years old. At the time I was with two girl friends and together we formed the main officers of the Gene Pitney Fan Club (Perth branch). The Capitol Theatre was a beautiful old building that was the venue for many of the Sixties acts of the time. The Rolling Stones and Roy Orbison on the same bill was an unusual combination. Two contrasting acts you couldn't

Peter Roper

believe would go together. Roy was supposedly the headline act. It couldn't have cost much as I was only earning seven pounds a week at the time.

Roy came on first, dressed in black and with the sunglasses of course, and was brilliant. The audience didn't move from their seats or make a sound as Roy sang. Everyone clapped each individual song, Crying being the standout. There was an interval and then, with everyone back in their seats and the theatre in darkness, the Stones got into their positions and opened with *Around and Around*. The teenagers swarmed the stage and lost control – a complete contrast to Roy. It was mayhem with all the noise. We got the sound of the songs and the riffs, but couldn't really hear the songs for the screaming.

We all congregated in the back alley after the show and pressed up against the windows of the limo transporting the group away to their hotel. A great night for young teenagers. No drugs around and no violence.

Rae Porter

Rae Porter *(age 15)*

I attended with my 20 year old sister. There were several Australian bands playing for the first half of the show and then there was an interval. I can remember coming back after the interval and Roy Orbison was already singing as people returned to their seats. I remember how small he looked. The thing I remember most about the Stones was how blond Brian Jones' hair was. He was always my favourite.

Vicki Brown *(age 15)*

It was the first pop concert I had ever been to and a group of school friends went together – all girls. We didn't dress in anything special, just our goodish clothes. We probably were not too trendy at all. I was surprised that everyone screamed as soon as the Stones came on stage. That was certainly something I hadn't expected. Also, girls started to cry and I found that a surprise too. I was also amazed that everyone stood on their seats and proceeded to jump up and down and break the seats throughout the whole show. I had never seen anything like that in my sheltered life. We had to stand on the seats too so we could see, but I hasten to add we didn't break ours! It was a really good show with all the favourite songs from those days and we were all picked up by our parents afterwards.

Christine Wansborough *(age 29)*

I was seven months' pregnant with my daughter. I went with my husband Philip. We sat up in the gods, which was the third level of the Capitol Theatre. I walked up all those stairs – it's a wonder I didn't have my daughter that night! I still remember Mick Jagger singing *Walking The Dog*.

Kevin Curnow

I lived in a country town and it was while visiting my fiancée in Perth that I *heard I Wanna Be Your Man* on the radio. I was blown away. This was totally new to me. I was shell shocked. My girlfriend at the time said "oh that is the Rolling Stones?" like it didn't have any importance. We broke up later.

I, like others, was swept up in the fervour that was in the capital of Perth at that time. It seemed like every young man wanted to be a Brian Jones look alike. Clubs in Perth for all things R&B and just plain blues were springing up everywhere. Perth was becoming an exciting place. Then came the news that the Stones were coming to Perth. There was no way I was going to miss this concert. Tickets were going to be sold to country areas first. I wanted to buy two but my girlfriend's mother would not allow me to take her away for the weekend. I have no idea why she didn't trust me!

The local radio station started playing more Stones and Beatles and other Sixties music than ever before. I knew I could not afford to be late, so I was dressed in my suit before I left. Sure enough I was the only one there in a suit. If you know what its like in Oz in February it's bloody murder driving for six hours and 400 miles with no air conditioning in your car in a suit. But I was going to see the Stones.

I arrived at the Capitol Theatre for the second show with just ten minutes to spare. I was offered a programme at the door but didn't buy one. I just wanted to be seated and relaxed for the show. I got my seat just six rows from the front, slightly left of centre – perfect!

Security was lined up shoulder to shoulder across the front of the stage and I thought about shows of the Stones I had read about in the paper. We didn't have TV where I lived. A local support band kicked things off. I forget who they were but they were not too bad. Roy Orbison kicked off the second half of the show and I became embarrassed. He never finished his set because the girls were screaming "we want the Stones" while he was performing. He gave up and gave over to the Stones.

When things got organised, the emcee informed the audience very forcefully that if any person left their seat and entered the aisles the show would be shutdown. And there was enough security there to see it shutdown. He left the stage and the Stones began to play *Everybody Needs Somebody To Love* as the curtain went up. The girls went berserk screaming. The band sounded perfect. I could not believe the adrenalin I felt. At one point Charlie got to announce the next song. No one could understand a word he said.

Then there was a slight break in the performance and I took a chance and yelled out "*Empty Heart*!" Mick replied "steady on, mate" not knowing, of course, who yelled it. After another couple of numbers, Mick turned towards Brian and Bill, said a few words and then they played *Empty Heart*. I could not believe it. Then the show was over and it was time to leave. Security was moving up from the front to clear everyone. I said to one security guard "how about letting me through to back stage as I have just travelled 400 miles to see them?" His reply was "you now have 400 miles to go home."

I had parked the car next door in an underground car park. When I got to my car I noticed there was an open door at the bottom of some stairs. Could this be a fire escape for the Embassy Ballroom which was between the car park and the Capitol Theatre? I took a chance and went up some stairs and a couple of passage ways. There were a few doors leading off it. I don't know what the door was that someone opened – maybe a toilet – but the person who opened it was Brian Jones. "Fuck," I said, "thanks for the great show." He said "glad you liked it." He was a bit stand-offish. I can't blame him. He must have thought I was a weirdo. At that moment a bloke too big to argue with came around the corner and I turned and left. He must have thought I was official as I had my suit on.

Kevin Curnow

On 1 April 1964, The Rolling Stones performed at the Locarno Ballroom, Stevenage, UK.

Right-hand page: Parr Hall, Warrington, UK, 25 November 1963

Brian Lawton

Brian Lawton

Laurie Stead interviews Brian Jones (above), Mick Jagger (above right), Bill Wyman (right), Keith Richards (below) and Charlie Watts (below right) 10 March 1965 backstage of the Huddersfield ABC, Huddersfield, UK.

Brian Lawton

Brian Lawton

Brian Lawton

DJ Dick Smith (behind Mick Jagger) in the Stones' dressing room at the Worcester Memorial Auditorium, Worcester, Mass. USA, on 30 April 1965.

The band on stage at the Worcester Memorial Auditorium, Worcester, Mass, USA, 30 April 1965.

*Above and right,
on stage at the
Worcester Memorial
Auditorium,
Worcester, Mass.
USA concert, 30 April
1965.*

*Brian Jones
performing at the
Convention Hall,
Philadelphia, USA on
6 November 1965.*

194

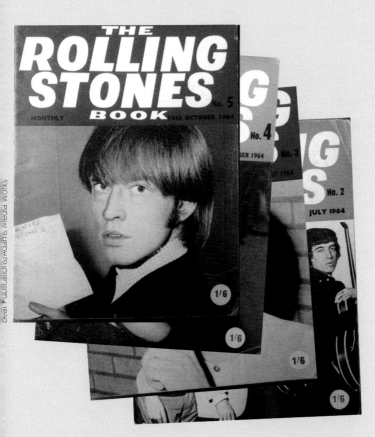

The Rolling Stones Book, the official fan magazine, appeared monthly from June 1964 and ran to 30 editions. It was produced by Beat Publications who also published The Beatles Book.

An ad for The Rolling Stones Book from the programme for the 1965 tour.

Also from the 1965 tour programme is this ad for Vox equipment.

BEAT CITY 79 OXFORD STREET, LONDON, W.1
FRIDAY, JULY 17th - 7.30 p.m.
THE TOMCATS and SUPPORTING GROUP
MEMBERS 5/- GUESTS 6/6
SATURDAY, JULY 18th - 7.30 p.m.
THE ROLLING STONES
ONLY LONDON CLUB DATE
SUNDAY, JULY 19th - 7.30 p.m.
JOHN MAYALL'S BLUES BREAKERS & THE REDCAPS
MEMBERS 6/6 GUESTS 8/- MEMBERSHIP 10/6
THE GREATEST BEAT CLUB IN THE WORLD

ODEON TELEPHONE 4881
ON THE STAGE
THURSDAY, FEBRUARY 20
6.15 : 8.45
ALL STARS '64
JOHN LEYTON ★ MIKE SARNE
The Swinging BLUE JEANS
THE ROLLING STONES
Mike Berry : Billie Davis
JET HARRIS
9/6 : 8/6 : 7/6 : 6/6 : 5/6
Now and Avoid disappointment.
Don't miss this Terrific Show! Book

KLIV presents
★ **IN CONCERT** ★
THE FABULOUS
ROLLING STONES
SHOW
SAT. DEC. 4
2 SHOWS - 7:00 and 9:30 P.M.
CIVIC AUD.
SAN JOSE
TICKETS: $5.50, 4.50, 3.50 - All Seats Reserved
Tickets On Sale:
San Jose Box Office — [St. Claire Hotel]
LOCKHEED **SHERMAN - CLAY, Oakland**

Kidderminster BIG BEAT **Sessions**
TOWN HALL
'IT'S A CRAZY WORLD' WITH
THURS.
MAR 5th **MARTY WILDE**
AND THE
WILDCATS
ENGLAND'S FIRST AMERICAN CHART TOPPERS
THURS.
MAR 12th **TORNADOS**
PLEASE NOTE FOR ONE WEEK ONLY
WE ARE OPEN ON A
Friday, March 20th.
WITH
THE EAGLES
The Fabulous
THURS.
MAR 26th **ROLLING STONES**
Our apologies for the rather high price, but
these fabulous Artists command fantastic fees. Adm 8/6
7.30-10.45 p.m. Adm 4/0
(Except March 26th)
2 GROUPS AT EVERY SESSION

*This and facing page,
fliers, posters, press
advertisements and
tickets.*

Tonight ARTHUR KIMBRELL 6.15 & 8.40
presents
THE ROLLING STONES
PETER JAY and the JAYWALKERS
PLUS TREMENDOUS ALL-STAR SUPPORTING ACTS!

HIPPODROME - BRIGHTON
8.00 **SUNDAY JULY 19** 8.30
ERIC EASTON presents
THE SENSATIONAL
ROLLING STONES
THE ECHOES | **KEVIN SCOTT** and The KINSMEN
PYE RECORDING STAR **JULIE GRANT**
MARTY WILDE and The WILDCATS | **KENNY LYNCH**
Prices: 12/6 10/6 7/6

A selection from Bob Lee's 1964 diary.

"OASIS"
The Rolling Stones
Plus
THE CRESTAS

PASS-OUT   30th. AUGUST 1963

G 29
Bristol Corporation
Colston Hall
SUNDAY
MAY 10th.
2nd House 7.45
Balcony
10/6
To be retained

WINTER GARDENS
BOURNEMOUTH
SATURDAY
FEBRUARY 22
8.30 p.m.
STALLS 10/6
JOHN LEYTON and ALL STAR SHOW
B 31 B 31

F 16 37
SEC.   ROW   SEAT
RESERVED $6.00
HOLLYWOOD BOWL
MON. EVE. JULY 25, 1966

209 D
SEC.   ROW
BALCONY $5.50
SAN JOSE CIVIC AUD.
1st SHOW
SAT. EVE.
DEC 4

34 J 4
SEC.   ROW   SEAT
ARENA $2.50
WASHINGTON COLISEUM
GOOD ONLY
SAT. AFT.
NOV. 13
ARGUS-SIMPLEX-
BROWN, INC., N.Y.C.

Enter Hall
by Door
City (Oval) Hall, Sheffield
ERIC EASTON presents
D **THE ROLLING
STONES SHOW**
Thursday, 11th March, 1965
SECOND HOUSE
8.50 p.m.
Doors open at 8.30 p.m.
STALLS, 8/6
(Front Entrance)
SEAT   No. 1
Row R

WORCESTER MEMORIAL AUDITORIUM
GOOD ONLY
FRIDAY EVE.
APRIL
30
1965
J 1
ORCHESTRA

RR 12
ORCHESTRA
Worcester Memorial Auditorium
WORCESTER, MASS.
Fri. Eve. at 8:00
APRIL
**ROLLING STONES
SHOW**
30
Presented By
D-B Enterprises
1965
Est. Pr. $2.82
Fed. Tax .18 Total $3.00
GLOBE TICKET COMPANY

RR 12
ORCHESTRA
WORCESTER MEMORIAL AUDITORIUM
GOOD ONLY
FRIDAY EVE.
APRIL
30
1965

APRIL, 1964
Saturday 18
Went to town in Kens car with Mike and Dave to buy tickets for the Rolling Stones show at the palace on May 3rd. Went to Speedway to see the Aces against Oxford had a bath Later Mike came.
R S

MAY, 1964
Rogation
Sunday
Sunday 3
The Rolling Stones were on Big Beat '64 Went to the palace (thr) to see them Live wich proved to be went one of the most exiting nights in my Life Met two girls called Paulinne and tina.

SEPTEMBER, 1964
Friday 11
Bought a ticket for the Rolling Stones show this time for the second show wich I will be going Twice Went in the Plaza in the Rest of my Dinner Hoar. Went to my Grandmas Strait from work for my tea and a Bath. Wait...

SEPTEMBER, 1964
Tuesday 15
Went to the fantastic Rolling Stones show twice Both house's also on the Show were Inez and Charlie Fox the Mojos and Mike Berry and the Inuccents. Inbetween shows I got beat up by a Copper.

Programme cover from the 1964 UK tour. The same design was frequently used with just the background colour changed. This one is from the de Montfort Hall, Leicester, UK, concert, 26 January 1964.

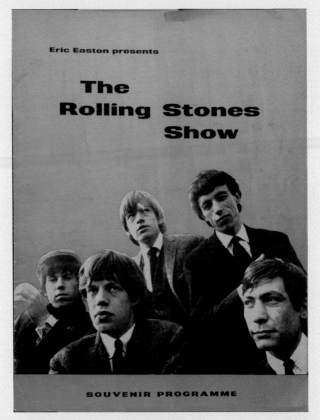

Autographed programme from the 1964 concert tour.

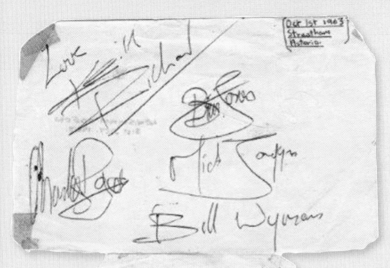

Memorabilia collected by Susan McLaren.

The Rolling Stones signed autographs on whatever came to hand.

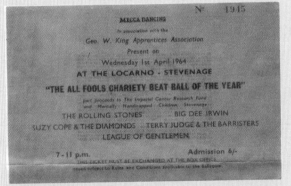

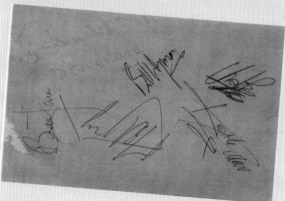

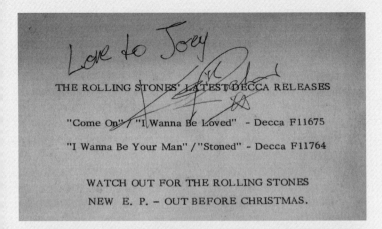

Love to Joey

THE ROLLING STONES' LATEST DECCA RELEASES

"Come On" / "I Wanna Be Loved" - Decca F11675

"I Wanna Be Your Man" / "Stoned" - Decca F11764

WATCH OUT FOR THE ROLLING STONES
NEW E. P. – OUT BEFORE CHRISTMAS.

© Leicester Mercury

Fans mob the Stones' car at the de Montfort Hall, Leicester, UK concert, 26 January 1964.

ROLLING.STONES

On April 30, 1965, the Rolling Stones rolled into Worcester. Girls and boys of all ages came to see Englands number 1, rock'n roll group. Many brought cookies, flowers and cakes, One girl brought a twenty five dollar cake, 1 foot by 2feet with the inscription " We Love You Charlie " on it. When she arrived with the cake at the stage door, the policeman would not permitt her backstage. She burst into tears and ran into the ladies room.

While she was in there the Rolling Stones walked in . They waved to us as we were the only girls there. We took fast pictures and got a few photographs. Just as the excitement was over and the Rolling Stones were well backstage the girl came out from the ladies room.

When we told her they had just walked through, she started crying again.

The Rolling Stones performed for twenty three minuites in front of 3,500 Worcester and Framingham teen-agers.Fans threw articles such as confetti, flash bulb, money and other such things. Mick Jagger,the lead singer, attempted to come down off the stage to arouse his fans, but one policeman pushed him back on the stage. Many girls burst into tears and hysterics at the sight of their idols. But in all the fans behaved well.

After the show was over, the Rolling Stones emerged from the same door they entered. Many fans saw their idols and tried to get at them. But the Rolling Stones fled into the limousines, and were on their way.

The Rolling Stones are far from being ugly and untalented. They're fab!

THE EDITORS:

JOANNA GICAS

BEVERLY ST.THOMAS

Review of the 30 April 1965 concert at the Memorial Auditorium, Worcester, Mass. USA, from a Freshman Newsletter by Beverley St. Thomas and Joanna Gicas.

Chapter 17

After shows in Australia, New Zealand and Singapore the Stones began another UK tour in March 1965. This tour, with the Stones headlining supported by Dave Berry and the Cruisers and The Hollies, coincided with the release of *The Last Time* which was to become their third British Number One single.

6 MARCH 1965
Empire Theatre, Liverpool

Trefor Jones
I was living in Ellesmere Port so a bit nearer to Liverpool than I had been the previous year when I'd seen them. The Stones were now more popular. I sent for two tickets and took my girlfriend Beth but we had to sit high up in the gods at the back of the Empire because the best tickets were gone. We counted ourselves lucky to be there. On arriving at the Empire there were hundreds of fans gathered outside, guys selling posters of the Stones and girls galore! After this, every time the Stones were due to do a show nearby and someone said "are you going?" I would say "nah, I've seen them twice already." The songs that seemed to stand out from this show were *It's Alright* and *Everybody Needs Somebody To Love* but the screaming girls spoilt a lot of them.

7 MARCH 1965
Palace Theatre, Manchester

Christine McDermott *(age 13)*
I had a seat in the stalls – seat C6 – for this show. Like most groups, when the Stones were in Manchester they used to appear on the Granada early evening TV programme. It was an easy bus ride from school down to the city centre and over to the Granada studios on Quay Street. One time as they came out in their car we chased it up to the traffic lights which as luck would have it were on red. Amazingly they had the rear off side window down and I launched myself through it and got Keith Richards', Brian Jones', Charlie Watts' and Bill Wyman's autographs. Mick was driving so I didn't get his. When the lights changed the car drove off and turned right with me still half in, half out of the window. Mick pulled over and let me out and off they drove.

June Lomas *(age 20)*
I worked at the Blood Transfusion Service as a nurse. My three friends and I worked late and went straight to the Palace in our uniforms. Our seats were in the circle at the front. Dave Berry was first on and sang the *Crying Game*. The noise was deafening then. When the Stones including Brian Jones came on it was impossible to hear anything for the constant screaming. The girls were climbing onto the stage and were being thrown off the stage by the dozen by the bouncers. After several attempts the Stones finally started to perform but it was mayhem with girls screaming and fainting. Then to my shock a girl came running past me, stood on the balcony in front of

me and then launched herself off shouting "Mick!" People expected us as nurses to help her but we were unable to get down to her because of the crowds. I read in the paper the following day that she only received minor injuries. She was so lucky! Despite all the drama and hardly being able to hear, it was still a great night and one I won't forget.

Jean Walker

We found out they were staying at the Plaza in Piccadilly. So hundreds of us ran to Piccadilly and they came on to the balcony at the Plaza Hotel waving at all us screaming girls. My boyfriend wasn't too pleased but did I care? No way! Best years of my life.

Penny Whitney (age 15)

I went to the first performance, at 6pm, and paid nine shillings (45p) to go in the circle. We went by train from Knutsford to Manchester. I have no idea how I came by the tickets. My brother Richard said he remembers going to a Stones concert with The Hollies supporting them and says he queued all night for tickets. I found that hard to believe as he'd only have been 14, but maybe he was with some 15 year old friends. It's difficult to imagine parents letting that happen. A few of us went. Mel and I had boyfriends in tow who were not Stones fans, and my brother and Mel's brother were with us too. I was wearing a light grey flannel skirt and knee high white socks with red and black stripes round the top over American tan tights and my navy

leather three quarter coat. Dead cool – I followed fashion in Honey magazine! My stand-out memory of the concert was Goldie and the Gingerbreads singing *Baby, baby, can't you hear my heartbeat?* They were wearing light blue satin bell bottoms. I cannot remember anything specific about the Stones themselves other than that it was great to be there. They'd only had a couple of albums at that stage and were only on stage for a short time as there were about half a dozen supporting acts each time. I don't recall them being drowned out by screaming a la The Beatles. That evening Mel's father Ted Phibbs, who owned the Highway Garage in Knutsford, collected us after the concert in a Dormobile and drove us home.

Martin Riley (age 17)

I think some of this concert featured on the Stones EP *Got Live If You Want It*. I went on my own to see them and I had an upstairs seat. I remember the support acts as it was a package tour. Goldie & the Gingerbreads were an all women band which was unusual at the time and they had a hit record out. The Hollies had Graham Nash in the line up. I remember Dave Berry & the Cruisers slowly coming out on to a pitch black stage with guitarist Frank White using a white double necked Gibson guitar which he had specially ordered from America. You could not hear the Stones because of the screaming going on. I came out onto Oxford Street afterwards deaf because of this!

> "I was wearing a light grey flannel skirt and knee high white socks with red and black stripes round the top over American tan tights … dead cool"

9 MARCH 1965
Odeon Theatre, Sunderland

Gill Dodd *(age 17)*
I worked at the Odeon. I was working my week's notice as I had another job to start. The next day when I went to work I was given a minute's notice because the boss said I had just stood watching the Stones all night. It was worth it though because they were brill – they had just found out that *The Last Time* had gone to the top of the charts.

The supporting cast were the Hollies, Dave Berry and Goldie and the Gingerbreads. I was an usherette but that night I was selling ices from a tray at the intervals as you did then. I remember on the afternoon the Stones were on The Hollies were walking up the rink passage which was not to be used by the public. The manager told me to stop them from coming in that way. They waved to me as they passed and I just stood there and couldn't say a word. I think that was one of the few times I saw Mr Ray the manager smile.

10 MARCH 1965
ABC Theatre (aka The Ritz), Huddersfield

Jenifer Taylor
I remember very well going to the Ritz, sometimes to see the concert and often just to hang around the back doors with my friends to see if we could get to see the stars. We did see quite a few this way but more often than not we handed our autograph books

over and they came back out with signatures in them. I still have my autograph book. I was lucky enough to see The Beatles, Cliff Richard and the Shadows, Adam Faith, the Bachelors, Dave Berry and many more.

I was still at school during this period of pop history and, because tickets went on sale early on a given day, I remember the queues starting the day before, certainly for the Stones and The Beatles. So to make sure we had a place in the queue for the Rolling Stones tickets we set up a rota system from our school, Huddersfield High School at Salendine Nook, whereby those of us who had free periods in classes would go into town on the bus and hold the place in the queue and then they would be replaced at regular intervals by other girls when they had to be back at school. It worked fine, and all this long before we had mobile phones.

Of course, when the doors opened on the morning of the sale, it was a free-for-all and the orderly queue nearly turned into a rugby scrum. I remember they opened all the doors across the front of the Ritz and there were then many queues instead of just the one for ticket sales. A bit dumb we thought at the time.

In the end I missed out on the Stones concert because both my best friend and I got the measles two days before. We were gutted. I remember pleading with my mum from my sick bed to let me go but to no avail. It was probably the right decision considering but I never have seen them despite being a huge fan in those early

"in the end I missed out on the Stones concert because both my best friend and I got the measles"

days, with pictures all over my bedroom walls and ceiling. My mum did take our tickets down to the Ritz to sell them back, however. I don't know how she managed it but I guess that there would still be plenty of kids wanting tickets.

Paul Rayner *(age 14)*

In those days you were either Beatles or Stones. I was always Stones right from the first chords of Come On. My brother's girlfriend worked for the local council and she got me a ticket from work so no queue. Only one ticket so I was alone, surrounded by teenage girls. Wow! I got all their records up to Exile but for me they were never the same after '69 when we lost Brian.

Laurie Stead

I was backstage at the ABC interviewing them all, plus Dave Berry. It's a long time ago and as it was such a daunting experience – I was very new to interviewing then – any memory of the event is difficult to recall, such was the madness backstage. But I have the proof of doing the interviews in the photos a friend took of us. There is

no photo of the group all together, but they are of me interviewing them individually. *(see p 000)*

Jenny Maskell *(age 17)*

I went with my mother who was only 35 and a great fan. My father couldn't understand why we liked them but we did, having previously seen The Beatles there as well. We queued all night for good tickets and again my father wasn't impressed. We had front row seats in the circle but it was so noisy we didn't know if they were actually singing or not! We were there though and that was important to us even just to see them. I have never forgotten that night.

Grahame Nasey *(age 13)*

I attended the evening concert with my 65 year old grandma. I attended several other concerts with my gran and this was the best. At the very least we heard some of the music – at The Beatles it was drowned out by the screaming. I had Stones records and the way they belted them out was great stuff. We had a great night and returned home on the number 60 bus to Crosland Moor where we both lived and had fish and chips in the paper from Gibson's shop at Park Road. I have two original official programmes from the concert. One of them has the autographs of all the Stones including Brian Jones. My uncle, Denis Morris, had a local group at the time called Denny and the Witchdoctors. Uncle Denny managed to get back stage and got the programme signed.

Paul Rayner

Brian Lawton

Laurie Stead (right) interviews Dave Berry

Angela Batty *(age 13)*

I went along with my 14 year old cousin Susan and my sister Judith, aged 11. The tickets cost ten shillings and sixpence (53p) and the seats were up in the circle. I just could not believe all these famous people I had only seen on television were actually on stage before my eyes. Of course when the Rolling Stones came on the place just erupted. Everyone began screaming. I had never done this before but I joined in with the rest of them and the next day I could hardly talk. Oh but what a night! The atmosphere and excitement were just something you had to be there to experience. A memory I will never forget is that after the show we ran to the back of the building shouting for Mick and he opened the window and sat for a while talking, laughing and shouting down to the crowd. He was really nice and he had a lovely brown corduroy jacket on, which I thought was fab. There was also a small window at the back of the theatre which my cousin said my sister, being small, would be able to climb in so we hoisted her up. But a man shouted to us to get down so that plan was foiled!

11 MARCH 1965
City Hall, Sheffield

Carol Owen, *(age 16)* and Barbara Sykes *(age 17)*

Our dad was commissionaire at the City Hall. We used to get into concerts for free. We used to go straight from school. It used to start at 6.20pm. We saw every

pop group possible. For a good five years we were going to City Hall once a month or maybe twice a month. At City Hall they had seats on the stage so we had to sit on the front seats and behave and when our dad wasn't looking we would scream. When we saw the Stones we were sat on the stage. And they'd turn round and sing to you and wave and things. Because we were young girls as well they weren't really interested in us as such.

There was screaming from the start of the show to the finish. So Dad managed to get us into the dressing room with the Rolling Stones. They were smoking and drinking and, with our Dad being the commissionaire, he said "come on hurry up and get out girls" because he didn't want us to be a nuisance to them. They would be smoking and drinking and "yes, you can have our autographs." They signed autograph books for us. They were friendly enough. We liked Brian Jones best. Better than Mick Jagger! When we came out of the show our ears were buzzing from the noise of all the screaming.

14 MARCH 1965
Odeon Theatre, Rochester

Chris Walledge *(age 16)*

My friend's father was the manager so we got in the back circle for free. Goldie and the Gingerbreads were one of the supports. We were sick of the girls screaming out to the male acts. So I shouted out in a high pitched voice "we love you,

Barbara Sykes

Goldie!" To two teenage boys that was funny at the time. The other memory I have was when the Stones appeared. I heard the intro to *Satisfaction* but then the screaming drowned out every note and every word for the remainder of the show. It was like watching TV with the sound turned off so I was glad I hadn't paid. Later I met a girl I knew who was in raptures because she'd seen Mick Jagger going in the back door so had rushed up and touched him on the side! I was completely underwhelmed.

Diane Merrick *(age 12)*
I went with my best school friend Lynne Butler. We walked to the theatre as there was no extra money after buying the tickets. We sat downstairs in the stalls and my friend and most of the audience spent the time standing and screaming at the Stones. Eventually I had to join the throng. It was a really great evening and amazing that, at the tender of age of 12, I was able to see such an upwardly famous group.

Margaret Madge *née Grace* (age 16)
I saw the evening show. I had not long started working for Sainsburys. They had organised the tickets. I went with my older sister Susan who was 17 and cousin Anthea, who was 16. We really enjoyed the evening. It was the first live show we had ever seen. I really loved Brian Jones and was very sad when he died. The best song was *The Last Time*. I don't think we realised they

would still be performing 50 years on as we saw them run down the steps of the Odeon and climb into a really scruffy old van. Of all the shows I have seen since that one sticks in the mind.

After their fifth UK tour, the Stones played shows in Europe, Canada and America.

16 – 18 APRIL 1965
L'Olympia, Paris, France

Stash Klossowski de Rola
I was playing with a guy called Vince Taylor. Vince Taylor was the inspiration for Ziggy Stardust for David Bowie. He was a black leather rocker and he was rather fantastic. He had this hit called Brand New Cadillac which The Clash and so many other bands have covered. I was in his band from '64 onwards. The first Rolling Stone I met was Charlie Watts who came to Paris to be with our drummer who was a very famous guy called Bobbie Woodman Clarke who had played with all the early greats. The likes of Billy Fury and so on. He was the first person to play double bass drums in rock'n'roll. People like Ringo and Charlie very much respected him as a drummer and Charlie came and spent a night partying with us. So I'd met him before. But he was the only one I'd had some acquaintance with.

We were absolute rivals with the Stones in a battle of the bands. We played the Easter weekend of 1965 against them, as it were – with them and against them. And their fans took to us

Diane Merrick

"that was funny because it would take about a second for people to realise that the Stones are actually right up close and had just walked by them"

like fish to water. We had a very sexy show and we were a great, great live band. A very good visual presentation. It wasn't just standing around singing and playing songs. It was a very dynamic sort of thing. We were able to do our entire act just like the Stones. Then there would be an intermission and the Stones came on.

We started on Good Friday and we ended up on Easter Monday having done all these different shows including, on Easter Sunday, a matinee. You can imagine how much interaction there was. The first gig we did with them they stood in the wings watching us like hawks and as we came off we were drenched with sweat. Mick Jagger tartly asked Vince Taylor "you been on?" "No, no. We've been rehearsing." And he blew right past him and we just smirked at them and walked on. Their fans were totally besotted with us. Young girls and so on. The Stones in those days – they only did twenty minutes. We did twenty minutes and they did twenty minutes. We often reminisced with Keith about those good old days when you could get away with doing just twenty minutes.

Any garage band now has almost better equipment in terms of amplification that was available in those days. The PAs were especially poor. The returns were non existent. All these kids who missed seeing Brian on stage, for the most part they would have been terribly disappointed because you couldn't hear anything. In Paris you could

to some extent and we certainly could hear them very well. The Beatles found it impossible and gave up touring because it was so bad with the screaming. It was quite exciting but musically speaking it wasn't much of an experience because you couldn't hear what the other people were playing and it was very hard to know where you were at. So the live gigs were exciting in a way but they also lacked a great part of the professionalism that is required today on the stage.

Dominic Lamblin
The second time they came to Paris they were very massive. They were doing three nights so they stayed longer obviously and we spent even more time together and we had a very good relationship.

In 1965 we were giving up the idea of entering the Olympia through the backstage entrance because it was so crowded. The fans knew about this entrance just like in London everybody knows where the backstage entrance for the Palladium or the Roundhouse or other concert halls is. So what we would do is we would wait for the show to start and wait for the supporting artists to be on stage, when everything was dark in the theatre. And then we would walk through the main entrance around through the Olympia and go to the door closest to the stage where you can access the backstage. That was funny because it would take about a second for people to realise that the Stones are actually right up close and had just walked by them or run by them so they'd be excitement but it was too late because we had already disappeared backstage. It was pretty funny to see the crowd reaction.

In 1965 we went for a sound check in the paddy wagon and when the sound check was finished we found out that there was no police car to take us back to the hotel and there were 200 kids around the entrance. So I told them "you know, the only way out we can get out of here that I can think of is my car is parked right across the street." It was a Simca 1000. "I think I'll get it out." And the minute I parked in front of the entrance I just revved, starting my car, and we just drove away. There was myself driving and the five Stones crammed in the Simca 1000 which is basically built for four people. It was pretty exciting.

I'd see them every time they'd come to Paris to visit. I would spend time with Brian when he was coming over to see a couple of girlfriends in Paris. He'd be coming to Paris pretty often. Same thing with Keith. All of them would come to Paris. We all know the aim of every Englishman is to finish his life in France, or to retire in France. Especially in the south of France. Keith owns a place. Mick owns a place. I think Bill sold his house in the south of France. And Charlie I'm not sure. I'm not sure if Charlie still has a place.

I kept on working with them. I was the head of Rolling Stones Records in France in the Seventies. When they signed with Atlantic Records in 1971 there was a provision in the contract that

in each of the major territories they should have their own label manager and so they said "well, in France why don't you hire Dominic? Because we've known him six or seven years and we've always worked well with him."

29 APRIL 1965
Palace Theater, Albany

Scott Miner
I was a sophomore at Niskayuna High School. It was afternoon and I was home from school but we hadn't had dinner yet. The phone rang and it was my best friend Jeff. "Hey Scott, you wanna go see the Rolling Stones?" "What? Are you kidding? Hell yeah!" That was my first reaction, quickly followed by the thought that my mother would never let me go. Jeff and I had managed to get into enough trouble together during our freshman year to last ten lifetimes. At one point I was forbidden to hang around him, which only made it more inevitable that I

Scott Miner

would. "Hang on man, let me ask." I turned with the phone in my hand to ask my mother who was standing at the kitchen sink washing vegetables for dinner. To my shock she agreed with a minimum of explaining, just wanting to be sure that Jeff's mother would be driving us. I quickly told Jeff I could go and within minutes was streaking down the street to his house three blocks away. This was during the wave of English bands in the early Sixties that would be known as the British Invasion. After The Beatles had played on the Ed Sullivan Show, it seemed like everybody was washing the Brylcreem out of their hair and forming rock bands. Anything and everything English was totally cool, and the Rolling Stones were right behind The Beatles in popularity.

I wasn't Jeff's first choice to go. He had asked a girl named Denise to go with him, but I found out just a few months ago when I spoke to Denise for the first time in 50+ years she was grounded. Her loss – my gain! I could hardly contain my excitement on the ride to the Palace. Jeff's mother dropped us off at the entrance with instructions to call her when the concert was over. We bolted out of the car into a loud animated crowd of teenagers hanging around the closed doors waiting admittance. The doors soon opened and the crowd surged inside. We managed not to get trampled as we fought our way up to the balcony. We had just gotten settled in our seats

"it was only by listening to the guitars that I knew what songs were being played"

when the emcee announced the first of the opening acts, a local band called the Sundowners. They opened with a cover of The Beatles' *Ticket To Ride* and the screaming began!

Everywhere were girls with teased black bouffant hairdos that resembled the Ronettes. Girls didn't look like that in our high school! This was heady stuff for a couple of suburban kids from Niskayuna. The Sundowners played several excellent cover songs popular on the radio before giving way to the second opening act, another local band called Buddy Randell and the Knickerbockers. They had a radio hit called Lies that sounded a lot like The Beatles, which didn't hurt airplay at all. They played several songs, all to screaming girls, before the emcee came back onstage to announce "the Rolling Stones!" It was non stop shrieking after that.

The Stones were dressed similar to their photo on the cover of the greatest hits LP High Tide and Green Grass. The screaming was so loud I could barely hear Mick Jagger's vocals and it was only by listening to the guitars that I knew what songs were being played. It didn't matter, though. There onstage were my long haired heroes – the Rolling Stones!

I noticed that many of the guys in the audience were throwing pennies at the stage. Not knowing why – this was my first concert after all – I found a few in my pockets and threw them as well but I'm sure that with my weak arm strength and the distance to the stage I didn't put Mick's eye out. Jeff and I couldn't stop grinning at each other. It would be years before I'd attend another rock concert but in 1965 – I saw the Rolling Stones!

Ralph Michael Spillenger

I went with a couple of my fellow 13 year old aspiring musicians. *The Last Time* was their only American hit at the time. I did not become a fan until Aftermath as I didn't get into R&B until later. The sound system was useless. All we heard were girls screaming. The only tune I recognized was *The Last Time*, because of the opening lick, and *Everybody Needs Somebody To Love* because Jagger pointed each time he said "I need YOU, YOU, YOU."

Mike Elmendorf

They played Albany in 2005. On the night of the concert I went with the Mayor of Albany and we presented the key to the city to the band. When we were with the band making the presentation Mick Jagger, was joking about the fact that they hadn't been there since nineteen sixty whatever, when they had played the Palace Theater. He was joking about the fact that the tickets were $3 and that the price had gone up slightly since the last time they were here. The tickets had to be around $300 for the better seats and I know they're even more than that now because I just bought tickets to go see them in Buffalo this summer.

30 APRIL 1965
Memorial Auditorium, Worcester, Massachusetts

Joanne Moninski Irish *(age 16)*
I was a junior in High School. We would save our allowance and part time job dollars and buy records. My parents allowed us to purchase records at The Mart, a Grafton MA department store. I assume that it was okay with them because in thinking back, my parents had a small record collection, so they must also have enjoyed current favorites during their youth. When the Stones were on *Ed Sullivan*, we sat a foot away from the TV watching this phenomenon. It was something I will never forget.

My father was pretty strict, not even allowing us to date at that time. However, he allowed us to go to a Rolling Stones concert. We bought tickets for the show from M. Steinert & Sons ticket agency in Worcester, which was the place to buy tickets. I didn't have my driver's license yet so my father drove my sister and me to the concert and dropped us off in the front of the Auditorium. My sister Nancy remembers running up the stairs to the Auditorium. We had pretty good tickets and were close to the stage. I yelled and screamed my lungs out until I couldn't speak, losing my voice.

The actual concert didn't start until 'past our bedtimes' and the dancers and singers prior to the Stones drove us crazy. We didn't want to see them and couldn't wait until they got off the stage and our loves – Mick, Brian, Charlie and Keith – performed

Joanne Moninski Irish

for us! I think they were local cheerleader girls who danced! I remember they sang *Time is On My Side* and *Little Red Rooster*. Most of the songs were drowned out by the screaming of all of us, including boys in the audience.

I took a photo at the concert on my Kodak Instamatic camera. It wasn't very good but it is evidence that I was there and sat pretty close to the stage. Those days were so different when it came to attending concerts. They weren't the Las Vegas type of performances that take place now. They were just concerts – the performers on stage without a lot of hype. My regret today is that I didn't keep all of the albums and also take pictures of all of the concerts I attended. It would be nice to have photos of the people and places from that time in my life. Some I'm sure I probably wouldn't have shown my parents at the time – if you know what I mean!

Sharon Ann Harmon
née McGrail (age 15)
Alaric Mills got tickets for me, him and my two best girlfriends, Donna Sherman and Donna Olson. We loved the Stones and none of us had ever got to see The Beatles so we thought this was the next best thing we would ever see. There were so many girls screaming we couldn't believe our eyes and ears. We sat to the right of the stage and maybe five or six rows back. They were great seats. We didn't scream – I thought it was rather silly and I wanted to hear them sing. When Mick came out on the stage I was thrilled and

also rather surprised that he was so short and slight. He was also dressed in what we called preppy attire. He had a checked shirt, which might have been green, and plain pants and his hair wasn't very long. His eyes were riveting.

Screaming continued throughout the whole concert. There was one part where a girl was screaming and I think some guy who was her boyfriend and who was jealous ran up on stage and tried to grab Mick but security guards pulled him off. That was exciting. Alaric took a home movie of the whole event. Sadly about seven years ago he passed away and I never got a copy of it.

Kevin Harvey *(age 17)*
There were only a couple of people in front of me in line that morning and I was terrified it would sell out before me. Top seats going for three and a half bucks, and a copy of the newly released The Rolling Stones Now! After waiting in the rain outside of the long gone Ladd's Music I bought two tickets within the first ten rows. What amazed me that night was that the hall wasn't sold out. At least the last dozen rows on the floor were empty. I didn't check on the balcony.

The set opened with *Everybody Needs Somebody To Love*, Jagger pointing out to each person he needed "I need YOU, YOU and YOU." I recall him taking off his sport jacket, gesturing as if to throw it into the audience and of course deciding after all to keep it. Brian Jones, with his other worldly hair and teardrop shaped guitar,

Kevin Harvey

Sharon Ann Harmon

was the visual center of the band. Jagger moved very little in those days, choosing to work the mic and actually sing. The highlight of the set was a mesmerizing *Little Red Rooster*. They closed with *I'm Moving On* and they did. Their latest single being *The Last Time*, the Satisfaction crowd had yet to catch up with them, which probably explains the empty floor seats. The Worcester show, pre aerobics workout and fireworks, remains a black and white marvel of a memory. As the saying goes, you really had to be there.

My father, a Worcester police officer who had the evening off, suited up and without informing me of his plans went backstage and watched the show from the wings. "These guys aren't like you think they are," he said. "They're very quiet and they don't eat the cookies and cakes the fans send back for them." I was stunned mute with this. He returned with four of the five band members autographs, Brian Jones' included, scrawled across a long since missing police report. Ah, well. Ladd's Music, a temple in its day, is also sadly long gone, as is the very street upon which it stood.

Ann Livingston *(age 17)*

This was my first concert. I went with two or three of my girl friends. I was about to graduate from high school. We sat on the first level, even with the stage, in the last row and the Stones appeared to be about two inches high. The concert went by fairly quickly and we stood the whole time on top of our seats.

Maureen Grogan *(age 14)*

The Auditorium was an old building with fancy seats and balconies – opera house or music hall style. I was there with my best friend at the time Lynne, her sister Kathy and one of her school friends. Lynne had just turned 14 and Kathy was 12 going on 13. Gosh, we were babies!

This was of course less than 15 months after The Beatles had come to America and been on *Ed Sullivan*. My sister and I along with Lynne and my friend Darlene – my best friend to this very day – were all insanely in love with The Beatles and as Beatlemaniacs had become obsessed with all things British. Hair. Clothes. Make up. And of course bands. It was the height of the British Invasion and we were totally swept up in it. Consequently, I only wanted to see the Stones because they were the next big thing from England.

We were way too young to get their more obvious sexuality. My favorite as of the concert date was Brian Jones – sadly not for his talent but because of his hair. But once there I was caught up by the music. I've always remembered Mick singing *Little Red Rooster* and *Time Is On My Side*. We were in Row I – which I assume was 9 – but during the show managed to get into some empty seats in the center section which were a few rows closer. It was my first, but far from last, concert standing on the seat screaming my brains out until the cops kept making us sit down.

I also remember Mick and the rest having more of a folk or blues club look with the turtlenecks, tight

Maureen Grogan

pants, and jackets on all but Mick. They all had such beautifully shiny long hair – much longer than The Beatles at that time. I remember a boy jumping onto the stage as we were directly center in the fifth or so row by then. I've never understood all the media claims that no one in the audience could hear the music or knew what songs were being performed. Totally not true, as we always wrote down the list of songs that had been played after a show.

Martha (Hamm) Serafin *(age 14)*
I was in Row 14. We went to lots of concerts then. I was in high school. The Stones were not exactly approved of by the nuns at our Catholic girls high school, but that didn't stop us. I doubt we paid more than $5 for our tickets. I don't remember much else except that Mick threw a tie into the audience and we made chains out of Black Jack gum wrappers to throw to Charlie Watts. It was kind of a big deal but I didn't realize how much of a big deal until years later. I also saw The Beatles at Boston Garden but I was nowhere near as close as I was to the Stones. Most people are surprised that the Stones were at the little Auditorium but in those days all the popular bands came to Worcester. And we could actually afford to see them.

Debra Bolz *(age 12)*
I will never forget my mother made me wear a pink and white seersucker suit with a skirt. I was not happy. She said if I dressed like a lady I would be treated

Martha (Hamm) Serafin

like one. I have no memories of the actual show. I do remember running to the stage after and scraping my hands over it. Then I made my father drive me to Harry's Drive In which was in Shrewsbury because rumor had it the Stones stopped there to eat.

Gary Dombrowski *(age 15)*
It's hard to believe this was my first concert. The Auditorium wasn't a great place to see a show but it was great to me – *Route 66, Not Fade Away*. My mom wouldn't let me go unless I brought my younger sisters – they were 14 and 12. Great memories.

Gary Shusa *(age 18)*
I was a senior at North High School, practically next door, and I went to the concert with a group of friends. If memory serves me well the hall was mostly full. Subdued quiet type girls I went to high school with were screaming their collective brains out. It was the first time I ever saw such a reaction. The Stones were great – not a long concert, but electric. Worcester obviously made a good impression on them as they came back years later to record and do another concert in a small local venue.

After the concert I went looking for my friends at the local Friendly's hamburger joint. Just as I was about to enter two slightly older guys, who I didn't know from Adam, grabbed me and asked me to help them with a big problem they had. It seems they had picked up three young ladies at the concert who wanted to 'party' but would only agree to do so if there was a third guy. Lucky me – I became long lost cousin Gary!

Dave Greenslit (age 14)

I played drums in a garage band called the Nozmo Kings – a play on the no smoking sign in my friend's garage where we practiced – and our group idolized the Stones. We covered many of their songs and the songs that they covered. I attended the Auditorium show with a friend. If memory serves (and frankly, at 64, often it doesn't) my buddy and I bought tickets for about $5 which got us seats in the back of the cavernous hall. I believe the Stones opened with *Everybody Needs Somebody To Love*. My friend claims it was *Not Fade Away*, because Mick Jagger was playing maracas. As soon as the curtain rose, the screaming drowned out the music. The acoustics in the auditorium were awful anyway. The next year we hitchhiked to Hartford for an outdoor show by the Stones, which lasted about as long as the Worcester gig, according to the lead guitarist of our band, who said when we recently talked about the show that Brian Jones was too shitfaced to play. The Stones were our favorite band because they were edgy and they represented the spirit of the times for kids like us in the Sixties. While my parents acknowledged that The Beatles could at least sing, they did not like the Stones. No adults did.

Beverly Paquette (age 15)

I was with my friend Linda. I truly enjoyed the screaming and the concert. I was seated in an aisle seat toward the front and Mick Jagger and the Stones were running up the aisle to get to the stage and I screamed "Mick! Mick!" And Mick stopped and shook my hand and I'll never forget that as long as I live.

Jen Forsberg (age 13)

I was barely 13 and my brother was barely 14. My sister who also attended had just turned 16 and she brought her friend, who was also 16 and her 14 year old brother. We were dropped off and went up the endless steps into the Auditorium.

This was my first concert and all the sounds, sights, emotions and feelings of anticipation left me breathless, anxious and physically excited. We lived only two towns away from Worcester so were in familiar territory. After we found our seats, my sister and her friend disappeared. Although I was curious it just seemed like another chaotic thing that can happen at a concert.

The noise was deafening with several thousand kids, mostly girls, all yelling in unison. Then above all that din there was loud screaming and sobbing from a single girl and when I looked down the aisle in back of me I saw my sister and her friend being led back to their seats next to mine by two security guard types. At first I thought that she had been hurt but she was just hysterical. As it turned out they were two of the

Gary Shusa

four girls that had hid out in the Auditorium garage and jumped the Stones. My sister could barely talk but she had scratched Mick's hand and grabbed his shoulder. A girl ran up to my hysterical sister saying "can I touch you? Can I touch you?" My head was spinning as I became catapulted into my sister's experience – and this all happened before the show!

The show itself was simply unbelievable. My sister became famous in our small town for a while amongst our peers. In 1969 I saw the Stones again at the Boston Garden with my best friend and our boyfriends. Although it was a longer concert and much, much bigger and very exciting it didn't come close to matching the Worcester concert. The Worcester concert had a more innocent air about it. Music was an absolute necessity for us as it was truly all we had.

"they didn't make it through twelve songs as there were too many girls rushing the stage"

Chester Clarke *(age 14)*

I attended with my friend Larry. Local top 40 radio station WORC, which is often credited with breaking The Beatles in America, ran a contest giving away every Rolling Stones album up to that point to the person who came closest to naming, in order, the first twelve songs the Stones played. Unfortunately they didn't make it through twelve songs as there were too many girls rushing the stage.

It really didn't matter to me. I couldn't name the six or seven songs that they did get through as I couldn't hear much over the screaming crowd. I recognized a little of *The Last Time* – and

nothing else. A good memory of an earlier day.

Denise Quaranta *(age 14)*

I was attending my very first concert. I remember the excitement because I sat in the second row on the left hand side of the stage. The ticket price was $10. The anticipation of seeing a British group was cool. The audience goers were in control but when the curtain opened I heard approximately four chords to *Mona* and the screaming was deafening. I stood on my seat but could not see well because the crowd ran towards the stage and others stood on the backs of their seats. You could only hear screaming and an occasional note.

Ron Whittle

When we found out the Stones were coming to Worcester we did everything we could to get tickets. We had balcony seats near the left side of the stage. I remember more screaming than I had ever heard before and it made it even more exciting to be there to witness it. It was an event to be seen at and something to brag about at school. I still can see Mick Jagger mouthing the words and being able to hear maybe every fourth or fifth word above the screaming. I remember leaving the Auditorium with my friend singing the Stones songs with the crowd on the front steps after the show, waiting for our ride home. I loved it. It was a time in my life I will never forget. It was a time in rock and roll history was made in Worcester!

Kenneth Bouthot *(age 13)*

Our local radio station was WORC AM radio – '1310 on your dial', as they advertised in a jingle – and during the British Invasion this station was at the forefront of featuring the rock talents that were just starting to release singles in the United States for radio airplay. I would be up early before school and listen to the station, which was very receptive to accepting calls on the request hot line, and I remember phoning in and asking politely to hear anything by the Beatles or Rolling Stones – and the Dave Clark Five. I would record them from the portable radio speaker with a small compact reel-to-reel that my dad had passed down to me. That was limited to the ever so small 3½ inch reels but – hey – at least I had access to some free songs.

I am sure that I heard about the future visit to and concert by the Stones in Worcester as a result of this station's promotions. They had a semi famous disc jockey, Dick 'the Derby' Smith, who was known to have bragging claims as one of the very first jocks to play music by The Beatles on American airwaves.

I remember clearly walking downtown after school to buy a pair of tickets for the event at a spot called Ladd's Music Shop which was located within 100 yards of Worcester City Hall after somehow amassing the staggering sum of $8 for a pair of tickets, as no way would I be allowed to go alone. Outrageous add ons like a service fee or convenience fee for tickets

was pretty much unheard of. One thing was for sure – there was no chance of Dad ever having the money to take me, so I bought his ticket. The Worcester Memorial Auditorium later became a favorite place for pro wrestling competitions where, thankfully, sonic quality and acoustics are not of prime importance. The venue featured an oval balcony which in hindsight may have been a better choice for me but I figured I would get as close as possible to the stage.

As I recall, it was an absolutely flat listening floor, meaning no slope at all. So if you were, like me, maybe 5 foot 2 inches then your line of sight might not be premium seating on anyone's scale. I remember a rather brief performance to say the least, lasting not more than maybe 11 songs, with most songs running maybe 2 minutes 35 in length and with deafening screams in between.

I recall a fellow trying to rush the stage who was grabbed by cops by his belt and flung off the elevated stage in a not so gentle manner. I think they played *Little Red Rooster*, as I recall the rather violent slide guitar action of Brian Jones back and forth on the neck of the guitar. If I had any ringing in the ears the next day it was from the incessant screaming and not because the public address system was loud or even adequate as it was surely not. I remember the band's amplifiers looking mighty small and few in number, the smaller Vox amps with the criss-cross grill cloths that the band used most of the time.

> "I remember clearly walking downtown after school to buy a pair of tickets for the event at a spot called Ladd's Music Shop"

Beverly St Thomas (left)

Beverly St Thomas *(age 15)*

I was a freshman at South High School. My best friend was Joanna Gicas and together we wrote the Freshman Newsletter for our class. We were associated with the radio station WORC and the DJ Dick Smith. We were granted backstage passes for many of the concerts that year, one of them being the Rolling Stones. We were not allowed backstage for their concert – not many people were – but we did get a couple of quick snapshots. *(see page 194)*

Rose Morton *(age 13)*

We had back stage passes to meet the Stones thanks to my friend's father, who worked in the music business. Myself and Pam Farrell presented a cake to Charlie Watts. It was pretty overwhelming. There was a lot of the press there. It was probably one of the most exciting moments of my life to actually meet the Stones. We had front row seats and the screaming fans were deafening. A night I will never forget.

Rosemary Ahmadi *(age 7)*

I remember being back stage, how I was a little disappointed that it wasn't The Beatles and how friendly the group was. I had two pictures taken with Mick Jagger but over the years the photos have disappeared. The person who took me was a family friend who had obtained backstage passes through his employer. I stood in the wings of the stage and could not hear any lyrics whatsoever! I was, however, able to see the audience and remember how crazy they were for the Stones with cheering and shouting – it really made quite an impression on me.

Clement Porter *(age 19)*

I had a band called Group Therapy and we appeared at the Auditorium a few months before the Stones concert in a 'battle of the bands'. My cousin worked with the stage manager, setting up concerts, and he gave me a call the day before the Stones show to see if my band would be interested in bringing our equipment backstage and possibly playing as an opening act if there was a problem, ie. an opening act cancellation or the Stones being delayed.

The next day we brought in our PA system and amplifiers. We never got the nod but left our equipment there just in case a last minute unforeseen thing happened. I had purchased my Stones tickets weeks before the concert on the third row back from the stage. The opening acts were done – now the big event. The announcement over the PA system came "Ladies and gentlemen, the Rolling Stones." The curtains were closed, but we could hear the music starting behind the curtain. This went on for a couple of minutes and then suddenly Mick Jagger pulled the curtain back just enough to walk out with microphone in hand. Then the curtain gradually and slowly moved back to reveal Brian Jones who was my favorite, Keith Richards, Bill Wyman and Charlie Watts.

A few days later my cousin called for us to pick up our equipment at the Auditorium.

I was shocked when he told me "guess what? Mick Jagger used your microphone." They had a problem with their PA system. A friend who was with me but in a different seat took a great picture of the Stones on stage that night. He had also taken pictures of my band on the same stage in the battle of the bands, so I have the pictures of Mick and me, both on the same stage although at different times, using this good old fashioned mic. (see page 193).

Clement Porter *(centre) with Group Therapy*

Michelle Wellen *(age 14)*

I was in eighth grade. My father drove myself and a few friends to Worcester, dropped us off at the Auditorium and we went in. We had balcony seats in the front row and had made a big sign. All you could hear was girls screaming. My dad came back at 11pm and picked us up. No violence, no fear. It was fun but you could not hear the band. And they looked very small. After that I stuck to folk concerts.

Rose Fitzgerald *(age 12)*

I was there in the front row. I went with my mom. She loved Mick Jagger, she loved all music. I also had a friend with me the same age. We sat in the front row at $4.50 a ticket. I remember the show starting and someone ran up on stage. The curtain came down but it continued. Brian Jones was with them and to me that was awesome. My dad was from Italy and very old fashioned but he did allow us to listen for a time. He didn't like it loud so we had to tone it down. It's funny the music

I listened to. My kids grew up with it too as I always had something playing in my house. To this day I still love the Stones. My mom, God rest her soul, still loved to listen to them too. She died in 2012 at 99.

Jody Tubert *(age 14)*

I have a photo of me and two school friends in our seats screaming. My brother Mark was backstage meeting them with my father. It was a priceless time. I also saw The Beatles at the Boston Garden in September 1964 along with three other siblings. My father, Jack Tubert, was in the interview room with The Beatles and got them to sign our programs. I also got to meet Herman and the Hermits, the Beach Boys, the Searchers and Bobby Sherman. It was wonderful to have a father whose assignment was "go cover those mop-heads"!

Neil McCoy *(age 15)*

I went with my cousin from Shrewsbury who could drive. I remember hearing the music very

Rose Fitzgerald

well in the middle of the Aud. The show was good enough. I don't remember much at all except that there were one or two songs that I wanted to hear that they didn't play. I had all their albums by then. I wanted to hear more bluesy stuff. I was a big Albert King fan back then.

Walter Kennedy (age 17)

I was a senior in high school and I snuck into that concert with a high school friend. I think it was pretty late when we got in by the side doors, which we knew about from hanging around there. I remember being on the main floor and seeing the band on stage but don't remember specific songs or the sound itself. The sound was not very good in those days. There was a lot of excitement – yelling and moving around. It was certainly not a quiet sit down concert.

Jean Johnson (age 14)

I went with a girlfriend. Our parents dropped us off and picked us up afterwards. It was great! There were many rock concerts at the Auditorium in the Sixties. We saw the Stones just once, but the Beach Boys three or four times, Gerry and the Pacemakers, Sonny and Cher, Peter and Gordon and others. It was wonderful to be able to see many of the top bands of the time at a small venue. The building is still there, but unfortunately in a state of disrepair and unused as a theater for many years. I still live in the area and it brings back memories every time I drive by.

Jean Johnson

Joanne Ferrecchia Willis (age 14)

My father would not allow me to attend The Beatles concert in Boston for fear of unruly crowds. But somehow, the Stones seemed less of a threat – perhaps parents were not quite as aware of the other groups in the British Invasion. I went along with three girlfriends all aged 14 and one of their brothers and his friend. We all hailed from Marlborough, about 18 miles east of Worcester.

Our front row balcony seats cost $4 each. When the Stones appeared on stage, the screaming and frenzy began immediately. We girls stood screaming and shouting as did the two boys with us. We heard *Satisfaction* and instinctively knew a hit was on its way.

If you can believe, little attention was paid to Mick Jagger. Brian Jones, dressed nattily and with a gorgeous head of blond hair, garnered the most attention, the most screams. He seemed to smile knowingly. After the concert ended, we rushed outdoors looking for any sign of the group leaving the auditorium. We circled the building looking at all the exits, but no sign. We waited for one of our fathers to come pick us, perhaps 30 minutes, but never caught sight of the Stones again. It was our first concert and, although I have attended many since then, it remains the most memorable and exciting.

Colleen Oliver (age 13)

I went with Patti, a friend from seventh grade. We both told our parents we were going with the other's parents so we could sneak off alone. Of course, our parents met at parent/teachers night and our plot was revealed – we were in big trouble and I think our punishment was a ban on concerts for a while. Luckily, the Stones had already appeared!

We had balcony or loge seats close to the stage on the left side of the house. Looking down at the auditorium, there was a walkway or aisle about halfway back from right to left. It was shocking to see that the second section was barely occupied but it was also exciting that we were seeing the Stones before others really knew about them.

When the last song – *The Last Time* – started we ran downstairs to the hallway leading to the dressing rooms. The police were not prepared. They set up folding tables between us and them for security. My friend was from the Bronx and considered very worldly so I followed her lead, flipping the tables over on the police. When they fell, we ran toward the dressing rooms. We were not successful, however, and were immediately removed so we ran to the garage and watched the performers leaving instead.

I can't remember whether my parents liked the Stones or not but I know my father really admired The Beatles. They drove me to the Manning Bowl in Lynn to see them again a year later so they must have at least been amused by the craziness. I'm not sure how the Stones influenced me except to expand my musical horizons to include the blues – I loved the early Stones!

Neil Faugno

I was at that concert with a group of guys. We arrived very close to the beginning and the place was jumping with mostly young females. A local DJ introduced some acts of local and regional talent, but in between these acts with the curtain closed you would hear a guitar playing the beginning of a Stones song only to be told another performer was coming on. It was a big tease.

Finally the Stones were introduced and the roar was deafening. Girls were screaming and the small arena shook with excitement. At the end of their performance a young guy made his way to the stage but a Worcester policeman lunged at him to keep him from reaching Mick and ended up straight arming him across the throat. Mick saw this and started to move towards the altercation but a hand – I believe it was Keith – grabbed Mick and pulled him behind the curtain.

After the last song ended the crowd ran to an area where they thought the Stones would be exiting but they never showed and the crowd dispersed. It was quite a night.

Diane Granger *(age 14)*

I remember standing in line waiting to buy my ticket. I was saving a place for my friend, Margie, who had to return a birdcage and use the refund to buy her ticket. I had my babysitting money. Later, Margie had a chance to get a ticket that was closer to the stage than ours so she sold her ticket to my older sister who was 20 at the time and glad for the

> "my friend was from the Bronx and considered very worldly so I followed her lead, flipping the tables over on the police"

Diane Granger

Lynn Couture

opportunity to go. We lived within walking distance of the Auditorium and walked to and from the show. A newspaper article said the performance was only 23 minutes but to me it seemed much longer.

I could not hear any singing over the crowd screaming but was glad just to see them perform in person. I remember the ringing in my ears all the way home. A few years ago, I found my stub to the concert and brought it to work to show my co-workers that I saw the Rolling Stones back when it only cost $4 to do so. They were impressed.

Gail Nason (age 17)

I went with my high school friends Alberta Martelli and Betty Rolls. We sat in the balcony and were able to hear them. I thought Mick Jagger was very young looking, even to me, and was quite thin and had a good voice. Of course, as now, his singing was very sensual. They of course had a tougher look than The Beatles. What an exciting time for music, so lively and upbeat, just what we all needed. Except, of course, our parents, who hated the look and the sound. I remember my poor brother Mick being so upset when my father shaved his long hair and gave him a 'butch' so he wouldn't look like a 'freak'. Now that is what you call a generational gap! I will never forget those years.

Lynn Couture (age 16)

The Rolling Stones were coming to Worcester of all places! This was something that I was not going to miss. I had already seen them on the *Ed Sullivan Show* and was totally smitten. I had

an after school job working as a dishwasher and kitchen assistant. At the end of my day I would return home greasy, sweaty and smelly. I used the money that I had made (50 cents an hour) and had diligently saved to purchase my ticket. I did not hesitate to spend 12 dollars on my ticket (tenth row, slightly left of stage).

I went with one of my friends. With a mouth full of metal braces and a head full of frizzy hair, I sat composed in my seat while young girls screamed throughout their set. Juvenile screeching was not for me. I took two photographs with my Brownie camera. My only disappointment was that Keith was situated on the other side of the stage. During the performance, Mick sang and gyrated toward our side of the stage. It seemed as though he was looking directly at me. Would I be invited back stage? How many other delusional girls thought the same? The night was wonderful and exciting and I had no regrets having spent my hard earned money on it.

Brian Barlow (age 16)

My first experience with music came with Ricky Nelson and Connie Francis. That's what I first got inspired by. And then Roy Orbison came out. Roy Orbison was my guy and I went to see him in 1962 and I couldn't believe how great he was. Then The Beatles changed everything. That killed me. I was in my car one day and all of a sudden they were playing *Love Me Do*. And I said "what is this?" and then *She Loves You* came out shortly thereafter so I was done. I can remember being in the car hearing the song on my father's radio and saying "what is this?" and I never stopped listening. Like many teens in the early Sixties I was obsessed with the new sound out of England when I first heard *Love Me Do* by The Beatles. My radio was on all day to local station WORC to hear more of this magical sound. I don't know what it was about the music but it was just great energy.

On 4 June 1964 I had my first taste of the British Invasion with a concert at the Worcester Auditorium featuring The Searchers. They were great and brought the new 'jangly sound' I loved from Britain. I have a magazine I bought in '64 and on the back of the cover it shows the up and coming band and it was the Rolling Stones. I'd never heard of them at that time. It was mostly The Beatles and American groups. And then the Rolling Stones were this new up and coming group. They were just kids. They were teenagers. America – the industry here – didn't want that music. They thought that guitar bands were dead.

They played the Loews about twenty miles from me in 1964 and they got hassle with the police for having long hair in the pool. They were playing to a half filled football stadium and then they got in trouble at the hotel because you were not allowed to have long hair in pools at that time. You had to wear bathing caps in this country. That was in the paper.

When WORC announced that the Rolling Stones were coming in April of 1965 to the same auditorium I already owned two records by them – *Time Is On My Side* and *The Last Time*. I was so excited that I played the 45 of The Last Time over and over in my room. I could not believe that my father, who was a big jazz fan, commented how much he liked the tune. I was vindicated!

To purchase tickets for that concert I had to take a bus to Lincoln Plaza from my High School, a 40 minute ride, which I did during the first week of sale. I was pleasantly surprised to purchase front row tickets for $2.50. My parents drove me and my brother, Stephen, to the auditorium where I would meet my cousin Linda and her girlfriend. I was let in early by the manager as he was a close family friend. My mom was always concerned about the crowds and potential trouble.

I sat down in the front with about 10-15 others in a very calm environment when suddenly the doors opened and the crowd of young girls raced in and hustled and jockeyed for their seats. The opening acts were not memorable as were the acts with the Searchers – Dick and DeeDee and Gene Pitney. However, the energy and anticipation of seeing a famous band kept us wired! In those days a DJ often introduced the band in front of a curtain and I believe the promoter of the show, Dick 'the Derby' Smith, was that man. He told me later he paid the band $3,000. He added

Brian Barlow

he wanted to bring them back the following year but the price was $30,000!

Anyway, the big maroon curtain opened and there they were. While there was a lot of screaming it always came at the end or beginning of a song or with some gesture by Jagger. One could barely hear him sing but the band came through. I was mesmerized by a very different sound than the Searchers or Beatles. This was driving, bluesy and sexy, not sweet and poppy. That show was one of the best I have ever heard in terms of how exciting it was and how tight the band was. It did not last long and we all dispersed to our rides home with a brief but amazing memory.

To date I had seen Roy Orbison, the Beach Boys twice, the Searchers, and all those bands. The Four Seasons I saw too. Then when I saw the Rolling Stones they were good. That band in '65 was as good as I have seen, really good. The only thing that might have topped it was the original Little Richard band that I saw. That blew me away. That was rock'n'roll. The Beatles wished they could be Little Richard, how good he was in his early days. The Rolling Stones were close to that. Very close to that. A different style entirely. But the energy! They really moved me that day. And I bought all their records.

I saw the Stones again when they played St Morgan's Cove in Worcester in 1981 – this little club. They came out on the stage and I'm right there and they put a piece of paper on this pillar that was like

"the Beatles wished they could be Little Richard in his early days. The Rolling Stones were very close to that"

in the middle of the stage. 'Set list', I thought. So I grabbed that set list after and there was one song on it which was the opening song which I think was *Off The Hook*. That was all they had. No plans. So here they are, the biggest band in the world, and no clue what they're going to play next.

It was organised by Gil Markle who had a studio called Long View Farm and the Stones took residency there in 1981. That was at Brookfield, Massachusetts and he's a friend of mine so we would visit and they'd play pool and we'd hang out and do different things.

I was out there once and said 'hello' and we just left, because it's their world. But they wanted to play a club so we recommended they do that and so I helped get the sound, helped get it together, but it was literally no plan. In fact, when I got there, there was no sound system so we just scurried up some stuff. And another guy did the sound and it was a mess.

They just were ok. I've seen better bands in that club. But Mick was working the stage like it was 20,000 people. And I'm right there and like 'over here! Over here!' He was running back and forth. It was great to see them. It was still good music. There they were. I couldn't get any closer. I've seen virtually every major act of the Sixties, Seventies and Eighties and have been a concert producer for the last 20 years. Despite that, few shows have ever rivalled that magical night in 1965.

Steve Smith

While I was too young to go to the show my father Dick Smith, a disc jockey and music director at radio station WORC, was one of the producers of the concert. It was his only venture into concert promotion and he barely broke even that night. I know there were a lot of unsold tickets around the house.

4 MAY 1965
Southern College Hanner Gymnasium, Statesboro, Georgia

Pratt Hill

I attended this show with my girlfriend at that time, Peggy Hartsfield, whose grandfather was Dean Paul Carroll, Dean of Students at Georgia Teachers College. We had front row seats and really enjoyed the evening. I remember the Romans and the Bushmen being excellent.

Glenn Bray *(age 16)*

I was a junior at Statesboro High School. My girlfriend and future first wife, Caroline, decided to go to the concert thinking that we would never get another chance to see the Rolling Stones. As soon as school dismissed for the day, we headed to Georgia Southern College. We went this early so we could get a spot near the front of the line. We knew we would be in line for three or four hours, but we didn't care. We were accompanied by Caroline's best friend, Sherry, who passed away several years ago. Her boyfriend played in one of the warm up bands. We were in the first 25 people to enter the

gymnasium that night and got great seats. The concert was sponsored and arranged by a local fraternity at the college, Sigma Epsilon Xi. The Bushmen and the Sons of Bach played first.

When the Stones took the stage, it was obvious from the outset that they were drunk or stoned or something. Their performance was raggedy and poorly executed. The music and singing were sloppy and disappointing. After playing three or four songs they left the stage. We all assumed they were taking a break and coming back soon. But they didn't.

The emcee, who was president of the fraternity, came on stage and uncomfortably announced that the Stones "had left the building". I remember that there were outcries of booing and unhappiness from the audience. And that was it. Caroline, Sherry, and I loaded up in my father's 1962 Ford Falcon and went home. I remember being disappointed at the time and thinking that the Rolling Stones put on such a poor performance because this was little unimportant Georgia Southern College and Statesboro GA.

Betty Wickham *(age 18)*

I was a sophomore at GA Southern College at the time and my roommate and several friends from my dorm attended. My mother was tolerant of all music and knew I was infatuated with the boy groups like The Beatles as well as 'my' Lettermen and Paul Anka! She wanted me to experience a concert. In those days the Student Activity fee was

Glenn Bray

Betty Wickham

Jagger could hardly stand when they finally got out there after several hours and no one was together, presumably using some of the other groups' amps and sound equipment.

They 'performed' maybe three songs and were actually being heckled because they were so vulgar and incoherent. The other groups filled in some but mostly we all left very unhappy. But with the music scene headed in a different direction we all knew this was not the last we would hear of them.

Lamar DeLoach

I was in the seventh grade at junior high school. There was a group of us kids that went to the concert and we understood the impact of this new wave of music because of The Beatles coming to America. At this time every kid in America watched the Ed Sullivan Show on Sunday nights with the family. We kept up with all of the alternative music styles that were happening here. The night of the concert the group that opened for them was called the Bushmen, a Georgia-based band that played at many school and college functions. Some people felt let down by the Rolling Stones but those who were younger knew there were many new acts on the way.

part of tuition so I don't think I had to purchase a ticket but you had to fight for one! I did purchase the program, which I still have, profiling all five of them with some backstage and recording studio pictures. This was by Peter Jones. I somehow knew to hold onto it even though it was a substantial part of my entire allowance.

As for the concert itself, it was dismal. They surely expected a large concert arena instead of a small gymnasium seating maybe 2,500. We were told some of their equipment did not arrive from Savannah and, to make matters worse, this was a dry county. So no booze within a 20 mile area and very little weed to be found. They were very pissed off when they heard this. Supposedly they were drinking and smoking pot on the way over in the limo and were already high on the trip over. Mick

Phil Blanchard *(age 20)*

There was lots of talk on campus about the Stones appearing. I didn't actually purchase a ticket. A friend, Billy Massey, and I decided that we would go to the Banner Gym to see if we could get tickets at the door. When we arrived a girl told us that a friend had heard that the band was seen outside the rear door of the gym. Billy and I wanted to see if they were still outside. We headed for the back door and there they were! Apparently they were trying to get a little fresh air as the gym was not air conditioned and it was May in South Georgia. After hearing those accents, we knew it was the Stones. Minutes later they began to make their way back in toward their dressing room.

Billy was the first to reach the door and was turned away by security. I was in the middle of the group and had longish hair. I think that's why I was able to get by security – I blended! After we got in the dressing room I asked if they needed anything. I think they assumed I was supposed to be there to assist them as they never questioned my presence. Mick Jagger replied "yes, a towel. It's fucking 'ot as 'ell in 'ere!" I had to go across to another locker room to get the towel. I returned, tossed the towel to Mick and he said "thanks a 'eap." I noticed a fifth of bourbon next to a locker. One of the group asked if I would pour drinks. I, of course, complied. The fifth didn't survive too long.

They changed guitar strings and Bill Wyman gave me the used ones. When I got back to my room, I put these things on a closet shelf. At the end of the quarter, when I packed to go home, the items had disappeared. Back at the gym front entrance Billy told a couple of co-eds that I had gotten into the Stones

Phil Blanchard

dressing room. Moments later girls were outside the window screaming to get my attention. Of course, they wanted autographs. Not expecting a positive response I asked if they would sign autographs for my friends. I was surprised when they yes. I located my registration form in my wallet, tore it in into several pieces and thrilled my co-ed friends with their autographs. I later found a couple of autographs – Mick Jagger and Bill Wyman – on the floor.

We chatted about their appearance on the Ed Sullivan Show. They asked if I was going into the concert and I said yes. They said for me to just follow them in. I followed them in and found a great spot on the floor in front of the spectator seats. The volume was so loud they didn't realize their microphones were not on but that was soon corrected. Also, the girls were screaming so loudly it made it difficult to hear the singing. Many of the guys began to boo in response to the screams. That continued through

Anne Staskewicz-Bojov

Kiki Morishita

to their final number. My parents didn't know I would be attending the concert. When I told them after the fact, they were not at all surprised about my experience.

16 MAY 1965

Long Beach Arena, Long Beach, California

Maureen Orcutt *(age 12)*
There were many bands that day but we were there for the bad boys. Girls were screaming – me too! Girls were running on the stage and climbing down the red velvet curtains trying their hardest to get the band's attention. The grand finale was being up close and personal to the car as it was leaving the arena. I touched it as I was pulled away by security. I was so thrilled to be part of the scene and did not know at the time but my mom had got tickets for four days later to see the Stones with Sonny and Cher on the TV show Shindig. We were up front for that show and saw them when they came out in a Rolls Royce to do *(I Can't Get No) Satisfaction*. What a week!

Andrea Tarr *(age 14)*
The Long Beach Arena show seemed tamer than the Civic Auditorium show of six months before. My friend's mother again came along. Like the Auditorium show it was packed out but the Long Beach Arena seemed to hold more people than the other venue. It was a long time ago and we were 100% thrilled to be part of these events and remember how exciting they were. These were standout experiences in our lives.

Anne Staskewicz-Bojov
I was in that pile of girls who swarmed the car at the Arena concert. However it was my compatriot who got the worst of it. The stories get embellished over the years but I believe my friend was clubbed off the car by the police. No hospital, though, just a bad headache. Exciting times.

My billy clubbed friend is a grandma now, though not the least bit old! We have stories about all the concerts in the LA area – all three Beatles' concerts, the last Doors at the Bowl, Country Joe, the Stones all-nighter at the Forum, Buffalo Springfield at Cal Poly Pomona, the Mothers at the Shrine dancehall, Cream at the Forum, Hendrix in the Valley and many, many more. Ah, the Sixties in Los Angeles. It was like nothing else.

Kiki Morishita *(age 12)*
Having been a Beatlemaniac but liking the Stones as well, they were for me the rebels and I found much exhilaration in songs such as *Satisfaction*, *Under My Thumb*, *19th Nervous Breakdown* and *Time is On My Side*. I think it was 1965 when I actually 'liberated' the album *Aftermath* from Thrifty's, a neighbourhood drugstore that had some bins of albums before Virgin Records or other popular record shops existed. So you could perhaps attribute this teenage 'lifting' to them.

I couldn't recall who had gone with me to see the Rolling Stones but a few years ago a former fellow student at that time called Janna said it was her. We were seventh or eighth grade. The show was very exciting and I remember the tumultuous energy throughout, with the passionate outpouring from the audience never subsiding and in particular the last song being *The Last Time*, their big hit at the time. When they began that, the mass hysteria sensed it was their final song and immediately began leaving their seats for the exits.

Since my parents had divorced I was living with my mother who was somewhat of a free spirit, although of Japanese descent. She had driven her very cool Corvair to pick us up after the concert was over. She told me that she had driven past the limo with the Stones inside and saw Mick at the window and then the horde of fans rushed past her in pursuit of the limo.

Walt Turley

I was present for this concert. My father was a plain clothes police officer working this concert and he was able to get me and my brother in to see it. Now, reflecting back, this concert was pretty unreal. It was the Animals, Paul Revere and the Raiders, the Byrds and the Rolling Stones. I can remember standing near the stage and girls and people sliding down the curtain trying to get on stage, going crazy over the Stones.

John Turley

I was one of the police officers in charge of the outside security at the Stones concert. Their limo was parked on the west side parking lot and we ran with the Stones to the

MAY 17

POLICE OFFICERS RIDE TOP OF 'ESCAPE CAR' TO HELIPORT
Police Officers John Turley (Plainclothes) and Jim Reed

TEN INJURED

Teen Girls Mob Rolling Stones

west exit and got them into their limo. There was already a large group of kids there. In order to move the limo, with it being already surrounded, I sat on the hood of it as it moved very slowly with me using my feet to push the ones in front away. We finally made it to the foot of Linden Avenue and the driver must have panicked as he drove really fast up the hill to Ocean Boulevard. It was a scary ride.

I was still on the hood when he made a left hand turn onto Ocean Boulevard. I had nothing to hold on to except my fingernails in the grooves of the hood. At a high rate of speed he drove fast along Ocean Boulevard, not stopping for signals at several intersections. At Golden Avenue he made another sharp turn to go south down a grade to where there was a helicopter waiting on the beach front. My intention was to drag out the chauffeur and do whatever to him. However I had to hustle the Stones to the helicopter. When I then looked for the driver he was long gone. Not too many people know this story and if I told this to anyone they would not have believed me anyway. I still do not know how I

Clipping from the police file showing John Turley (left)

hung onto the hood of that limo. I guess my legs hanging over the front helped.

29 MAY 1965
Academy of Music, New York, NY

Lynda Smith *(age 15)*
I do not remember how I got the tickets. I think we purchased them at the door. I went with a girlfriend who also loved the Stones sound. I did not tell my parents I was going to the concert until after. They were a little upset that I had taken the bus into NYC without telling them. I was living in the suburbs, about an hour long bus ride into the city.

I remember the really loud screaming and carrying on of the largely teenage girl audience over Brian Jones. The screaming was so loud that it was hard to hear the music. And the pushing of the audience as the girls tried to get up to the stage was very annoying. The concert was held in the 14th Street Academy of Music which was an old time movie theater with floor seats and a balcony so it was really easy for the audience to get out of hand.

The Stones were the first group I got into that incorporated American blues with rock'n'roll. I loved both forms of music and could not get enough of the Stones. As soon as a new album was released I was always sure to get it. It was so long ago but, being it was the first Stones concert I went to, the memories are still clear.

Joanne Brooklyn *(age 15)*
The Stones played the Academy of Music in NYC in October 1964. It

Margaret MacLeod

was Bill Wyman's birthday. I was going to go but my brother decided to get married on that day and I was a bridesmaid. I was 14 and very disappointed. In May of 1965 I finally got to see the Rolling Stones at the Academy of Music in NYC. I was over the moon when Brian Jones and I coincidentally wore the same outfit which was white pants and a black sweater. I was sure it was a sign we were meant to be together. Lol – he was already 23!

Following their third US tour the Stones returned to the UK to take to the stage in Scotland in June 1965.

18 JUNE 1965
Caird Hall, Dundee

Margaret MacLeod
My friend and I worked in Wilsons Restaurant then and we were asked to go along to the concert with sandwiches, etc, for the Rolling Stones and the Hollies, which we did with a police escort. We were allowed in the Stones and Hollies' dressing rooms. I got all their autographs and I foolishly gave them away, which I now regret. We also got to watch the show from the side of the stage. It was a night to remember and we will never forget it.

Dorothy Thomson *(age 17)*
It was my first live concert. Although I was mad about Cliff Richard, I was also mad about the Stones. What a contrast! I went to the Saturday show with a couple of friends and we were upstairs at the side, overlooking

the stage. When Charlie Watts led them on stage, I grabbed the nearest steward and almost threw him over the balcony! And, yes, I screamed all the way through but I loved every minute.

Brenda Wilson (age 18)

I was there, near the front with a group of Bell Street College of Technology students. I was a student nurse at Dundee Royal Infirmary. I remember Mick Jagger strolling on to the stage. I was so close I could see him very well. The others sort of straggled on. I don't remember a screaming frenzy – not like The Beatles, where the noise was deafening. The whole concert struck me as rather sedate. I remember clapping in time to the music, especially to Satisfaction. There was some screaming at the back of the Caird Hall but not around us. Bill Wyman and

Brenda Wilson

Charlie Watts hardly moved a facial muscle. I was fascinated by Mick Jagger as I had never seen such a performance on stage. The singing, the posturing, the movements, the music – I was hooked! It didn't appear overly loud and I could make out the words of his songs. I think they played *Little Red Rooster*. Keith Richards just stared at Mick, occasionally coming up front to sing his bit. Brian Jones looked bored, as if playing to a rural backwater was not his scene. I remember clapping politely to the music. I even kept my coat on!

Mari Phillips

I was in the second row, having saved my milk round money up for the ticket, and was still a fourth year school pupil. The band so nonchalantly strolled on, one by one. So cool then. Mick's cool moves. Bill Wyman dead pan, guitar held high. Charlie Watts. The late but oh so talented Brian Jones and, of course, Keith Richards. I recall the screaming and also the St John's ambulance men looking stunned at the hysterical audience.

I also recall going home to my then teenage years' home, in a poor housing estate in Dundee, just on Cloud Nine. No one I have ever spoken to about their Caird Hall gig seems to remember how they simply and casually strolled on to that stage and then that bass guitar started up! Something big was happening outside Dundee in the rock world and I, a screaming teenager, had just been part of it. It is a night I just never forgot.

Chapter 18

The Stones embarked upon a short Scandinavian tour before commencing a further UK tour in July 1965.

17 JULY 1965
The Guildhall, Portsmouth,

Bruce Horn

I had previously seen them at the Gaumont in Southampton. By the time of the Portsmouth show they had learnt some crowd control and said they wouldn't start the next song until the crowd was quiet.

Michael Smith *(age 23)*

I think they must have been the whole of the second half of the show. They played twelve tunes. Ten of them, I don't think anybody knew what they were because the girls were just screaming everywhere. The noise was such you could just make out *Satisfaction* and *The Last Time*. But the other ten I don't think anybody knew what they were playing. It was that noisy, all the stupid girls screaming their heads off all the time. I mean in the run up they only had to mention the Rolling Stones and that set the screamers off again. The band just came on and jumped about and played the music. They weren't worried about all the noise.

25 JULY 1965
ABC Theatre, Great Yarmouth

Sheila Roll

Unlike when we saw them in Lowestoft a year before, here we were sitting – well, standing and screaming from our cinema seats – with no chance of getting near them. The cinema was full of screaming girls. The best song was *Everybody Needs Somebody To Love*. Mick Jagger bent down and pointed as he sang "I need you you you and I need you you you." There were incredible screams every time he did it. Each girl hoped he meant them. Wonderful. We couldn't get anywhere near them that time so I treasure my autographs from 1964.

David Tate *(age 22)*

I worked at the ABC Regal for several years as a film projectionist and then follow spot operator, controlling the stage sound and lighting until I eventually became the stage manager. On the day the Rolling Stones played there I was on the sound desk situated at the rear of the stalls.

The in-house sound system was very basic compared to modern day sound rigs. It only amplified the vocals. There were six on stage mics, one off stage, and three rising mics. Stage monitors, now a very important part of a sound rig, were limited to one off stage speaker. Drum kits were not miked up and the guitars relied on the amps brought in by the bands. Successful bands like the Stones had roadies, but many turned up in an old Transit style van and humped the gear in themselves, with our help of course.

Each of the two Rolling Stones performances had around 1,400 screaming fans drowning out the sound of the band. It was all about atmosphere, not sound quality. My wife also worked at the theatre, doing several duties including box office and secretarial work for the artists. On the evening of the Stones concert, working as an usherette, the theatre management required her and other staff members to stand at the front of the balcony to stop crazed female fans jumping down into the stalls. They had all decided to stand aside if this happened, fearing for their own safety. Fortunately, it did not happen. It was quite a high balcony with a steep seating area, providing good sight lines.

A team of first aiders were at the front of the stalls rescuing the fainting fans from being trampled upon. After being revived in the orchestra pit, the fans were placed back among the seething mob. At the stage door fans crowded around and a group of young girls removed a double extension ladder from the back wall of the theatre. They then attempted to gain access to the dressing rooms. Order was restored by theatre staff and, again, fortunately no one was hurt. Overall, it was quite a night.

Carol Scott (age 15)

I went with a school friend and we went to the early show as we had school the next day. It was amazing – it was the first gig I had been to. We sat about five rows from the front. I remember Mick Jagger walked down from the stage and we all tried to move from our seats to go and touch

David Tate (third from right) and fellow stage crew members

him but so did half the audience! They were so good live even in those days. I can't remember each song they sang but they did my favourite, *Satisfaction*, and I'm sure they were looking at me whilst singing. After the show we went to the stage door to try and see them leave but were told they had already gone.

John Bullock (age 16)

I had just started work at a shipping company in 1965 and in the evenings, to earn extra money to buy a Mini, I worked at a holiday camp in Hopton on Sea. The boss's daughter, Susan Caster, who was sweet 16, came with me to the Rolling Stones gig. As I did not have a car at the time we caught the bus and Susan's mum took us back to the holiday camp after the concert.

I remember just walking into the booking office and buying two tickets for the circle – numbers A1 and A2 – with an excellent view of the stage. Bill Wyman started off with *Everybody Needs Somebody To Love* on his haunting bass guitar and smoking a cigarette which he placed in the upper neck between drags. I am sure the show also finished with Wyman again playing the same number as Mick and the rest of the band disappeared through the stage door. We both enjoyed the whole evening and people were dancing in the aisles to quite a few numbers.

Helen Plane *(age 14)*

I was there along with my cousin Wendy. I remember queuing early in the morning and my mother getting in the queue for me as I had to go to school. We sat five rows back. Wendy swapped her own maracas at the stage door for Mick's. I have the programme – Bill Wyman's head has black pen round it. He was my favourite Stone. I have two records – *Got Live If You Want It* and *Five by Five*. *Five by Five* is not bad but *Got Live* is a bit warped. They've not been played for 40 years, I guess. *Five by Five* is a cracking sleeve.

Wendy Williams

and new. Mick's were red with a hole in one of them. I still have them to this day.

22 AUGUST 1965
Futurist Theatre, Scarborough

Derek Cook

My sister Pam worked in the booking office at the Futurist Theatre and, partly because of her, my band The Methods played on the same bill. Also on the bill were The Roving Kind, Keith Powell, Alan Field and Lulu and the Luvvers. Alan Field was the compere. We actually did two spots. We opened because somebody didn't turn up. Lulu was fantastic and the Stones couldn't be heard vocally because of the lousy cinema PA system and the girls screaming. A gig to remember! My drummer at the time, Kelvin Robertson, enjoyed a good chat with Charlie about drums and drumming.

Mick's maracas

Wendy Williams *née Betts (age 15)*

I went with my cousin Helen. I had, prior to the concert, bought a new pair of green maracas out of my pocket money in a music shop in Regent Road in Great Yarmouth in the hope of swapping them for Mick Jagger's. After the concert, I went to the stage door at the rear of the building and the road manager came out, so I asked if he would swop mine for Mick's, which he did. Mine were green

Kelvin Robertson (age 17)

I was in a band and we did a gig at the Futurist in Scarborough as the stocking filler. They wanted a cheap local band to start each show off. We did 20 minutes at each show and in the interval I sat on Charlie Watt's drums and chatted with him. I think he was new to independents, which is the art of playing something different with each hand, and feet when you are up to speed. So I demonstrated the technique as I played it for Pink Champagne. Charlie has a band of his own playing jazz and, who knows, maybe I was his inspiration! Lulu was the closing act for the first half and she kept calling them the 'Rowlin' Bownes.'

Pam Hayden (age 18)

I met them once in the theatre I was working in. The Futurist Theatre could hold about two and a half thousand. They put on pop shows followed the wrestling craze. I met the Stones as they were preparing to do a show in the night time. My brother Derek was on the same show. They were asked to find a local band to appear on the show and somebody came up with Derek's group and they went down a storm because they were well known in Scarborough. I was in the office but they asked me to go in the booking office for the day. The show was a sell out but if there were any cancellations then they needed somebody to sell the tickets. So that's when they'd come in and have a chat. One of them chatted me up – Charlie, the drummer. He was married at the

Derek Cook, Kelvin Robertson and The Methods

time, so I told him where to go. I was surprised how scruffy they all were when they came in. We thought they were going to get changed but they never did. They went on stage as they came.

It was a bit of a let down. I preferred them to The Beatles. I went up to the back of the circle to watch. I could get in and just stand and watch everything. They were all screaming teenagers. I couldn't believe it.

8 SEPTEMBER 1965
Palace Ballroom, Douglas, Isle of Man

Philip Ryder (age 10)

My recollection is of meeting the Stones was in 1965 at the Castle Mona hotel on the Isle of Man. I was 10 at the time and we arrived on the Saturday to start a week's holiday with my grandparents. During the afternoon we went to the gardens of the hotel and the Stones were there having afternoon tea. My cousin and I approached them nervously and asked for their autographs, which they gave us. We then sold them to the fans waiting

> "I can remember Mick wearing these white jeans and this tee shirt with horizontal blue and white stripes"

outside for 2/6d (13p) and spent our profits at the toy shop. What fools. If only we had kept them!

11 SEPTEMBER 1965
Halle Münsterland, Münster, West Germany

Hanns Peter Bushoff (age 14)
I was living with my parents in Münster when the Rolling Stones played their first ever German concerts, one at 5pm and one at 8pm. It was my first concert and I had to beg my parents for weeks to go there. I went to the afternoon show. It was a package show with some other bands and later on I read that the Stones played only half an hour or so. For me it was an eternity. I don't have the ticket stub anymore and I didn't take pictures. I wish I had, but I would have been far too excited to hold the camera straight!

26 SEPTEMBER 1965
Colston Hall, Bristol

John Leighton (age 14)
I lived in Bath at the time. My uncle who lived in Bristol bought tickets for me to go and see them at the Colston Hall. And it just sort of blew me away really. I had good seats in the upper circle and it was when *Satisfaction* had just come out. It was absolutely amazing. Brian Jones was still with them and I can remember Mick wearing these white jeans and this tee shirt with horizontal blue and white stripes. That's all I wanted to buy afterwards.

The support band was Unit Four + 2 and they were good but no one was interested! It was just absolute pandemonium. The Stones were only on for about an hour. If I'd have been downstairs with my uncle, his wife and my cousin I don't know whether they would have stayed. It was just screaming girls and people trying to get on the stage and everything. But where we were sat we had good vision, reasonably good sound, and it was absolutely fantastic. Because all you'd ever seen was grainy black and white images on the TV and you'd be listening to *Radio Luxembourg* at night to the *Teen and Twenty Disc Club* or whatever. As a fourteen year old you just go home with it in your head and I had to go and get one of those tee shirts. I had to get the white jeans. That's all I wore! It was superb.

On the back of that I bought their first album. It left a lasting impression on me. I've taken my boys to see them. I took them to Wembley in '95 and my eldest son decided he had to play guitar. He picked up the guitar got a few chords I bought him an electric one and now he earns a living playing guitar. And a lot of his stuff is Stones based. I've been following the Stones ever since. The buggers have cost me a fortune!

27 SEPTEMBER 1965
Odeon Theatre, Cheltenham

Joan Hemming (age 17)
I saw them twice at the Odeon. Brian Jones' grave is in the cemetery in Cheltenham. I often park alongside the grave when I go to any funeral there.

29 SEPTEMBER 1965
Granada Theatre, Shrewsbury

Elizabeth Day née Morgan
I attended a Rolling Stones concert in Shrewsbury. The bus was organised by the Young Conservatives and as we had to leave Ludlow early some of the young men, who I think were bank clerks, were still in their formal suits and looked over dressed. As I had just left college and started work, I went along more out of curiosity and as a means of getting to know people than as a fan of the Stones.

We were seated in rows in the theatre and, as the evening warmed up, some of the girls in the audience showed their appreciation and were getting rather noisy. The most memorable part of the evening for me was when a girl sitting behind me leaned forward, tapped me on the shoulder, and asked "why aren't you screaming?" Every time I hear the Rolling Stones or see their picture in the papers now, I always visualise Mick Jagger performing somewhere on a stage below me and remember that nameless girl and her comment.

1 OCTOBER 1965
ABC Theatre, Chester

Alan Powell (age 14)
Years ago I bought and started a Beatles scrap book. I painstakingly cut out everything I could find on the Fab Four. Then one day I was hit by a bolt from the blue and, reversing the scrapbook, I started pasting in cuttings of the Rolling Stones. I used to watch Top Of The Pops avidly but was mocked by my father who derided all the acts as rubbish – especially "the bloody Rolling Twerps" as he called them.

Then it was announced they were going to play the ABC Theatre in Chester and a big boy I knew said he was going to bunk off school and go for tickets. I begged and pleaded and he got me one! I still have the ticket, which cost twelve shillings and six pence (63p). I got the bus from Ellesmere Port. You didn't want to miss the last one back or you'd be stranded in Chester – the big city! There were two performances and my ticket was for the second one – front stalls, seat H2. The audience was a mixture of boys and girls.

There was a full supporting cast of The End, The Original Checkmates, The Moody Blues, The Habits, Charles Dickens and the Spencer Davis Group, with the teenage prodigy Stevie Winwood. The Stones went down a storm. The screaming – from boys as well as girls – was deafening. All too quickly they finished with Satisfaction and people tried to rush the stage. We were so close.

The side door doors opened and we rushed out for the last bus and separated only by a line of bobbies parallel to us ran the Stones into their car. We stretched our arms. Brian was right there in front of us, laughing as he dived into the car. Oh yes – we got the last bus! I have the cutting from the Chester paper the following week. I wrote the track list down in my special exercise book. Years later I met Bill Wyman and he read through the set list, nodded, ticked my work and signed the page!

> "we stretched our arms. Brian was right there in front of us, laughing as he dived into the car"

3 OCTOBER 1965
Odeon Theatre, Manchester

Bernard Caswell

I think I paid 12/6 (63p) for my seat on the front row of the balcony. Contrast that with what you have to pay now to see them. I can't for the life of me remember who – or indeed if – there were any supporting acts.

My main memory of that night is of the loud and incessant screaming from the girls in the audience, which I didn't really expect. I saw The Beatles at the Apollo in Ardwick the previous year and, although the screaming there was loud and to be expected, the noise at the Odeon was louder. However the songs could be heard despite the cacophony and I thoroughly enjoyed the night.

They played all their hits up to that time but the only one that sticks in my mind is *It's All Over Now* and the fantastic guitar riff intro, which is still one of my favourite intros of theirs. My one regret is not keeping the ticket stub or the programme. The money I'd get for them now would be a very welcome supplement to my pension.

4 OCTOBER 1965
Gaumont Theatre, Bradford

Christopher Roper

My father dropped me off in town outside the then Gaumont as he also had the previous year for The Beatles. He had a Morris Minor with the trafficators coming out of the side. Paul

Deanna Sargent

and Barry Ryan were one of the support acts – I had been at the same school as them for a couple of years a short time previously. I attended the show alone and I was downstairs in an end of aisle seat about halfway from the stage.

5 OCTOBER 1965
ABC Theatre, Carlisle

Deanna Sargent *née Boertien (age 14)*

I went with my friend Jennifer Hyslop. It was a school day and we could barely concentrate on our work. We were both from outlying villages so had to be transported each way and therefore couldn't hang around for a glimpse of their arrival at the ABC. However as it turned out they were late as their car broke down on the motorway. Meanwhile the supporting groups were in place including Paul and Barry Ryan. During their performance one of the brothers dropped his microphone next to his brother who was lying on the stage singing and walked off in a fit of jealousy.

After what seemed hours there they were – Mick Jagger made his apologies and their performance was in no way affected by the delay. We thought they were fantastic. We were quite near the front and I remember thinking how young they looked. They were a bit more reserved in their appearance in those days. There was no trouble, no drugs, no alcohol. I don't even recall seeing a policeman. It was great!

7 OCTOBER 1965
City Hall, Newcastle

Philip Jopling (age 16)
My girlfriend at the time and who went to the concert with me was older. We went with two other couples. I remember our seats were mid way from the stage in the stalls but everyone was standing on their seats for the whole of the concert as you simply could not see anything when seated. In addition, the noise of everyone screaming drowned out the music but the atmosphere was still fantastic.

8 OCTOBER 1965
Globe Theatre (aka ABC Theatre), Stockton-on-Tees

Ian Gilfellan (age 15)
Jagger was hit in the eye by a coin at one of the concerts. PP Arnold was in the Ikettes with a cast on her arm. Spencer Davis were still unknown and someone came on dressed as a Dalek!

David Carter (age 15)
The Stones were supported by the Spencer Davis Group and Unit Four + 2. The compare was Ted Rogers. Someone threw a coin on the stage which hit Jagger just above his eye but he carried on while throwing blooded tissues into the crowd. What a night!

Barry Parkin (age 18)
On the same bill as the Stones was a young Marianne Faithfull. As the Stones finished their spot, Mick Jagger introduced her. As he walked off stage she walked on and he gave her a kiss in the

Philip Jopling

middle of the stage. Rumours were around that they were seeing each other so you can imagine the reaction from the crowd!

9 OCTOBER 1965
Odeon Theatre, Leeds

Pauline Gerrard (age 17)
My then boyfriend Tony Oliver and I begged and borrowed enough cash from our parents to buy two tickets in the front stalls for the Rolling Stones. The begging was so worthwhile. After taking a two hour journey involving three bus changes from Royston to Leeds we joined the long queue outside the theatre to see our favourite band. The atmosphere was electric and when the Stones, dressed in their bizarre outfits, bounced onto the stage they could scarcely be heard above the screams and excitement of the audience.
Jagger was phenomenal, covering every inch of the stage whilst performing his outlandish moves, but the loudest outburst came when Brian Jones was

239

introduced – sultry, smiling, hair flopping over his eyes. Every female in the audience immediately fell in love with the broody guy.

They played all their well known songs but it was hard to decipher which song was being sung above the screaming audience. I had already seen The Beatles but the Stones gave them a good run for their money and I don't think one person in the audience that night regretted the price paid, the long journey, the queuing or hearing only snatches of songs. Everyone left the theatre on a high.

11 OCTOBER 1965
Gaumont Theatre, Sheffield

Andy Thompson

Andy Thompson *(age 16)*
I remember Unit Four + 2 were on with them, and maybe the Nashville Teens. At that time Jagger was wearing the sweatshirt with horizontal lines on. I remember them doing *Johnny was a rockin.' (Around and Around)*. Brian Jones wore a white polo neck sweater. The screaming was slightly toned down compared with 1964. You could actually hear them.

14 OCTOBER 1965
Odeon Theatre, Birmingham

Liz Wolsey *(age 12)*
They were playing with Ike and Tina Turner and maybe the Yardbirds. I so wish I had written it all down. I was nearly 13 years old and it was so exciting. I was on the third row but all I remember is Mick Jagger taking off his tie and throwing it into the audience and girls going crazy.

16 OCTOBER 1965
ABC Theatre, Northampton

Pauline Lever *(age 14)*
I had just fallen head over heels in love with Brian Jones and the music and singing of the Rolling Stones. I lived in a small village seven miles from Northampton, the Rolling Stones were coming to town and a lady in our village had arranged a coach load of us to go and see the Stones perform. I remember I was so excited I felt as though I would burst. My friend Kay was in love with Mick so we were beside ourselves.

We had seen other groups perform in town – even The Beatles – but no group or pop singer had ever made us feel like the Stones. We loved the rebellious attitude and the casual look and long hair, growing all the time. The music was sensational. Once inside we sat through a good line up, which we didn't really appreciate at the time. Unit Four + 2 were on and to be honest we hardly listened to them. Charles Dickens and another group called the Habits performed, and the Spencer Davis Group were on and very good. Stevie Winwood sang *Every Little Bit Hurts*. But they had the job of performing just before the Stones and by then we were at bursting point. Suddenly, towards the end of the second half, compere Ray Cameron started to whip up the crowd saying "come on let's have a great big welcome for The Rolling Stones."

Suddenly we all erupted into a frenzy, screaming and shouting. We just found ourselves joining in with the hysteria that threatened.

The curtains came up and there they were – our idols, the best ever group, and the most gorgeous boy I had ever set eyes on. We screamed and shouted and my eyes were firmly on Brian. Things were being thrown on stage and suddenly I was aware that Keith Richards had collapsed on stage, face down. Brian called for the curtains to close, Mick ran over and Bill turned off the electrical equipment. We didn't know what had happened. Our hearts were pounding and we were horrified at the thought that they wouldn't come back on. The crowd sort of hushed, although there was a shout of "fake!" from somewhere, and Ray Cameron came on and said Keith was fine and ad libbed some jokes of sorts.

Then the curtain went up again and we screamed and suddenly I had the urge to get to Brian. I was about five feet tall but I could run and climb so I vaulted the stage and hoisted myself up – I can't imagine trying that now! Suddenly a policeman grabbed my foot and pulled and I was aware that he was determined to get me off and it would hurt. The stage was almost my height and there was just a hard floor beneath me so, aware that I could be seriously injured if he was going to pull me off the stage legs first, I waved to him and said I would get down. He helped me down, threatened me and then went after some other hysterical girl. Subdued, I stayed close to the stage, eyes fixed on Brian and still screaming.

The bouncers and police were very rough but I suppose they

had not come across this sort of adulation before and were unsure what to do. One girl lay on her back kicking her legs screaming for Mick and some bouncers sat on girls to keep them down. After the show, totally exhausted and still hyped up, we were ushered back to the bus. My friend and I sat and sort of cried and giggled and hugged each other but made little sense.

When I got in my mum came and said "well, was it good?" The adrenalin was settling and I was in a cold sweat and squeaked an answer at her. I could hardly speak. I remember Mum saying "you silly little devil, what a state to get yourself into. Whatever will Mrs Hayward think?" Mrs Hayward was the lady who always organised the coaches and tickets.

The newspaper reporter the next day stated that it was not a bad show at all and that the Rolling Stones stole the limelight but that the fantastic performing audience came a close second.

Pauline Lever

17 OCTOBER 1965
Granada Theatre, Tooting, London

Janet Hobson (age 19)
It was in Tooting Broadway at a cinema which was very plush inside. I went with my girlfriend and we had to queue for tickets on a previous day. I wore a grey mini dress with Peter Pan collar. It was a great night with lots of screaming! Mick Jagger was jumping around on stage – as he still is – and Charlie Watts with that deadpan face. I kept the tickets for years but have misplaced them now.

Chapter 19

Following their sixth British tour the Rolling Stones returned to the USA and Canada for their sixth North American tour.

31 OCTOBER 1965
Maple Leaf Gardens, Toronto

David Shaw
The first time I saw them there was screaming but not bad compared to The Beatles when hearing what was being played was an impossibility. Problem was, I had no Stones albums yet so I had very little idea what was played that night. The main thing I picked up on was the fabulous drone put on by Brian and Bill. Keith Richards had his back to the audience for much of the show, seemingly keeping an eye on Charlie Watts, and Mick Jagger was quite sedate.

They returned less than a year later. They'd had some hits then and I had a much better grasp of what they were playing. *It's All Over Now* was a standout, with Mick doing some amazingly acrobatic dance moves, seemingly levitating from one side of the stage to the other, and Brian and Bill providing an even better drone effect than the previous time.

Brian was playing a Vox teardrop guitar and was dressed in black turtleneck and red cords as he appears on the High Tide and Green Grass album cover. Keith still had his back to the audience most of the time. Mick was much more active than he had been during that earlier show.

6 NOVEMBER 1965
Convention Hall, Philadelphia, Pennsylvania

Tom Sheehy *(age 15)*
I never felt more alive than on the night I saw the Rolling Stones at the Convention Hall. I was planning on going with my friend Jim Fury but at the last minute he had a hot date so bowed out. I went to the show solo. Opening the concert were Philadelphia's own Patti and the Bluebells. Patti would go on to become a superstar as Patti LaBelle and Bluebell Sara Dash would years later join Keith Richard's X-Pensive Winos side project. Keith once remarked that he had his eye on Sara ever since that night in Philly.

It was not only the first time I saw the Rolling Stones. It was also my very first rock'n'roll show. Needless to say I was consumed with anxiety, because I sensed something significant was about to happen in my young life. From the moment the lights went down and I heard the opening chords of *Everybody Needs Somebody to Love*, my heart started pumping and didn't slow down until I got home.

The Stones not only sounded amazing, they looked mesmerizing as well. Mick Jagger kept pointing to girls in the audience and calling out "I need you, you, you!" which caused young women to scream, rush the stage, climb upon it and grab Jagger. Brian Jones was my fave member of the band and he looked so cool in his black turtle neck sweater and his striped plaid trousers. Both Bill Wyman and Charlie Watts came off as the pensive lot, as they made very little facial moves which suggested they were just taking it all in. And then there was Keith Richards flailing away at his Gibson as he smiled at the audience continuously. Highlights were *That's How Strong My Love Is*, where Jagger fell to the stage, laid on it and sang from the floor James Brown style.

I was blown away when I heard the opening notes of *The Last Time*, because I could clearly see that it was Brian who played the lead on that song with Keith supplying the rhythm parts. As the set progressed, it was quite obvious that they were saving the best for last. They closed the show with *(I Can't Get No) Satisfaction*. I saw Keith step on some pedal in front of him on the floor, which I later found out was a fuzz tone, and then he hit those immortal opening notes. It was the most powerful moment of the evening, and when I got home and my family asked me how the show was, they all laughed at me because I think I was speaking in tongues, as someone might do when they just went through a dramatic religious experience.

9 NOVEMBER 1965
Lincoln Motor Inn, New York, New York

Barbara Neumann Beals
I think they were staying at the Lincoln Motor Inn this time. And my sister said "would you like to meet them?" And I said "are you kidding? Of course!" She

didn't have to ask twice. So she said "just dress nicely and just act calm. Don't act like you're about to meet the Stones." Which was very difficult to do. So we went upstairs and went inside, and I was just knock kneed and frozen. They were five storeys up and had a little terrace outside. They'd been throwing things down at the fans.

Mick Jagger appeared at the window. He knocked at the door. Apparently he was locked out. So my first vision was Mick Jagger, those blue eyes and that stunning face. He was pointing at the door to me, you know, "can you unlock it?" and I couldn't move. I literally froze to the spot. And someone else had gotten up and opened the door and he said to me "cat got your tongue? But you do have nice knickers." He was very charming. He could see I was nervous as hell. I'd never met anyone famous before and he was just trying to talk to me. I didn't even get to tell him how I danced like him. In my mind beforehand I was thinking "oh, I'll show him a few moves." Ha ha ha! I couldn't even move. I was so stunned.

And then I met Charlie and Keith and Bill Wyman. On our way out my sister knocked at Brian's door. Oh my God – that was bizarre. That was when he was with Anita Pallenberg and they had those famous fights. And he answered the door with little more than his underwear on. You know, people used to call me Brian because I had the same hair, the same blonde hair and bangs and everything. It was like, he looked at me for a second and was like "is

> "and he said to me 'cat got your tongue? But you do have nice knickers.' He was very charming"

that my doppelganger" but then he went on "I can't talk now – we're fighting, we're having a big fight" and when they did play next time he had a broken rib.

10 NOVEMBER 1965
Reynolds Coliseum, Raleigh, North Carolina

Al Slaughter (age 16)
I went with a buddy of mine called Sonny Watkins. We were best buddies. I lost my driving license and couldn't drive for sixty days on suspension. He hauled me around everywhere and he told me he had some tickets to go and see the Rolling Stones and I said "well, we might as well." I worked at an A&P store for 90 cents an hour. We'd save up our money and go to the soul shows – James Brown. Around here we were big into R&B and rock'n'roll and soul music back then. We were a couple of farm boys who got tickets by accident and went over there. We'd heard of them. We'd seen The Beatles.

We were in high cotton when we went over there. We got over there and we were right by the side of the stage. They were really great tickets for a couple of high school kids. We were amazed how little they were. They were so small. We were 16 and we were six foot tall and 180 pounds back then. They were a different breed. All those guys. The Rolling Stones were totally different. It was just an atmosphere that night. It was quite a treat to get a free ticket from your best buddy who hauled you around when you didn't have a driver's license.

12 NOVEMBER 1965
Coliseum, Greensboro, North Carolina

Catherine Cochran (age 13)
I was so lucky to see them. I won two fifth row tickets through the local radio station. I had seen Herman's Hermits a few months before – my first concert – so I went with my 11 year old brother. I like The Beatles but when I heard Around and Around – that was so rocking compared to The Beatles! Also at that time the stage came down so low that the stage was only about a foot off the floor. But the clincher for me to be a loyal fan for 50 plus years was when Mick sang *Everybody Needs Somebody To Love* and looked me straight in the eye, pointed at me and said "I need you!" It was instant love for me. I have seen them now more than ten times. My room is a shrine, just like I was still 13. It is a dream come true for me to be in my sixties and still able to see them live. They are like family to me.

13 NOVEMBER 1965
Washington Coliseum, Washington DC

Bill Currier (age 17)
I was 17 and a Junior in High School. I had all the albums released at the time, *England's Newest Hit Makers*, *12X5*, *The Rolling Stones Now* and *Out of Our Heads*. I took a city bus in the morning to the event alone. None of my friends wanted to see this English group but me. I purchased a ticket at the door for $4.50.

Remember I was only making $1.25 an hour then so it was like a half day's work. The show was early in the day – the Stones had to get out of town and play in Baltimore that same night. The crowd was on its feet the whole time. I don't think it was sold out.

The Coliseum was in the ghetto, the slum area of DC, and held about 9,000 people. The sound system wasn't great. It was a Sixties show and I was about 20 rows away and the thing you could hear was guitars, drums and a very loud crowd. Brian was jumping all over the place and was awesome on the harmonica. What I remember about Brian was his hair was so neat and clean looking, like a perm, compared to Jagger and Richards. I loved every second of it. Just me and the Stones and about 8,000 crazies. It was my first concert and, like a first girlfriend, one you never forget.

Bill Currier

was almost spiritual and it took some doing to get the live focus off of him. His hair and style really made him stand out in spite of Mick's dancing. Brian had a glow around him somehow and his spirit and passion were undeniable in that live stage performance. It was a life altering experience to be remembered with perfect clarity forever. Brian exuded such elegant class and grace; he was clearly the Stones creator and different from the rest. It's burned into my memory like it was yesterday. I have seen the Stones numerous times with Mick Taylor and with Ronnie but seeing Brian – wow!

14 NOVEMBER 1965
Civic Coliseum, Knoxville, Tennessee

Sonny Thrower (age 11)
I got to see a lot of acts through having a dad with two radio stations. There were about 250 people there for the Stones show – East Tennessee hadn't really gotten into them yet. Brian was there with his white Vox Teardrop and I was hypnotized. I was already in a band before that and studied the Stones appearances on Sullivan, Shindig, Hullabaloo, etc. so I knew what to expect. But getting to see Brian was miraculous. His stage presence

21 NOVEMBER 1965
Will Rogers Memorial Center, Fort Worth, Texas

Frederick Goggans (age 15)
Fort Worth was my home town where I grew up. I went with a girlfriend. The Will Rogers Center was actually known as being the location of the world's first indoor rodeo with professional cowboys and all that every January. And the arena was set up like a pavilion for the rodeo. So it's a kind of elliptical building and it normally has a dirt floor where the cowboys

Frederick Goggans

ride the broncos and things of that nature. At one end of it are gates where they have the chutes for the animals that the cowboy comes out on top of a horse or a bull or whatnot. So one end is where everything comes in to the arena. This concert was in November so it was three months before all that. I remember that they used it all for various other performances and the dirt was all taken out and they put sheets down on the floor.

My recollection of the Stones concert is that they had a platform or a stage that was circular and rotated and it was in the middle of this arena. They had the dirt removed and there were chairs and the Stones came in in a Brinks armored car through a little pathway through the crowd. It was totally sold out. You have the arena floor where normally in the rodeo there's no seating. You have a lower level for boxes like theater boxes and a small area behind that. Then there's a walkway and then there's an upper deck which goes all round which is larger. And that was very full.

The crowd was quite enthusiastic. There were lots of girls screaming. I think it was much more of a mixed audience than you'd find at a Beatles concert. The armoured car was there for protection. There might have been a theatrical component to it. And they also departed in the same vehicle.

Rodger W Brownlee
Totally sold out? Far from it! I should know – I was there, and spent a little time with the Stones before the concert while they waited to go on stage. I was a member of a local band called ThElite and we were slated to open for the Stones at this appearance. The concert was sponsored by KFJZ radio and their top DJ Mark Stevens, who happened to be our local handler, had negotiated with the promoters to have ThElite open the show. At the time we were playing numerous venues sponsored by KFJZ and emceed by Mark and we were a top draw. We could put 1,500 – 2,000 people in one of their venues and I'm sure that was part of his reasoning. Plus, being one of his bands, he wanted us to get this exposure. A day or two before the concert, Mark contacted us and said that "Madison Avenue types from New York blew in and nixed it", so we were out – they didn't want any local band in the show. Disappointed, we nevertheless decided to go to the concert.

Having played at the Will Rogers complex on numerous occasions, we knew most of the Fort Worth cops who pulled security, so when we showed up at a back door, they opened it for us. We walked into the area that was used as stock pens for the rodeos, one of which had recently concluded – the smell still lingering strongly in the air. It was mostly dark but we headed for a light coming from one of the tack room doors. We went in and there were the Stones waiting to go on. They looked somewhat dishevelled and tired and complained of being hungry.

They sent an old porter out for food. We chatted them up and took a few photos. They were all nice, quiet, hungry guys – not all that different from ourselves. When the armored car arrived at the tack room, we decided to make our way into the Coliseum and find a good vantage point to watch the concert.

What we saw from an upper tier of seating was almost stunning; rather than the sold out concert that everyone expected the turn out was dismal. We guesstimated at the time that there were fewer than a thousand people there. The floor seating was not even full, much less the tiers of balcony seating around the arena. When the armored car came out of the end of the arena through the gates usually used for the rodeo grand entry, there were screaming girls all right but the armored car was hardly needed. There was no crush of female humanity.

Throughout their performance there were screaming girls around the stage, but the concert overall was a disappointment from an attendance standpoint. At the end of the show, it was widely rumored that Mick Jagger stated "I'm never coming back to this fucking hick town" or words to that affect, and they didn't, for another seven years.

ThElite subsequently made numerous appearances at the Will Rogers Coliseum, opening for the like of the Beach Boys and the Byrds among many other top groups. Most of those shows were sold out but, sadly, not for the Stones on their first trip to Cowtown.

27 NOVEMBER 1965
The Gardens, Cincinatti, Ohio

Paula Brock (age 12)

This venue was used a lot for basketball games and sporting events. What sticks in my mind the most just a little over a year from seeing The Beatles at the same venue is that it was sold out for The Beatles and we had to sit in the seats that were assigned to us. At the Stones concert it must have been more than half empty. After first sitting in our assigned seats we realized we could sit anywhere that we wanted because there were so many empty seats. There were seats on each side of the stage with only a metal railing separating us from them.

I sat on the right side of the stage with my older sister and her best friend. We happened to be on Bill Wyman's side of the stage, much to my disappointment as I was in love with Brian Jones. Brian was on the left side, Mick in the middle and Keith and Bill on the right side and of course Charlie in the back. There were only a few yards between us and them. There were no security guards or police on the stage or near us.

Their current hit on the US charts was Get Off Of My Cloud. I am not sure just how long they played, but it was probably about 30 minutes. I remember while they were playing they turned on the spotlight and shone it around the seats and it showed off the pitifully half empty arena. Even though the place was not sold out by any means the crowd was loud and the girls, including myself, were

Paula Brock

going crazy. I have no idea to this day what made us girls scream and cry when we saw them or The Beatles. It was just a natural reaction.

My sister's best friend told her that she was going to jump over the railing after their last song. I will never forget her going over the railing, her bright red satin slip showing as she vaulted over the railing. She liked Keith the best and she disappeared behind the curtain so fast following the boys that I didn't even realize it at first. It all happened so fast. I remember my sister and I going outside and waiting to see if we could find her. I remember crying hysterically over Brian and knowing that I was so close to him but didn't get to touch him.

Our friend finally showed up outside and was so excited. She told us that she ran backstage after Keith and grabbed onto him around his waist. She said that a cop was trying to pull her off and she said that Keith told him to leave her alone. I will never know if that really happened for sure, but I really think it did. She was as quick as a rabbit vaulting over that railing.

29 NOVEMBER 1965
Coliseum Auditorium, Denver, Colorado

K Arlan Ebel *(age 14)*
I was just learning to play the guitar. The Stones were my favorite band. I had the first three albums and *Out Of Our Heads* had just come out. As we were being let into the auditorium proper there was a stampede of rushing, screaming kids and my friend got knocked down and almost trampled. It took all of my 14 year old strength to lift him back up safely onto his feet. We were drenched with sweat before the show even began. The opening band was The Ramrods. They all had dark curly hair and wore jean jackets. They mostly did Dylan covers including *Like A Rolling Stone* which had just recently been released. They were actually pretty good. What I remember most clearly is Brian Jones' hair and how well he played the harmonica. I was enthralled by the guitar playing, but I couldn't always tell who was playing what between Brian and Keith since we were a little ways back from the stage. I loved the concert. They played all my favorites except for *Little Red Rooster*. And I remember that we had a good laugh because on the way to the concert, we saw a place called the Rolling Stone Motel. One of the kids said "that's probably where they're staying!" and we all cracked up.

4 DECEMBER 1965
Civic Auditorium, San Jose, California

Bobby Asea *(age 12)*
Before the British Invasion I was fortunate enough to have an older sister who was in her teens and who was also very much a fan of the most popular band around at the time – the Beach Boys. Having moved from the East Coast to the West Coast in Northern California it wasn't long before both of us got bit by the surf sound bug. The

K Arlan Ebel

Beach Boys were our idols. Luckily for me, the band came to our town and my sister was nice enough to bring me along to see them in concert twice; pretty good for a ten year old in 1963. For me the Beach Boys were kings.

Then out of the blue came this new group called The Beatles from Liverpool, England that everyone was talking about. They were going to appear on the *Ed Sullivan Show* the next Sunday night. Being open enough to check it out but not mature enough to accept their greatness I, along with the rest of the country, tuned in. We were truly blown away. The memories of that night are some that will stay with me forever. But in spite of how great and interesting those four lads were I was determined to stay true to my idols the Beach Boys. In my head I was thinking "how dare these foreigners come here to this country and take over with their popularity and number one hits?" But inside I knew they were great and I dug them. I just didn't want to admit it.

This behavior carried on for a while until I heard of the Rolling Stones. When I heard their music and saw their performances on shows like Hollywood Palace, Shindig, Hullabaloo and the *Ed Sullivan Show*, I thought to myself "this British band is like no other." I fell in love with their music and everything about them from that day on. My life was changed! My sister Dorothy still preferred the Beach Boys so when the Rolling Stones came to town I didn't have a chaperone to escort me to the

Bobby Asea

concert in the spring of 1965. Luckily for me, they came back to San Jose in December of that year. By then I was the ripe old age of 12 and also a veteran of the concert scene thanks to my sister taking me to see the Beach Boys a couple of times. Somehow my parents allowed me to go with my best friend Joe, who was also a Stones fanatic.

The Civic Auditorium holds around 3,000 people and they played two shows. We went to the early one. With the stage curtains closed behind him, as the announcer was in the process of introducing the Stones, it seemed like Mick and Keith were tugging at the curtains, which in turn made the young audience react in a wall of screams. The place was sold out and, just like Beatlemania, us Rolling Stones fans screamed our lungs out. Even though there was a lot of screaming going on, I remember being able to hear the music. *Satisfaction* was their latest hit and of course they played it live. Other songs I remember clearly are *That's How Strong My Love Is*, with Brian playing electric organ, *Get Off Of My Cloud*, *Mercy Mercy*, *Play With Fire* and *The Last Time*.

Bill was on the far left, Brian next to him, Keith far right, Charlie on a platform and of course Mick all over the place. Brian seemed to be enjoying himself. I distinctly remember Mick doing his James Brown imitation dance and going from one end of the stage to the other. At one point he took off his jacket, stood on the edge of the stage and swung it out towards the audience as if he was going to fling it to a lucky fan in the seats. Of course he didn't and the jacket kept going until it landed on his shoulder. I think he fooled everyone. The show was all too short – about twelve songs.

On our way out we ran into some friends waiting in line for the next show. We were so excited to tell them about the greatest show we had ever seen.

Michael Funke *(age 18)*

That 1965 US tour promoted their fourth US LP *Out of Our Heads* and a few of the stops included two shows in one night. San Jose was one of those. My friend Glenn and I had tickets to the first show. I still have the $5.50 ticket stub— Section 209, Row D, Seat 5 in the balcony, facing the stage. I was a bigger Stones fan than Glenn, but it was his first Stones show, and we were a pair of excited 18 year old white bread suburban kids that night. Glenn favored Keith.

I was – and still am – a Brian Jones fan. While we knew what marijuana smelled like, neither of us had smoked pot (yet) and our first trip to a psychedelic dance hall was three months away. We were there for the music, for the Stones, and we restlessly sat through several opening acts – the Rocking Ramrods, the Embers, Vibrations, Patti LaBelle and the Blue Belles and more. And, finally, the Stones! 'Dam deedle dee dam dam, little girl where did you come from?' They quickly rolled through a dozen songs, ending with their huge 1965 hit *Satisfaction* a little over 30 minutes after they kicked it off with *She Said Yeah*.

I'm not sure what happened next. We were simultaneously pumped about the show and disappointed that it was so short. It was probably Glenn who suggested we try to find a place to hide while ushers cleared the auditorium for the second show.

Anyway, we ended up in a men's restroom with maybe half a dozen other guys. We were all

Michael Funke

milling around, talking excitedly, determined to find a place to hide but clueless about where that might be. Suddenly a guy wearing black engineer boots, a black leather jacket and sporting a ducktail – a 'greaser' in the language of the Fifties – strutted in and up to a small square door in the far wall. He lifted his leg and kicked the door open. We all piled in. The greaser – our hero now – and a few other guys pressed their bodies against the door and he told us to shut up. We sat mutely, looking up at the tiered seats of the balcony above us. Finally we heard someone enter the restroom. We all seemed to press forward against the door and held our breath. There was a rap on the door. Another one. A grunt as someone pushed against it. Then footsteps, followed by silence.

I don't know how long we waited, but eventually we all piled out, smiled at one another in the bright lights of the restroom and went our separate ways. Glenn and I headed back to the balcony. The seats were rapidly filling up. We gazed down at our shoes and tried to look inconspicuous as ushers checked ticket stubs and rent-a-cops stood by. We stood in an aisle so we weren't blocking anyone's view and watched as the opening acts paraded out and performed identical short sets to kick off the second show. It seemed to go on forever. Finally, Patti LaBelle and the Blue Belles closed their set with *I Sold My Heart To The Junkman*, just as they had less than two hours earlier. By now Glenn and I were

vibrating with anticipation. This, we said, is going to be so cool. The auditorium was packed and everyone was ready to rock with the Stones. Finally, there they were back on stage. "Dam deedle dee dam dam, little girl where did you come from?"

Mick was prancing around like crazy. Well actually, pretty much exactly like he had pranced around in the first show. Wait a minute. Didn't he twirl the microphone cord at exactly the same time in the first show? Twelve songs later, after the last fuzzy tone of *Satisfaction* had faded away, Glenn and I looked at one another and essentially said "what a gyp". We knew next to nothing about the music scene and never considered that the Rolling Stones would be playing the same set night after night on their tour of the States. We know better now.

But despite the brief and repetitive shows, Glenn and I were more than satisfied. It was the Stones, after all, and we had heard some great tunes – *Hitch Hike*, *Mercy Mercy*, *The Last Time* and their latest single *Get Off of My Cloud*. So for two guys who had never smoked pot we were feeling pretty high as we hit the street, where we were suddenly surrounded by crazed, boisterous people, their faces painted day-glo, dressed up like clowns. The Merry Pranksters. They were passing out wildly drawn handbills that asked 'can you pass the Acid Test?' Well, even though we had never smoked dope we knew what that was about and our answer was "fuck, no."

Cynthia Porter

5 DECEMBER 1965
Sports Arena, Los Angeles, California

Cynthia Porter *(age 14)*
I went with my friend Jackie. Tickets were $5.50 and we didn't have a lot of money so I pulled weeds in my neighbours' yards at 25 cents an hour. I also cleaned hotel rooms. My mom drove us and went for a coffee across the street while she waited for the show to finish. I don't think Jackie's dad would have taken us. I think the reason I liked the Stones was because Mick was so weird. The other bands were in suits but the Stones wore tee shirts and sweatshirts. We were trying to get on stage but the security pushed us back. They were very gentle, not like they are today. I threw my bracelet at Mick. I would have thrown my bra on stage if I'd been wearing one but at 14 I didn't have any boobs! I loved Mick. I didn't like Brian because his hair made him look like a Beatle. I love Mick. I still do.

1966 started quietly for the Rolling Stones, with no performances until they arrived in Australia in February for their second tour Down Under. It was to be a quieter year generally, with fewer than 90 shows worldwide and only 23 in Britain. Something of a contrast to the height of their gigging activity in 1963 and 1964, when they routinely played more than 25 shows a month.

18 – 19 FEBRUARY 1966
Commemorative Auditorium Showgrounds, Sydney

John Dillimore (age 18)

I was born in England but was living in Sydney, Australia. I took a girl called Bridget. I recall a large crowd lining up to get in and an exciting atmosphere. I had got good seats and was only rows from the stage. The Searchers were the support band who were quite big at that time and sang Needles and Pins, a hit for them in those days. But primarily we were there to see the Rolling Stones and it was electric when they did come on. They wore white pants. Mick played tambourine. They sang 19th Nervous Breakdown and Satisfaction. Everyone was stoked and happy at that gig. I wish I still had the ticket.

21 FEBRUARY 1966
City Hall, Brisbane, Australia

Paul Chesher (age 15)

It was my first ever concert. It was held at the Milton tennis courts in Brisbane, an open air concert with the stage at one end of the arena. I was in the stand directly in front of the stage and we were so excited. The first set was fantastic and the crowd went wild. During the second set it started to rain

and the Stones kept playing for a few minutes and then stopped. We were sitting in the rain wondering if it would be cancelled and then Mick Jagger came on stage and said "if you guys can sit and listen in the rain then we will play in the rain." The crowd erupted. Despite the obvious dangers – the roadies must have been working feverishly to keep the electrics dry – they finished the concert with Jagger singing in the rain for the rest of the concert. We were all soaked to the skin but on such a music high. It was one of my most memorable experiences and demonstrated the group's dedication to their fans.

22 FEBRUARY 1966
Centennial Hall, Adelaide

Gus Howard

The band was more confident, had bigger amps and seemed more business like. They played That's How Strong My Love Is, Mercy Mercy, Get Off My Cloud, She Said Yeah, 19th Nervous Breakdown, The Spider and the Fly, Play With Fire, Satisfaction, and Not Fade Away – slightly more original Stones material this time but still some covers. I remember Brian had that same odd insecure look like he'd just stolen something. There was nothing in the show

> **"the announcer said the concert would be called off if people left their seats. That was our signal to go up front before everyone else did"**

or his playing that indicated the wide variety of instrumentation he was introducing to the recorded material of the band at the time. I half remember seeing him on that stage with a sitar, but I am not sure that's reliable. They must have been incredible pressurised then.

The shows were sandwiched by a just few days between appearing on *Ed Sullivan* in New York and returning to LA to complete the sessions for *Aftermath*, so the flat out professional Stones stage delivery may have also carried a bit of a 'where are we?' element.

After Australia, the Stones were back on tour in continental Europe in March and April and then off to the USA again in June.

24 JUNE 1966
Manning Bowl, Lynn, Massachusetts

Brian Grange *(age 14)*
It was drizzling a little bit and they were getting shocked with their guitars. They tear gassed the crowd and the wind blew the tear gas back to the stage. I saw Keith push a cop off the stage. Chairs were flying. Headlines the next day said 'Stones get stoned' because rocks were being thrown at the limo when they left. The stage was rushed twice. After the first time the local radio DJ grabbed the mic and said if that happens again the Rolling Stones will fly back to London. They played ten songs, 30 minutes, and it was over.

When we were walking in the limo passed us. I could see Charlie in the back seat next to the

window on the driver's side. Like Jagger said later "it wasn't very secure." Great show!

Gary Dombrowski *(age 15)*
What I remember most about that show was standing on the folding chairs watching Brian Jones sitting on the stage with his sitar, Mick announcing to the crowd "Lady Jane in the rain" and the smell of tear gas.

Colleen Oliver *(age 14)*
My parents drove me and my best friend, Arlene, to Lynn to see the Stones and planned to have dinner out while we were at the concert. Our seats were terrible – far back and on the ground. We couldn't see anything! I think it was during the intro for the Standells that the announcer said the concert would be called off if people left their seats. That was like our signal to go up front before everyone else did and that's exactly what happened. We were right in front and there were only saw horses and police between us and the Stones. Back then, the stages were very low so we felt like we could almost touch them. What an experience!

I vaguely remember them saying they were cutting it short due to the rain but I can't swear to it. What I do remember is the crowd pushing forward and us being pushed into the police. The next thing we knew tear gas was being thrown and we had no way to escape it – the crowd was behind us and the police and Stones in front of us. The tear gas was awful! I was separated from my friend and we spent hours looking for her. My poor parents were beside themselves but all ended well, thankfully. At the time, there was a photo published where we could pick ourselves out of the crowd but I don't think it exists anymore. We were also getting a reputation. What fun!

27 JUNE 1966
Dillon Stadium, Hartford, Connecticut

Don Massey (age 18)

I was a high school student at the time, and we were all caught up in the British mania of the period, and rightly so. Dillon was at that time a rather simple stadium of rather small dimensions and nothing close to what is now defined as stadium or arena that would be appropriate for shows, just a small bleacher seat space overlooking a field that was often used for high school football games and the like. There were no performance spaces suitable for shows in Hartford. It would be a number of years before a civic center would be built.

The excitement for Connecticut fans like me and my friends grew pre-show, as one would expect. The very idea that a British group would appear in our humble capital city was amazing in and of itself. The fact that it was going to be a Rolling Stones concert made the atmosphere thick with tension and pleasure.

By today's standards, there were relatively few uniformed officers arrayed around the stage but they were not likely to be pressed by crushing crowds, since those in

attendance were really quite tame. I recall thinking that the crowd was not very loud or rambunctious and I guess I expected that we would all combine our excitement into one powerful rush of sound, coupled with a rising tide of motion toward the stage but there was very little of the sort. Frankly, that surprised me. This was the Stones and they were right there in front of us. The Stones took the stage and it was obvious that the crowd was delighted.

As bands go they were as good as one would expect, their talent and execution honed very well by live shows in prior years in Britain. They looked as we expected – a touch of Carnaby Street evident in their costume choices. Sadly the show did not go its full length. From the very first the speaker system was quirky and irritating, prone to intermittent cut outs that left Mick Jagger singing largely to himself at stage front. A number of times the vocal audio simply stopped and each successive time made Jagger more and more frustrated. Even from my bleacher seat halfway back from the stage,

Don Massey (left) on bass guitar

it was obvious to me that Mick wanted a better sound system than was present that night, and his irritation grew with every interruption.

I have read that it was primarily because of the fans pressing toward the stage that led police to request that the show be terminated. I recall nothing intrinsically dangerous or threatening to either Mick or the fans down front that would have led a wary police force to cut the show early. In fact, Jagger voiced his displeasure with the sound system several times during the show, well before the culminating moment. I felt for Jagger and his band mates because the desire to provide the best show possible was being thwarted by the sound system. Each effort to correct it had failed. So, having reached his limit, Jagger simply stopped singing, tossed the mic stand into the crowd below and left the stage in a huff. The band never said anything to us before leaving the stage – they simply walked off. They were at the mercy of the production team who provided the sound.

Stunned as we were to realize that the show had come to a premature halt, we accepted it and filed out of the bleachers. Of course, a mic stand being thrown from the stage by a rowdy British singer whose anger was evident even 50 yards from the stage was a new thing for us. In my case, I empathized with Jagger and clung to the memory of his having tossed the stand from the stage as an appropriate gesture of his frustration and outrage. Now the

> **"am I glad they came to our city? Yes. Am I glad I went to the show? Absolutely"**

police might have contributed to the decision to end the show early, but the Stones were never in any physical danger and the crowd loved their work. I could not have accepted the sound issue if I were on stage to perform. The show ended because of the sound, and that's all there is to it.

Am I glad they came to our city? Yes. Am I glad I went to the show? Absolutely. Each time they return to Hartford or a nearby city, I am led to the memory of the Dillon show and the first evidence of Jagger's sexy surly nature that would contribute to the definition of the man and the band in coming years.

Rob Marona *(age 16)*
My band decided to go to see the Stones. The oldest of us had just turned 16 and nobody had a driver's license yet and none of our parents had volunteered to take us, so we hitchhiked all the way, just like the song. It was to be our first concert, with our number one heroes. What could be better than that?

The concert was at a college football stadium. Stones concerts in stadiums bring back memories for hundreds of thousands, if not millions, of people. But few have a memory like this one. I've never had good luck when it comes to the Stones. This had to be one of the worst concerts ever. First of all, it was the middle of the afternoon in the blazing sun, and only about 200 hundred people came. The stage was set up in the bleachers at the 50 yard line and the audience was made to sit in the bleachers on the opposite side with the empty field in between. There were a couple opening acts which we weren't interested in, and then the Stones arrived.

Three limousines drove out onto the field to the front of the stage and out they came. Apparently they were already experiencing conflicting ego problems. Surely they all could have fitted in one, or at most two, limos? Or maybe they had one as a decoy. They had to run for their lives from the girls sometimes back then. But not this day. They started playing and it soon became obvious, even from that distance, that something was wrong with Brian Jones. They played *The Last Time* and he just couldn't play the signature guitar lick right. And that seemed to amuse him. They played three, maybe four, songs. After about 10 or 12 minutes they quit, got back in the limos and left. I was very disappointed. I guess that's the way they did shows back then but by today's standards, and even then, it seemed like a rip off.

None of us remembers exactly how we got home that day, but we got right back to practicing, undaunted by the experience and no less committed to learning Stones tunes.

Roger Wiley

I attended the Rolling Stones concert at Dillon Stadium in Hartford. They arrived by helicopter. A very strange young woman dressed totally in black sat next to me and made very dark pronouncements to nobody

in particular. I suspect she may have been a prototype for the Goth era.

Linda Rinaldi *(age 15)*

Our local music shop in Meriden CT organized a bus trip to Dillon Stadium, about half an hour away. I remember folding chairs were lined up neatly in the outside ball field at Dillon Stadium. Everyone sat quietly and very well behaved, so different from a few years later when concerts were a free for all.

Chuck Sheketoff *(age 11)*

That was my first concert! My father took my brother and me. I was only 11 and my brother was almost 13. My memory of the details is vague although I've always imagined my dad was sitting with us smoking one of his cigars while older kids around us smoked pot!

1 JULY 1966
Steel Pier Marine Ballroom,
Atlantic City, New Jersey

Mary Jones

My Mom said I could go because she felt bad that I wasn't allowed to see The Beatles in 1964 in Philly. Six of us went. My friend Char said that we took two buses to get there. It probably took us three hours. We left early, about 6 am. Normally it would be one and a half hours by car.

Peter and Gordon opened and they were watching the show. At the intermission we ran so fast to see if the Rolling Stones were with them and all of our food dropped as we were running. What a day!

> "something was wrong with Brian Jones. They played The Last Time and he just couldn't get the signature guitar lick right. And that seemed to amuse him"

Natasha Conn

2 JULY 1966
Forest Hills Music Festival, Queens, New York

Stephen Conn

My mother, Natasha Conn, saw the Stones in concert in Forest Hills. Her girlfriend threw flashbulbs to make a couple dancing in front of them sit down and afterwards they noticed many dolled up girls waiting to be let into the band's hotel.

24 JULY 1966
Civic Auditorium, Bakersfield, California

Liz Beavers

My memories of the Stones at the Bakersfield concert in the Sixties were not that fond. Mick wore a white t-shirt and pink trousers. The singing was great but Mick sang with his back to the audience almost the entire time. He would prance back and forth occasionally and briefly turn around. I took it as a snub to Bakersfield. But, that was also back in the day when you expected a performer to face the audience. I think Johnny Cash was the first one to turn his back on the audience while singing.

25 JULY 1966
Hollywood Bowl, Los Angeles, California

Cynthia Porter

I wasn't near the front when I saw them at the Hollywood Bowl. I was sat next to Humble Harv. Humble Harv was a deejay with Radio KHJ in Los Angeles and he used to play *Goin' Home* by the Stones on his radio show every night at a quarter to twelve. It was fifteen minutes long and he'd close the show with it. I can remember cruising along Downey Boulevard to the first ever McDonalds listening to *Goin' Home*.

I think the reason I didn't try to get on the stage at this show was because I was sat next to Humble Harv. I had Humble Harv sign my playbill. To begin with I thought 'I don't want this messing up' and then I thought 'but it's Humble Harv!'

11 SEPTEMBER 1966
Ed Sullivan Theater, New York, New York

Joanne Rogers

I saw them with Brian at the *Ed Sullivan Theater*. For some reason I remember Tom Jones being on the same bill. If you look it up it says that they were on the same bill together on 2 May 2 1965 but I know I did not go on that date as it was my brother's birthday and in an Italian family – in mine, anyway – you celebrated each other's birthday.

We had no tickets to get in but we waited outside to see them. I remember a police officer grabbing Brian's long blond hair as he mistakenly thought that Brian was a female fan trying to run in the entrance of the theater. Of course, seeing the Stones without the whole entourage they travel with now was so refreshingly beautiful. Just them and their music.

The Stones returned to the UK to perform what would prove to be their last British tour of the 1960s.

23 SEPTEMBER 1966
Royal Albert Hall, London

Stephen Moyce *(age 16)*
I was 16 in September 1966 when I paid the then exorbitant sum of £5 to see the Stones play at the Royal Albert Hall in London. The package tour mindset still existed then and supporting the Stones were, incredibly, the Yardbirds featuring both Jeff Beck and Jimmy Page, and Ike and Tina Turner.

As the evening progressed, the atmosphere and tension building up in the Hall was almost palpable – we were going to see the Stones for real! Seeing them on TV and playing their records was great, but this was different. At last they were on – the hall erupted in total chaos with the deafening

Stephen Moyce

noise from the screaming girls, many of whom rushed the stage. They were continually repelled by the security guys and, amazingly, concert promoter Tito Burns. The Stones played on regardless.

My seat was about thirty feet from the stage and I could clearly see Brian Jones, resplendent in a purple velvet jacket. He was smiling at all the mayhem as his rhythm guitar chords helped power along all the hits – the Stones had notched up six number ones since 1964. The vocals were virtually inaudible. The Hall in 1966 had yet to receive the necessary saucer-shaped acoustic baffles and Mick Jagger's best efforts just disappeared into the vast roof space but it didn't matter. The experience of it all was totally overwhelming. What a time to be a teenager! The next twelve months would see the Stones embroiled in the Satanic Majesties album and Brian's sad decline accelerate alarmingly. But on that early autumn evening they were peerless – and I was there!

Brenda Parker
Brian just stood quietly playing his guitar and staring up at the ceiling, seemingly in a world of his own. Mick was the centre of attention and now that he had his James Brown moves down pat he was the one everyone looked at and the others just played behind him, almost as if they were his backing group. Not

"if he wanted me to come he should have made special arrangements including sending a limo to pick me up"

that it mattered as before they'd even played a note everyone was already screaming at the top of their lungs!

Stash Klossowski de Rola
There was a famous show I went to with the band where the girls stormed the stage immediately and it was over in a matter of moments. Very often they ended like that. They totally lacked crowed control so it just turned into a mess. I've seen them dozens and dozens of times in various venues. I don't even go any more.

Mick Jagger was wondering why I hadn't come when they played in Rome last year and I said "well, you know, if he wanted me to come he should have made special arrangements including sending a limo to pick me up here at Montecalvello." Because I wasn't about to brave those crowds to go to a Stones gig. The last time I went to a Stones gig was in LA for A Bigger Bang. And although I was invited it took me two hours to get to the gig when it should have taken an hour from my house. It took an extra hour to approach and find a place to park.

There was a special VIP section with the sound box and it was great to see the show. But either you went with them in buses for the guests and then you had to miss three or four numbers or you went with your own transport but then it took you another couple of hours to get to where you were going. By the time I went to the hotel Keith had gone to bed.

24 SEPTEMBER 1966
Odeon Theatre, Leeds

Brian Robinson (age 21)
My job was travelling all around the country and I happened to be in Leeds in 1966 selling decorating materials and all that sort of stuff. We were in a hotel and saw that the Rolling Stones were on in a cinema just round the corner. So we went and got tickets. It was probably ten shillings to see them and it was the Rolling Stones, Ike and Tina Turner, the Beach Boys.

We were sitting on the second row in and when they'd finished the concert we were very close to the emergency exit doors on the side, and me and two mates who I was working with opened the doors because we wanted to get out quick and there was an alleyway down the side and a big stretch limo and I ran out first and bumped straight into Keith Richards. And they got in the limo and drove off.

25 SEPTEMBER 1966
Empire Theatre, Liverpool

Alan Powell (age 15)
I was in row V. The price was 17 shillings (85p). Well, they had to pay for those outrageous clothes somehow. The opening acts were Ike and Tina Turner and the Ikettes, The Yardbirds with Jeff Beck and Jimmy Page on guitars, Peter Jay and the New Jaywalkers and Long John Baldry. The Stones played tracks off Aftermath and were awesome. I remember that the lighting was very good. Charlie introduced Lady Jane and Brian,

his hand bandaged, played his dulcimer with a big white feather. They had so much energy. The place was bouncing and it was over too soon. We later saw the footage of the London Albert Hall gig from the same tour and it brought it all back.

Christine McDermott

28 SEPTEMBER 1966
ABC Theatre (aka The Apollo), Ardwick, Manchester

Christine McDermott *(age 14)*
I was sat in the stalls – seat E2. The Stones had Ike and Tina Turner as one of the support acts. Having been to see The Beatles twice in Ardwick, when it came to the Stones concert I knew that for artists to get away from the theatre quickly they went out of the stage door and through the back yard of a terraced house that backed on to the theatre and out through their front door where their car was waiting for them. I found this out because I was friends with Eric Stewart's sister, he from the Mindbenders. They lived near me in Ardwick and Eric went to school with my cousin. Knowing this we were able to get out of the theatre and round to the house just as they were coming out into their car.

Like most of the concerts back then you didn't hear much of the music for all the screaming but the Stones were one of the bands you wanted to hear so the later ones weren't too noisy that you could hear quite a bit of the songs. I count myself lucky to have been a teenager and lived in Manchester during that period.

It was such an amazing place for music, clubs and concerts. I prize my autographs, especially the Brian Jones one. I also have Otis Redding's autograph as I saw him at the Ardwick ABC on his last tour before he died.

29 SEPTEMBER 1966
Globe Theatre (aka ABC Theatre), Stockton-on-Tees

Ian Gilfellan *(age 16)*
I had to hitch a ride from work to buy the tickets as I only had enough for them and no fare to Stockton – that was in July, about the same time as the World Cup finals. Jimmy Page and Jeff Beck were in the Yardbirds. I remember Jeff tried playing his guitar over his head and didn't notice he'd pulled his lead out. We ended walking back to Middlesbrough.

George Morland *(age 17)*
After seeing them in 1964, the next time I saw the Stones was at the ABC in 1966 ticket price 15/- (75p) where we sat in the circle. I went with my girlfriend – now

my wife of 45 years. The show was excellent apart from the non stop screaming when the Stones came on.

Barbara Gibbon *(age 19)*
My friend Jean and I were at the Globe when they played with the Yardbirds, Ike and Tina Turner and I am sure Billy J Kramer and The Dakotas were also on that night. We decided to go to Stockton early on the morning of the Stones gig. We walked from Middlesbrough. Venues for groups and artists in the Sixties weren't large arenas like they are today, and you were quite close up to the artists in the theatres then. So we decided to go early to find a way into the building so that we could see and talk to the Stones, and mainly Mick Jagger.

Our plan went really well. We sneaked in and looked round the place. The only place we could find where we could hide and not be seen was a dressing room with a wash basin with a curtain round. We got under and pulled the curtain over. We hid there for quite a while and then some people came in and were talking. We don't know what they were doing but later assumed they were getting ready for the show because all of a sudden the curtain was pulled back and there was Keith Relf of the Yardbirds with a drier in his hand. He must have been looking for somewhere to plug it into. We just crouched there looking amazed and never said a word. Neither did Keith – he just walked away. We weren't bothered about the Yardbirds at

the time, all we wanted was to see Mick Jagger just like we had seen Keith.

A good few minutes later some man who worked in the Globe came in, pulled back the curtain and told us we weren't allowed in the dressing rooms or anywhere else in the theatre until the doors opened for the show. He took us to the stage door entrance and said that was the best he could do. It was okay with us as when the Stones did arrive although there were other screaming fans with us by then, we got to actually see them close up and touch them. It was a brilliant time.

We had tickets four rows from the front. What a good view we had. Of course we were all screaming so you couldn't hear the words of the songs. What a fantastic show. When the Stones had finished girls were throwing things on the stage to them. I had nothing to throw so I took one of my shoes off and threw that. Mick picked it up and threw it back. Was I glad! Not only had Mick Jagger touched my shoe and thrown it back, but it had never entered my head as to how I would have walked back to Middlesbrough with only one shoe.

30 SEPTEMBER 1966
Odeon Theatre, Glasgow

Gordon Rennie *(age 16)*
I saw the Rolling Stones at the Odeon Cinema in Renfield Street. Long John Baldry compered the show. The support acts were Peter Jay and the New Jaywalkers, the Yardbirds and finally the Ike and Tina Turner Revue – quite a

> "although there were other screaming fans with us by then, we got to actually see them close up and touch them. It was a brilliant time"

line up. I don't think I heard much of the Stones due to screaming. The cost of this show was 12/6 or about 63p in today's money.

6 OCTOBER 1966
Odeon Theatre, Birmingham

Penny Edwards (age 14)

There were no big venues or anything like the NEC etc that there is today. This was held at the Odeon Cinema on New Street in Birmingham city centre. It's still there. The Stones were very scruffy and still are, but the sound – wow! I was with a girl friend and I'm not sure how much we paid but it wouldn't have been a lot then. We stood at the side of the cinema, perhaps because it was cheaper, but we rocked for three hours. The most vivid memory was being deaf for three days afterwards. No health and safety spoiling your fun in those days. Plus we couldn't hear our parents moaning!

Pauline Lever (age 16)

After seeing the Stones in Northampton in 1965, my friend Kay and I were itching for more. We looked at tour dates and discovered that they were appearing at the Birmingham Odeon in October. We booked tickets and thought we would worry about getting there nearer the time. As time drew near we asked my friend's dad for a lift there. He refused and my parents didn't have a car and we were getting concerned. My boyfriend at the time came up with an idea and the day before the concert

we spent an agonising few hours waiting to see if his friend could find somewhere to hire a car. He was 17 and most places said no. However he did get one and on the day we were picked up at 5.15pm and we were on our way. The lad put his foot down on the motorway and we drove at speed towards Birmingham.

Kay and I soon found the Odeon and we snooped about trying to find someway to perhaps get into the building. We were moved on a few times and eventually tried to get into a pub close by. Once inside I looked around and noticed a blond young man standing with a group by the bar. My heart almost stopped but a closer look revealed he was not Brian. I said to my friends "he looks like Keith (Relf) of the Yardbirds (who were also appearing) but his hair is too short." Later at the show it was revealed Keith had in fact had his hair cut shorter and it must have been him. However we were soon spotted and thrown out of the pub.

Time soon came around for the concert to start and we went into the Odeon, hearts beating and feeling very excited, the only thing was we were not in the stalls but upstairs in the circle. The show itself was very good – the line up was Long John Baldry, Peter Jay and the New Jaywalkers, The Yardbirds and Ike and Tina Turner, but we had come to see The Stones, and the others were poor comparison. However Ike and Tina were fantastic and The Yardbirds were also very good. The tension inside us was building

> "the line up was Long John Baldry, Peter Jay and the New Jaywalkers, The Yardbirds and Ike and Tina Turner. But we had come to see the Stones"

up and when the Stones came on we almost burst with excitement. My eyes fixed on Brian and I screamed and shouted and just ran for the edge of the circle. I remember looking down at the stalls and longing to be there. I actually remember wondering if I could climb down and even – if I jumped would I be ok? Which of course was silly and I would probably have been killed. A bouncer came and grabbed me and said "I hope you are not thinking of jumping" and he sent me to my seat and said if I moved he would throw me out.

The Stones were fantastic. They sang *The Last Time*, *Paint It Black*, *Lady Jane*, *Under My Thumb*, *Get Off Of My Cloud* and *Satisfaction*. Towards the end other girls from the circle started to go to the edge and we also went and stood by the edge and waved and screamed. Downstairs all hell had let loose and we longed to be there.

The show came to an end and we filed outside where people were selling posters. I queued, watching as the posters of Brian were disappearing quickly, but I purchased my prize and we met the boys. This was the Sixties and the drink driving law hadn't come in. The boys had been drinking and they were listening to our constant talk about the show which probably distracted the driver. He went out of a side road and we saw a bus coming and knew there was no way we were going to miss it. We went straight into the bus, causing a huge dent, and skidded to a halt.

The police arrived and were lovely. They made a huge fuss of Kay and I and laughed because I was crying and saying "I have creased my poster of Brian". We were basically unhurt – just bumps and bruises. They took us to a garage and the car was towed there. When we arrived they made us sweet tea and arranged for someone from the hire company to come and get us. They asked if we should phone home and I suddenly realised I had lied to my parents and that they thought Kay's father was taking us. They would not have let us go with the boys.

We got home about 5.30am and immediately Mum asked if Kay's dad and the car were OK and I had to come clean. The car was written off and something was mentioned about a court case but I don't remember anything about whether it took place. I got into a lot of trouble for lying but we had seen the Stones again and survived the crash. After sleeping for about an hour I was dragged out of bed to go to work – at 16 I had been working for about six months. What an experience we had had, but it was all worth it to see the Rolling Stones, the best ever group, and to see my blond hero, albeit from a distance.

9 OCTOBER 1966
Gaumont Theatre, Southampton

Graham Kesby *(age 16)*
I couldn't get away from work because I was working by then. I went down to the box office in my lunch time thinking they'd

all be sold out and I was able to get tickets. I think the PAs had improved a little bit but it was still a mass of screaming in '66.

Michael Smith (age 24)
It's now called the Mayflower but it was then the Gaumont and they had a bit more stage presence then because Mick just turned round and said "shut up everyone otherwise I shan't sing any more. And I wanna do a quiet one." It was *Lady Jane* and he got absolute quiet before he started on that one. It was just all these screamers and they just didn't worry about being able to hear what they were playing. Mick just came on and said "be quiet otherwise we won't carry on."

There were a lot of girls there. There was a good mix of ages. I suppose there was from about 16 to about 30 there would have been. At the time you were either a Beatles fan or a Rolling Stones fan. The Beatles were all right to start with but to me they just went

off. When they got to *Sergeant Pepper* I thought that was a load of rubbish. I liked the Stones right from the start and stuck with them.

When I got the tickets for the Gaumont my girlfriend at the time was more into classical music. And I said "I've managed to get tickets for the Rolling Stones." And her reaction? "I don't like the Rolling Stones." I said "well I've got tickets now so we're going!" "Well," she said, "I'll come with you on one condition. That you come with me to a concert I want to go to." And I said "yeah, fine." So I had to sit through the Vienna Boys' Choir. At half time when the lights came up I sank down in the seat so that no one could see me in case anybody I knew was there and thought "what's he doing there?" Some of it was in English and some of it was in Austrian. I took Sally to see the Rolling Stones and then I had to put up with the Vienna Boys' Choir. It was worth it to see the Rolling Stones.

> "I took Sally to see the Rolling Stones and then I had to put up with the Vienna Boys' Choir. It was worth it to see the Rolling Stones"

Chapter 22

1966 saw the end of the Rolling Stones extensive touring schedule within the UK. 1967 was to be another quiet year for the group in terms of live performances. Apart from a 27 show tour of Continental Europe, which included the first performances by a Western rock music band behind the Iron Curtain, the Stones did not play live. Instead, recording and other off stage interests increasingly pre-occupied the different band members.

15 JANUARY 1967

Ed Sullivan Theater, New York, New York

Barbara Neumann Beals

So we got to go to *Ed Sullivan*. My sister Lynne took us to the hotel and they were not there. So she said "just poke around. Take anything you want." I was like "what?" So we each took a pack of cigarettes. And I just happened to take Mick Jagger's harmonica. Which I still have! I still have it proudly in my room and I still can't believe I did that when I was – what – 14, 15 years old. But I did. And I think we each took one little bit of clothing. We didn't steal like money or anything like that. Just little mementoes.

So then we had to hurry and we got in the audience for *Ed Sullivan*. And that was the famous night when the Singing Nuns refused to go on. They were to appear the same night as the Stones but they took offence at the lyrics for *Let's Spend The Night Together* and they told Ed Sullivan that they would not go on unless the lyrics were changed. So I got to hear all this going on. It was fascinating. And finally they changed the lyrics. But Mick leered at the camera when he said "let's spend some time together." It was absolutely hilarious. And of course the audience was in on the

whole thing. So we just continued screaming "Mick! Keith!"

Carol Siegel

I met the Stones outside Colony Records in NYC a couple of hours after the *Ed Sullivan Show* where they had to change the lyrics to *Let's Spend The Night Together*.

Carol Siegel with Brian Jones and friend

Barbara Neumann Beals

My sister Lynne made herself very useful to cement the friendship between her and the Stones. She invited Charlie's wife Shirley to go clothes shopping. They went to Bloomingdales – naturally – and Arnold Constable, which is now defunct but was very popular at the time. Lynne told me Shirley was very shy, very sweet and overwhelmed by the fans, none of whom recognized her. They had a great time!

She'd do small errands for various Stones, since it was hard

Carol Siegel with Keith Richards

for them to sneak out. She went with them to Arthur's, near the 59th St Bridge, one of the first huge clubs for rock stars. She brought my brother Eric to meet them there, before he shipped out to Vietnam. Obviously he was thrilled and brought me a souvenir – an Arthur's ashtray. I always wanted to meet Keith in the 1990s or 2000s to present him with this rare souvenir – ha ha! Unfortunately it broke recently, so that's that. I have nothing but wonderful memories of that magical time, actually meeting the Stones, long before it became synonymous with the name groupie or other derogatory assumptions. For Lynne and me it was such a special time during the Swinging Sixties, wearing the Carnaby Street look and being the envy of friends.

They were just charming and smart and it was just nice. They couldn't have been more polite. That's what struck me. They were just so polite. So nice and I think at that time they just had a lot of respect for younger fans. And they knew I was a rabid fan. My sister told them she had to do the talking for me. Because I literally just couldn't speak. I was so scared. They were joking around saying "come on."

There were no drugs, not that I saw at the time. It's not like they were offering me drugs. It was all very sweet and very innocent. My sister during all this time had stayed in touch with the Stones and she really became quite chummy with them. She dated Keith for a while but it wasn't

the great love affair or anything like that. And I think she ended up really liking Andrew Oldham. But just for those few years, a period of about four years, I got to meet them. I talked to Keith on the phone one night. He had a blackout back then and my sister was there and she said "Keith has nothing to do I thought we'd give you a call." I said "what?" So I was on the phone with Keith for about half an hour I thought "who's going to believe that I'm talking to Keith Richard?" and I was trying to sound like I knew what I was talking about. I did grow up with the old blues so we were talking about blues and Muddy Waters and he said "oh you like that stuff?" and I said "yeah, I sort of grew up with it" and "we loved that stuff. My parents used to go to the Cotton Club." He was intrigued and he was so nice. They were all so nice. There was never anything like 'oh, I'd like to screw your sister'. There was never ever, ever anything like that. It wasn't raunchy. It was just very in the early stages. They just wanted to know how they were doing.

They were hoping that they'd be a bigger success. And when that happened we absolutely lost touch with them. As my sister went on to other groups and they became more famous then it all kind of faded away, little by little. The minute they became so big it was a whole different world. For those few years of the early swinging Sixties, with the English mods and the early part of the British Invasion – when we tried to dress like Patti Boyd or

> "it's not like they were offering me drugs. It was all very sweet and very innocent"

Jane Asher or Marianne Faithfull – it was quite a charming and relatively innocent time. It was just quite a thrill. But my sister went on from there to meet Eric Clapton, the Animals and the Kinks. So all I know is I remember getting a lot of front row center seats for a lot of concerts that were pretty darned good. I just consider myself very lucky.

I haven't gotten any big phone calls from Keith lately but that one phone call I treasure. Those were really special times. I'd like to thank the Stones for changing our lives in the most positive, friendly way.

6 APRIL 1967
Palazzo Dello Sport, Rome

Stash Klossowski de Rola
Brian was then with Anita and so I saw a lot of the other Rolling Stones as well throughout '66. In the fall of '66 I went to Rome and then in '67 the Stones came to Rome. And I went with them to the gig at Pallazo Dello Sport in Rome which was a big gig. It was memorable.

It was a very, very good live concert by the Stones. It was amazing. The sound was very good. There was still some screaming but the hysteria had somewhat subsided and so you could actually hear the songs. And I remember how everyone was impressed with Brian playing the dulcimer, playing all these different instruments. And I actually rode in their car with them and went with them. And in fact I was actually expecting to go up with them

at one point and play with them on stage but in the excitement it just didn't happen. There we stood with Gina Lollobrigida and so on. It was wild. And then the management of the Piper Club said "oh, you're friends with the Stones? Can you invite them down on our behalf?" And we all ended up staying, with the exception of Keith who took a plane and went straight back after the gig to be with Anita because that's when that split had occurred between Brian and Anita. So there was some tension.

I was going to do a film in America with my then fiancée Romina Power who was Tyrone Power's daughter. She'd gone on ahead to America. And I was supposed to do a picture with her with John Huston. And Brian said "listen, we're going on to Greece. If you're stopping in London stay at my house and I'll put my car and driver at your disposition." And Brian then asked me to go with him to Cannes, to delay my departure. That otherwise he wouldn't go and did I think he had a chance to get Anita back? Which I believed he did. So we went to Cannes and it was fun, although it didn't quite work out as Brian had hoped. And then Brian and I went back to Paris. We'd both been flirting with Suki and we called Suki and made her join us in Paris at the Lancaster Hotel and then Suki and Brian went together and then we went back to London. Brian and I were alone and I was preparing for my last few days in London when we were busted and history was completely changed.

JUNE 1967

Halland, Lewes, East Sussex

Charlie Watts purchased a mansion in Halland near Lewes in East Sussex.

Bob Fairweather

My brother and I were asked to erect a prefabricated building for Charlie Watts at his home in Halland, Sussex. We found his house and woke Charlie up and he made us a cup of tea. He showed us where he wanted the building erected. The prefab was for Charlie's wife to do her sculpture in. It was a carry of about 75 yards through mud. As the prefab weighed about seven and a half tons in all we were not happy. I said if he helped us we would do it and he agreed. I must mention here that Charlie was an animal lover and had dogs of every breed running around.

We worked until midday, when he had to go off for a recording session. His wife took him to Uckfield station because Charlie couldn't drive. Before he went he lent me his wellies as the sole had come off my shoe. I had to telephone my firm at two o'clock and he said I could use the phone in his house and had left the door undone for me. At 2pm I went down to the house, opened the door and was confronted by white carpets, so I had to take my wellies off. I made the call, opened the door to come out and was met by Charlie's dogs. They were snarling and wouldn't let me get to his wellies. They had followed me most of the day with no trouble

Bob Fairweather

and it suddenly dawned on me that it was Charlie's wellies they liked and not me. Once I took them off I was doomed.

I had to make my way through the house and get out through a window. I ran back up to the prefab in my socks and got up on the roof, where I stayed until they lost interest and wandered off. While we were unloading the prefab Charlie told us that when Keith Richards used to call he would drive his Jag up the drive at 100mph and do a handbrake turn, scattering gravel all over his flower beds. In the newspaper that morning was an article saying that the Stones had become millionaires. I told Charlie this and he just shrugged. I don't think money meant that much to him. He also told me he used to live in a prefab with his parents. He had no airs and graces. He was one of the nicest blokes I ever met.

JULY 1967
King's Road, London

Stephen Conn

In 1967 my mother Natasha Conn was living in London to study ballet. One day, sitting in a coffee shop on the King's Road, she overheard some school girls say "oh, look a Rolling Stone! A Rolling Stone!" She turned to see Brian Jones talking to the Russian dancer Rudolf Nureyev. While she found Nureyev the more magnetic of the two, she distinctly remembers Brian wearing a purple jacket, with white cuffs practically flowing to the floor.

SEPTEMBER 1967
Courtfield Road, London

David Kirch

The Rolling Stones rented a large flat from me in London in Courtfield Road, South Kensington. The living room was oak panelled and it must have been at the time that they were accused of taking drugs because there was a raid at my flat, which involved the removing of the panelling, as presumably drugs might have been hidden behind it. Anyway, no drugs were found and the panelling was put expertedly back again and they paid all their rent so it was not really a problem to me.

NOVEMBER 1967
London Clinic, London

Annette Williams

I am from Western Australia and came to the UK for six months and stayed 13 years. Most of the Sixties I spent in London and worked as a nurse at the London Clinic. In November 1967 I looked after Linda Keith, and Brian Jones was a frequent visitor. At that time I was – and still am – a Beatles fan but my 12 year old brother Denis back in Australia was a Rolling Stones fan. I bought a Stones 45 record for him with a view to asking Brian to autograph it for Denis. When I saw Brian on his visit to Linda Keith I asked him if he would autograph the 45. He looked at the record and then said "I will give you a special sleeve and autograph it."

A few days later Brian came in to see Linda. He gave me the sleeve and autographed it for me. The sleeve was *2000 Light Years From Home*. Long afterwards I discovered that the first 45 I had asked him to autograph was by someone called Paul Jones. I admire Brian and what a gentleman to save me from acute embarrassment and then giving me his own sleeve that he had designed. He was truly a kind person and a dedicated musician.

I left the UK in 1971 to return home. In 1991 I read Bill Wyman's Stone Alone and was amazed to read about the sleeve Brian gave me. Later I was in need of a new stereo system and I thought 'I am sure Brian would not mind' so I put the sleeve up for auction. It went for $1,400 and I received a cheque for $1,000 and bought a great stereo. Thanks Brian – I really enjoy my music.

12 MAY 1968
Empire Pool, Wembley

As the band increasingly experimented with drugs much of the latter part of 1967 and early 1968 was taken up with police interest and media scrutiny of the band's off stage interests, including occasional court appearances. Time spent in the recording studio, not always productively, outweighed that spent performing live. Then in May 1968 the Rolling Stones made a surprise and unbilled appearance at the annual New Musical Express Poll-Winners' Concert performing *Jumping Jack Flash* and *(I Can't Get No) Satisfaction*. It was their first live performance anywhere in the world in over a year.

Graham Kesby
The Beach Boys were the top of the bill. But the Stones came on just before the Beach Boys. And then the Beach Boys came on after the Stones.

11 DECEMBER 1968
Wembley, London

The Rolling Stones decided to produce a concert film based around a live performance by the band with a circus theme. The aim was to make a full length TV show that would provide sufficient transmittable footage such that the band would not need to travel to TV studios around the world to perform, a task made more onerous by the convictions for drug related offences that Mick, Keith and particularly Brian had accumulated in the two years they had been away from live performance. It was to be Brian's last public appearance as a member of the Rolling Stones.

Graham Kesby
They were all in the room in front of me. With all the other people who were on there.

Stash Klossowski de Rola
It was really, really tragic with Brian because downers make you lose your ability and he lost musical ability, considerable musical ability, in that process. It didn't get any better. He had sparking moments. He played brilliantly on *No Expectations*. But to me it's very painful to watch the Rolling Stones Rock'n'Roll Circus because Brian is a shadow of himself. He doesn't do any of the introductions properly. I'm just aghast when I see him on that. He can barely hold it together. Brian. This amazing force. This amazing beacon of light that he had been was a sorry caricature. I miss him a great deal. I loved the guy.

Chapter 23

After their May 1968 appearance at Wembley the Rolling Stones did not perform live in front of a paying audience for the remainder of 1968 or for the first six months of 1969. Recording for their next album *Let It Bleed* took up much of the early part of the year, although sessions were sporadic with band members arriving at different times. Brian Jones, increasingly ostracised by Mick Jagger and Keith Richards, made only limited contributions to the new album. Mick and Keith, wanting to tour the USA again but aware that Brian's drug convictions meant he was unlikely to obtain a visa enabling him to appear with the band, took the decision to sack Brian and, along with Charlie, visited Brian at his home in Sussex to break the news. Brian left the group in June 1969 and announced that he would instead devote his energies to other musical projects. The band announced a return to live performance with a free concert in London's Hyde Park. Two days before the concert was due to take place Brian Jones was found dead in the swimming pool at his home in Sussex, apparently the result of drowning. The band elected to press on with the Hyde Park show. Their last performance in Britain in the 1960s was hastily rebadged as a tribute to Brian, the founding member of the Rolling Stones.

5 JULY 1969
Hyde Park, London

Elaine Spinks *(age 19)*
I went to Hyde Park in 1969 the day of the free concert by the Stones just after Brian Jones had died. The memory of walking in Hyde Park towards the stage with thousands of other fans still brings goose bumps now. The atmosphere in the park that day was amazing – there was no trouble and my friend and I were right at the front side of stage. We saw Mick Jagger and Marianne Faithfull get out of a car back stage and he waved. There was almost silence when they walked on stage, Mick with his white smock on and new guitarist Mick Taylor. Jagger spoke emotionally about the band's loss and then released some doves – you could have heard a pin drop and then everyone cheered. What a day!

Andy Thompson *(age 20)*
I went down on the midnight train from Sheffield and got to Hyde Park about quarter to seven in the morning. It was a really hot day. And we were possibly eighty yards off stage in the park for 6.45am. The Stones didn't come on until around 7.00 pm, a long wait but well worth it. But they were absolutely rubbish that day. They were in an air conditioned caravan because it was such a hot day and they tuned all the guitars and when they got on stage all the tuning went out. They weren't very good at all.

Jilly Williamson *(age 20)*
It was a boiling hot day. Anticipating a huge crowd, myself and friends left Aylesbury on the first train having been up all night to make quite sure we did so. We were at the park well before 8am

and found a good position not too near the stage on a slight rise to give us a good view. There were a few people around the stage and a couple of dog walkers. We slept. I still remember the amazement of waking in a crowd that stretched as far as the eye could see. It was a great show apart from the fainters from the heat. These were man-handled over heads to I don't know where. I didn't need the loo – which was just as well.

Bill Shelton

I was so far back and over the brow of a hill that I gave up and went to the Albert Hall to see Chuck Berry and The Who. When I asked for tickets at the box office they told me that Chuck had been taken ill and would not be appearing. Chuck is my all time hero so I gave up and caught the train back early! The following week I read a review in the Melody Maker which said that Chuck did perform that night so the day had turned out to be a complete flop.

Guðbjörg Ögmundsdóttir
(age 17)

Nothing could dampen my spirits that day. There was not a cloud in the sky. Within me I still felt the deep sorrow for Brian's sudden passing. But today was a celebration of his life and his music. A Danish friend from work was going with me. When we got out into the street outside the hospital where we had been working we were filled with suspense and excitement. Almost immediately we noticed the headlines of the day on every

other street corner. We stopped and bought some papers and saw pictures of people lying in sleeping bags in front of the enclosure in front of the stage. We had not realized that people had started arriving at Hyde Park the evening before and the police, afraid they would have a riot on their hands, would let them stay in the park throughout the night. This was unheard of – Hyde Park was always locked at night.

We hurried down the Underground and made the short journey to the nearest station to where the concert was being held. The trains and the sidewalks were filled with young people around our age and some a little bit older, a few a lot older. Everyone had long hair. We had never seen so many hippies walking along the streets and they were coming from all directions. When we

Guðbjörg
Ögmundsdóttir

reached the area in front of the stage where people were already sitting and lazing in the sunshine, everyone was really cool and friendly. By this time my heart was beating so fast I thought I would have a nervous breakdown. I felt I needed to calm my nerves. To my surprise my friend pulled out a bottle of valium. She said she was going to take one and I took one too. We pulled out a sandwich to eat and a beer to drink with it and some of the people around us broke out in laughter and made some comments at us for being really uncool to have brought beer.

We really felt embarrassed. Of course we had smelled all the incense and joints in the air and when a joint was handed our way we accepted and took a drag or two and gave out sandwiches or fruit in return. No one wanted our beer. Everyone was really nice and friendly and it was a tremendous joy to be there among the crowd. I was amazed at the size of the crowd. It just went on for as far as you could see.

A few guys near us announced they had seen what they had come to see and it was time to split – the Rolling Stones were sell outs and not worth listening to anymore! The announcer explained Mick was going to read something for Brian and he was asking all of us to be quiet while he did so. Then thousands of white butterflies would be released. The Rolling Stones walked on stage and the roar of the crowd was unbelievable. They all looked so cool. Mick was wearing this incredible outfit.

> " thousands of beautiful white butterflies were released into the air. It looked so fitting and beautiful and I could feel my heart fill with joy"

The next day the headline across the front page of one paper read 'Where Did He Get That Frock?' He was all dressed in white and when he spoke everyone went quiet. It was the weirdest thing. But he didn't think the crowd was quiet enough. So he said "are you going to shut up or not?" After that you could have heard a pin drop. Then he read Shelley's poem in remembrance of Brian. It was very beautiful. I could feel the pain stinging in my heart. I really felt like crying.

Right afterwards brown cardboard boxes were brought out and thousands of beautiful white butterflies were released into the air. It looked so fitting and beautiful and I could feel my heart fill with joy. This was a moment in history that would not be forgotten. The Stones were on stage for over an hour, performing lengthy versions of most of their songs.

I felt empty inside after they left the stage. It almost seemed as if the sun had left the sky. Emotion was overcoming me and I suddenly felt all the anticipation, excitement and the experience of the day overwhelm me. I staggered off the path and sat down under a great big tree. My friend followed me and I told her I needed to take a moment to take all this in. Emotions absolutely overtook me and I started shaking and crying. Tears were streaming down my face. Almost at the same time I started laughing uncontrollably. All the grief of Brian's passing that I had been holding in and the joy of seeing the Stones perform just had to come out. I felt unspeakably happy and sad at the same time.

A couple of young guys came by and started asking me what was wrong but I couldn't talk. At last one of them said he thought he knew what I was feeling, that I was crying for Brian and laughing due to the happiness of having just seen the Stones perform.

Bob Lee

I was working at the AA. I think there was a big football match on at the same time. All the trains and all the coaches were full. So I thought 'I'm not going to be able to go'. By this time I was married. And the AA, for reasons that I can't understand, had a personnel manager for Manchester who in actual fact lived in London. And I knew this and I knew also that he commuted back at weekends so I dropped hints like bricks, you know, and he sussed this out and eventually he offered to give my wife and myself a lift down when he was going back on Friday. He kindly offered to put us up at his house as well. So that's how we managed to get down there. He was a big music fan but he was a jazz fan.

He ran us into Hyde Park as well. And that, again, was incredible. We didn't see an awful lot because we were quite far back but you could hear them clear enough. And I remember walking round London and we heard this record coming out of somewhere and I said "listen to that – it's fantastic." It was *Honky Tonk Women* which came out that weekend. That was

the first time I heard it and it just blew me away.

Thomas Marschik *(age 20)*

I had just finished my sophomore year in college. I missed meeting Keith Richards by 15 minutes as he came by the small hotel I was staying in near Paddington Station which was about a ten minute walk to Hyde Park. I slept in Hyde Park the night before the concert. There were perhaps maybe a hundred of us in my area which was right in the area where they were constructing the stage.

Someone had a radio and I must have heard *Honky Tonk Women* two dozen times that night as the song had just been released that Friday. There was also an announcement that because we were orderly the police would not come in and evict us, as Hyde Park at that time was always closed at night and no one was supposed to be there overnight. This caused someone to break apart a lawn chair and build a small fire. Luckily we were not evicted.

If you watch the concert video on *YouTube* and freeze it seven seconds in, there is a guy sitting in the middle of the frame in a blue jacket kind of by himself from the back. That I believe is me. Pretty cool.

Trish Cole

I went with a gang of lads; my then boyfriend and three or four of his mates. We drove up from Ashtead in an open topped Land Rover and, if I remember correctly, we were able to drive into the

> "I must have heard Honky Tonk Women two dozen times that night as the song had just been released"

> **"the screaming had mercifully stopped and the music was being taken seriously now"**

Park and actually leave the Land Rover quite close to the stage. I had long straight hair with a fringe then and someone yelled out "it's Marianne Faithfull!"

We were quite near the stage, where the ground began to rise away from the flat. People were mostly sitting and lying on the ground, with the odd person dancing. We were all very aware of the death of Brian Jones and I was interested to see how Mick Taylor would fit in. I remember when the butterflies were released, although I believe that many of the butterflies died. I can't remember anything about the quality of the performance but I liked Jagger's white 'dress'!

Brenda Parker

Hyde Park was like closing a chapter and turning the page and moving on into a new and very different decade. Everything had changed by then. It wasn't pop music anymore. Now it was rock and the Stones truly were 'The Greatest Rock 'n' Roll Band in the World'. The screaming had mercifully stopped and the music was being taken seriously now. Brian's recent departure had been a blow, but the word was that he was putting his own band together so that was something to look forward to and the announcement that the Stones would do a free concert to introduce his replacement was met with great excitement.

My friend Robert and I were really looking forward to it and were eager to see what the new Stones would be like, but of course Mick Taylor's debut was completely overshadowed by the terrible news of Brian's death and at first no one seemed to know if the concert would now take place. When word came that it was going on as planned, albeit now as a tribute to Brian, I felt it was the right thing to do.

It was such a strange and surreal day, firstly because the weather was so hot and secondly because I think we were all still trying to process the fact that Brian was dead. We weren't used to our rock stars dying then. Brian was the first and so it was truly shocking. I remember coming out of the Marble Arch tube station and seeing a veritable army of us all in our hippie finery streaming across Park Lane from every direction and heading into the park.

I was directly behind someone dressed from head to toe in heavy black velvet, maybe in mourning for Brian, and I remember thinking to myself "she's going to be so uncomfortable in such a heavy outfit in all this heat". I don't remember what time the concert was scheduled to begin but Robert and I got there only a couple of hours before the allotted time and had no trouble finding a place to sit only a few yards from where the stage was being set up. Everything was so much simpler then – can you imagine doing that now? And then we just sat there and waited for what seemed like forever.

Looking back on it I can't believe that we sat there for all those hours in the broiling heat with no food or drink. And if there were bathrooms set up anywhere, I don't remember seeing them! And yet it didn't bother us at all. As the time passed we could see that we'd been joined by heaven only knows how many thousands of people, some of whom had climbed trees way behind us.

It was literally a sea of people but everyone was friendly and good natured, although the mood was subdued because of Brian. At the sides of the stage the crew had set up a pair of massive pictures of Brian from the photo session for the inner sleeve of *Beggar's Banquet*, which I thought was an odd choice, but he had a big grin on his face so I guess that's why they'd been chosen.

It took forever before the Stones finally showed up and before they did we had to endure the Battered Ornaments, The Third Eye Band (or maybe the Third Ear Band? They were so boring I really didn't pay much attention to their name!) and Alexis Korner and the New Church, who I found very disappointing. Apparently King Crimson also played, although I have no recollection of them at all. I remember seeing Marsha Hunt in the area just in front of the stage all dressed in white fringed buckskin and looking fabulous but none of us knew then about the affair she was having with Mick. The security people made her move and she was obviously annoyed – apparently the security people didn't know about the affair either.

The security people were a bunch of bikers and I've always thought that it was because they did the security at this concert that the notoriously bad decision was made to use bikers as security at Altamont. The Brit bikers were pretty harmless but I don't think anyone realised that the Hell's Angels in California were just a bunch of vicious thugs and were actually nothing like their UK counterparts.

Anyway after what seemed like a really, really long time Sam Cutler finally announced the Stones and out came Mick in his Mr Fish white 'dress'. Knock offs showed up in the Oxford Street boutiques within days! He looked very serious and said he was going to say a few words for Brian and read a poem by Shelley but the sound system wasn't great and I think a lot of people thought he said he was going to read a poem by Che! And then the white butterflies were released. It was a nice gesture. I took a picture while they were being released.

A lot of the songs were from *Beggar's Banquet* and *Let it Bleed* and during *Midnight Rambler* a bunch of people sitting a couple of yards in front of us got up and blocked our view. Everyone was trying to get them to sit down again and when it became apparent that they weren't going to several people began shouting out to Mick asking him to make them sit. They got Mick's attention but instead of him shaming the standees he just shimmied his way to the other side of the stage as if to say 'hey, not my problem!' Fortunately they did eventually sit down, but it was no thanks to Mick. By the end of the concert Mick had ditched the dress in favour of the pale mauve sleeveless tee shirt he was wearing underneath it. He was full of energy and running and dancing all over the stage, but the concert itself was a bit ragged and I didn't think Mick Taylor looked very comfortable. And then it was over, it had been an emotional and very tiring day but it really was the end of an era. I still love the Stones and I always will, but I never went to see them again.

John Philpott

John Philpott

My sidekick Chris Poole and I had managed to convince the concert organisers Blackhill Enterprises that our local paper the Rugby Advertiser needed to cover the event. Our barefaced cheek had paid off as after a few calls two sky blue tickets for the press enclosure arrived in the post. Chris was the main mover here, for he had struck up a friendship with concert promoter Sam Cutler, the man who not only oversaw that historic London gig and who went on to become the Stones chief road manager.

That Saturday Chris and I rose early and made our way to Rugby Midland Station only to find that all the Euston bound trains were full. Somehow we managed to convince a guard that our mission was urgent, and he allowed us to ride in the mail carriage. The sky was as blue as our tickets when we joined the crowds heading for Hyde Park. Being in the press enclosure meant we were in the

company of the emerging rock aristocracy. In my case, that meant sitting next to pop starlet Marsha Hunt, a vision in white buckskins topped off with an Afro halo of hair.

All manner of bands prepared the way for the Stones, most of them now little more than musical memories. Pete Brown's Battered Ornaments, Third Ear Band, Screw... who knows what became of the musicians that helped to make history on the boiling hot day all those years ago? A crowd of nearly half a million listened to them politely, if a little dutifully, and then around mid-afternoon the Stones strode on stage. The footage has been played many times – Jagger in Greek soldier's ceremonial frock, Richards a living skull and the rest looking rather bewildered. Introduced by Sam Cutler as 'the greatest rock'n'roll band in the world' they were hopelessly out of tune, a vision of jaded rebellion that even then was showing signs of being very much part of a new Establishment.

They came and went. As Chris and I filed out of Hyde Park in the dusty heat of that July day, I reflected on the fact that my only sustenance all day had been a hamburger and Coke, both bought for what seemed like an extortionate amount. This had been the first big rock festival and the rip-off merchants had been more interested in LSD of a different kind! We caught the train back to Rugby, suspecting that we had witnessed history in the making.

Alan Powell (age 18)

We had to get the bus from Ellesmere Port in Cheshire. It was my first ever trip to London. Hyde Park was packed when we got there – strangely dressed people lying on the floor smoking long roll ups. There was nothing like that in Ellesmere Port, and no free love either! We climbed a tree but it didn't help so we sort of wove our way forward, stepping on the occasional ankle.

The British Hell's Angels didn't look that tough, a bit like some of the hard knocks at home.

We watched the exotic girls climbing up on the stage and sit by them as they played. "Was that Marianne?" "There's Suzy Creamcheese!"

We saw Keith with the Gibson V – so cool. The press said that they were out of tune, that Jagger had a dress on, that the butterflies they planned to release were already dead. But we loved them and this was a rare chance to see them. They were getting so remote and untouchable. They'd been in the papers facing jail. We bloody loved them – leave 'em alone!

Postscript

Hopefully this book has given the reader a flavour of what it was like to attend one of the early performances given by the Rolling Stones. In compiling this book I have endeavoured to contact as many people as possible, but in the UK alone the Stones played more than 750 times between 1963 and 1966. There will be many more fans out there whose story hasn't yet been heard. If you witnessed one of those early shows or know someone who did I'd love to hear those memories and can be contacted on stonesinthe60s@gmail.com

One of the less pleasant discoveries in researching this book was finding out just how many of Britain's fabulous provincial cinemas and theatres have failed to escape the wrecker's ball over the years. Too many of my contributors concluded their reminiscences of seeing the Stones in their home town with the words 'it's not there now'. Even those venues that are still standing are routinely subjected to redevelopment proposals from avaricious developers who face feeble resistance from over stretched and under funded local authority planners. Either that or they are boarded up and neglected in the hope that funds will someday arrive to enable them to be restored to their former grandeur.

It is sad and a little ironic that, if the Stones were today to offer to play some of these theatres and donate their fee that they can now command to the venue's restoration, the desperate struggle to fund to return of some of these magnificent buildings to their former glory would be ended overnight. Mick Jagger has thrown his weight, if not his wallet, behind a few such restoration campaigns but the list of buildings which remain vulnerable to redevelopment remains too long.

The Futurist Theatre in Scarborough, where Pam in the box office was chatted up by Charlie Watts, is just one example of a building where we should be erecting a plaque to celebrate our musical heritage and preserving a venue in which bands of the future might tread the road to stardom rather than talking about replacing it with an amusement arcade.

Acknowledgements

I could not have written this book without the help of many people, foremost amongst them the journalists and features editors of the many local and regional newspapers – around the UK and beyond – that I approached with my original plea for help. Most happily printed my letter asking people who saw the Stones play their local theatre, club or ballroom to come forward. Several kindly ran features on my search for fans and were good enough to forward emails and telephone numbers of people who got in touch with them.

I'd like to thank all of the people who saw the Rolling Stones in the 1960s and were kind enough to share their memories with me and scour attic rooms and cardboard boxes for the photographs that appear in this book.

I'd particularly like to thank: Robin Mayhew for his reminiscences about the Red Lion in Sutton and for putting me in touch with others who were able to contribute to this period of the Stones' story; Alan Ford from Stevenage Museum and David Menconi from the Charlotte News Observer for doing the same; Sarah Stoner from the Sunderland Echo for an early lesson in researching the facts and for making me aware just how many times the Stones played in the North East of England; Alan Trew for allowing me to see his Stones memorabilia and take up a slice of his Sunday morning to do so.

For permission to reproduce extracts from their memoirs I'd like to thank: Rodger W Brownlee of 'TheElite' © for recollections of the Stones appearing at the Will Rogers Memorial Center, Fort Worth; Dawn Young for permission to reproduce an extract from *Not Fade Away*, her memoir about life with Brian.

One task I omitted to carry out early on was setting up a searchable database of the Stones' concerts that would have enabled me to check and cross reference information that my contributors provided. I found myself referring to Nico Zentgraf's excellent database about the Stones' early activities more times than I cared to remember.

I would like to thank my long time support group of Jenny Parks and Diane Finlayson, who I know will be eager to reconvene our writing group just as soon as the pubs are open, and Elesh Makwana, whose IT skills came into play when I needed help in rescuing some photographs. I would especially like to thank Julie Bounford and Trevor Bounford, who saw the potential for this book to make it into print. Finally I would like to thank Kate Sullivan for the coffees, meals and all round love and support to enable me to apply myself to the task of writing this book, and Bill Houghton to whom I seem to have passed on my enthusiasm for, and shared love of, the greatest rock'n'roll band in the world.

And I must not forget my Dad. If he had not disliked Mick Jagger so much, I might never have become a Stones fan and so never have thought to write this book.

Index of venues

Index of contributors

*Richard in the Sixties
with his Dad, who
was no fan of the
Rolling Stones*

Richard Houghton lives in Manchester, England with his fiancée. He's
been a Rolling Stones fan since watching Mick Jagger strut his stuff to
Brown Sugar on the BBC's Top of the Pops. Richard didn't see the Rolling
Stones live in the 1960s although his mother did take him to see the 1964
Beatles Christmas Show – he was four years old. Richard has seen the
Rolling Stones live 20 times.

You Had To Be There: The Rolling Stones Live 1962–69 is the first in
a planned series of titles to be published by Gottahavebooks.

www.gottahavebooks.co.uk